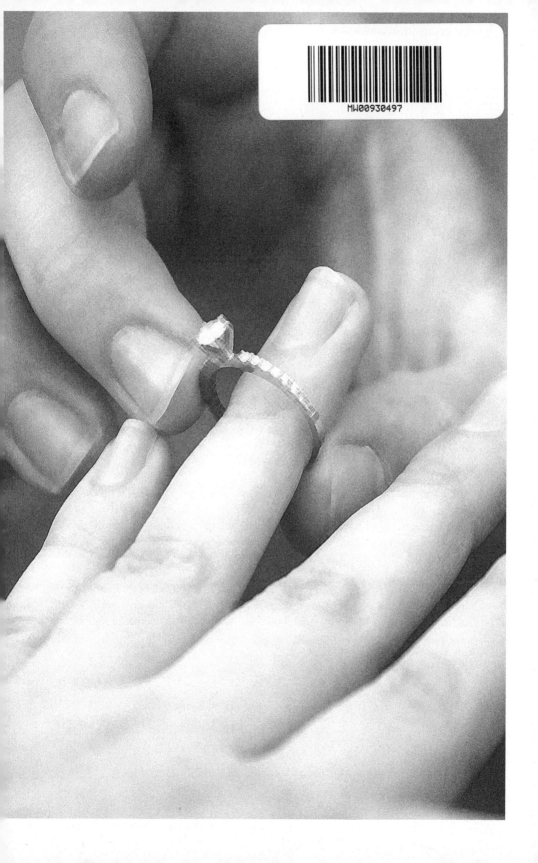

FROM THIS DAY FORWARD
Longing for a Miracle
Saved by the Sheriff
Home to His Heart
For the Love of Sophie June

Cover Design and Interior Format

From This Day Forward

Contemporary Romance
Novella Collection

Ruth Logan
Herne

Longing
for a
Miracle

Ruth Logan Herne

*For Natasha Kern, with great thanks for being Greek,
awesome and wise. I thank God for you daily!*

"He called a little child to him, and placed the child among them. And he said: "Truly I tell you, unless you change and become like little children, you will never enter the kingdom of heaven."
Matthew 18: 1–3

CHAPTER ONE

"MIMA, YOU CAN'T POSSIBLY MEAN to keep all this stuff, right? Can't we donate some?" *Or rent a dumpster?* Tasha Sorkos kept her real opinion firmly to herself. Ninety percent of what they were sorting should be tossed. The other ten percent could be donated. Mima Petropollis could buy new, comfortable furnishings and clothing for the two-room suite she'd be moving into in Grolier Garden apartments, a senior living facility located three miles north and a lifetime away.

"Or burn it," muttered Tasha's mother, and she purposely said it loud enough for Mima to hear.

"Mom. Really?" Her mother was spoiling for a fight from the tip of her sprayed-and-coifed hair to the soles of her never-bought-knock-offs in her life shoes. "Be nice, okay?"

"This isn't my idea of fun, there's no reason Aunt Nikki and Athena couldn't have handled this on their own, and I have two clients waiting upstate in Newtown. My January budget depends on deals cut before the dearth of holiday sales leaves me penniless."

Her mother's overly dramatic Realtor's lament was a common December occurrence, which made it easier to tune out. Tasha hauled another box onto the bed while her mother grumbled, answered her cell phone when it gave the most annoying three-note-ring tone known to man and motioned she needed to take the phone outside.

"She probably staged the call." Tasha's cousin Athena lugged an arm full of loaded hangers into the room. "These are from Papa's room, and every time I ask Mima anything, she glares at me like I'm trying to ruin her life, steal the silver and bilk her bank accounts."

"That's guilt talking for not visiting like you should. Mima loves you."

"I do make the best *gyros* known to man."

"There's that," Tash agreed, then cited the obvious, ignoring the still jagged pain to her heart. "And you gave her two beautiful great-grandchildren."

"Tash—"

Tash held up her hand, avoiding the conversation. "Let's not go there, okay? We've got a lot going on today, and dealing with Mom's anger issues for the next forty-eight hours is enough to handle. You know it, I know it, so let's get things done and move on."

"I was warned against fraternizing with your mother a long time ago," Athena replied, "which means you've spent way too long as the buffer zone. Allow me to say I'm sorry you drew the short straw on the parental end of the equation and offer you chocolate from the Kandy Kitchen."

"Rula's chocolate? I'm totally in. I thought she'd passed on years ago." Tasha examined the piece in her hand more carefully. "How old is this chocolate, exactly? Are we talking pre- or post-millenium?"

Athena laughed as she began sorting Papa's old clothing. "Totally fresh. I stopped by on my way over and Rafe hooked me up."

Rafe Karralis was here? In Grolier Springs?

He couldn't be. Rafe moved away before she did, when his father developed a sophisticated yet simple computer program that used a UPC-type code to track packages around the world. Why would Rafe be here? They'd gone from working class normal to uber rich in a heartbeat and the last she heard, he'd been acing courses at Stanford University while she tackled a medical business degree at Wharton in nearby Philadelphia. She set a pile of discards into a large box and bit into the chocolate.

Soulfully good. A blend of smooth milk chocolate over a truffle-style center that tasted like… mango, she realized, smiling. The outside of the perfectly blended shell was dredged in tiny flecks of something crunchy, familiar but indefinable. "This is to die for." She moved some more things into the box and did her best to make the next question sound off-hand. "So… What's Rafe doing there?"

"Forty-seconds, not bad." Athena's smile said she wasn't fooled, and because Tasha wasn't the only high school girl who pined for Rafael Karralis to notice her over a dozen years before, Tash figured she was in good company. "And you added a distinct note of casual to the question which only makes me love you more. Well done."

"Answer the question, troll."

Athena laughed, then sighed. "He's making chocolate and running the family diner because they've hit some hard times."

Tash understood that scenario. A crumbling economy had taken its toll on trickle-down businesses across the country, and the deterioration of her grandparents' neighborhood was a result of that collapsing infrastructure. "It's a tough time for a lot of people, that's for sure."

"And your job?" Athena kept her voice down, and Tash appreciated her sensitivity because Mima didn't need to worry about this on top of everything else. Their weekend goal was to get her packed, and moved while they disposed of things quietly. Which meant they might be able to order a dumpster for Monday, once Mima was tucked into a safer environment than 4th Street now offered. The background sound of sirens underscored the neighborhood's decay, a sad commentary in many older cities.

"Business and research don't always fare well in tough times, but ours is fine. I'm doing okay."

"I've got baklava!" Aunt Nikki sang the announcement as she charged up the stairs. "I was running past Anastasia's and thought it would be a nice treat while we worked."

"So far I only see two working," scolded Mima as she marched down the hall from the third bedroom, "which means I thank God for my granddaughters and say phooey to my own girls. One is busy shopping for food and the other?" She raised her shoulders in a glum shrug. "Who knows what Marina is doing? Who has ever known what Marina does? It is a mystery, always, and always with that phone to her ear, as if everything— her life, her job, her time— is so vitally important."

Mima's cryptic comment didn't faze Nikki. She winked at the girls and motioned downstairs. "We'll take a break when this room is done. I'll carry the transfer boxes downstairs and we'll have coffee and baklava."

"I'm out of coffee." Mima made the announcement almost as if she was proud of the fact that she had a house full of helpers and hadn't bought coffee. Tash was pretty sure she did it on purpose.

Nikki waved that off. "I knew that so I bought some."

She'd bested her mother and Tash thought Mima's gaze held a hint of approval, but it disappeared quickly. Approvals were scarcely given and short-lived. "Then I might have a cup with you. In a while. When we get more accomplished as you move me out of my own home."

Nikki went on as if she hadn't heard her mother's oft-repeated lament. "And I ordered lunch, it's being dropped off at one, so that gives us nearly three hours of work time after our baklava break."

"I can't remember the last time I had baklava." Tash wrote 'donate' on the box at her feet, then added a tiny star to the box top before she moved on.

"With all the Greek restaurants in Philadelphia, you never have baklava? That's taking dieting to an unhealthy level, girlfriend."

Weight concerns didn't keep her from the melt-in-your-mouth Greek dessert. Memories did.

"Then this will be a double treat," Aunt Nikki offered as she lugged the first box downstairs. "I'm going to pack the stuff we're moving into my SUV. The few items of furniture we're taking will fit in Rafe's truck."

"You got it? Good!" Athena high-fived her mother, and the two of them, acting like normal people, sent a wave of nostalgia over Tash. She'd wanted normal for so long. She'd hoped, she tried, she'd failed. And that failure had cost too much. It hadn't just broken her heart, it fractured her soul.

"That saves us renting one for the afternoon," Athena added, "Is he bringing it over?"

"Later, yes. I'll be back." Nikki disappeared down the turned stairway. She returned quickly and dusted flakes of snow off her hair. "Looks like the weather is cooperating for the holidays."

"Snow! Come on!" Athena grabbed Tash's hand and tore down the stairs like they used to when they were kids. She dragged her through the front door, dashed down the steps in sock-clad feet and waved her arms like a thirty-year-old lunatic.

"It's weather, Athena. A fairly common occurrence. And it's not like we haven't seen snow before." Tasha turned to go back in, but Athena grabbed her hand.

"The first snow is magical, Tash."

"I believe it's only magical when it's the first snow *and* Christmas snow. I distinctly remember Frosty's directive."

That voice. Still strong, still deep, still...

Rafe.

She turned, willing her lungs to work and her heart to beat, because just the sound of his voice, like smooth gravel, total guy, took her back to school girl crushes and gazes from afar, total tenth grade nonsense.

Neither organ cooperated fully, but they joined forces to a degree and that gave her enough aplomb to reach out a hand and act somewhat normal. "Rafe, what a nice surprise. I never expected to see you here. I thought the West Coast tied you up on a permanent basis."

His expression faltered, then he shrugged. "Permanence is a questionable state of being these days, isn't it? Good to see you, too, Tash. I brought the truck over early because I was coming this way and Aunt Ro was able to follow me."

"We could have given you a ride back." Athena gave him a little punch on the arm, the kind of thing an old friend did when they weren't still crushing on the cute Greek guy that made John Stamos look plain. "I know how crazy busy the Kandy Kitchen is this time of year. I bet Ro and Pete are glad to have you."

"It keeps me busy." The look he shared with Athena said more.

Ro pulled into the narrow, cracked concrete drive, and Rafe moved that way.

"We'll drop it off later, Rafe. Thank you!"

"No problem." He waved a hand but didn't turn, as if making chocolate for the upcoming holidays was life-saving work.

It's really good chocolate... her conscience mused. *And chocolate and holidays go hand-in-hand.*

He started whistling on his way to Ro's car, an old, familiar carol that would be aired way too often over the next four weeks, a tune she switched off whenever it came on.

She didn't like to think of Christmas and hope, of children and miracles. Presents under a tree and little girls, growing up to wear princess dresses and sparkly shoes.

"You okay?"

Athena's gaze probed too deep, so Tash raised her chin and nodded. "Fine. Let's get back in, okay? My feet are freezing and I've found that as I've gotten older, I can appreciate the snow from inside as well as outside. More, even."

"You think we can get Mima settled over the next few days?" Athena kept her voice low as they moved back up the steps.

Tash waffled, then shook her head. "I took extra time off, so I can stay through the week."

"You're a lifesaver." Athena grabbed her in a quick hug. "What made you think of that?"

"Holidays. They're tough on families, I know my mother will be more hindrance than help, you've got kids and a job and family stuff to do because it's December—"

"Two plays, a holiday dance recital, indoor soccer tournament, church services, piano lessons and all the family fun that goes on between Thanksgiving and New Year's," Athena's litany reminded Tash of their combined youth, crazy busy and so much fun when they were together. They'd shared everything until their roads forked down distinctly different paths. "December and June are chronically crazy, every year."

Tash knew that. She took a breath that got lost somewhere between her empty heart and her aching soul.

"Tash, I'm sorry."

Tash didn't want to hear this. She didn't want Athena to say it out loud, to commiserate with her loss. It had been three years, three long, empty, "you'll-get-over-this" years and her heart still felt like someone snatched it out of her chest from the end of October until the winds of January moved her beyond the glitz and glimmer of fake cheer. "Athena—"

"I know we don't talk about it, I know you like your privacy, but if I could go back and change things for you? I would. And I pray for you, every single day, because if Nora hadn't been down with a cold, she'd have been in that car, too."

"Why did I think it was so important for a four-year-old to dance?" Tash stopped, turned her face into the snow and sighed. "Why didn't I just say 'hey, the weather's bad, let's keep Zoe home for the night?'"

"It wasn't your fault, and no one knew it would rain hard enough to flood streets and knock out electric. You can't blame yourself, Tash."

"I know that." Tash winced, remembering. "But I'm not blameless, either, because I knew I had work, and I knew Grandpa didn't like driving in the city. I could have stopped it if I'd just decided to skip her dancing lesson, but I didn't, and I spend a tiny part of each day wishing for a do-over."

Athena tried to hug her, but Tash stepped back, one hand up. "Don't sympathize. Not now, not here, when Mima lost just as much that day. I can barely look her in the eye, thinking that if I'd made other choices then, our lives would be so different now."

"It was an accident, Tash. No more. No less. Don't make it into a life-long sacrifice."

Her words pierced because that was exactly what Tash intended to do. She'd loved and lost, and the bitter taste of sequential loss was nasty medicine. Her grandfather and her daughter, gone. The husband who promised to love her, off with another woman before his baby daughter had even been born.

You and me against the world...

She used to sing that to Zoe when she was a baby, a sweet song of single motherhood, crooning about love, time, memories and loss...

And then she'd insisted that Zoe go to dance class even though Nora was sick, and Grandpa had taken her, like always, because the lesson time didn't work for Tash's busy schedule.

Gone, in one fateful moment, one bad, everlasting decision.

"Coffee's ready." Nikki's voice and the smell of fresh coffee took her back to a time of crazy family dynamics, noisy days, busy nights, cousins, parents, grandparents.

"I'm going to hold off on baklava." She met Athena's worried gaze and nodded upstairs. "Save me a piece, okay?"

"I will."

She dashed up the stairs, hoping no one was up there, wishing for a few moments of peace and quiet, time to re-group and re-center her emotions.

Zoe was gone. The years marched on.

And that's how it had been for thirty-eight months of burying herself in fund procurement, research and development and top-secret crusades on cutting-edge battles to cure cancer.

She'd pledged her life to two things: Being alone, because alone was never as bad as saying goodbye...

And making a difference in the world.

Atonement?

She shoved the nudge of conscience aside as irrelevant. There was no atonement for bad choices that left two beloved people dead. But she was smart and educated and in the right place at the right time to make a difference now, and she'd do it to the best of her ability.

Alone.

Simply put... it hurt less to just be left alone.

CHAPTER TWO

*Y*OU HAVE NO OTHER CHOICE. *Plant a freakin' smile on your face, walk into the room and pretend there's hope.*

He'd thought so at first. Statistics bore that out. Now, after two rounds of chemo and a failed bone marrow transplant?

Not so much, but Rafe took the internal scolding to heart, strode down the hallway of his grandmother's ranch house and peeked into Alexia's room. "Hey, pretty girl. You awake?"

"Daddy!" She turned quickly, happy to see him. "I was just fixing my dolls' hair before their treatments."

His heart clenched. His insides coiled into a tight, angry mass of helplessness. No kid should have to re-enact chemo with their dolls. No kid should have to fight a killer disease for two years, a disease that seemed determined to thwart medical knowledge. He choked down the ball of anger that owned him most of the time. "Will they be as brave as you?"

Her expression said yes and no. "Aubrey's scared, but I told her it will be okay in the end. Brooke's not a bit scared but she's really, really mad."

So was he.

Why Lexie? Why weren't the new standard treatments that generally kicked A.L.L. to the curb working? When he heard the words "ninety-seven per-cent remission rate" two years ago, he'd never imagined that Lexie would fall into that three per-cent.

But she did, and her prognosis had turned grim.

"Can we put up the Christmas tree tonight, Daddy? Please?"

"Of course, baby." He choked on the words because the oncologist had made his point very clear. With the now rapid progression of an angry disease, this would be the last tree-lighting he'd share with his beautiful daughter. "Do you want to go get a tree with me like we always do?"

She answered him with such care that he knew she was trying to protect him. A five-year-old, guarding her father's emotions. His heart tightened again, but he wouldn't rage or lament in front of her. He tipped his head, waiting.

"I think I'll stay home," she answered thoughtfully. "Me and Gee-Gee K. can get the decorations down. He said he could use my help."

God bless Rafe's grandfather.

His father was too busy garnering more money he didn't need by installing his package tracking software in emerging nations' delivery services while showing his third wife a Caribbean Christmas holiday. His mother was in a West Coast treatment facility that catered to the *nouveaux riche* who got overwhelmed with sudden wealth. The spa-like facility was happy to help them in the form of elongated therapies and feel-good-about-yourself exercises that bilked bank accounts to the max.

But Gee-Gee K and Mima were here in Grolier, filled with old-fashioned love and Greek food, willing to help him make a home for Lexie. If this was going to be her final holiday on earth, he wanted it to be traditional perfection. And there was no place like Grolier Springs to do that.

"I'll see you in a little while then, okay? Do you want a fat tree or a skinny tree?"

She smiled, remembering their yearly debate. "I want the tree that needs us most."

"Will do." He turned, refusing to let her see his moist eyes. Others first, including the tree. She'd been that way from the time she was born, always looking out for others.

But who was looking out for her? Who was making this call to take her from the arms of the father who loved her so much? God?

God loves her as you do. More, actually.

He shoved that thought aside. If God loved her, would he let her suffer through unsuccessful treatments? What kind of love was that?

You let her suffer through those treatments, too.

Of course he did, because it was necessary to save her life. Only...

He stopped, stared around the driveway, then realized the restaurant van was being used by Athena and her cousin Tasha right now. He'd promised Lexie a tree and had no way of getting it, so how smart was he?

He pulled out his phone to call and rent a truck for an hour, but paused as a white van pulled up to the drive. "Tasha."

She climbed out of the front seat and waved his keys. "Here and thank you! We were able to get the lamps and Mima's blanket chest and her pictures and her favorite chair all in one trip. I told Aunt Nikki and Athena that I'd wait for them at the apartment, so if you wouldn't mind dropping me off, that would be wonderful."

"At Grolier Gardens?"

She nodded. "I said I'd hang out and start making the place look more homey. Put Mima's things around. Do you mind?"

"No." He shook his head, accepted the keys, then opened the passenger door. "Hop in."

She pulled herself up with ease, smiled when he closed the door, then winced in apology as the radio came on full-bore when he turned the key. "Sorry." She reached over, shut the station off and made a face of regret. "Billy Joel's "Scenes from an Italian Restaurant" came on and I forgot it wasn't my car. My bad."

"I love that song."

"Really?" She turned slightly and looked surprised. "My dad was a fan and he played Billy Joel and The Boss constantly when I was little."

"For me it was twelve years of piano lessons. I thought I'd be an updated version of the "Piano Man" someday, until I realized I was better at other things."

"From what I remember, you were good at everything." Tash ticked off her fingers to make her point. "Football, basketball, school, piano, track, and now I hear you've added chocolate making to your elongated list of attributes."

"It's peaceful." He ignored the long list of yesterday's news and zeroed in on the chocolate. "Following Gee-Gee K.'s instructions, learning to work with the chocolate and the molds. More like a retreat than a job right now."

"A chocolate retreat sounds like a beyond wonderful thing to contemplate."

He started to answer, then noticed that the Christmas tree lot was lit up across the corner. "Hey, do you mind if we stop by the tree lot, first? I know they're closing soon and I have to grab a tree tonight. If you're all right with that?"

She hadn't done a Christmas tree in three years.

She hadn't strung a light, put up a Nativity or decked a hall. She avoided church services and anything and everything to do with the holiday Zoe would never know again, but she couldn't very well explain all of that to Rafe. "Not a problem. I'll wait in the truck."

He nodded as if that wasn't a strange choice, pulled into the small parking area off the side street, and climbed out. He lumbered toward the tree display set up in the parking lot of a quaintly decorated strip mall. The mall hadn't gone for the politically correct white twinkle lights and refined greenery. They'd chosen a total North Pole look, with candy-cane striped utility poles, jewel-toned lights, fresh green swags adorned with clutches of pinecone and scarlet ribbon. Christmas music heightened the seasonal feeling with outdoor speakers mounted at six separate sites, ensuring that everyone would be surround-sounded with some sort of holiday cheer no matter which store they frequented.

She stared out, through the windshield, watching families stroll through paths of trees while others did a sing-along at the far end of the busy parking lot.

The sound of their voices, raised in prayerful song, came over the speakers. Tash reached out to close the van window more securely, but it was rolled up tight and snug and still the lifted song of praise filled the cab.

She reached over, ready to turn the engine on and find more Billy Joel or Springsteen or something to shut the faith-filled song of anticipation out, but Rafe had taken the keys with him.

Anxiety started somewhere around her feet and climbed rapidly.

Was she whacked? Probably so, but she deliberately kept herself out of situations that reminded her of what she'd lost. It was a safety mechanism, a strategy she'd learned from her hospital-recommended grief therapist, but lately the tactic failed more than it succeeded.

Because you need to move on. For your own health, it's time to move forward.

She shut down the internal reminder like she would a snooze alarm on Saturday morning. No one and nothing could force her to move on if she didn't want to. She knew who she was, what she'd done and what she failed to do, and if she wasn't woman enough to shoulder her responsibility, then how could she even think to look her grandmother in the face?

She tried the window again, sure it must be open, because who would play Christmas music that loudly?

She turned abruptly, searching the tree lot for Rafe, but wherever he was, his tall, strong, dark profile was hidden from her view.

Anxiety escalated to panic and surged forward. She was just about to jump out of the truck and walk the ten blocks to Mima's new apartment complex when a tap on the driver's window stopped her.

Rafe opened the door once he had her attention, and she breathed a quiet sigh of relief, right up until he opened his mouth. "Can you come out for just a minute, Tasha? Give me your opinion?"

She couldn't, no. The last thing in the world she wanted to do was immerse herself into the festive, artificially created world to help Rafe Karralis pick out a Christmas tree. It was on the tip of her tongue to tell him she'd rather poke hot pepper slivers under her fingernails when she met his gaze.

Grief.

She recognized it because it paralleled her mirrored image each morning, before she put on her "I'm okay-You're okay" happy face and fought through the day.

Deep-set pain shadowed his eyes, his expression and his tone, but he tried to mask the emotion and that only heightened it for her because hey… it takes one to know one.

She stared at him, not knowing his story, unwilling to share hers and then drew a deep, slow breath. "Sure."

"Thanks."

He didn't come over to open her door for her, almost as if doing that would take too much effort and he was already at the end of his reserve. She rounded the front of the van, zipped her jacket higher, and faced the brightly-lit lot. "Let's go."

He trudged ahead, leaving her to follow behind, and she did, but um, hello? Hadn't he just come and requested her presence? Wasn't a little casual conversation or at least an acknowledgement in order? Obviously not.

He turned down one row of gorgeous Douglas Firs, angled left through Scotch Pine and turned another sharp left at the juncture of the elegant, pricey and prickly Blue Spruce. "Here we go." He tipped up one ragged excuse for a tree with his left hand, turned himself and the tree in a full circle, then did the same with an equally ugly offering with his right hand.

She eyed the trees, then him. "Is this a joke?"

"It is not."

She stared at him, trying to get a read on whatever was eating at him, but then realized she'd be better off fixing herself before making a lame attempt to help someone else. "Well. They're equally needy."

"Not helpful."

She shushed him with a frown. "You asked for my opinion. I'm giving it. Be quiet."

He started to open his mouth, but then acquiesced. "Take your time."

She didn't want to take any time at all, she didn't want to be here listening to how folks would only dream of being home for Christmas. She didn't want to be stuck in the middle of a Christmas tree lot, surrounded by someone's over-the-top idea of holiday cheer. She'd rather be home, with a good book and a fairly dark room, shades drawn, leaving herself on the outer edges of joy-to-someone-else's-world. But she *was* there, so she examined both trees. "The one on the left is skinnier."

"My left or yours?"

She nodded, understanding. "Yours. But the one on the right is kind of begging for a home, very "Peanuts"-friendly."

"You're sure?"

He wanted her opinion, now he was questioning it? She bit back what she wanted to say and stayed polite, even though it half-killed her. "But if you choose that one, I feel like I've doomed the one on the left to the wood chipper destiny. No one else is going to pay thirty-five dollars for that tree."

"People do strange things."

She knew that, and avoided them as much as possible for that very reason. "Are we good?"

"Yes." He set the tree on the left against the taut rope with careful hands, as if the sad excuse for a tree had feelings, and gripped the tree she picked. "We're good."

She walked back to the van, climbed in, and waited while Rafe paid for the tree. He carried the skinny thing over to the van, opened the back and slid it into the empty cargo area with ease, then shut the door.

The sweet nostalgia of pine-scent gripped her by the throat and wouldn't let go. She breathed deep, the strong scent sending a wealth of emotions speeding along, like watching "The Polar Express" race along the tracks to the North Pole. The smell probed a sense of holiday immediacy, as if this whole season of expectation, waiting and wonder meant something.

It didn't, but her senses picked up on the beautiful fragrance and carried her back to a time when Christmas was good and kind and golden.

"I love that smell." Rafe climbed into the seat beside her and drew a long, slow breath. "It reminds me of growing up here, and Gee-Gee taking me to the diner on his shoulders, letting me crush the nuts for the baklava and mix the cheese for the spanakopita. I hated mincing the onion but he made me do it and he'd say 'Rafael, there will be much in life you may not like, but still must do. May God's blessing make chopping these onions be the worst of those things.'"

"Were they?"

He turned, one brow thrust up. "Hmm?"

"The onions." She led him back to the conversation he'd instigated. "Was mincing onions the worst thing that ever happened to you?"

"I'm afraid that was just one unanswered prayer out of many."

She understood that, too, but then a stroke of conscience broadsided her. She hadn't exactly done a lot of praying or church-going once she left Grolier. School, internships, work, life, marriage, divorce, death…

Naw, she pretty much shrugged church off and now she downright hated the thought of it so she was totally in league with the idea that answered prayers were a rarity and a coincidence. End of story.

He steered the van out onto the side road, flipped the signal to make a right turn as Tash reached into her small purse to grab the keys to Mima's new apartment.

Nothing.

She groped around the inside of the small, leather bag and came up with one cough drop, an eye-liner she thought she lost, a pen, her wallet and the keys to her car. No apartment key to be found.

Could this day possibly get any worse? She laid her head back against the neck support, sighed and then turned to face Rafe more fully. "I don't have a key."

He made the turn back onto the main road, pulled the van to the curb and faced her. "To the apartment?"

She nodded, feeling pretty stupid and more than a little tired. "That would be the one."

"Does Athena have it?"

"She must. Which means I either wait in the cold or you drive me back to Mima's place."

He glanced at the time and his expression said that the ten minutes to Mima's place didn't make the short list. "Listen." She pulled out her phone. "I'll just have Athena come get me. It's no biggie."

"You wouldn't mind?"

She did mind.

She minded that he needed to stop and get a really ugly, horrible, no good, very bad tree instead of driving her to Grolier Gardens where she would have discovered she was keyless nearly forty minutes before. They would have called Athena and she'd have hurried to the old suburban neighborhood to rescue Tash. Now? Tash was stuck, out of her comfort zone, and ready to pop someone in the jaw because no matter how good-looking Rafael Karralis is or was, he could at least be polite. "It's fine. A few minutes either way won't make a difference."

Clearly the minutes meant more to him than they did to her. His jaw relaxed. His eyes went soft, and for the space of two quick breaths, she thought she saw the sheen of tears in those big, brown eyes, but he reached out, patted her hand and said, "Thank you, Tash. Thank you so much."

They pulled into his grandparents' driveway. He stopped the van quickly, hopped out, and went around back to remove the sad excuse for a tree. He carried it up the side steps, opened the big wooden door and called, "I've got it!"

He started in, realized she wasn't with him and swung back. "Come on, come see my Mima and Gee Gee K. He might even make you a vanilla Coke if you're good."

She drank vanilla Cokes at the diner all the time back in high school. It was her thing, and she never expected Rafe to remember, not with the parade of girls that trouped into the Kandy Kitchen daily.

She glanced at her phone and hit Athena's number on speed dial. It went right to voice mail, so she texted her instead. "Must have left key in your purse or on table. Bring spare to Rafe's house."

She hit send, climbed down and followed Rafe and the tree into the house.

The difference in the air hit her as soon as she walked in the house. Somber, playing at joyful, like the bad chords of a dysfunctional rock band.

Gee-Gee K. ambled forward, older, stouter, and wearing the big smile that welcomed families into the quaint twelve-booth diner, but the smile didn't reach his eyes. Rula followed him. She grabbed Tash into a hug and the scent of laundry soap, bleach and hand lotion hinted that Rula still ran a house where cleanliness was next to godliness.

But then another voice called out. Small. Young. Joyous.

Her heart leapt, longing to answer that call, a spontaneous response that took her by surprise because she'd done her best to avoid small children for a long, long time.

"Did you get the tree, Daddy? Is it here? I can't wait to see it!"

Rafe had a daughter? Tash's heart reached out even as it crumbled inside.

Her voice, so like Zoe's. The joy, the cadence, the lyrical question as if she'd been waiting all day for this one special moment, a chance to see her father and the family Christmas tree. Footsteps came their way, not with the swift dash she'd have expected, but the soft tread of quiet feet.

"We're in the living room, honey."

"I'm coming!"

Rafe carried the scrawny fir into a fun and cluttered room, set it into a decent-sized holder, then frowned in realization. "It's too thin."

"Or the stand's grip is too wide." Gee Gee K. stated the obvious as the adults stared at the tree and the holder.

"That's not a tree, it's barely a stick," observed Mima.

"And ugly to boot," noted Gee-Gee K., but when the little girl turned the corner and entered the room, she clapped her hands together in glee.

"Oh, it's perfect, Daddy! So perfect! It's just the one I would have gotten if I'd been there."

"Well, good." Rafe palmed the girl's bald head and turned toward Tash. "Tash, this is my daughter, Alexia."

His quick intro didn't give her time to pretend. The sight of the little girl, her face swollen by steroids, the lack of hair, the port line scar on her chest beneath the soft pink flannel pajama top said too much. Fierce regret tightened Tash's tongue.

"Hi." Lexie gazed up at her, waiting for her to respond, and Tash tried, but nothing came out. She stood there, staring at a small child ravaged by the treatments of a wretched disease and choked on the normal pleasantries anyone else would offer.

Rafe stared at her. So did Gee Gee K., as if wondering what her problem was.

She moved forward, a hand out.

The little girl pushed closer into her daddy's leg, clearly unnerved by Tash's silent reaction.

Ashamed, Tash took another step to close the gap, but Rafe directed the child to her great-grandmother's side. "Lexie, it seems we either have a tree that's too skinny or a holder that's too big. Can you help Mima figure this out while I see Tasha out?"

"Sure!" She sent one more tentative glance Tasha's way and skirted the table. "Who's putting on the lights this year? Daddy usually does it at our house, but Gee-Gee if you want to do it, I bet my dad won't mind."

"Won't take more than a string, and prob'ly have to loop that twice," the elderly man teased. He sat alongside Alexia and pretended to study which way to turn the tree to best see it, until he made a show of throwing up his hands and backing off a step. "Equally bad on all sides. The perfect tree!"

"And we gave it a home!" Excited, the girl hugged her Mima, then sat in a comfy-looking, over-sized chair as Tasha left the room. "Goodbye, Tasha! Nice to meet you!"

She tried to force a smile, but the look on Rafe's face said it was more of a grimace and unwelcome at that. He got to the door with her, saw the lights of Athena's SUV pulling in the end of the driveway and swung the door wide. "Your ride's here."

"I see that. Rafe, listen, I—"

"Goodbye, Tash."

She had no choice but to step through the door, wishing the last five minutes back. If she had them back, or if someone had given her fair warning, she'd have either avoided the confrontation, a skill she'd perfected, or she'd have practiced her moves. Ashamed, she started to turn, but Rafe shut the thick, wooden door with a firm click.

She stared at the door, mentally revisiting the scene inside. The retro-room, crowded with Greek pictures and statues, the religious hangings on the walls, the sweet older folks, the needy tree and the dying child.

You hurt her feelings.

That realization broke her heart.

Fix it, her conscience prodded.

She couldn't, of course. There was no way to fix the awful first impression she'd made. Why didn't Rafe tell her? Why didn't he—

Really? You're going to blame him? Might want to think about that a little more, Pumpkin.

She climbed into the passenger seat of Athena's SUV, glared at her and said, "Why didn't you tell me Rafe's kid was sick?"

Athena frowned as she backed out of the driveway. "I didn't mention that?"

"Not a word."

Understanding lightened Athena's face as she recalled their earlier conversation. "We got interrupted." She worked her jaw as she turned onto the main road, heading toward Mima's apartment. "Sorry. Most of us know so it's common knowledge. They tried everything in California. Multiple rounds of chemo, and a bone marrow transplant. Nothing has worked and now they're out of options. He brought her here for a traditional Christmas with her Mima and Gee-Gee K. Heartbreaking," she added, shaking her head. "The whole situation is just absolutely heartbreaking."

Tash agreed because her heart had puddled the moment she heard the girl's voice. Then the sight of her, mis-shapen from treatments aimed at quieting the angry power of cancer. The thought of Rafe's child, going through multiple rounds of chemo, bone-marrow testing, then a transplant…

What was worse, she wondered as Athena pulled into the driveway of Mima's new suite. To have your child snatched away with no warning, or watch her slowly and painfully fade from sight?

Tears came from nowhere. Athena turned, saw, and came to her side. "Tash, I'm sorry. I should have warned you, I never even thought of it because you were just dropping the van off and grabbing a ride back here. I'm truly sorry, honey."

She wrapped her arms around Tash as a neighboring tenant flicked on a sweep of Christmas lights surrounding a small outdoor Nativity scene. The hug and the lights and the back-lit star shining down on the empty manger made things worse.

What form of god would take small children? If there was a god, and if he cared, how could such things happen? To snuff out a child's life, a life that hadn't even been lived?

It was wrong, therefore it couldn't be true. A loving deity's protection would safeguard all, which made the whole story of an infant king's birth in a cave-stable nothing more than a well-propagated and overly commercialized myth.

"Come on in, let's get warm." Athena opened the door with her key, and tugged Tasha inside, but the reality was that Tash hadn't been warm in three years and was pretty sure Mima's central heating wasn't about to change that now.

CHAPTER THREE

"IT'S SPANAKOPITA NIGHT AT THE Kandy Kitchen." Tasha's "Mima" gripped her two-decades-old purse and jutted her chin on Thursday night. "Rula always makes spanakopita for the Thursday night special and I go there every week at five o'clock. This week will not be different."

Tash didn't want to face the Karralis family again, but Mima's car was in the shop and she was slated to help her for another twenty-four hours, and then Athena would take over for the weekend. But right now?

That meant taking Mima to the popular local eatery to get her feta, onion and spinach filled pastry. She drove slowly, unsure what to say. How could she apologize properly? Or was she better off just ignoring the whole mess and focusing on Mima?

She parked down the street from the diner and took Mima's arm. "The temperature's dropping and this looks icy."

"Budget cuts." Mima frowned but didn't shrug off her help, a nice step forward. "I expect Gee-Gee or Rafe will salt this down once we tell them it's a mess."

Rafe wouldn't be here. He'd be home, caring for his little girl, of that she was certain. She opened the big, oak-framed glass door and held it wide for Mima, then stepped in behind her.

"Mima, come in, let's get you seated." Rafe appeared at Mima's side, ushered her to a wide-booth that made it easy to climb in and out, and made a joke of handing her a menu. "If you're not having the beef kabob special with the spanakopita, tell me now and save me the heart-attack of surprise later."

Mima blushed like a twelve-year-old, then reached out a hand to cover his. "And our little angel, Rafael? How is she doing?"

He was turned toward Mima, leaving Tash nothing but a view of his strong, broad back, but the slight hesitation said he hated the question or the answer. Possibly both. "Holding her own for right now. As we were told. Thanks for asking about her, Mima."

"I pray." Mima gripped his hand hard between both of hers. "I pray for her and you every night, and I ask my Mikos to pray with me. He is with Jesu now, which means he is so close to the throne! I believe God hears my prayers Rafael. I believe with all my heart."

Tash slid into the opposite side of the booth, and saw Rafe's reaction. Gratitude and resignation marked his face, but resignation won, and Tash knew what that meant: He'd accepted his daughter's prognosis. He'd stopped fighting.

Her heart ached for him, and for every parent who lost a child, the aching emptiness unfilled by even the sweetest of memories because there were too few. He turned toward her, and she expected at least a flash of anger because of her behavior the previous weekend. She started to stay something but stopped when Rafe squatted next to their table, reached out and took her hand. "I had no idea, Tash. I was on the West Coast and pretty wrapped up in my own life for way too long." Troubled eyes gazed into hers. "Mima and Gee-Gee explained things on Saturday night."

Warmth emanated from him, mixed with sweet sincerity. Meeting his eyes, she felt like someone truly understood the empty ache in her heart, the hollow depth of her soul. "I—"

He squeezed her hand lightly, the kind of gentle grip that said words weren't needed. "Lexie loves the tree. Thanks for helping me."

She hadn't been a help, not really. And her attitude sucked. She bit back words of self-recrimination and said simply, "You're welcome, Rafe."

"I've never understood calling you Rafe when Rafael is such a strong, vigorous name!" Mima smacked her hand to the table, but she didn't look all that mad, she looked… interested. Which meant she was paying too much attention to their back-and-forth. "The name of angels and kings, a name to pass on to future generations. Your parents did well in the naming. Not so well in the rest. But you, Rafael, you are a gift from God to so many."

He winked at Tash, reached out and hugged Mima, then stood.

"I'll have Cass bring waters. Do you want drinks, ladies? I expect a vanilla Coke would be a nice walk down memory lane on this side of the table." He tapped the faded wood in front of Tash. "Coffee, Mima? Or is it too late?"

"It will be if we keep talking!" Her quick smile took the sting out of the words, and as Rafe moved off to seat the next family in the door, she faced Tash directly. "You helped pick out their tree?"

"I was in the wrong spot at the wrong time."

"Perhaps not." Mima smiled as Rafe's younger cousin dropped off their drinks and a plate of lemons for their waters. "Perhaps it is time to stop avoiding life and join in the dance, Natasha."

"I have no desire to dance, and my life is just fine."

"You change my words with purpose because your heart is still sad, but you know what I mean. Life goes on. For you, for me. And God wants us happy."

"Right." Tash made a face. "Mima, you have every right to believe as you choose, but I'm not the pig-tailed kid who bought into the whole religious scenario I was force fed. I grew up."

"Growing up does not have to mean growing away."

"It does when fate hands you a really crummy hand." She took a sip of her water, hoping the effort of swallowing would choke the anger stirring inside. "I don't want to talk about this."

"You never do, but it has been a long time and you and I both lost much that day. It is time to talk, Tasha. Time to heal."

Mima spoke of healing as if it was possible, but it wasn't. Especially not now, when twinkle lights marked windows, doors, wreaths and poles, when Christmas music rang from the rafters of every retail space and the thought of another empty Christmas morning made her long to sleep for long, long days and wake up sometime in January.

"You go back to work on Monday?"

The change of subject slowed her anxious breathing. "Yes."

"And your month is busy?"

She nodded. "Research and I have one thing in common. We don't recognize holidays."

Mima studied her, then shrugged. "We have different ways of handling life, Natasha. And your way gives me much concern."

"Because?"

"Life is so much more than sorrow. You are my beautiful one, *agapite mou*! I long for you to be at peace."

Her aged grandmother wanted her darling girl to be at peace, when she was responsible for her grandfather's early death? The irony wasn't lost on Tash, and when Cass came by to get her order, the last thing she wanted was food. She hesitated, read her grandmother's look of warning, and duplicated Mima's order.

Regal to the max, Mima dipped her chin in approval. "You will love the tender beef and the vegetables. The spinach pie might help put some meat on your bones." She snapped her napkin into place to punctuate the statement. "Few make a better spanakopita than me. Rula is one of those who gets it right."

"Do you cook now Mima?" She meant to leave the subject alone, but it seemed okay to talk about food and being alone because they were both in the same boat. "For yourself?"

"I do and I don't." Mima frowned into her coffee cup, picked it up, then set it back down without sipping. "It's a bother, and I don't like being bothered. And it's lonely."

Tash knew the truth of that.

"But then I got mad at myself for being an old woman feeling sorry for herself."

"Grieving isn't feeling sorry for yourself, Mima. It's part of life."

Mima's expression said maybe it was and maybe it wasn't. "A time for every purpose under the heaven." She clipped the words with all the tenderness of a Greek dock worker. "Learning to read the signs of the times, to forgive and move on, this is what God expects of us."

And they were off on the God-thing again. Maybe the food would come quickly, they'd ordered the special, so it was probably mostly pre-made, wasn't it?

"So what I need from you…"

Oh, no. Tash glanced around, hoping someone would appear with something, to get Mima off this tangent.

"Is forgiveness."

"Huh?" Tash stopped fiddling with her fork, sat straight and frowned because if ever a conversation had taken an inside out turn, it was this one. "Mima—"

"Your grandfather loved you children. He loved you all so much, you were his pride and joy."

"We loved him too." Why were they talking about this and

where in the name of Sam Hill was the food? How long could two kebobs take?

"He would have done anything for you. Now Marina liked to take advantage of that."

Tash's mother was a user to the max, that wasn't exactly news.

"But not you or Nicolette or Athena. You were all looking to do for others, always helping, doing your best."

"Mima, I'm not following you."

"I should not have let your grandfather drive that day. The day of the accident."

A wave of cold washed Tash's skin with goosebumps. What was it with everyone wanting to talk about the accident all of a sudden? What was wrong with them? Couldn't they respect her privacy or did invasive Greek families have a time limit on minding their own business?

"He wasn't himself that day. He had a headache, his sinuses were bad with the rain and I had a meeting with the ladies that afternoon, to set up the Greek food table at the church bazaar the next week. I was busy, but what was I thinking?" She drew up her shoulders, and her face grew pensive. "That food was more important than my husband's health? Than my great-granddaughter's lessons?"

"Mima, don't do this."

"I must, because until we speak of things, Natasha, we can't move beyond them. And this stands between us each time we meet and we need to see it for what it is, dear one. I have to confess to you as I have already done to the priest and to our God because if I had skipped my meeting that day, my husband and your daughter would be alive."

New guilt swamped Tasha. Her grandmother had spent these last three years carrying unwarranted guilt on top of her grief. "Mima, none of this was your fault. You couldn't have known, we get storms all the time, who would have predicted such an outcome? No one."

"And yet, I knew his head hurt, and I knew he didn't like driving in the dark, in the rain, but I shrugged it off and went on with my day. And then?" She shrugged, eyes round. "The unthinkable. Whereas if I was driving or told him not to go, our lives would be different now. And I am sorry I did not take that action then."

"I'm the one who insisted she go, even though Nora was sick and it would be just Zoe going to the lesson. Papa never told me 'no', it wasn't in him. And I knew that. So if anyone's to blame—"

"Does someone have to be to blame?"

Rafe's voice interrupted their earnest confessions, and from the sound of his voice he was both sympathetic and surprised. He set plates down in front of them, squatted beside the table and frowned. "How come someone needs to shoulder the blame for an accident involving flooded roads, an unforeseen stalled low pressure system and a clogged storm sewer? Isn't that why we call them accidents?"

"And yet—" Mima drew out the second word and Rafe shook his head.

"I'm facing something that makes me cry every day."

The thought of this big, Greek guy confessing his grief humbled Tasha.

"And yet I don't let a morning go by without thanking God for the time I've had with Lexie. That I loved her when her mother didn't. That I've been blessed with over five beautiful years with her. She taught *me* courage, because she was so strong going through those rounds of treatments and surgeries, always believing that our choices were in her best interests. And you know what?" Eyes damp, he raised his shoulders lightly. "They were. They may not have done what we hoped, but I made each decision in her best interest, just like you, Tash, wanting your little girl to have her dancing lesson. You can't hate yourself for wanting her success and joy. That's what a parent does."

The cook called his name. Rafe turned, waved, then covered her hand with his one more time. "I can't say I understand it, Tash, any of it. But I can say that these years with Lexie have been the best possible years of my life and I thank God for that chance, the chance to be her daddy, because she's made me happier than I ever thought I could be."

Her heart melted, then froze.

His words humbled her. Here he was, facing the unthinkable, and talking about gratitude for the time he had. Was he crazy or just that nice and wise?

"The poor shall eat and be filled..." Mima's soft voice intoned the evening grace Tash had learned at her table decades before.

"Those who seek the Lord shall praise him. Their hearts shall live forever."

Hinted meaning probed her soul. Was her precious child somewhere other than here, maybe in the arms of the Savior? Could such a thing really be or was it all rhetoric of fearing-death nonsense? But the thought of Zoe's heart and soul, living forever?

A thread of peace let her shoulders relax, her chest loosen up, and the smell of seared beef seasoned just right smelled good. She faced her grandmother, determined that if nothing else, she would put the elderly woman's regrets to rest because life was too short for someone Mima's age to walk each day in the shadows of sorrow.

Good advice at any age, I'd say.

She shrugged off the mental wisdom and tasted the food. Wonderful. Warm. Enticing. Greek. And when Rafe walked by, smiled and winked at her, a wink that said we're in this together, the tiny rise of sweet emotion said her heart might have started working again, which was ridiculous.

Or was it?

CHAPTER FOUR

"NATASHA, YOU'RE BACK, I KNOW you kept up with things from the 'burbs, but the staff's schedule just had a make-over." Mary Hanson kept her face turned toward Tasha, but shifted her eyes to the left.

Natasha looked beyond her assistant, amazed. "Bjorn is here? From Sweden?"

"Something's breaking. Something big. He's here to meet with heads of research and development and two of the doctors in the HIV study."

"Hold everything. And can you make fresh coffee in the conference room, Mary? And order up a *Dannoli* tray from Frangelli's, please. Bjorn loves good pastry."

"I'm on it."

Tasha stowed her purse behind her desk, then strode into the glass-walled meeting room to her left. She paused inside the door, letting the vibes of excitement hit her. Whatever had brought the researchers out of their work areas and Bjorn all the way from Europe had them happy, which meant her fundraising and grant-writing job just got easier. "I've never seen this kind of reaction in the eight years I've been here, so are you going to make me wait?" She crossed the room, hand outstretched and grabbed each person's hand individually. "I'd order champagne but it's morning and we're working, so coffee and cannoli-stuffed donuts by Frangelli's will have to do."

"You know your boss." Bjorn laughed and clapped her in a big hug. "I took a red-eye when I was told of our accomplishments, and sleep is the farthest thing from my mind right now, but coffee and sweets will help me when physiology takes precedence over emotion."

"What's happened?"

"The altered virus with the therapeutically-targeted T-cells has put a hand full of last chance patients into remission. At long last, the possible miracle we've been waiting for. It worked, Tasha."

She stopped. Stared. "It worked?"

The answered grins were enough of a reply.

"Side effects?"

"Miserable at this point, because we'll need to fine-tune amount, timing, all of the things that affect each patient, but that's like tweaking a fine recipe in an Italian restaurant. The amount of fresh basil and grated Parmesan changes the flavor, but sauce is still sauce. And we have achieved the miracle we prayed for."

The miracle we prayed for.

The younger researcher's words hit hard. Their team had worked diligently for years, searching for a systemic approach for the body to kill its own cancer, eventually eliminating the need for chemical warfare, amputation and radiation. If the body could be taught to recognize the cancer at the cellular level, then it would heal itself.

And as that reality hit, another image came to mind. Alexia Karralis, age five, dying, forty-five minutes away.

Adrenalin surged. Her heart beat hard, against her chest, and as the three doctors who'd administered the life-saving technique ten days before came into the room in their typical scrubs, she knew what she had to do.

When the hub-bub of success died down, she would go to them on their own turf and beg for Alexia's life, because this time the choices were not obscured by circumstance and weather. This time the options of life and death were clear and looming, and the worst the team could say would be no.

But fate or Providence or God...

The very thought of that possibility made her half-cringe, half-hope...

Had put her here, now. And if she could help save Rafe's daughter? That's exactly what she would do.

She placed a call to Rafe that evening. "Rafe, it's Tash."

"Back to work and you missed the old home town already?" His voice teased, and then teased again, but softer. "Or maybe you missed me, Natasha."

The gentle suggestion nudged her heart, but she went straight to the point. "Can you have all of Lexie's medical records forwarded to me here at Geisert? I have two doctors who want to review her charts." It was a lie, she hadn't spoken to the doctors yet, because she wanted the information on Alexia Karralis in her hand when she did.

"What's this about, Tash?"

"About re-examining the procedures to date and seeing what might be available on this side of the Mississippi. Just get me the records, Rafe. Please."

He clicked his tongue, an old habit she'd forgotten until he did it now, so she knew his hesitation was deep rooted. "She's gone through so much. Maybe too much," he added, "despite what I was saying last week. There comes a time when you have to look at the odds versus the quality of life. And that's what I'm trying to do. Thank you, Tash, your concern means a lot to me, but—"

"Get the records, Rafael, or I'll come there myself and watch you make the phone calls, and don't think for a minute I'm afraid to do it. Don't route them through yourself, have them sent directly to me at this address via overnight messenger or have them fax them through to me at this number." She spieled off the number for him. "Got that? And my e-mail is N_Sorkos@Geisert.med. I'll watch for them. If anyone gives you trouble, call me back and I'll go crazy on them. I need those records ASAP."

"You're serious."

"Always, unfortunately." She didn't elaborate, but she paused, took a breath, and added, "It is the season of miracles, Rafe."

That tipped the scales. She heard it in his breathing, then his voice. "I'll have them all to you by Wednesday at the latest."

"Perfect." She hung up before she was tempted to say more. At this point nothing was brought together, but in her head she saw the amazing opportunity of timing and she'd never forgive herself for not taking it. She laid her clothes out for the morning, an old parochial-school habit, and went to bed, but before she fell asleep, she found herself doing something she hadn't done since those parochial school days. She prayed.

And it felt good.

He couldn't sleep. He couldn't eat. Was it the clear deepening of his daughter's life-threatening illness or Tash's hope-stirring phone call, an emotion he'd tanked about five weeks back?

Her voice, upbeat. Her tone, insistent. Bossy, even.

That thought made him smile slightly, which was weird because there hadn't been much to smile about in the past six months, and not all that much before then. But at least they'd been able to play the optimist about Lexie's treatment early in the fall.

Optimism hadn't been an option for long, autumn weeks.

He walked to the back door and stepped outside, despite the bone-chilling cold.

Set to timers, most of the neighbors' Christmas light displays switched off around midnight, but the Ogallis family's white silhouette Nativity display stayed lit all night, a beacon of faith in the damp darkness of December.

The pentagon-shaped manger, the gathered people, a camel, two sheep, a donkey and a cow... and a feed crib, waiting for the Christ child.

His heart ached. His hands chilled, but he barely felt them as he trudged forward.

"And God gave his only begotten son..."

He didn't want to give Lexie. In this and all instances, he'd give the win to God because he didn't have the strength to say it was all right to take his beloved daughter. He was selfish enough to want her here, with him. He wanted to watch her play soccer, teach her to ride horseback, shop for her first prom gown, dance at her wedding. He wanted it all, unashamedly.

She was mine first... The nudge of the Holy Spirit bit deep.

He knew that. Believed it. But he still didn't want to give her back to heaven. Burying a child went against every ounce of natural order, and yet...

Tash had done that.

He'd been so angry at her last week. Her reaction to Lexie cut him to the quick because he expected better from a smart, beautiful woman like Natasha Sorkos. It took all of his strength not to ream her out as she left, and when Mima had explained her circumstance later?

He'd been glad he kept his big mouth shut for once.

He stood before the manger scene, watching, praying. Did God hear? Was that really how it worked?

He didn't know, but if God was listening, Rafe wanted him to hear his plea, tonight. He wanted God to save this precious child and let her experience life on earth to the full. That alone was his Christmas wish.

He made the requested phone calls the next morning, and had the records sent directly to Tash's office in Philadelphia, and despite the fact that he told himself he wouldn't hope, he did. And he kept his cell phone with him, charged and the ringer on full, just in case she called on Wednesday.

She didn't.

Tash had Mary hold her calls on Thursday morning. She took the thick sheaf of folders and made her way around the labyrinth of University City medical buildings until she came to the research wing she needed. She arrived at the meeting first, which was good because keeping busy doctors waiting didn't make the short list. When the two doctors walked in together, she handed each of them a folder, and handed the other two to the research specialists, then launched her well-rehearsed spiel. "Alexia Karralis, age five-and-a-half, treated at three separate highly acclaimed West Coast facilities for the last twenty-seven months, now receiving comfort care forty-five minutes north of Philadelphia with her father and great-grandparents. Typical ALL presentation, a-typical response..." She went on as they leafed through the papers, citing the grim statistics of Lexie's looming demise, and ending with, "I want you to consider using CART-19 on Lexie. Please."

Three doctors shook their heads instantly. "It's too new. Untested."

"She's little, how do we dose her?"

"We'd most likely kill her."

And then the fourth doctor, staring at the opening page of the medical records, the page with a picture of a beautiful little girl staring back up at him, raised his gaze. "But perhaps we would not."

The two men and one woman turned and stared.

He shrugged. "She's already dying, she'll be lucky if she makes it to Christmas with these numbers. Does this child have anything to lose?"

"We risk our success being shoved aside if we lose this child now." Lines of resignation marked the older researcher's face. "We're riding high momentarily," he continued. "We've just had some major success, with a treatment we're devising as we go. Can we afford to kill this little girl?"

His blunt approach drew frowns, but Dr. Orrington, the renowned oncologist whose work was lauded internationally, made a face. "I recognize the need to secure funding from multiple sources ASAP. But Howard," he turned to meet the older researcher's gaze, "can our souls afford to say no?"

Again three faces peered into his, as if wanting to find a flaw in his argument. They couldn't or didn't and he handed Tasha a card. "Get her here today. Time is short."

Rafe's phone rang at ten-seventeen. He saw Tash's name and picked it up after clamping a steel grip on his emotions. No matter what she said, he understood the current reality of Lexie's situation and he would do nothing to jeopardize one last Christmas with his precious child. "Tash. Did you get everything I sent?"

"I did, and our team wants Lexie here now," she replied quickly. "Can you bring her straight down to the city, Rafe?"

A knot formed in his middle, the kind of clench that said fear and hope just met head-on. "For what, though, Tash? I've been thinking about this, thinking hard, and the reason I brought Lexie back to Grolier Springs was to —"

"Die."

Her interruption made him examine his choices more closely. "To have one last Christmas, yes. I promised myself I wouldn't do anything to mess that up, and to build up hopes again..." He drew a breath, his shoulders tight, his chin taut. "I can't, Tash."

"You can and will, because what if I told you this might not be her last Christmas? What if I told you that they might be able to give you all the Christmases you can imagine, but not if you don't move your stubborn Greek feet to the car, with the kid, and get down here. Park in the garage, and bring her through to the back entrance. It's quieter. I'll meet you there and take you to meet the doctors. And Rafe?"

"Oh, you're allowing me to talk all of a sudden?" He wanted to be angry about her strong-armed tactics, but instead of stirring up angst, her mini-tirade kindled hope. He hadn't allowed himself to hope in weeks. Months, actually, when it was clear that the last course of treatment hadn't arrested the rogue cell growth. "I'll be there in an hour."

"I'll be waiting," she promised. "Drive careful."

Not a bad reminder, and two-fold, remembering what she'd experienced. "Will do."

He headed straight down I-76, got off at South Street and parked in the garage opposite the Children's Hospital an hour later. He still wasn't sure this was the right thing to do, but Tash's insistence said he had little choice, and when he saw her waiting inside the rear entrance, his reaction to her smile, her face, said that maybe he was trusting too much, too soon.

And yet it felt right.

"You made it." Tash motioned to the wheelchair next to her. "Your chariot, madam."

"You said we weren't going to do any more hospitals, ever." Lexie's despairing eyes said she hadn't expected him to turn the tables on her.

"I explained on the way down that Tash's friends have some new advice for us."

A weary gaze stared up at him, and she almost cried, and Lexie rarely cried despite the rough hand she'd been dealt.

He stopped, ready to do an about face, but the feel of Tash's hand on his arm kept him still. "If you two decide this isn't what you want, that's fine. But you should at least listen to the doctors. Let them explain what they've discovered."

He couldn't meet his daughter's eyes. If she wanted to leave, he'd have to do it, and despite his promise to her, his job as a parent wasn't always to make her happy. It was to do the best thing for her, and so he gripped her hand, raised it for a kiss and said, "Let's head up."

Tash led them to an office adjacent to the pediatric oncology unit, and within minutes they were joined by a middle-aged man with wire-rimmed glasses. "Mister Karralis. Alexia." The way he said Lexie's name, as if it was something sacred and special stirred

Rafe's heart, or maybe it was his soul… In either case, the man's graveled but kind voice relaxed him. This wasn't a punk-doc, fresh out of the lab, ready to use his beautiful child as a notch on his belt. This was a man, probably a father, just like him, someone who knew the score and understood the end-game well. "I am Dr. Ottinger, I work here," he indicated the unit with a quick nod, "but also I work with our research team on new ways to fight cancer. At this moment, we are experimenting." He stressed the word with a pointed look to Rafe, and his honest choice of words helped again. "With differentiated T-Cells specifically targeting the cancer cells. The job of the T-cells is to charge after the cancer cells in Alexia's blood. We send them in on the attack, and they dash around the body like an army on a mission, finding those bad cells and getting rid of them. Then the body cleans up the residual mess left behind like it does after any viral attack."

"Viral attack?" Rafe had learned enough medi-speak over the last two years to know that T-cells were naturally produced within the body, but clever cancers fooled the warrior cells into thinking they belonged there, thereby avoiding the body's natural response to invaders. "I don't get it."

"The T-cells are sent into the body via a viral host which uses a virus's natural course to carry them to every possible area. The T-cells then encounter the cancerous cells, attack them, and destroy the cancer at its own level."

"I read something about this," Rafe said. He leaned forward. "How doctors used a heavy-duty measles virus to send targeted cells into a body, with mixed results. Some good, some bad."

"The drawback for measles virus is the gift of immunization," Dr. Ottinger explained. "Most of the population has either had measles or been vaccinated, making the body pre-programmed to fight the measles virus. Using that can impede the goal of full body contact. We have chosen a different virus, one that most humans have not seen and has no immunization."

A prickle of unease teased Rafe's spine. "And that would be?"

"A specially altered version of HIV."

Rafe's hands clenched. His throat went tight. He knew he had to bite back his response because Lexie was sitting right there, watching him, but to intentionally give his daughter a dose of HIV? Not gonna happen, not on his watch. "You can't be serious."

"I am quite serious. And we would only consider such a new, radical treatment in the most special of cases." He smiled at Lexie, a beautiful, older gentleman's smile of benediction and Rafe knew the look, oh he read it loud and clear. The middle-aged doctor believed Lexie was near death's door. Well, tell him something he didn't know. "We have enjoyed the benefit of a clear success with this treatment on a handful of patients." Dr. Ottinger went on. "All are showing no traces of cancer and have no incidence of HIV. While I cannot promise results, I can promise we will do our best if you decide on this course of action. Time is precious, of course, we'd need to start cell growth right away to maintain the body's current strength levels."

Translation: She's growing weaker by the day, acting now gives us the best possible chance of a good outcome.

"The HIV virus we use has been modified. Even so, the body's reaction is very strong and made more volatile by the weakened immune system."

"Side effects?"

"High fever, joint pain, illness, typical anti-viral physical response."

"Odds?"

The doctor hesitated, then exhaled softly. "Undetermined due to lack of data. We have six success stories to date, and are offering the treatment on a case-by-case basis once we've ascertained that conventional wisdom has come up short."

"How long have you been doing this, doctor?"

"Three months. Our successes have been in the recent weeks."

Three months? He wanted to try a treatment they'd just started using— no, make that experimenting with—short months ago?

He couldn't do this, he couldn't possibly allow this. What was Tash thinking? Why did she dangle a thread of hope before him, only to offer the choice of injecting his daughter with a deadly virus, loaded with tiny scraps of genetic information that promised to do The Charge of the Light Brigade on Lexie's out-of-control blood cells? What if he said yes to this course of treatment and Lexie never came out of it, missing the one thing he promised her, a nice, normal Christmas?

He stood, needing air, needing…

Something. Something concrete, something written in stone, a guarantee. Yes. That's exactly what he wanted, a guarantee, a promise, something absolute to hang onto because the thought of saying yes and having Lexie not make it through made his heart shrink to tiny, Grinch-like proportions. "I need to think about this."

"Of course." The doctor stood as well. "Might I suggest we get Alexia's blood work done and go from there depending on your decision. Having everything ready to go buys us necessary time."

He swallowed hard. A part of him wanted to grab Lexie's hand and head north to Gee-Gee and Mima, putting tempting thoughts of cures and remissions behind him once and for all. But another part, the calm, sensible side that learned to examine business prospects with quick analysis forced him to stop. Think. Consider. And so he bent over Lexie, kissed her head, nodded to the nurse, and strode out the door. "I'll be back."

CHAPTER FIVE

T ASH WATCHED HIM GO, THEN grasped Lexie's little hand, and oh... the feel of a child's hand in hers, the soft skin, tiny fingers, and cool touch.

Zoe's image flashed through her mind, a funny, unpredictable four-year-old, dancing in the wind beneath the trees in Fairmount Park. She loved to go there, she loved the green grass, the statuary, the big trees, deep and green for long months of spring and summer, and somehow, picturing Zoe with Lexie's hand tucked tight in hers, didn't seem quite so bad. She bent low. "May I stay with you?"

A spark of longing brightened the child's face. "Oh, please."

"Done." She hung out with Lexie for the next couple of hours, and when one of the staff nurses brought them matching princess coloring books with brand new crayons, they declared a coloring contest, and that's how Rafe found them mid-afternoon. Tash had tucked Lexie into a big, comfy chair, tossed a couple of her favorite toys alongside, but neither one acknowledged his presence when he arrived because they were head-to-head in a coloring competition and the clock was running.

Rafe should have been irritated that he went unnoticed, but the sight of them, woman and child, heads bent, industriously coloring matching pictures, made him smile. "Hey. We don't even look up and say hello to the old man?"

"Daddy. Shh. We're in a contest."

Tash slid a look to her cell phone on the tray table, but kept working as she spoke. "It's timed. Tash's nurse gets to judge based on three factors. Amount completed, skill level, color choice. There is a slight and I mean *very slight*," she emphasized the words and Lexie giggled out loud, "handicap allowance due to age, and that was the nurse's idea, not mine. I figured go big or stay home."

Lexie giggled again, but she didn't look up. Fingers moving, she deftly and carefully shaded in the princess's signature blue dress, then outlined the border in a slightly deeper blue. Glancing at Tash's work, he saw she'd done the same thing, and the thought of Lexie, copying Tash and learning from her felt good at a moment when everything around him seemed wrong.

The phone alarm signaled the end of time.

"Grrrrrr!" Tash stared at her princess, chagrined. "I wanted to get the flounce done, and the trees. How'd you do, kid?"

Lexie turned her more childlike offering their way.

"I love it!" Tash high-fived her. "And you didn't get the trees done either. It's such a trick to know how to work fast and carefully, it's one of those skills you don't realize you need to sharpen until it's right smack-dab in front of you. And then?" She shrugged. "Oops. Too late. It's always good to be ahead of the game, in my book."

Rafe believed that philosophy. He'd lived that attitude as a single father until Lexie's cancer dead-bolted his choices. Seeing her now, working with Tash, competing and loving it, gave him a glimpse of the future she could have if this treatment proved successful.

And if it isn't successful? Have you then wasted the last few weeks she has on more pie-in-the-sky treatments with no positive results?

He'd come back to this wing, determined to say no to the experimental offer, grab his beautiful child and go home, but seeing her actively engaged with Tash stopped him.

Maybe they were wrong not to fight tooth and nail. Maybe the nudge to come back to what he knew first, Grolier Springs, his family hometown, was God's way of putting this choice before him at Children's Hospital.

He understood odds and percentages, and to have a chance meeting with Tash, who happened to be some kind of money-procuring bigwig on a cancer research team, had to be more than luck or chance.

It had to be God.

Dr. Ottinger came up alongside him. He said nothing. He paused and watched Tash with Lexie, just like Rafe did, and when Rafe turned his way and gave a quick nod, the doctor breathed deep. "I'll send the order to initiate cell growth."

He thought he'd feel scared or hopeful, but a simple calm acceptance washed over him instead. He'd made a decision, and for the life of him, he didn't know if it was right or wrong, but it was done and there was comfort in that. He moved across the room and took a seat opposite Tash. "Lexie, I've thought about this, I've prayed about it, and I've decided to let them try this new treatment. I know I promised no more treatments—"

She made a face and waved him off as if this wasn't life and death, a huge deal in his book. "I already told them I wanted to do it. It feels funny to sit around Mima's doing nothing." She scrunched up her little face and frowned. "Like we were giving up and I don't think we ever want to give up on things, do we, Daddy?"

They didn't, no…

"So I told the nurses and Tash I'd talk to you because doing something is way better than doing nothing."

The child's simple courage confirmed his decision, but Rafe was no fool. He understood the gravity involved, the risk he was taking. It would take them at least a week to grow and train the needed cells for the treatment. A week of waiting, hoping, praying… "Can I take her home in the meantime?"

"Absolutely. We'll call you when we're ready for her, probably seven to nine days."

"We'll see you then."

Tasha shared a few words with the doctor, then caught up with them. Rafe turned her way inside the elevator. "What are you doing tonight?"

Surprise widened her eyes. "Sleeping?"

Lexie giggled and Tasha slanted her a grin.

"Before that?"

"Working. Why?"

"I'm going to take Lexie down to the Christmas Village. That way she can see the Christmas lights along boathouse row on the way home later. You in?"

Tasha's heart surged, then shrunk. She couldn't do this. Could she? Go out with Rafe and this precious child, knowing what the future might bring? If she was so mired in her own past, how could she be good for Lexie? Or Rafe? But she took one look into Lexie's excited eyes and noted Rafe's anticipation and caved. "Hang out downstairs. Give me twenty minutes and I'm all yours."

"We can grab food first, give it time to get dark. Lexie, are you hungry?"

"Can we get ice cream?"

"Anything you'd like, sweet cheeks."

She dimpled, and Tasha had a brief image of what she'd looked like before treatments left her cheeks rounded and her scalp bald.

"If we're making this a night, let's go to The Franklin Fountain first," Tasha suggested. "Everyone should go to The Franklin Fountain when they're in the city."

"Agreed." Rafe met her eyes and smiled. "Soda shops are always in style."

She blushed, which was ridiculous, but the warmth of Rafe's smile made her remember sitting in the Kandy Kitchen, sipping a vanilla Coke, hoping he'd notice her. He didn't, then, but he was now because he wasn't afraid to look into her eyes and identify with her loss. "I'll be right back."

"We'll be waiting."

She hurried up to the offices, checked in and out with Mary, and rushed back to the elevator, and it wasn't just because her high school crush was waiting downstairs. It was because a child waited with him, a girl who might only have a matter of days to have fun. She stepped off the elevator and saw Rafe sitting with Lexie in his arms, sound asleep.

"Oh." She crossed the floor and sank into the seat next to him. "She looks too peaceful to disturb."

Rafe scoffed. "Nope. She can sleep tonight. Right now? It's party time. Or it is once we get to the Fountain. Is your car here?"

She shook her head. "I carpool with a neighbor. She drove today."

He stood, balancing Lexie with strong but gentle grip. "Perfect. It's been a long time since I've had two pretty girls to impress."

"You don't have to impress me, Rafe." She paused before they got to the door and looked up.

"What if I want to, Tasha?" He met her gaze, then dropped a

sweet kiss to his daughter's forehead when she stirred. "What then?"

If Rafe had wanted to impress her twelve years ago, she'd have fallen over in teenage girl disbelief. But now, the thought seemed beautifully normal. How could it when nothing about their situation was normal? "Will she wake up when you put her in the car?"

He shrugged. "Maybe. Maybe not. But if she doesn't, we'll wake her when we park down on Market Street. I'm pretty sure the ice cream shop isn't going to be teaming with business in December."

They parked in one of the small business lots nearby. Old City, Philadelphia was busy as business people left work for home, but Rafe was right. The soda and candy shop was fairly quiet.

"Let's awaken the sleeping princess, shall we?"

"Rafe."

He was bending through the back door to awaken Lexie, but he stopped and turned. "Yes?"

She looked down at the sleeping child, then shrugged. "She just seems so peaceful."

"She does, I know. But Tash, if this might be the last week of Christmas she has, I don't want her to sleep through it. We're here. The Christmas Village is only a short drive away, and the boathouses are on the ride home. I want her to feel every bit of Christmas joy she can before they treat her next week. And then?" He shrugged, but his face showed the struggle of "then". "We'll see."

"All right."

She stepped back, and when the chill late-day air stung Lexie's cheeks, she stirred and opened her eyes. "Where are we?"

"We're going to get ice cream, like you asked."

"Really?" She sat up higher in his arms, and looked around.

Twinkle lights surrounded them. Christmas motifs brightened the quaint walkways, while a Salvation Army bell ringer tolled nearby. "Oh, I love the bells, Daddy! And the lights! And even the cars look all Christmasy."

The city traffic heading toward the expressways reflected the jeweled tones of the Christmas lights trimming each window.

"It's so very pretty. Isn't it, Tasha? I always like colored lights the best. They sparkle more."

Tasha had feared she wasn't ready to see Christmas through

another child's eyes. Zoe had loved the colored lights, too. That was probably normal for kids, the gay mix looked cheerful and fun, but seeing Lexie's excitement didn't mar Zoe's memory or make her feel disloyal. It felt good and healing to see Lexie tip back in her father's arms and scan the buildings for the prettiest lights.

They chose cozy seats in the back of the soda fountain, and when their order was ready, Lexie's broad smile matched her round eyes. "That's such a big sundae!" She grabbed Tash's hand. "You have to help me eat it, Tasha. I'll never eat that much ice cream."

"I'd be honored," Tasha told her. The ice cream clerk brought a second spoon, and Lexie watched carefully as Tasha took her first taste. Tasha paused on purpose, letting her face show her happiness, then sighed out loud. "The best ever, Lexie!"

"Isn't it?" They shared back and forth, laughing. Teasing. The beauty of the normalcy wasn't lost on Tasha, and when they finished their treat, Lexie gripped Tasha's hand on one side and her father's in the other. "Isn't this just so much fun?"

"It is." Rafe grinned down at her. For this moment, that's all it was. Sweet, family-style fun. And when he went to pay the bill, an older gentleman waved him off.

"You come back when the little girl feels better and I'll let you pay then. For tonight?" The man shrugged like it was no big deal. "Merry Christmas to you and your pretty wife and your little girl."

Merry Christmas. Pretty wife.

He turned and saw Tasha teasing Lexie about something silly and girly and most likely pink. He couldn't hold back a prayer, and he'd stopped doing that weeks ago when he promised God acceptance, no matter how hard it was. But now, with another thread of hope dangling before him, he sent up the one-word prayer he'd discarded weeks ago.

Please. And then he moved back across the mostly empty room as the entreaty re-stamped itself upon his heart. "Ready, girls?"

"Yes!" Excitement raised Lexie's volume.

Tasha replied in a more refined tone. "Me, too. Let's go see what the Christmas Village has to offer."

They took the car up to Love Park and let Lexie have a peek at the fun of an old-fashioned Christkindl. Wooden booths, scenic displays, bright lights, joyous music… and when a vendor displayed a beautiful music box with a gathering of children, playing at a festival, Lexie's face showed the enchantment of the moment. "Oh, Daddy." She stretched out a hand to the dainty box, then drew back as if it was too special to touch. "Have you ever seen anything more beautiful?"

Rafe hugged her close and fought the quick clutch of emotion teeming inside. "Yes, darling. You."

She turned and met his gaze, saw the damp eyes, and placed two little hands alongside his cheeks. "You mustn't worry anymore. You promised. Okay?"

"I won't."

She sent him a very determined look. "You've said that before."

"I mean it this time."

"Okay." She aimed a smile at Tasha, then yawned. "I'm tired, Daddy."

"Then we'll head home." He snugged her close as they walked to the car, and when they arrived at Tasha's house in Mount Airy, it wasn't hard to tell which one was hers. Tucked in a family-style neighborhood of decorated homes and corner shops, Tash's cream and brown house stood dark, stark and lonely.

"Tasha, where are your Christmas lights?" Lexie peered out from the back seat, perplexed. "Did you forget to buy them?"

Too late, Rafe realized the backstory. Tasha had lost her daughter just over three years before. Facing holidays after a grievous anniversary could be a wretched circumstance. He started to intercept Lexie's question, but Tasha turned and faced her from the front seat.

"I've got some," she admitted slowly. "I just haven't gotten them out in a while."

"Because you're busy," determined the little girl. She slapped a hand to her forehead and aimed her look toward her father through the rear-view mirror. "Dad, we've got time to help, don't we? And then Tasha's house can look pretty, like all the rest."

Rafe hesitated. "I'm not sure, honey. Tasha's schedule is tight."

"Well, ours isn't." She folded her arms across her chest and for that brief moment she looked and sounded like the healthy child she used to be. "We can help her in a few days, when she's got a day off, couldn't we? Like Saturday?"

Rafe decided to take Tasha's lead, and when she turned his way, he read the struggle, but something else, too. Strength. And kindness. "I think that would be a great idea, Lexie. Rafe, is that good with you? To bring Lexie over on Saturday and you guys can make me look more festive?"

"You're sure?" He held her gaze so she would know he was willing to make this all go away. "We don't have to do this, Tasha."

"But—" Lexie looked up at him, puzzled.

"I think we do." Tasha drew a breath, let it out and smiled back at Lexie. "I think we really do, Rafe." She climbed out, opened the back door and leaned in to kiss Lexie's cheek. "Good night, honey. Thanks for hanging with me today."

"It was fun." Lexie smiled up at Tash and the ice cream clerk's words ran through Rafe's mind again. *Your wife and your little girl.* At this moment, that's exactly what they looked like, smiling down at one another.

"I'll see you Saturday, okay? Ten o'clock good?"

"Ten's fine." He wanted to re-ask the question, reassure himself that she knew what she was getting into, but she moved up the steps, applied her key, and let herself into the unadorned house. A light winked on, and as they started to back out of the driveway, Tasha tipped back the front curtain and waved.

Lexie waved back, excited, and as they drove home, she didn't fall asleep like usual. She chattered about Tasha this and Tasha that and when they slowed down to view the lights along the Schuylkill River at boathouse row, she was starry eyed at the sight. No matter what else happened, he'd be grateful to Tasha for making Lexie smile and laugh. That in itself was a sweet, tiny miracle.

CHAPTER SIX

TASHA USUALLY IGNORED THE NEIGHBORING decorations when she came home, eyes forward, gaze locked. But tonight the twinkling lights called to her, as if seeing them through Lexie's eyes. Bright and bold or simple and sweet, a good share of the homes had decorated and the festive neighborhood took on a joyous air throughout December.

She'd blocked out happiness for years. She'd let guilt stifle healing. She'd turned a blind eye to her grandmother's emotions, and if Mima hadn't opened up last week, she'd still be going through life, chin down, pretending oblivion.

Now she couldn't. *Wouldn't*, she decided. Mima's words and Rafe's example pushed her into moving on. "Why does it have to be someone's fault?" Rafe had wondered, and he was right.

A light flashed on across the narrow street. She moved to the window and tipped back the curtain.

The Jackson's Star of Bethlehem had come on, and cast its pale amber glow over a plastic resin Nativity scene below. The scene showed signs of wear and tear in the daylight, but none of that was visible now. A stalwart father, a young mother, bent, nurturing her child. A bed of straw, and a scattering of animals.

Mary, the mother of God. Mary, young but willing to accept the challenge offered. Mary, knowing the scriptures, and understanding what might lay before her firstborn son.

Did she ponder the future on that cold, starlit night? When choruses of angels announced the birth to common men of the fields?

Or did she just marvel at the perfection of her blessed child before her?

Tasha wanted Mary's courage. She needed that kind of strength, the inner core she saw in Rafe. In his grandmother. In Mima.

Peace I leave with you. My peace I give to you.

She watched the lighted scene a few moments longer, then let the curtain slip back into place, as she sent up a rusty prayer for Lexie's recovery. She knew the odds better than most, but some hope was better than none. Until this morning, none was exactly what Rafe and Lexie had.

"I brought food," Rafe announced when she opened the door on Saturday morning. "And a kid."

"Then the kid better be hungry because I got food, too." Tasha laughed as she swung the door wide. "Clearly we could have coordinated our efforts, but whatever is in those bags smells wonderful!"

"What did you get?" Rafe walked straight through the entrance hall and into the vintage kitchen. He spotted a tray on the table and grinned. "Bagels. You drove to 3rd Street to get us bagels?"

"It's a special day."

"It is." Rafe helped Lexie tug her warm jacket off, and he breathed deep. "And I smell apples."

"And cinnamon!" Lexie turned toward the stove. "You made hot applesauce?"

"Nope. You and I are going to make hot applesauce," Tasha told her. "Just like in the book Mima read to you."

"I'll be just like Betsy!"

"Yup. I've got all the apples peeled and cored here. I'm going to put them on to simmer and we're going to check them every little while. When they're soft and they've cooled a little, you'll get to mash them."

"I've been waiting to mash apples all my life."

Rafe's grin said he appreciated the drama of her words. "That long, huh?"

"Oh, Daddy, you know what I mean." She looked around the house for the first time and then turned to face Tasha. "You're not kidding about needing help. There's nothing here."

"Lex—"

Rafe looked chagrined, but Tasha stooped and nodded. "Exactly why I called in the experts. I saw how wonderful you made things at Gee-Gee's house and I was hoping you could help me. So, to that end—" She set paper, scissors, glue, glitter and patterns on the table. "Wanna get artsy, kid?"

Lexie's eyes grew wide. "Yes!" She slid into the chair and within seconds had picked out several simple patterns to cut out. "Tasha, this is the best idea ever."

"And if you paint glue into the little patterns on the ornaments, you can selectively glitter any part you want, using any color you want." She showed her an example, and Lexie grabbed hold.

"This is so pretty! Did you do it?"

"When I was about a year older than you. My Mima liked to do these things with us and it was fun to have handmade ornaments for the tree."

"One problem. You don't have a tree." Lexie made the statement carefully as if guarding Tasha's feelings.

"And I think getting one for just me would be silly," Tasha agreed. "So I thought if Dad and I hang up garland and lights around the windows, we could hang the pretty ornaments from the garland."

"Oh, that is a really excellent idea!" Lexie's grin said she approved. "I'll try and do a bunch so they dry in time to hang them later."

"And these," Rafe held up two boxes of outdoor lights. "Are for the porch, I expect?"

"Yes."

"Well, come on, woman. I've no intention of getting cold alone."

"Lex? Will you be okay?"

"I'll be fine!" She looked fine right now, despite the effects of the treatments she'd endured. She looked… delighted. And when Tasha thought of all she'd been through, the idea that a fun glitter project made the girl so happy humbled her.

"Okay." She turned, tugged on an Eagles sweatshirt and moved to the door. "Let's do this."

Rafe looked around once they got outside. "Do we have a ladder?"

She grimaced. "No." She brightened. "I've got a chair. Would that work?"

He eyed the arch and was just about to consider it when a neighbor's door opened across the way. "Tasha, you're putting up lights! Need help?"

She waved to Mr. Jackson and started to say no, but Rafe called out, "Got a ladder?"

The middle-aged man nodded quickly. "Be right there!"

As he descended his driveway carrying a nice six-foot aluminum ladder a few minutes later, Mrs. Jackson came out of the front door. She hustled down the steps, caught up to the man, and climbed the steps to Tasha's porch while the two men propped the ladder in the front yard nearest the house.

"I saw you have garland and I have these extra bows, honey!" She handed Tasha six slightly tattered red velveteen bows. "A mouse chewed a bit off that one, but from the road, who will know?"

"No one." Rafe smiled up at her and when Mrs. Jackson looked at him— really looked at him— she about swooned. Her reaction said no matter what the age, women weren't immune to Rafe's good looks, which took Tasha right back to high school.

"Mother, why don't you run across and get those little lights we had extra. They'd be perfect on Tasha's bushes here. Then no one will even hardly notice they need pruning, but there's always next year, right?" Mr. Jackson settled the ladder, then insisted on holding it while Rafe climbed to affix the lights in the year-round screwed-in holders.

"These are handy little things," he noted, looking down at Tasha, and when Mrs. Jackson saw Rafe's look, she drew a deep breath, squeezed Tasha's arm, sent her a look of pure joy and bustled back across the street to gather the extra lights.

"Tasha, you're putting up lights?" Jenny Rood from next door popped her head out a window. "How wonderful! And I've got just the thing for around the doorway! I'll be right over!"

Rafe's snort said he was choking back laughter, but when Jenny hurried across the narrow concrete driveway carrying an extended length of thin, pre-lit garland, the only look she saw on his face was appreciation. Tasha met Jenny on the top step and realized that she was giving away a decoration she'd used for years. "Jenny, I can't take this." Her neighbor was on disability, she lived in her parents' house, and money was always tight.

"You can too!" Jenny took the chair from one side of the porch and moved it to the left side of the doorway. "I even brought my handy-dandy little hammer and a couple of corner nails so we can have it up in a heartbeat."

It might have taken a few extra heartbeats, but the pre-lit, dollar-store style garland was hung quickly, the moth-eaten bows were tacked at the four arch corners of the front porch lights, and as they re-tested the lights to be sure they worked, the front door opened from within. "You guys are pretty noisy out here." Lexie had her jacket draped around her shoulders, and paused when she saw the three strangers on the porch. "Oh, sorry. I didn't know we had company."

Tasha hesitated, unsure how to explain, remembering her own awkward first meeting with Lexie, but Jenny Rood was way ahead of her.

"How cute are you, sweet thing?" She crooned the words like you would to any five-year-old, then pointed to the mish-mash of lights and greenery. "What do you think? Awesome, right?"

Rafe climbed the steps, lifted her into his arms, then carried her back down to view the entire effect from the yard. "Now it will be showier at night of course," he began, but she waved off his words.

"It's so beautiful even now!" Her unfettered pleasure put smiles on the faces of Tasha's three neighbors. "Tasha said she needed help decorating and you all came over! This is a great party!"

"With an amazing amount of food," Rafe joked.

There was, Tasha realized. She pushed open the door and waved the neighbors in. "We've got plenty," she insisted, and when Jenny and Mrs. Jackson exchanged glances, Tasha folded her arms across her chest. "Really, this is perfect. Lexie and Rafe came over to help me decorate. And since this is the first time I've done it in a while," she hesitated, then shrugged her shoulders lightly, knowing she needn't say more, "it would be a nice thing to celebrate, don't you think?"

"Count me in," declared Mr. Jackson. He followed Rafe and Lexie inside which meant Mrs. Jackson had no choice and Jenny got swept up in the stream.

"You're sure you don't mind, Tasha?" She turned just inside the door. "No one wants to put you on the spot."

Facing her next door neighbor, Tasha realized she wasn't being put on the spot, she was being helped. The understanding made her smile. Her neighbors had been tiptoeing around her sadness for three years, and God bless them, they'd done a good job of it. "You have to come in, Jenny. I drove over to 3rd Street and got bagels and Rafe brought baklava and spanakopita from his grand-parents' restaurant. And a fruit tray. We've way too much, but with you guys stopping in, it's not too much at all. It's just perfect."

"Tasha? Do you have a bottle opener?" Rafe poked his head around the corner, and Jenny's quick sigh said she knew a good thing when she saw it. "I brought some sparkling grape juice to make this a real celebration."

"Top drawer, left of the sink."

"You've got lights for in here, too," Jenny noted. She gripped Tasha's arm. "I'm so glad."

Rafe poured the sparkling juice into a mismatched bunch of glassware, then raised his glass on high before touching it to Lex-ie's. "To a very merry Christmas!"

Lexie giggled as people touched their glass rims to hers, and by the time they'd eaten and swagged lighted garland around the front windows, the five-year-old looked worn out, but happy. And happy was the important thing. Rafe bundled her into the warm car, then bounded back up the steps to say goodbye. He swept the decorated porch a quick smile, then reached out and pulled Tasha in for a big, long hug.

"Thank you." He whispered the words against her cheek, her ear, and when he drew back, the look he shared said more than words. "You made her happy today. That means everything to me, Tash."

"I'm glad." She whispered too, because talking about a child's happiness was worth the respect of a whisper. "Thank you for coming over. For the food. For—"

His kiss stopped her little speech, ramped up her heart and reig-nited her pulse into high gear. The strength of his arms, the chill of his cheeks, and the warmth of his lips combined to put her world on a whole new orbit. The kiss melded the joy of the day with the heart of the season, and Tasha would be okay if it never had to end. Of course it did.

"Gotta go."

"Yes, get her home."

He stepped back and held her gaze for long, slow seconds, then raised his palm to her cheek once again. "I'll call you later."

She wanted him to. She wanted to sit and talk long hours, shar-ing all the things she'd stored up for the last couple of decades, but she simply blinked up at him and offered a gentle smile. "I'd like that. A lot."

"Me, too." She stood in the door, watching them leave, and when they were out of sight, she went back inside.

The front room had been transformed. No longer austere, the windows were draped with garland. Mrs. Jackson had run home and gotten spools of wired ribbon, and she and Jenny had crafted pretty bows while talking around the kitchen table. The six windows had a bow wired at each corner. Green garland swagged across the tops with two of Lexie's glitter ornaments hanging from the greenery. When the heat switched on, the forced air warmth sent the paper ornaments dancing beneath the twinkle lights.

She went back to the kitchen to put the last cups into the dishwasher and spotted a folded paper on the table. She opened it, smiled and sighed.

"Thank you for the memry, Tosh!"

Would there be more memories for Lexie Karralis? Would the treatment work? Would the doctors know how to dose her properly at her age and size?

She sank onto the couch and studied the room. The extra light and the scattered decorations lent a feel of Christmas, but knowing what Lexie was about to face, she longed to do something to help. But what?

Church bells tolled the hour down the road. She went to her computer, plugged in the church name and saw a Mass schedule for that weekend. If she dressed quickly, she could make the five o'clock service.

She stared at the door, unsure.

She'd shrugged off anything to do with faith or religion years ago, long before she lost Zoe. Too busy, too important, too self-absorbed...

But hearing Rafe's take on faith and life was like a breath of fresh air. Maybe she wasn't as smart as she thought she was. Maybe she needed more than herself and her job. Maybe she needed—

She wasn't one bit sure, but she hadn't been sure about a lot of things lately so she changed into good clothes, slipped into a warm coat, pulled on boots and gloves and walked to church for the first time since her wedding day, nine years before, but this time she made the trip because she wanted to. And that made all the difference.

CHAPTER SEVEN

"I LOVE YOU, DADDY."

Lexie was prepped and ready for the treatment a few days later.

Rafe wasn't. A part of him, a very big part, wanted to yank the IV tubing out and race for the hills of suburban Philadelphia. What if things went bad? What if the treatment took what little life she had left? Was it worth giving up those weeks?

Fear gripped his heart and grappled his soul. He'd made a decision to avoid more interference. Why hadn't he stuck to his guns? He'd promised her a beautiful Christmas, and if she didn't make it through, what kind of father did that make him?

He was on the verge of literally pulling the plug on his permissions, when Lexie peeked up at Doctor Ottinger. "I'm ready."

"As am I." He smiled down at her and spoke softly as the treatment was administered, explaining that she was going to get sick first... and then better.

Lexie made a little face as Tasha walked into the room. "Well, I've done that before!"

"Yes, you have." The doctor smiled at her, stepped outside and spoke to the nurses, then motioned Rafe to the hallway.

"Now what?"

"We wait. We make her as comfortable as possible. And we pray."

He wanted to be strong.

He felt weak.

He longed to be prayerful, because that came easy to him most days, but the thought that he'd made this decision with Lexie, stuck square in his chest. What-ifs plagued him.

He put on his best face and re-entered the room. When Lexie looked up, the smile on her face said she was willing to fight. How could he do any less?

"You're staying on-site, aren't you?" Tasha moved a checker to be kinged and looked really proud to be beating Lexie, but then Lexie jumped two of Tasha's men and squealed as Tasha looked his way.

She read his emotion. He saw it in her change of expression, but he sucked a breath and nodded. "Yes. That way I'm here to annoy the kid all I can."

"Did you see the decorations the nurse's put up, Daddy?" Lexie pointed through the windowed wall. "I'll fall asleep looking at them and wake up looking at them. It's perfect."

It wasn't perfect. None of this was perfect, but there was no backing out now. "I love it, honey."

She squealed again when she beat Tasha, and when Tasha groaned as if she'd just lost an Olympic medal, Lexie gave her a half-hug with her free arm. "Can we play again?"

Tasha tapped her watch. "I have to get back to work, but I'll come back and play more later, okay?"

"Good. Daddy, can I watch TV?"

"Sure." He picked up the remote and aimed it at the suspended set. "What would you like to see?"

"Something with Christmas."

His gut knotted. His chest went tight, but he found a princess show celebrating the holiday, then followed Tasha into the hall.

"You're scared."

He couldn't deny it. He also couldn't talk about it.

"They'll do everything they can for her, Rafe. And then it's up to God."

"It always has been," he corrected her, "but I feel like I'm sec-ond-guessing him. Should I have left well enough alone?"

"No."

His grunt said she didn't know what she was talking about.

"You're giving her a chance, and that's the best any of us can do. It's not wrong to give her a chance, Rafe."

He wanted to believe that, believe *her*, but when Lexie's fever spiked into the stratosphere forty-eight hours later, Rafe wanted to punch someone. Code-colored lines on the monitors said her body was under siege. Her pale skin took on a grayish cast. Her pretty eyes, so full of life, stayed tightly shut, and when she did move, it was in obvious pain and distress.

He'd done this to her. He'd made this decision and seeing the result, he pretty much hated himself, Tasha, the doctors and God.

"How's she doing? Any better?" Tasha tiptoed into the room on the twenty-third, and Rafe lost it.

"She's dying."

Tasha stopped in her tracks and looked from Rafe to the nurse and back again.

"You called me all hepped up about this new treatment, this new chance and I was so freakin' desperate that I took the bait, Tasha." He turned her way. It didn't matter that she looked broken-hearted. It didn't matter that he was taking out his angst and guilt on her, all that mattered right now was that he'd broken the promise he made. He'd brought Lexie back to Grolier Springs for a sweet, old-fashioned Christmas, and what did he give her?

A death sentence.

"Rafe, I—"

"Don't talk."

The nurse stared at him. So did Tasha, but then she took a step back. Her gaze went to Lexie, barely clinging to life despite the machinery and technology of the Pediatric Intensive Care Unit. She stared at Lex. Her chin trembled. Her hands clenched. And then she took three more steps back and left the room.

He'd hurt her, and he'd done it on purpose, which made him a bigger jerk, and seeing what he put his precious daughter through, the week before Christmas?

He hadn't thought such a thing was possible.

Tash's heart started beating again about the time she got back to her office. Mary took one look at her, and followed her into the room. "Not good?"

"Not good at all." She sank into her chair, closed her eyes, and put her head in her hands. "She's close to full system shutdown. Her vitals are weak, her body's at war with itself. What have I done?" She brought her head up to meet Mary's look of sympathy. "Why didn't I just mind my own business? I ran around, begging favors, bringing Rafe in when he was already reluctant. I stole the last few weeks he had with his daughter, and I can't forgive myself for that."

"You stole nothing." Mary stayed pragmatic. "You offered a one-in-a-million chance, Tasha. And you know how things went down with the initial adult patients. They got real sick, too."

"Not like this." She cringed, remembering the look of Lexie's body. "I don't know how this can be fixed, Mary. And the look on Rafe's face…"

"He blames you."

"With good reason."

"Then my prayer will be that Lexie turns a corner." When Tasha made a face, Mary gripped her hand tightly. "We've watched miracles happen these last few weeks. Five adults are now cancer free because of work we've done here. A major drug company is putting all of its resources behind this research because we might be able to kick cancer to the curb in the next few years. Tasha, listen."

Tasha met her gaze reluctantly.

"I can't predict any of this, and Lexie is under the care of the best team of doctors in the biz, but she's got something else going for her. God. And if this treatment works, if they can definitively thwart cancer in this little girl, the entire world will celebrate and I think our world could use some good news these days. So keep praying, and no matter what Rafe says now, cut him some slack. You know better than most how difficult these times are."

She did. She understood the anger and the wrath. The bitter disappointment and the yawning emptiness.

"Stay kind and supportive. Don't let him get to you. And keep praying."

She would. It felt strange, but it felt good, too, so she'd keep doing it because honestly? It made her feel better which made Mima's take on God and faith right all along. But right now, she wanted one thing only: For Lexie Karralis to come out of this crisis and live life to the full, God's promise. And that didn't seem like a likely scenario at the moment.

Commotion around Lexie's bed yanked Rafe awake. A medical team surrounded her, but none of the oft-heard danger tones had gone off. Had she slipped quietly away while he slept nearby?

He shot out of the chair and nearly toppled the nurse nearest him. "What's happening? What's going on?"

Dr. Orrington held up a hand of caution. "We may have isolated the cause of the over-reaction. If we're right, this medication should ease the body's response to the treatment."

"More treatment to fix the already almost lethal treatment?" Did he sound bitter and tired? Yes to both.

Dr. Orrington's gaze wasn't affronted. Instead, compassion filled his eyes and softened his jaw. "It is always hard to put our faith in the unknown. But if Dr. Warren is correct, this medication might calm the reaction. On the positive side, the virus is doing exactly as it should. It is destroying cancer cells throughout her body."

Rafe wasn't impressed. What good were dead cancer cells if Lexie didn't survive? He started to speak, but paused as Tasha slipped into the room. She crossed to his side, put a wrapped gift on the tiny table in the corner, then sat, head bowed.

The doctors offered instructions to the nurse, then Dr. Orrington turned back to Rafe. "You're a praying man."

Rafe nodded. "Usually." Fear put bite into the single word. No matter how ready he thought he was to let Lexie go home to God, now, at the moment of truth, he'd do anything to save her.

Dr. Orrington put a hand on his shoulder. "Don't stop now."

He slipped out of the room with Dr. Warren. They were here, in the middle of the night, trying to save a child's life. His child's life.

The nurse was checking all of Lexie's apparatus. He sat back down, next to Tash, and wandered what to say to her. He'd hurt her deliberately.

Why did she come back? Why did she come back now, in the early hours of Christmas Eve? With a gift, besides. "Why aren't you sleeping?" His voice sounded gruff. He didn't care.

Tash lifted her head. "I woke up and something told me to come here. So I did."

"Something?"

She shrugged. "The Holy Spirit, maybe? Remember how Sister Angelicus used to talk about those whispers of inspiration, how important it was to listen? And then to act?"

"I remember."

"I decided that if a smart woman like Sister Angelicus could listen to those nudges, so could I."

He stared straight ahead, then dropped his head into his hands. "I don't want to lose her, Tash."

"I know."

Emotion gripped his shoulders. It put a stranglehold on his neck, his jaw. "I told myself I was ready."

The soft, quiet touch of her hand on his arm said she understood his struggle, and more than anyone else, she *would* understand.

"But I'm not. Which means all my talk about accepting God's will was basically meaningless because I'd do anything right now to save her."

Her hand grasped his, and the feel of her cool, smooth fingers blessed him. "Then we pray together, Rafe."

He gripped her hand, gripped it hard, and the touch of someone else who'd faced this struggle gave him courage. "Our Father…"

"Who art in heaven…"

"Hallowed be thy name."

"Thy kingdom come…" He struggled, choking on these next words, words he'd uttered all his life without weighing the true meaning behind them. "Thy will be done. On Earth as it is in heaven."

Thy will be done.

Four tiny words, ripe with meaning, layered with trust. Could he trust again? With Lexie so sick, struggling more with each beat of her little heart? Could he place her into God's hands, his care?

Do you have a choice?

Tash squeezed his hand lightly and whispered the rest of the prayer for him.

He wasn't sure when he dozed off, but when he woke, Tash was gone and Dr. Orrington and a nurse were standing alongside Lexie's bed.

And they were smiling.

His heart leapt. His throat convulsed. He stood, and as Dr. Orrington moved slightly left, Rafe got a clear view of the monitors registering Lexie's vitals. And they looked much more promising. "She's doing better."

"Much better." Dr. Orrington reached over and put a strong hand on his shoulder. "This is the improvement we waited to see. As of now, her body should begin normal clean-up procedures to rid itself of leftover waste."

"When will she wake up?"

He shook his head. "We'll give her time. Her body has been through a great deal. Normal rest is good. And we'll monitor everything, but Mr. Karralis, this—" he motioned to the new display of vitals. "Is what we've been praying for."

He strode out, shoulders back, head high, and if joy could be measured by footsteps, the quiet doctor's happiness was soaring.

Rafe turned to the nurse. "When did Tash Sorkos leave?"

She glanced at the clock. "About half-an-hour ago. She said she was going to work and to call her if anything changed."

Rafe stepped out of the room, moved into the far corridor and pulled out his cell phone. He texted two words. "Doing better!"

Almost instantly a response came through. "On my way!"

He wasn't sure if she brought roller blades to work or got dropped on the helipad above the new wing, but she arrived back on the floor far quicker than humanly possible. He heard the elevator doors open, turned, and there she was. "You were on your way back."

She nodded. "I know you're mad at me for all this, but Rafe, if you don't mind, I can't stay away. I tried to work." She hooked a thumb toward the maze of research facilities to the southwest of the hospital. "But I can't concentrate. So is it okay if I stay down here? With you?"

"Yes. And Tash…" He wanted to apologize for his outburst yesterday, for his outrageous behavior, but she raised her right hand and put it against his mouth.

"Don't say a word. Don't apologize, don't do any of that because I get it, Rafe." She went through the gowning process and as the big double doors opened to re-admit them to the PICU, she faced him square. "I get it."

The nurse stepped out as they slipped in. Tasha breathed deep. "Her color's better. So much better."

"And her vitals." Rafe pointed. "Heading toward normal."

"Oh, thank God." Tasha sank into the chair, hands clasped, and despite her brave words in the hall, tears slid down her cheeks in a free-fall of emotion.

"Hey." He sat next to her, handed her a clutch of tissues and waited while she mopped her eyes and blew her nose. "What was all that brave stuff in the hall if you're going to come in here and fall apart on me?"

"Happy tears don't count," she scolded. "They're different."

"Just as messy."

"Yes." She aimed a watery smile his way. "But much more welcome."

The nurse returned with a tray of food. She moved the wrapped gift and slid the table their way. "A little holiday treat from the kitchen. Turkey sandwiches and cranberry sauce. I figured you guys hadn't eaten in a while."

"You're a life-saver." Rafe smiled up at her.

"Well, we'll give that credit to God and the researchers, but I do what I can. Food is the easy part," she joked. She adjusted one of Lexie's lines slightly, then left again.

"Did you call your grandmother and Gee Gee?"

He winced. "No. I called you." Her smile said the thought of him calling her first pleased her. "I'll call them now."

He went through the whole stepping out process again, asked his grandmother to inform the family and every prayer chain they could, and then returned. "Still sleeping?"

"Peacefully."

Relief calmed him. He wasn't sure when he fell asleep, but he knew exactly when he woke.

"Daddy?"

The half-whispered question made him smile.

"Daddy?" In his dream, Lexie's voice sounded stronger. Louder.

Rafe blinked his eyes open. Tash's head was on his shoulder, but she moved at the exact same time.

"Daddy, my throat's sore. Can I have a freeze pop?"

"Lexie?" He stood, hit the nurse call button and grinned down at his little girl. "Hey, honey. Merry Christmas."

"Is it Christmas day? For real?"

"For over two hours." Tash came alongside the bed and when Lexie's eyes lit up to see her, Rafe's heart did a little dance in his chest. "Hey, sweet thing. How're we doing?"

"Better." She blinked up at them, owl-like, yawned and sighed. "I feel better."

"Good." The nurse bustled in, smiling, and within a few minutes, Dr. Orrington and Dr. Warren came through the door.

"It's Christmas," Rafe told them.

"Best present I could imagine is right here." Dr. Orrington exchanged a knowing smile with Dr. Warren. "Alexia, how are you feeling?"

She smiled up at him. "Good! Can I have a freeze pop?"

"I've got it right here." The nurse handed her a lime freeze pop and smiled. "I think you told me green is your favorite, right?"

Lexie nodded. "And orange is my second favorite. But it's almost my first."

Her words made them laugh, but Rafe didn't try to mask the tears in his eyes. Twenty-four hours before he'd railed at God and Tasha, regretting his decision. Right now, with Lexie's bright-eyed smile looking up at him, he was pretty sure God, the doctors and Tasha were beyond amazing.

He swiped his sleeve to his eyes and turned as Dr. Warren touched his arm. "We won't have definitive results for weeks. We'll test her blood periodically to search for markers and the t-cell presence, but right now I want to wish you both a Merry Christmas from the entire staff. Seeing this." Dr. Warren indicated the wide-awake child with a smile. "Makes our day. Merry Christmas."

"Merry Christmas, to you, too, Doc." Rafe shook his hand, then Dr. Orrington's. "And thank you. Thank you so much."

"Is that a present?" Lexie peeked behind Tasha and Rafe. Anticipation brightened her gaze. "Is it for me, maybe?"

"It is." Tasha crossed to the little table, brought the brightly wrapped gift over and set it on her lap. "Wanna open it?"

"Well, yes!" Lexie handed Rafe what was left of her freeze pop. When her hands fumbled the wrapping, Tash reached in to help slide the sparkly paper off. Lexie opened the box carefully, then stared inside. "The music box with the little children, playing. Santa brought me the music box I loved so much."

Rafe started to correct her, but Tash directed an elbow to his side and he hushed up real quick.

"How did he know where I was?"

"Super smart guy." Tash's look said that was a given. "I don't know him personally, but I've heard from others that he's always on the ball."

"So it would seem." Rafe smiled her way.

"Can you wind it, Daddy? Please?"

Tash smiled at him, and in her eyes he read the sweet joy of holy days, children and miracles. His heart lifted, lighter and happier than it had been in years. "I sure can, honey. I sure can." He wound the hand-carved box and as the music played, the tiny wooden children frolicked in time, spinning and turning as they rotated around a decorated tree in a Christmas of dreams. And when Tasha slipped her hand into his… and held on tight… one of those indefinable nudges told Rafe his dreams had just come true.

EPILOGUE

"WE FIND NO TRACE OF cancer in Alexia's blood, and no after-effects from the HIV."

Rafe had prayed for this outcome. He'd convinced himself that this was exactly what he'd hear today, but when Dr. Orrington said the actual words, the final noose around his neck broke free. "Nothing?"

"No. And the t-cells are still there, ready to take up the charge if it tries to come back. Mr. Karralis, we're happy to tell you that as of this moment, for all intents and purposes," Dr. Orrington smiled at Lexie, "we think Alexia is cancer free."

Happy emotion rose within him. He stood up, clasped the doctors' hands in turn, then turned to Tash. "You did this."

She laughed and winked at the doctors. "Well. They helped."

He moved closer, serious. "You know what I mean. You knew I'd accepted Lexie's fate, you knew why I brought her home. But you wouldn't let me give up, Tasha."

"I was in the right place at the right time."

He moved another step closer. "Which wasn't an accident."

"No." She smiled and reached up a soft hand to his cheek. "It wasn't an accident or a coincidence. It was a set of lost keys, a really bad tree and a precious little girl. And God."

"So." He swept the doctors a quick look to include them in on the conversation before he turned back to Tasha. "What if Lexie and I didn't go back to California? I can set up my office here as well as there."

Tasha's heart beat faster. She'd faced this day of Lexie's clean bill of health, knowing it would mean Rafe and Lexie would be free to rejoin their interrupted lives on the West Coast. But—

"You love your job."

"I do," Tash admitted. "And right now, seeing the hope come alive around here? I love it even more."

"So what if we stay here…" He slanted a grin down to Lexie and she hopped up and down, excited. Nodding.

"Hurry up, Daddy! You take too long! Ask her!"

The doctors grinned in tandem.

Lexie grabbed hold of Rafe's arm and Tasha's hand. "Tasha, will you marry us, me and my Dad? We think it would be a really good idea, and then you'll always have help with your Christmas decorations and we can make applesauce together whenever we want!"

Rafe tipped a smile down to the girl, then brought his gaze up as he cradled Tasha's cheek with his free right hand. "Yeah. What she said."

"Really?"

He laughed out loud and it felt wonderful to hear him laugh, to see his joy. Yes, she wanted to be part of that, now and forever. He let go of her cheek, lifted Lexie into his left arm, and dropped down on one knee, balancing her. "Tasha Sorkos, would you do us the honor of marrying us? Well, me, actually, but she's part of the deal. Consider it a buy-one, get-one-free kind of deal."

"I do love free stuff," she teased, then she met Rafe's eyes. His gaze, his expression made promises she thought were forever gone. They weren't because she saw them there, reflected in his big, brown eyes. "Yes, Rafe. I would be honored to marry you and raise this cute kid together."

"And if God sends one or two more, I wouldn't be opposed to the idea," he added as he stood. He met the doctors' grins with one of his own. "You're witnesses. No way she can back out of it now."

"No way she wants to," she whispered as she stepped closer.

Dr. Warren cleared his throat. "And that would be our cue to leave."

"I want an invitation to the wedding," declared Dr. Orrington. "And a dance with the flower girl!"

Lexie clapped her hands together as Rafe claimed a kiss. "I will love being a flower girl! Can we pick out dresses soon, please? And can we wait until I have more hair?"

"Absolutely, darling." She picked Lexie up and kissed both cheeks. "We will wait until your hair is long enough to make you happy each time you see the pictures, and yes." She turned her attention to Lexie's father. "I think it would be lots of fun to see about some siblings. When it comes to Christmas decorations, I can use all the help I can get."

He kissed her then, properly this time, with Lexie cuddling into Tash's shoulder.

She'd gone to Grolier Springs to help her grandmother turn a new page in her life, and stepped into a brand new story of her own.

And it was good.

DEAR READERS,

I LOVE THIS STORY! A STORY of hope and healing, of second chances and bends in the road.

Rafe Karralis is a man of faith, but he's being grievously tested right now as the loss of his only child looms. Natasha Sorkos is done with God, faith, family and has pretty much let grief and guilt run her life for three long years.

The circumstances that bring them together, the Holy Spirit nudges, the combination of Christmas, proximity, and timing isn't a coincidence… it's destiny. And as Rafe and Tasha feel their way through a holiday run amok with emotion, the simple faith of a child sets the tone for the happily ever after they so richly deserve.

Like most of you, I've lost family and friends to cancer. I've watched people fight the good fight, enduring surgeries, chemotherapy and radiation. For most of my life that's been the path we know, but hope for a new normal is coming alive in research facilities all over the country.

Lexie's story was inspired by the beautiful story of Emily Whitehead, a young girl with no options remaining when she entered the CART19 program (now known as CTL019) at Children's Hospital of Pennsylvania. Her cure using a new and controversial treatment, showed us what can be done! Hallelujah! Here's a link to Emily's story: *www.chop.edu/stories/relapsed-leukemia-emilys-story#.VEOigvnF8xE*

THANK YOU SO MUCH FOR reading this sweet story of faith, hope and love. I love to hear from readers, and whether this is your first "Ruthy-book" or one of a long list of favorites, I'm so grateful for your time! Feel free to contact me at *loganherne@gmail.com* and come visit my website at *ruthloganherne.com*. Friend me on facebook and we can laugh together, pray together and watch the antics of little kids around our farm in upstate New York. And if you love inspirational fiction, my buddies and I have a great blog called SEEKERVILLE: *www.seekerville.blogspot.com* where we talk writing, books, reading, HEROES!!! ☺ I'd love to have you stop by! Giveaways are only part of the fun, it's just a real nice "feel good" place to hang out online!

God bless you and Merry Christmas no matter what time of year you're reading this!

Saved
by the
Sheriff

Ruth Logan Herne

This delightful book is dedicated to all my fun friends in Seekerville. I love you guys so much... Getting to know you, sharing your ups and downs, your epic fails and your successes! Working side by side with you blesses me every day! Thank you!

CHAPTER ONE

Mɪʟᴋ CHOCOLATE EYES STARED UP at Deputy Jim Kar-ralis.

The young woman's expression said she knew she was about to die.

Jim dug his heels into unforgiving ground to make sure that didn't happen. Not today, anyway.

The car's perilous balance offered credence to her expression, which meant he better act first, ask questions later. "Can you hear me, miss?"

She blinked once for yes, which meant what? She couldn't talk? She was afraid to talk?

Jim had no idea, but the strong derecho wind meant the car, the woman and the child strapped in a rear-facing car seat could all be swept over the thinly forested embankment at any time. "I'm getting the baby first."

Yes.

She mouthed the word and blinked again.

He took a stance, his right foot balanced on a horizontal branch of the sideways tree, and one foot on the hill as he reached to ease the back door open. The child slept, chin down, eyes buttoned shut, as if the world wasn't about to fall out from under him. Jim eyed the restraining device, the car, and assessed weight distribution mentally. Removing the woman's weight from the front would likely send the car and the child down the steep, rocky embankment. But how to get the child out without rocking the car? And did he dare wait for the rescue team, with the early-summer storm initiating so many calls?

No.

He braced himself against the sapling at his back, grasped the car door handle, and eased it open against the fierce west wind, but what would hold the door open once he leaned in to retrieve the child? One blast of wind against the open door could send all three of them to their deaths.

A gust barreled through the narrow, wooded roadway not far from I-76. The car teetered, and Jim was pretty sure it shifted in the wrong direction.

Pray, Dimi! Pray hard, when things get bad and everything seems dark. Pray hard!

His grandmother's words and her old-world faith bolstered him.

He'd pray, and pray hard, too, because one way or another, he was saving this kid and this woman.

He adjusted the tether he'd wrapped around his waist to the tree, then leaned in. With fingers far more nimble than normal, he pressed the release button of the drop-in system holding the infant in place. Not daring to breathe, he lifted the handle, praying.

The seat came loose.

Holding tight, he eased the seat through the door. When he had the seat fully extracted, he wished for two things. A partner, but budget cuts had put their sheriff's units in single response cars, with a much wider patrol.

The second prayer was for him to get his right foot back to the hillside while holding the baby carrier.

A blue flashing light came toward him.

He paused, still praying, fairly certain he'd earned points with no small number of angels and saints.

"Jim, that you?" The volunteer firefighter pushed through the brush, gained visual and stopped abruptly. He didn't pause to sweet talk Jim or make eye contact with the woman in the front seat. He grabbed his radio, keyed the mic and barked an order. "Priority status, Dexter Road, east of I-76, rescue in progress, need full response, stat. I repeat, rescue in progress, two victims, infant and woman, need equipment stat."

He didn't wait for a response. Like Jim, Ernie Fallon had done a quick assessment and voted to act first.

He climbed the last few feet, eyed Jim's tether, and reached out. "Without moving any muscles you don't need to, hand me the kid."

Jim took Ernie at his word. He didn't try to make eye contact or small talk, he simply kept his gaze locked on the car and shifted the infant carrier to the left.

"When I take it, you're going to need to toe grip that branch, got it?"

Ernie didn't bark the order, but he sounded like he wanted to. "Agreed." Jim clenched the branch as tight as he could through work shoes. The grip wasn't all that tight, but it helped because when Ernie took the weight of the baby from Jim's left arm, his body tried to shift to make up the difference. The toe hold bought him three important seconds to regain his center of balance.

Ernie disappeared through the brush. Jim heard his engine turn over. A few seconds later Ernie returned. He angled his work-truck crosswise. He withdrew a tether from his hydraulic winch, crossed the length of space separating his truck from the car, then bellied forward to attach the heavy duty cable to the teetering sedan. Flat on his back, Ernie slithered underneath the car, muttering unhappily about the lack of good old-fashioned steel parts.

The car had three options. Stay where it was, fall forward and crush Ernie or tumble backward down the cliff.

God if you've got an eye on this, let's go with option number one. I know I'm a jerk sometimes. I don't pray like I should and I don't go to church when I'm supposed to, and I shouldn't smoke cigars on the golf course, so if you get us out of this, help us save this woman, I'm a reformed man. Whatever it takes, God. I'm yours.

No further word came from Ernie beneath the car, but the sound of metal on metal said something was happening.

He thought he heard a shuffle, but a blast of wind drowned out everything for long, drawn-out seconds. Then Ernie came back into his field of vision, backing toward his horizontally-parked vehicle. He hit the switch on the hydraulic winch and the small engine kicked into life. Jim breathed easier, knowing they were about to enjoy a successful ending. The wind paused, and the creak of the metal draw came through loud and clear, but then something went wrong. Very wrong.

The winch jolted.

The tether snapped.

The distance Ernie had gained started to slip away. The cliff was about to win the war, and no way was Jim going to let that happen. He pulled open her door, mindful of the small tree behind him and the precarious foothold. "Grab me."

She did.

He grabbed right back. When gravity and momentum started to lean the car downhill, he countered by pulling back, withdrawing her quickly. And then the corner of the door caught hold of her windbreaker.

Jim held tight, one set of toes biting to grip wood, the other pushing against Pennsylvania mountain rock.

The weight of the car pulled the tearing jacket, but Jim wasn't sure what would give way first. The slippery fabric or his arm?

A final groan of the car's undercarriage said the sedan was about to succumb. With one arm gripped around her waist, he spun that jacket up and off in a move that would have earned him the audience vote in a dance competition, and then held her… and his breath… while the car careened down the mountainside.

"Don't look down. Look right here. Right at me," he instructed softly, and when she did, those milk chocolate eyes took hold of him, heart and soul, and he was pretty sure they weren't about to let go.

And maybe?

He didn't want them to.

She'd escaped with her life twice today.

But the day wasn't over, and Salena Ramos knew that reality first-hand.

Stop. Think. Calm yourself down and tell this guy what's going down. What's the worst he can do?

Jail.

But right now, with the Miami thugs of the Los Hermanos human trafficking racketeers looking for her and the baby, jail might be the safest place to be, although the shelter of this man's arms seemed pretty nice at the moment.

An ominous crack beneath their feet said she might have counted her blessings too soon.

"Don't move." He whispered the words, a warning and a comfort. Since she wasn't about to move and cause the slender branch beneath them to break further, she was okay with being bossed around. For now.

"Ernie?" The cop raised his voice but never moved a muscle.

"I'm here. I see. I'm going to extend this big branch to you, miss. I want you to grab it, then walk your way up these last few feet, okay? You're going to have to let go of Jim—"

She didn't wait to hear his instructions. Instinct told her to grab the branch, ease off the horizontal tree that was giving way beneath them, and get herself up the hillside if she ever wanted to hold that baby again. She turned carefully, a dancer's move, grabbed the branch, and eased one foot, then the other, up the knobby slope.

The branch whined beneath the big cop.

He'd tethered himself to the narrow tree to save her and the baby, and now that tether might spell his death. If that slim tree gave way, he had no way out as long as that tether held. He and the tree would tumble down the cliff together.

"You got that, Jim?"

Stress stretched Ernie's voice with fear as the sapling root and thin trunk listed further.

"Mechanism's stuck."

Ernie's sudden intake of breath was her cue. He didn't think the big guy could get out of the harness belt before the ground gave way beneath him. Ernie stretched out, on the ground, reaching, but Salena moved first. She reached into her boot, pulled out the short, sharp knife she kept there, and dance-stepped her way back behind the sapling. "Hold still."

His body went taut on demand, but she felt the tension rolling off of him like waves on the Florida shore. "Get back up there. I saved you once. I have no intention of doing it again."

By the time he was done scolding, she'd sliced the well-made tether with the sharp blade, then pitched herself backwards.

He took a broad leap up, toward Ernie, and when his foot hit solid, level ground, the rest of him landed in a whoosh of relief as the slim tree fell over, pulled by the broken branch and pushed by the driving, straight-line wind.

He pushed up quickly, grabbed her and hauled her up along-side him. "Are you okay? Are you hurt? What were you thinking, doing that?"

He sounded gruff and unsure, but mostly gruff so she met his eyes coolly and said, "Tit for tat. You saved my life. I wanted to return the favor."

He stared down, hard, then grabbed her into the biggest hug she'd had in years. "You sure did! Good job! Okay, where's that baby?"

"Squalling in my pick-up," answered Ernie as several sets of flashing lights came their way. "He's got a good set of lungs, Miss—?"

"Salena," she told him as she hurried to the truck. "Oh, Isaac, come here. Come here, darling. You must be starving."

"Do you need a place to feed him?" the cop asked. "We can give you some privacy in my cruiser."

"That would require milk and a bottle, neither of which I now have." She tipped her gaze toward the nearby cliff and made a face.

"Oh. Sorry. I thought—"

"That I would be nursing him."

He shrugged, embarrassed. "My cousin's got a little guy about his size and she's still nursing. Again. Sorry."

Now or never, sweet cheeks. Tell this guy the truth before someone figures out where you turned off the interstate. "He's not mine, actually."

The officer got a little bit taller and broader as her words registered. "Oh? Whose baby is he?"

She hauled in a deep breath because she'd had limited options a half hour ago. Now she had none. "He was my sister's child. She was stolen by the Hermanos brotherhood in Florida over a year ago. She had a child, little Isaac. She got word to me about him, and said they were going to kill her because she tried to escape before the baby was born. She didn't make it. They let her live long enough to deliver Isaac, and then they had her killed."

He stared at her, impassive. "And how did you come to have Isaac with you?"

"I stole him," she admitted. "And now they want me dead and the baby back. Which means we're all in danger right now."

Ernie came closer. "You mean what you're saying, Miss? That the brotherhood is after you?"

"I've never been more serious in my life."

"I'm still processing the part about being a kidnapper and crossing multiple state lines with a stolen child."

"Arrest me," she urged him, "but whatever you do, keep me safe and don't let them near that baby. The Vaccaros and their little band of brothers don't like to be bested. They don't mind using women for whatever purpose suits them at the time, and they like to keep women in line by showing them what they're willing to do to innocent children. Isaac will not become one of their barbaric examples and I'll risk my life making sure it doesn't happen. He's the only thing we have left of Roslyn."

Two more police cars pulled in from one direction as a rescue ambulance approached from the other. She stared up at the broad-shouldered sheriff, praying he'd believe her, because at any moment, Julio Vaccaro's henchmen could show up. "Get in my car, with the baby." He swung open the back door of the cruiser. "Ernie, advise the guys that I'm taking Miss—" He pointed at her to fill in the blank.

"Ramos. Salena Patricia Ramos. I am—"

"The dancer's daughter."

She stared up at him, surprised. Most men knew her famous football-playing father, killed in a high speed crash nearly ten years ago. But why would a man recognize her name by relationship to her mother? He held out his hand. "Hand me your weapons, Miss Ramos."

"Hand them over to you? Why?"

He sighed as if she was questioning the obvious, and he was right. She reached into her boot and extracted the knife, then took her loaded 9 mm. handgun she had affixed to her waist band.

"Anything else?"

She frowned, then withdrew a second blade, smaller, but just as sharp. She handed it off with a dark look, folded her arms and sighed.

A walking artillery.

He scowled as she handed over the second knife, jerked a thumb to the car and waited while she climbed in beside the crying baby.

His earlier prayer was to save her and the child.

Mission accomplished.

But if Salena Ramos was speaking the truth, it would take little for brotherhood collaborates to join forces to end her life. The uptick in racketeering-related deaths had spelled trouble for donut-hole plagued cities throughout the northeast and upper Midwest.

The problem wasn't as bad in his more rural/suburban patrols, but real enough to command law enforcement respect across the entire country. Police leaks along the I-95 corridor meant he didn't dare radio the situation. He'd work quickly and quietly under the radar for the moment, and let command make the big choices. But first he had every intention of getting to the nearby Wegman's grocery store to get baby formula and a bottle.

Easier said than done.

They strode into the suburban supermarket, found the baby aisle with comparative ease, and he stepped back, letting her take lead. When she stared from one can to another, he got a better take on their dilemma. "You don't know what kind to get, do you?"

"He didn't appear to like the one I had." She made a face, scanning the labels quickly. The baby squalled loud and long. The spectacle of the big, uniform-clad deputy with the diminutive honey-skinned woman and the crying infant was drawing attention. The last thing Jim wanted was to be noticed. "Get one of each."

She looked intrigued, saw the price and shook her head. "I managed to lose most of my cash and credit cards when that car pitched over the cliff. Not to mention his diaper bag." She cooed to the baby and winced as if she was pretty sure the situation couldn't get much worse.

"You figure out milk. I'll get diapers." He strode further down the aisle, then came right back. "How much does he weigh?"

She looked blank, so Jim carried the baby to the back of the store, plunked him down on the bulk food scale, then smiled as he picked him back up. "Twelve pounds, two ounces. All right, little man, we've got something to work with now." He went back to the baby supplies aisle, proud of his accomplishment.

Salena was gone.

He hurried down the aisle, realizing he'd made a rookie mistake and he hadn't been a rookie in over ten years. Just when he was about to radio in an alert, she hustled back into the aisle. "Sorry. Had to use the ladies' room. Did you get diapers?"

He hadn't because he was pretty sure she'd hoodwinked him.

She didn't and he almost felt ashamed, but the thought that she could have was a wake-up call. He was believing a gun-toting, knife-carrying woman's story without a shred of evidence to support it, and why was he doing that?

Because he felt sorry for her, she'd almost died and yes, he was admittedly attracted to her. The cute kid was a bonus, but right now the tiny boy was shrieking again which meant they needed to soothe the baby's needs.

Or buy earplugs.

"Let's try this one for delicate stomachs and this one for enhanced brain function."

"It says that? For real?"

"So it claims." She grabbed the two cans, then a three-pack of four-ounce bottles. "We need wipes."

"Wipes." He stared, not understanding.

"You know to clean up his bottom when he—"

"I get it. Say no more. Please."

He moved back down the aisle, secured the size one diapers and a box of wipes, and moved up front with her. "I'll take care of this stuff."

She faced him, reluctant. "I don't mean to make you do that, but if I flash my debit card here, it's like asking them to locate me. Cash is invisible these days."

She was right about that, but he had to wonder why she knew so much about covering her trail, stealing babies and driving down obscure roads. For the moment, he'd settle for feeding the kid and gaining some needed peace and quiet. But then, he had every intention of finding out how bad the situation really was.

CHAPTER TWO

O H, IT WAS BAD ALL right. And about to get worse, Jim decided back at the sheriff's office in Allentown.

"What do you mean she's not wanted for kidnapping?" Jim hissed as his section commander showed him the print-out. "She must be. She told me herself, she stole the baby."

A detective came up alongside. "She probably did, but there's no way the Vaccaro crowd will go to the police to procure the child. They deal on their own terms and their own turf and they're not afraid to use torture and death as a deterrent to others."

"That's what Salena said."

His captain's look of interest sharpened.

"When she was explaining her reasoning," Jim explained. "She said the baby was the only thing she had left of her sister and she wouldn't let them use him as a lesson to others."

"I've got Miss Ramos in interrogation right now. She's either the gutsiest thing I've ever met or she's in on the whole thing."

"How do you figure?"

The detective handed him a sheaf of papers. "The Miami commander said they've been trying to infiltrate the brotherhood for nearly five years with little to show for their time. He said the likelihood of a young woman showing up out of the blue, pretending allegiance and allowed anywhere near the baby would have been impossible."

Was the Florida commander correct? Or did Salena have so much at stake that she was willing to push the limits?

The latter, he decided as he watched through the two-way window. And when the interrogator asked him to step in, he did it with measured reluctance. Seeing Salena in the small, narrow room played the guilt card, but what did he have to feel guilty about? She was a confessed felon, except he was pretty sure she wasn't, except that she was, even if extenuating circumstances pushed her to take matters into her own hands.

He entered the room quietly and stood along the wall.

Her eyes met his. Quick emotion deepened her gaze, but she stemmed it. When she spoke, her tone was polite and grateful. "Thank you again for saving our lives. Isaac and I would both be dead right now if you hadn't gotten to us when you did. I'll be in your debt forever, deputy."

"Just doing my job, ma'am."

She acknowledged that by tilting her head slightly. "I'm glad you were there to do it." She shifted her attention to the detective. "Can you keep Isaac and me safe in lock-up?"

"Why would I be locking you up, Miss Ramos?"

"There must be something," she told him. "Because if you let me out and the brotherhood has figured out where I am, then we've got a situation."

"There's no record of this child's existence."

Intense, she leaned forward. "That way he's untraceable when Vaccaro uses him as an example to keep his people in line. Home births are attended by nurses working on the side to augment their income. On the down low." When the detective looked doubtful, she handed him a tiny disc drive. "Everything's on there. Have your people look at it. I don't lie, I don't cheat, I don't steal but my father taught me to protect what's mine. That baby is pretty much all I have left of my family. Vaccaro will only get him back over my dead body, but I'd prefer we not come to that."

The detective motioned Jim over to a seat, then he stood and moved to the door. "I'm going to have our people check this out. I'll be back in a few minutes."

Jim faced Salena. She arched one brow, sat back and said, "So he leaves a more sympathetic ear in here with me while we're being watched, hoping you might get more out of me, or tempt me to say something more to incriminate myself. Except I've given you everything I've got."

"You watch too much NCIS," Jim said mildly.

"I love Gibbs," she admitted, smiling. "But more to the point is that you're all wondering what to do with me. I don't want to die," she went on. "I don't want them to get their hands on Isaac. I actually have a career and a life I'd like to return to eventually, but unless Vaccaro is neutralized by death or prison—"

"Or deportation," Jim offered.

She scoffed. "Anyone living along the border knows that re-crossing the border back into the U.S. is a simple car ride and payout. And when your Mexican alliance owns a significant amount of the border area through terror and tyranny, you pretty much come and go as you please. But you keep thinking that, deputy."

"I thought we were on a first name basis."

"We were until I realized that no one is taking me seriously," she replied. "And I'm not going anywhere without my nephew, so if you people think you're putting him in the system, you're wrong."

"You claim to want his safety." Jim emphasized the verb, letting doubt edge his tone.

She frowned. "Not claim. I do want his safety."

"Then maybe the system is the best place for him right now."

"You can't mean that."

He shrugged. "What if we put Isaac in a safe house, away from you? Away from any connection?"

"There is no such place," she whispered, staring at him, and when she did? His heart seized again. "Jim, you can't be serious. Other than full-blown witness protection, there's no system that can guard his identity."

"According to the wire, he has no identity."

"Not in the standard system, no. But if you check the bottom of Isaac's left foot, you'll see their mark. The brotherhood marks their own."

He didn't want her to be right, but her intensity said she was. And when he had command check the baby's foot, they found a tiny, curved scar just below his little toe.

"She could have done it herself," the detective reminded them when Jim excused himself from the room a few minutes later. "But I don't think she did. Somehow Ms. Ramos inserted herself into the inner sanctum and has done what no one else has managed to do. She's given the police an inside look at the Vaccaro brotherhood."

"You've checked the flash drive?"

"I saw enough. She got herself in deep enough to get names, faces, voices and a visual. Miami P.D. will love her forever."

"What about now?" Jim stared at one detective, then the other, finally resting his gaze on his captain. "We can't put her out on the streets with the baby. That's like offering target practice."

"Miami's contacting the feds."

That meant federal marshals stepping in, taking over. "Witness protection?"

"They want her alive to testify. The only way to guarantee her safety is through them."

Jim knew that, but the thought of putting her and the baby in a system seemed like undue punishment. Most people put into witness protection were criminals testifying against other criminals. Salena Ramos wasn't a criminal. "She's not a typical candidate."

"Ms. Ramos isn't the norm," agreed his captain, but again the eyebrows shot up. "But she doesn't have a wide range of choices, Jim. She got in, she got out, and she brought Vaccaro's son with her."

"Are we sure he's Vaccaro's son?" asked Joe Jackson. "There's little honor among thieves and the brotherhood has their brand of scum."

Detective Frank Sykes tapped a pencil against the desk. "Let's run a DNA check on the baby, see if it matches Vaccaro."

"I'm on it." Detective Jackson moved across the room to make the request.

"Jim, let's fill out an application for federal protection and get that ball rolling," the captain directed. "If she's unwilling, there's little we can do. We can't keep her here."

"I understand."

She looked up when they re-entered the room. Her look of acceptance broke his heart, as if she'd resigned herself to her fate as long as the baby was safe. "You've impressed the Miami P.D. and the F.B.I. Well done."

"I wanted Isaac protected. If I could take down a ring of horror at the same time, I was okay with that."

"How'd you do it, Salena?" Jim sat across from her, hands splayed. "You couldn't have just walked in there."

"But I did." She stared at him, then sighed. "I'm a registered nurse from just outside Nashville. I worked obstetrics for three years. Roslyn had gotten involved with drugs and men about the same time I was working my way through nursing school."

"Working your way through school?" Jim stopped her, perplexed. "Your father made millions in his football career."

"All of which is in my mother's name," she said softly. "I declared my emancipation when I was eighteen so I could apply for college loans. I'll get a legacy from my father when I'm thirty in three years. He did that because my mother's habits set the example for Roslyn to follow, and she'd already started abusing drugs before he died. Once he was gone, money didn't get wasted on things like tuition when drugs and alcohol were available."

"I'm sorry you had to deal with that."

"Yes, well." She shrugged. "It taught me to talk the talk. That helped when I was inside the Vaccaro network. I think it might have been God's way of preparing me."

"You still haven't told me how you got in."

"I transferred to Miami General's O.B. unit, mentioned that I was paying off my mother's debt and that I needed extra work." She lifted her eyes to his. "The fact that I'm Latino probably helped because they like everything and everyone to blend."

Jim couldn't imagine the beautiful woman before him blending with anything, but he kept that opinion to himself. "You're telling me you can just show up at the door, walk in and pinpoint their location?"

"They hide in plain sight," she told him. "It's the best way. Julio's family loves the crazy, busy life in Miami. They're not the type to hole up in an out-of-the-way compound in the middle of nowhere. The cab pulls into one of their hotels with an underground garage, you're taken through a convoluted mix of halls and floors, and then you're in the family wing which only has family as needed for medical treatment."

"Then how did you find the baby?"

"Listening." She shrugged. "You listen to the maids and the hired help. Maids know everything. Every family has a stupid person or two who say too much the help's invisible to them. From there it was my job to figure out the schedule, pinpoint which woman was caring for Isaac, and make my move. It didn't take long to realize the new baby boy in the Vaccaro wing was my nephew. They'd changed his name, but the staff found the reaction of Julio's wife amusing. The last thing she wanted to do was raise his half-breed baby."

"And if they killed you?" he asked coolly, because it certainly seemed like that would have been a more likely scenario. "How much help would you be to Isaac if you were dead, Salena?"

"And how would I live with myself if I never tried?" she countered.

He started to fall in love with her right then, because how many people risked life and limb for anyone else these days, but he chalked up the rise of emotion to lack of sleep. "It's about the most courageous thing I've ever heard," he admitted. "I don't know that I could have done it."

"You risked your life today to save two perfect strangers," she whispered. She leaned in and locked his gaze to hers. "You're exactly the kind of person that would have done it."

The lights blinked off, then on, then off again. They came up a few seconds later, but Jim stood and moved to the door. "Come on, we've got a power outage. We need to get you somewhere safe and see what this storm's got in store for us."

"It's not good," offered a deputy, overhearing Jim's remark. "We've got downed power lines all over, tree fall, accidents and a brand new two-alarm fire caused by lightning."

"And the National Weather Service says this line of storms is being fed by warm Gulf air and might last for hours."

"Let's get that baby and tuck you somewhere while I work." Jim hooked a thumb down the hall. "Lieutenant, can you get the baby for us, please?"

"I'd rather slide hot pepper slivers under my fingernails," the old guy grumbled, but then he smiled and winked Salena's way. "I'll be right back with the little guy. And he likes to be walked when he burps."

"Good to know." Salena exchanged a quick look with Jim and frowned. "I know nothing about babies, so this is going to be a crash course in child welfare."

"I'm taking you someplace where they know lots about babies. Just make sure you wear what they tell you to wear and play the part."

"The part of what?" she asked as the lieutenant brought the baby down the hall.

"A nun."

Her mouth dropped open, then closed. "That's brilliant."

"Only if you stay completely out of sight," he warned her. "Aunt Kathy would kill me for putting little ones in danger, but they don't have a placement right now."

"But won't we be putting *them* in danger?" she asked as they took the back stairs down to the parking lot. They stepped out into breath-snatching wind and torrential rain. He paused at the door and looked down at her. "They wouldn't have it any other way," he told her. "Do unto others as I have done for you. That's their creed and when I told her our situation, she and Sister Anne jumped on it."

"Jim." She looked overwhelmed, then blinked, catching herself. "Thank you. I don't know what else to say."

"Wait here while I get the car. I'll pull up and you hop in. Artie installed a car seat from the fire department for us."

He crossed the parking lot through the storm, pulled up to the curb outside the back entrance to the judicial office building, got out and opened the door for her.

"You're getting soaked."

"Better me than him."

The baby stirred when he said that, blinked, then dozed back off. "Safe, sound, fed and dry. That's the preferred list around babies according to Aunt Kathy."

"She sounds sensible." Salena settled into the car and sighed. "I could use a good dose of sensible right about now."

He bet she could.

He eased the car out of the lot. The storm would make travel to the converted convent tricky, but once Salena and Isaac were safely tucked away, he could get back into service. Could the Vaccaros track them down to the worn church on the outskirts of Allentown?

Possibly.

But the pre-Civil War church had been an instrumental stop on the Underground Railroad, helping Southern slaves to freedom. A soundproofed, underground tunnel led from the church to the convent and then diagonally across the road to the old mercantile. The mercantile had long since been converted into ground level shops with apartments above, but the long unused passageway remained. The two sisters had shown Jim, Dante and Rafe the tunneled chambers years ago, lauding how many lives the secret passage had saved. And now Jim wanted it to save two more.

That underground passage provided the perfect temporary hiding spot for anyone being hunted. No one had ever been discovered while there in the past and Jim had every intention of making sure that track record held.

Salena was pretty sure they'd taken a left at Armageddon and hooked a right at the Apocalypse because she'd never gone through a storm of this magnitude in her life, and she wasn't any too sure they were going to survive this one. Except…

Jim Karralis had already saved her life that day, and Isaac's, so if he thought this was a good idea, she was all in, one hundred percent. Right up until he pulled into the parking lot of an old brick church complex that had been needing restoration funds for decades, minimal.

She bit her lip, stared at the building, then the baby, and didn't right her features before Jim noticed. "What's wrong? Do you have something against church? Against the Sisters of St. Agnes? Because they're about the greatest women known to man."

"No, it's fine, I'm just surprised." She started to detach Isaac's seat, but Jim motioned her ahead. "Go in, I've got to bring the whole seat along and it's heavy and awkward. Use the door right there with the red knocker."

The door swung open before she got anywhere near the knocker and two small, impish women waved her in. "Come in, get dry, that's a monster storm out there and there's nothing to block the wind at this entry, but it's way more private than bringing you through the front, especially with Mass being said."

The soft sound of Communion bells took her back a dozen years.

They'd gone to church often as a family when her father was alive, even during the football season. If Reggie wasn't there, the nanny would gather her and Roslyn up and take them to church in their very best clothes. Her mother didn't bother going, attending Mass was always too early or too far or too stuffy or too chilly… And when her father lost his life in a multi-car accident on the interstate, going to church became a thing of the past.

She'd left it like that, pushing faith aside on purpose. Life took on two distinct sides. Before her father's death when she and Rosie were children of a gilded age, and after when their mother's illicit habits eventually put them in mental, emotional, physical and financial danger. And that's when Salena emancipated herself, fought for an education and a career and moved on with her life, but the soft, melodic chime of sanctuary bells brought back sweet memories of a better time.

"Come this way, dear, we'll show you around and you can see where everything is."

She expected cell-like rooms and austere settings, so when the sisters emerged into a cozy but good-sized kitchen filled with modern conveniences, she was amazed. "This is wonderful."

"Oh, it is." Sister Kathy smiled as she moved down an adjoining hall at a quick clip for an older woman. "Sponsors and former patrons take good care of us, that's for certain. Here is the living room, and through that door there is the first baby room."

"I'll take Isaac in there." Jim kept his voice soft, moved beyond the three women, and tucked the car seat with the sleeping baby into the first nursery. He turned, saw her look of surprise and smiled. "Pretty nice, right?"

"Beyond that." She turned to the sisters, confused. "You take care of babies here? Why?"

"Struggling newborns and infants, actually," Sister Anne explained. "Babies that can't be placed in regular foster homes come here because we've got the time and patience to see to their needs. We take care of those with significant difficulties."

"Oh, that's marvelous." Salena had worked the obstetrical unit for several years. She understood that some babies were high risk at birth and not all parents were equipped to handle special needs infants. "But you have no babies now?"

"Anne had a hip replacement some weeks back."

"I'm doing fine," the petite woman declared and she did a little dance step to show just how limber she was. "But the doctor signed me out for six weeks, which means we can't take a placement for at least another ten days, so this is perfect!"

"I don't see how harboring a woman and a baby who are being hunted by drug-dealing human traffickers can be considered perfect, or even slightly good," Salena corrected her, but she was taken aback when Sister Kathy waved that off as if it was nothing.

"God's timing," she declared. "If we had babies now, we couldn't have done this, but Anne's surgery, her quick healing, and Dimi's phone call all make perfect sense now, don't they?"

"Dimi?" She raised a brow to Jim and he shrugged.

"Dimitrios Stefanos Karralis."

"But you go by Jim."

He nodded. "Easier. But you can call me Dimi if you want to."

Her heart swelled and she was pretty sure her breath caught, because she did want to call him something sweet and special, the name only people close to him used. Was that because she owed him so much this day? Or was it because she hadn't allowed herself time for any kind of romance since Roslyn started making really stupid choices almost five years before?

She wasn't sure but he moved toward the door after hugging both older ladies. "Call me if you need me, okay? And can you show Salena how to access the tunnels if needed?"

"First thing," Kathy promised. "Go with God, Dimi. You are beloved."

"Same to you," he told them, then he lifted his gaze to Salena, across the room. "I know you don't have a cell phone. That's probably best right now. Aunt Kathy has a relay system she can use to get messages to me. It sounds awkward but it works and it's not easily traced. I've got to go."

Suddenly it wasn't all right that he was leaving, and not because of the quaint pair of sisters and the unusual convent or the prayer-filled church. It was simply because she felt better when he was near.

She swallowed that emotion and nodded. "We'll be fine."

He turned and went back through the kitchen, and once the back door was shut, she turned toward Sister Anne, surprised. "You can't hear the storm in here."

"Virtually sound proof," Anne told her. She handed Salena a soft, small blanket. "Use this like a sweater. It will get warm later, but when you're wet and the day is dark, the chill takes hold."

The crocheted cotton shawl felt wonderful.

"Sit down, dear." Sister Anne motioned to the soft sofa separating the room into two sections. "You must be exhausted, I've got baby Isaac's bag and Kathy's putting together bottles. We find it's always better to be proactive when it comes to babies."

"He goes from happy to ballistic in a matter of seconds, so I totally support your reasoning," Salena replied. She sank down onto the couch and for the first time in days felt like she could relax. Her lids grew heavy, and the last thing she remembered was hearing the sister's voices lifted in some sweet hymn of prayer. And then nothing as welcome sleep claimed her.

CHAPTER THREE

J IM PARKED OUTSIDE THE CHURCH in time for Mass the
next morning, then veered right, toward the hallway leading to
the attached convent and rectory on the far side of the complex.
He checked the door to the outside, found it locked securely, then
moved down the hall. When he came to the convent door, he
knocked twice, paused, then knocked twice again.

He waited, patient, sure that Anne and Kathy were checking
him out, and when the door swung open, he was surprised to see
Salena on the other side. "Hey. You look better."

She made a face at him, and he laughed and backtracked as he
shut the thick, wooden door. "Rested. Showered. Clean. And with
new hair. Nice color." He grimaced, took off his deputy hat and
ran his fingers through his hair, laughing. "I'm going to stop now."

"Please do. What's in that bag? Please say food."

"It is food because it occurred to me that you probably haven't
eaten since yesterday morning, have you?"

"The night before, actually, and if you don't open that sack real
quick, I will not be held responsible for my actions."

"Usually the sisters are up, making breakfast," he noted as they
crossed through the broad living room and into the kitchen. "What
have you done with them?"

"Sister Kathy is at Mass and Sister Anne has Isaac right there."
She pointed to the big, wrap-around rocker where the aged nun
and the infant slept, cuddled together. "How precious is that?" she
whispered.

"Oh, man. That's one of those pics you love to get on facebook,
but if we post it there, that would be super dumb on our part,

wouldn't it?" He smiled her way as he withdrew three tubs of cream cheese, and eight bagels. "I got a variety and I brought some of my cousin Rafe's specialty breakfast sausage, the kind his dad makes for their Greek restaurant."

He formed patties while he warmed up a square griddle on the stovetop, and when the sausage began sizzling and snapping, he was pretty sure her mouth watered. He couldn't tell for sure because she was too busy eating a sun-dried tomato bagel with garden salad cream cheese in rapid-fire fashion. "I'm sorry I didn't think of food yesterday afternoon."

"I was too wiped out to think of it myself," she confessed. "Coffee?"

"Yes. Absolutely."

She glanced over her shoulder as she brewed his cup. "Did you stay up all night?"

He shrugged. "Storms don't run on schedule, and this one did a lot of damage in a two-county area, then swept right through North Jersey into Manhattan and toppled a bunch of stuff here, there and in between. A lot of people lost sleep last night."

"Not me." She sent a guilty look toward the sleeping nun curled in the rocking chair with the tiny boy snug against her chest. "I fell asleep as soon as I sat down and the sisters took over. I never heard the baby or them and I didn't wake up until ninety minutes ago."

"You needed sleep." Sister Kathy came up through the back entrance, saw Jim and beamed a wide, open smile. "I thought you'd come by even though you should be home resting. You brought us fresh bagels from Hiram's shop, aren't you the most blessed boy?"

He smiled as she hugged him. "I will always be a boy in Aunt Kathy's eyes."

"Precious, no matter what the age," she told him. "So. Let's sit down and figure this out. What's our plan?"

Salena looked from him to his aunt. "I'd like to hear this, too."

"We don't have one yet."

"That's not acceptable," Kathy told him, and her tone said she meant it. "A woman and a child are in danger. There should always be a plan."

"Explain that to Mother Nature," Jim told her. "There's going to be days of clean-up in our county alone and that splits forces. The department has to maintain a presence on roads, at overpasses, as well as answering calls. In the meantime, the captain has contacted the U.S. Marshals to do an intake on the Federal Witness Protection program."

"Please don't tell me you're serious."

He nodded, grim. "Los Hermanos and the Vaccaros might be thwarted for a while, but in the end, they will continue to look for you, Salena. We might call it a rescue, but in their eyes you stole a child and gathered valuable information that could take them down. Why would they even consider leaving you alive if they can find you?"

"But witness protection?" She sat back, eyes round, and if shell-shocked had an image, it was stamped across her face. "To leave my identity behind? Become someone else? Be sequestered away?" She looked overwrought, and he couldn't blame her because the very thought of stepping fully into the unknown with nothing and no one didn't sound like a whole lot of fun to him, either.

"I don't see another way around it, and I thought about it all night," he said softly. "If you do anything in your name right now, you can be traced and killed. And Isaac, too. The only way I see to prevent that is for you to go all in and accept the protection. If it's offered."

"If?" Aunt Kathy brewed herself a mug of coffee and scowled. "There can be no 'if' involved. When a woman risks her life, her home, and her livelihood to rescue a child from the evils of drugs and slavery and lawlessness, there are no 'ifs' to keeping her safe."

"There's protocol to follow, I'm sure," Salena told her.

"There is always protocol," Kathy replied, determined. "And there are times when protocol should be conveniently forgotten in the name of safety."

"Be careful what you admit in front of me," Jim warned her, smiling. "It's better that I don't know everything that goes on."

"Now that's something we agree on." Kathy smiled his way, then rose as Sister Anne started stirring in the living room. "Anne, let me take this sweet baby from you."

Sister Anne sat up, looked around, and sighed. "The best sleep of all is with a child in your arms. Maybe that's why I always liked those statues best. Mary, holding Jesus, cradling her perfect son."

"It is a beautiful sight," Kathy agreed, "but this little one needs a complete change of clothing, which means so do you, Anne."

"Not the first time, won't be the last," Anne said as she moved toward their bedroom wing. "I'll be back and I'd love a plain bagel, toasted."

"I've got your name on it, don't you worry." She watched as Sister Anne left the area, then turned toward Jim. "She's not spry enough to move quickly if there's trouble no matter what she says."

"I agree. So then we make sure there's no trouble."

Kathy frowned into her coffee. "Evil isn't choosy, Dimi. You know that."

"Do you want us to leave?" Salena asked the obvious as Jim turned the sausage one last time. "I would understand if you did, Sister."

"I think it is better if you and the baby split up," she advised softly. "It might seem harsh, but it's much harder to find and identify a small baby than it is an identifiable woman with a baby."

"Aunt Kathy, I—" Jim started to argue, but Salena raised a hand to stop him.

"She's absolutely right. No one's going to think it's odd for the sisters to have a baby here. That raises no suspicion because it's the norm. But to have me here sends up red flags." She turned and faced Sister Kathy. "Can you keep him safe?"

"I would die trying."

"Bless you. So." She turned toward Jim after kissing the little fellow goodbye. "I'm taking two of those sausages in a bagel to go and we need to hit the road."

"You're sure?"

"Safety first, and as long as we don't think we've compromised the sisters' home, then I suggest we leave, access something of mine somewhere far from here to throw the wolves off-track, and leave the baby in peace until everything has been resolved."

He'd decided she was gutsy yesterday, and he'd been right, but now he was seeing another side of her strength: sacrificial love, a quality his grandmother rued as forgotten these days. He saw it now, plainly, in the eyes of this wonderful woman. "Grab your sandwich and let's hit the road. Aunt Kathy?"

She hugged Salena goodbye and looked up at Jim.

"Be careful, okay?"

"As always. And you know we've had our share of trouble here over the years. Anne and I are old hands at making things come out all right. In God's name."

"Amen." He held open the door, closed it quickly behind them, and then did the same for the second door.

"This place is built like a fortress."

"Which is why it was perfect for transporting slaves," he told her. "The double doors, time to unlock them, silent rooms… everything done for a reason, to protect and save."

She climbed into the car and didn't let herself look back. Eyes forward, she motioned west. "If you have a car I can borrow, I'll drive two hours west, make a couple of purchases with the debit card in my pocket, then I'll double back. Maybe we can gain a little time if Julio and Hector's boys go on a wild goose chase."

"You can't possibly think I'm letting you out of my sight."

She was adjusting her seat belt until his words registered. "But you have to work."

"Yes."

"And you can't chauffer me around 24/7," she continued.

"It's been cleared with command. Nobody wants you dead, it seems." She angled him a scorching look. "Seriously, until we have the ability to get things square with the feds, I've been assigned to keep you safe. Here." He handed over a burner phone. "For emergency use only, of course."

She set the phone on her lap and stared at him, remorseful. "Do you regret seeing my car go out of control yesterday?"

Face forward, his jaw twitched. "Well, now, that depends. I've actually been considering getting to know you better, Salena Ramos, but if your life is always edge-of-your-seat exciting, you might be out of my league." He stopped at an intersection and chanced a quick glance her way. "So what do you say? Think you can tone things down a little at some point? Take a chance on a hometown guy? Because that might be fun, don't you think?"

Sincerity laced his words, but right now she couldn't think of anything beyond finding some realm of safety for Isaac and herself, although the offer of getting to know Jim— *Dimi*— Karralis made her feel almost normal again, like the woman she'd been before Roslyn disappeared.

Could she be that woman again? Normal? Kind? Funny?

She could come close, maybe, but the fury of the last year had left its marks. But then, hadn't her life been a series of unlikely events? Yet she was still here, so maybe there was an underlying reason for it. Maybe her safety and Isaac's life were somehow tied to a greater good. Or she just got lucky multiple times.

More likely.

"You wolfed that sandwich."

She laughed softly. "I was so hungry. Yesterday I was too tied in knots to eat or even think of eating, and Isaac wasn't fond of his bottle and between lack of food, being hunted and a crying baby, I thought my head was going to explode."

"But you handled everything with forthrightness and grace," Jim noted. "I wouldn't have known you were hurting. That's a neat trick."

"I figured that one out early in life. Keeping my complaints subdued kept my mother at bay."

"My mother is Greek. Nothing keeps her at bay," Jim told her. He grinned as he hit the interstate heading west. "But she's a great lady. Tough as nails, always working, and never steps out of the house without her hair done and full make-up."

"You're kidding." Salena slouched in her seat. "Now I'm embarrassed. I haven't seen make-up in weeks because I wanted to go into that complex looking like a hard-working immigrant."

"Is this your natural hair color?"

She slanted him a quick look. "You could tell it wasn't natural? Because I thought it looked good."

"I assumed it wasn't," he corrected her, "because you went the distance to assume a different identity. So my guess is that you changed it up before taking the job in Miami."

"I did."

"And then worked at the Miami hospital with your acquired identity. Did you change your name, Salena?"

She grimaced. "I used a partial name so I wouldn't have to file legal papers. Legally I am Salena Patricia Ramos-Fernando. I used Tricia Fernando in Miami. They say to stick as close to the truth as possible and my nursing license was in my full name."

"I'm surprised they didn't catch it on a background check, though." Jim tapped his fingers on the steering wheel. "If they've got cops on their payroll, wouldn't they have identified you as Roslyn's sister?"

"You think I got lucky? Or do you think I had help?"

He didn't hesitate. "Help, definitely."

"That means someone there knew who I was." She leaned her head back against the headrest and sighed. "Olivia."

"Who's Olivia?"

"One of the Vaccaro nieces. She was tough as nails, a real witch to the help, I wanted to hate her, but she was the one who dropped bits of information like kids leaving a crumb trail in the forest. I thought she was vicious and stupid." She turned his way and frowned. "It turns out she was helping me all along, and playing a part. Just like me."

"Why would she help? What's in it for her?"

"Guilt? Penance? Cleansing her immortal soul?"

"The usual answer is money, but I'll let you believe what you will." He pulled off the interstate and held out his hand. "Give me whatever card you've got in your pocket. We'll grab gas here."

She handed him the card, and when he climbed back into the car a few minutes later, she glanced around. "Doesn't it rattle you? Knowing someone's looking for me, for us? That someone is hunting us right now, and that you're targeted just because I'm with you? Why don't you just drop me off somewhere, turn around and go on with your life, Jim? Because I hate the thought of something happening to you."

"Oh ye of little faith," he chided, smiling. "Maybe I've got a trick or two up my sleeve. Maybe I'm like a combo mix of Ninja-warrior-deputy and Gibbs all rolled into one."

"I don't want innocent people hurt on my account."

"I concur. So let's figure out steps two and three. Anyone tracing the police call from yesterday and the rescue of a woman and infant child can put two and two together."

She'd thought that too, but she hated to hear him say it.

"So that means they can see the responding officer's name. That means I've been discovered already. Hence today's assignment."

"Jim, I'm sorry." She put a hand on his arm, apologetic, but the grin he flashed her said it was all okay, even if it wasn't.

"I'm not. Gives me a chance to get to know you, Salena. Anyway, an old buddy of the captain's has a hunting cabin in the hills. It's rough and off the beaten path, but it's virtually untraceable. I'm going to get you up there with a few sacks of food—"

"And my gun."

He didn't argue. "And the gun and we'll see if the wheels of justice can turn fast enough for Miami's police to make some arrests."

"Do you think being arrested will stop the hunt?" She made a face. "I don't think Julio and Hector give up easy."

"It might not stop it, but it could slow things down," he told her. "Even well-oiled machines don't like to draw extra attention to themselves when there's already mounting evidence. You were an eye-witness. Racketeers and cartels like to make an example of those who cross them."

"So even with the arrests, killing me makes sense."

"When you put it that way, it does." He flashed her a comforting look from the driver's seat as they headed toward the western part of Pennsylvania. "That's where Witness Protection comes into play, although I understand the reluctance. What happened with your sister, anyway? How did she get into a position to end up with Los Hermanos? Most of the women associated with them from outside the family have an interesting list of priors."

"Drugs. Sex. Alcohol." Salena frowned. "Once my father died, our lives were surrounded by all of the above. Roslyn tiptoed into my mother's habits. I stayed as far away as I could possibly get. Then Roslyn contacted me that she was in trouble. Big trouble. And then she was just gone and you know what happens when a twenty-four-year-old drug using woman disappears?"

Jim's expression said he knew, all right. "Not much."

"Exactly. She was like a non-person. Oh, I get it from the numbers angle, there are only so many police and so many leads and people who put themselves deliberately in harm's way should expect consequences. But I didn't realize how little could be done across state lines and through regular channels."

"Not like TV, is it? Where everything is wrapped up in a sixty minute segment."

"Huh." She paused and stared out the window, remembering that last communication. How desperate Roslyn sounded. "Then she got a message to me in Nashville that she was pregnant and trying to run away, but got caught. Oh my heart just broke to think what she must be going through, because what if Daddy hadn't died? What if she'd gotten a break back then and had a normal life with at least one parent who cared? Life could have been so different for her. She always wanted to be a princess. If my father hadn't died when he did, she could have had her wish."

"I'm sorry." He sounded truly sorry, and that sympathy brought tears to her eyes, but tears would get her nowhere. "I'm sorry you lost him, and sorry everything went bad, but look at yourself through all of this, Salena. You hung in there, you made the right choices, you did what you needed to do to thrive. Couldn't Roslyn have done the same?"

"Of course. But she wasn't strong like me. She was needier. More delicate."

"That's not your fault," he argued firmly, and the strength in his voice said maybe she didn't need to carry a full load of guilt. "She had options. No one said it's easy to make the tough choices."

His words lent power to her tired heart.

She'd longed to help Roslyn more, but by the time she had graduated with her R.N., her sister had taken long strides down a dangerous path. "I know all this, but it's kind of you to remind me."

"Where is your mother now?"

She shrugged. "Who knows? The estate was divided up into three equal shares. Roslyn and I were scheduled to get ours on our thirtieth birthdays. Mom had gone through the bulk of hers in a few years. She moved while I was in college, and there was no forwarding address."

"She didn't contact you or your sister to tell you where you lived?"

"It didn't matter, not really," Salena replied. And it hadn't mattered, because she'd had enough of her mother's me-first lifestyle by the time she moved out at age eighteen. "We never really had a mother, as odd as that sounds. And Daddy was gone. The one person who truly cared about us after his death was our old nanny, Tanté Dolores. And eventually my mother got rid of her and there was no one."

"I'm sorry."

His simple words touched her heart in a way she'd forgotten long ago. "Thank you, Dimi."

He smiled when she used his Greek name. "Great name, right?

Dimitrios!" He proclaimed the name with a little fist pump into the air. "When I asked my mother why we Americanized it to Jim, she reminded me of Saint James in the Bible, a man who loved God and believed we needed to show that love every day. That actions spoke louder than words."

"And you became that kind of person," she observed.

"It fit. So for today our actions are to take them off the trail like you suggested…"

"I'm going to bet you thought the same thing, but thank you for the credit."

"You're welcome. And then get to the cabin, get set up, and bide our time."

"Our time?" She turned more fully toward him. "You can't stay up there with me. Can you?"

"Did you think I was going to leave you alone?"

"Well. I—"That was exactly what she'd thought, actually, because how could the department give Jim the time to stand guard?

"I'd like to say I'm altruistic, but you're a star witness in a major crime that crosses multiple state lines. If it wasn't for the storm, there'd be more of us guarding you right now. According to my boss, the Vaccaros have their fingers in gambling, drugs, human trafficking and prostitution across a dozen states while they live the life of kingpins in Miami. Multiple departments have been aching to take them down and you've given them the key with your flash drive. Keeping you safe isn't just an honor, Salena." He angled a look of understanding her way. "It's a duty."

"Freedom, justice, honor, duty, mercy and hope."

His smile widened. "Churchill's list of great things that can be shared in a single word. You like history or just great quotes?"

"Both." She paused as he turned the unmarked SUV up a some-what graveled, mostly dirt drive. "This isn't a road."

"Logging trail."

"A mudwash in the rain, I expect."

"Yes."

"Jim, if we get cornered, how do we get out? Is there another way in?"

CHAPTER FOUR

T HERE WASN'T.
Sensibility said there was no way anyone could find them in the Pennsylvania Wilds. The Wilds were where folks went to make people disappear. If Bigfoot had a regular stomping ground, ensuring his privacy, it would be the Pennsylvania Wilds, home to millions of acres of dense woodlands, unexplored. But she was right to question the terrain because with only one way in, there could be only one way out, and from a police perspective, that wasn't good. "We'll scope things out once we get to the cabin." And when they pulled up to a ramshackle old building that had seen better days about three decades before, he stopped the SUV, set his jaw, and climbed out. "Wait here."

A slight, unhappy hum from Salena's side of the car said she wasn't impressed, and neither was he. They were most likely unfindable, but also indefensible.

A spark of unease crept up his back and tingled his neck.

This was out-of-the-way and off the beaten track to the max, but it was also target practice for anyone who might track them.

He was being ridiculous, of course. The captain had sent them here, he'd relieved Jim of duty in order to guard Salena...

Jim and no one else...

Misgiving stabbed him crosswise in the gut. He moved back to the car, motioned for her to get out, put a finger to his lips and then lay on his back and butt-crawled through the bug-filled leaf clutter. When he found the tiny tracking device magnetized to the undercarriage of the car, he understood how far the reach of Los Hermanos extended. "Get in," he told her quickly. "We've got to get out of here." He threw the device as far as he could through a narrow line of the forest growth, and hoped its location near the cabin would keep the hunters on track.

Unless they'd already made the turn onto the logging trail in which case...

He pulled out his gun, motioned for her to do the same and put a finger to his lips.

Her face had paled, but when he casually asked her opinion about baseball and catching a possible game sometime, she took a breath and waded in. "I'm not a huge baseball fan. We were raised on football. I think my dad always wanted a boy, and when he got two girls, he wasn't afraid to teach us how to run, jump and catch."

"You play flag football?" Jim put surprise in his voice purposely as the car careened back down the mountain trail.

"Who said anything about flags?" She laughed, sounding normal under the circumstances. "We played tackle with pads, miniature helmets, the whole thing. We even had a goalpost in the backyard. We switched to soccer after Dad was gone, but playing football with him was so much fun. Those were the good times."

"Well, if we get to keep you around through the summer, maybe we can go down to an Eagles game in Philly," he suggested. "My brother and I have season tickets."

"That's a long drive," she protested as he aced the final turn leading out onto the two-lane highway. "But I'd love to go to a game, Jim. That would be fun, although I'll probably be in witness protection by then, don't you think?"

She'd played the card beautifully, sounding just like she should. Disappointed but willing to do whatever it took to take care of things and put Los Hermanos away. "Most likely." He wrenched the wheel to the right, onto the open highway, heading for the interstate, but he wasn't stupid. If the captain had planted a locating device, he may have planted a microphone, too, but where?

Someplace easy for him to remove it before an investigation found it, which meant a hand swipe should locate it.

They'd have to be close for that, though, and thwarting their staged forest showdown bought him time. But where to go? And what to do? And if Captain D'Marino was on the take, who else had been bought? The sheriff, himself? The lieutenants?

At the moment he could trust no one, but as he angled the car onto the I-80 entrance, he changed his mind.

The interstate was easily tracked via multiple means. The wilds?

No one tracked those so he continued west, then north, then east until he'd stuck them deep into the back roads of grub land.

The SUV was a problem. If the captain put out an APB on it, someone would notice them. Deep in the Pennsylvania mountains, folks minded their own business as a general rule and everyone drove a truck or an SUV, but driving a vehicle on a well-advertised BOLO was never smart.

He pulled off onto a narrow lane and parked where they wouldn't be noticed, then motioned for Salena to get out of the car.

She did, followed him about twenty feet up the path, and stopped when he did. "You think it's bugged?"

"I'm going to check and see although there shouldn't be anyone close enough to hear us now. Better safe than sorry." He scoured the car and found the tiny, sensitive device attached beneath Salena's seat. The realization that they were being targeted and tracked by people he'd trusted until an hour before infuriated him.

"Someone in your department set us up."

As dire as that sounded, he couldn't deny it. "So it seems."

Despite the growing warmth of the late spring day, she crossed her arms and hugged herself. "How can one group have so much power?"

"Money." He almost spat the word because the thought that people dismissed life over money sickened him. "And control. If they're the supply line for interstate drug trade, they'll launch an all-out attack to protect their interests."

"Will anyone suspect what's happened? That we're being set up? And is there anyone we can trust?"

"Family. Aunt Kathy. But I can't get any of them involved because of the danger there."

"What about the baby?"

Jim frowned.

"You were there this morning, with the car. If they were tracking us, then they know he's there."

"Unless they think we have him. But at this point, I don't think it's the baby they're after, Salena. I think it's you."

"And now you." She scowled, walked ten paces away, and then strode back. "We need to do something."

"As in?"

"I don't know!" She stomped her heel into the ground in anger. "How could I have fallen into trouble in the one jurisdiction along the interstate owned by Julio and Hector?"

"Except what if it's not the one police force?"

She uttered a small, urgent prayer under her breath.

"All it takes is one desperate person in a position of power. The captain's wife has a degenerative nerve disease. My guess is he caved to make money to cover her drug payments, and college tuition."

"Whereas the honest person goes out and gets an extra job."

He couldn't argue that. The Karralis family had worked hard since emigrating six decades before. His grandparents, his parents, aunts and uncles, all embracing a solid work ethic. "We need to find a place and stay put or change vehicles."

"We seem to be short on cars at the moment."

"And places to stay. How much cash do you have on you?"

Salena pulled folded bills out of her back pocket. "One-ten."

"I've got a hundred." He frowned, wishing he was more like Uncle Louie. The man avoided anything plastic and kept money beneath a loose floorboard in a closet. Now there was a man who always had money in his pocket. "We've got to go on the assumption that they'll keep looking for us, and my guess is that the department will issue an APB on me for taking you hostage or some such thing. That way they can blast our pictures everywhere and create a dragnet."

"Who can we trust?" They exchanged glances and came to the same conclusion. "Kathy."

"How do we get in contact with her?"

"The burner phone. Once she knows the score, she'll do whatever she can."

"They'll be watching her."

He nodded. "But Aunt Kathy's not your average sister. She and Sister Anne were watching a baby in a custody suit several years ago. The father's family staged a coup to snatch that baby and when they finally got into the convent, there was no sister and no baby."

"She hid in the tunnels."

"Nope. She dressed as a priest and walked right past them while

Father McEvoy put on her clothes and bustled around inside as if he was her."

"What if they kill her?" Salena asked as they climbed back into the car and eased it back onto the road. "How can we live with that?"

"Let's hope it doesn't come to that. Aunt Kathy would be the first to say she's lived a long life and would give it up in a heartbeat to save someone else. Let's grab coffee from that mini–mart up ahead. I'll wait in the car while you go in. You're less noticeable than I am right now."

She skewered him with a dark look. "Thanks."

He smiled despite the dire situation. "I'm in uniform. Your hair is changed, less likely to identify you."

"And all Latino girls look alike, right?" She opened the car door swiftly. "If it's good coffee, it's worth the risk, I suppose." She looked calm and cool as she entered the convenience store, and Jim began to understand how she'd made it through the Vaccaro stronghold. Good acting was essential in undercover ops, but what if she was using the acting on him, too? Was he getting the truth, a well–scripted scheme, or was she great at improvisation? And if that was the case, to what end?

She returned minutes later, hopped into the car, and said, "That was weird. Let's get out of here."

"Weird? Why?"

"Because they had a television on in there, and everyone is looking for us. We're considered armed and dangerous."

He'd figured this would happen, but he hadn't counted on it this soon. "Did they recognize you?"

"They didn't seem to."

"My family will be ballistic." He put the car into gear and headed back into the hills. "Which is actually good because D'Martino will have a much tougher job on his hands with two generations of Karralises rallying. They know better than to think I've done anything wrong."

"They'll stick up for you?" The winsome note in her voice said the thought surprised her.

"Yes. Noisy, loud and disruptive, which means two sides of the story will be getting out. As long as we can stay alive long enough to let them be heard. Does the phone have a signal?"

She checked the phone on the console between them. "Yes."

"I'm pulling off up here and letting the family know we're all right."

"Won't they peg the phone with that new tracing software?"

"Not if I text to e-mail."

"Brilliant."

He texted Sister Kathy the predicament, the danger and the captain's involvement, then did the same to his cousin Rafe, instructed him to buy a pay-as-you-go phone, and call him in two hours.

Two hours later the phone rang. "Dimi, what's going on? How did this happen? Ernie Fallon came by the house a few hours ago and said something bad was going down because he helped you rescue a woman yesterday. And now everyone's after you. You being set up?"

Leave it to his cousin Rafe to add up the numbers accurately. Relief loosened the tensed muscles along the base of Jim's neck. "Yes. We need money. I don't know who's clean in our department, Rafe. D'Martino set us up to be killed this morning. Salena turned in a flash drive yesterday loaded with incriminating evidence against the Vaccaro drug operation out of Miami. It was supposed to go to the feds and MPD to strengthen their case against Los Hermanos, but my guess is that it disappeared before it ever got there."

"Of course, if you have a back-up—"

He stared as Salena waved a second flash drive in the air.

"You backed it up?"

"Twice. I wasn't taking any chances. The other one is in a Miami storage locker." She rattled off the number and location and he repeated them to Rafe. "Rafe, if you can get hold of the feds, they're less likely to be infiltrated. They'll want this collar badly. This could topple an entire ring. But we need protection for that baby with Aunt Kathy and we need money. And a place to hole up."

"Head north to 12501 Milton Road outside of Bear Spring," Rafe told him. "Milt Herschmeier lives there with his wife. I'll let him know you're coming. His parents were hidden and kept alive in Germany during World War II. He'll consider it an honor to return the favor."

"You're sure about this?" Jim didn't doubt his cousin's sincerity, but it wasn't just his life they were talking about. It was Salena's, and keeping her safe was becoming more important as time went on. He'd examine why that was later. For right now, he had to cover all the bases.

"One hundred percent. And if you need to leave, Milt will trade cars with you so you can ditch yours."

That was an answer to prayer right there if the county sheriff's office was blasting their photos and the car all over the news and the Internet. "I'm on my way."

"How do you know this guy is all right?" Salena asked as he drove deeper into the wooded hills. "How can your cousin be sure?"

"We'll find out soon." It felt weird to be flying blind, unable to check things on the radio or the scanner, unable to connect to the Internet or see the news, but then he realized that law enforcement used to do this all the time. *Trust your senses. Tune in.* Easier said than done, but it was sound advice.

"Bear Spring, there." She pointed left and he made the turn onto the narrow road, drove through town and hung another left on Milton Road. When the road veered right, a house set well back from the road appeared, and the package-sized mailbox bore the Herschmeier's name and number. "This is it."

He hoped Rafe was right. No, he prayed Rafe was right, and that meant putting himself in God's hands, something he'd been lax with lately. Right now, prayer seemed like the best possible thing to do as they approached the white clapboard split level set into the trees.

An older gentleman walked out of the house, hooked a thumb around back, and by the time Rafe got there, the door to an empty garage bay was open. He drove in, parked and glanced at Salena.

She looked trapped and scared.

He felt the same way, but at some point he needed to trust someone. He got out of the car and strode toward the man. "Mr. Herschmeier?"

"Milt," the old man told him with a firm clasp of his hand, and when Jim met the older man's eyes, he knew they were okay for the moment. "Come inside, mother's got food for you and fresh coffee. I've parked my car there, the tank is full, the keys are in it. If for any reason you need to get out of here quickly," he continued as they moved toward the back door, "There's an access road that runs to County Road 17 from behind the garage. The path winds through a few patches of thick forest at first, but then opens up enough to drive easily and meets the road just above the western side of the village."

"Got it, and I hope I don't have to remember it," Jim replied. "Milt, this is Salena Ramos."

He gripped her hand and smiled. "Miss Ramos, it is an honor. I am a big football fan and my heart broke with the tragedy over your father, years ago. It is my pleasure to help his daughter."

Her eyes grew moist, and if Jim had second-guessed himself about her sincerity and integrity before, seeing her response to the elderly man's words pushed him to trust. He recognized the unlikelihood of a woman infiltrating an operation like Los Hermanos but he also understood the heart of a warrior, man or woman. Salena Ramos was a warrior.

The first bullet slammed into the fence post to Salena's left.

The second one caught her arm before Jim was able yank her behind the house.

"Do not think, go," Milton hissed, as he yanked a gun from behind his back. "The car. Go. Now."

And then the aged man popped off three rounds toward the woods just east of his house, holding whoever was there at bay.

Jim didn't hesitate. He grabbed Salena's good arm, and they raced for the car while old Milt Herschmeier held off whoever had followed them.

He jerked the car door open and hopped in while Salena dove into the other seat. He turned the key and the sound of a well-tuned engine sprang to life. He took a breath and held it as he steered the car around the garage and onto the thin lane threading between the trees. Just when he was pretty sure the car couldn't make it through, the lane widened.

Clear sailing.

No bullets.

And no time to check Salena's wound.

"How did they find us? How did they track us?" she demanded, and he realized she was more angry than hurt.

"How bad is your arm?"

"Flesh wound, I'll live. Blood is sticky." She reached into the glove compartment and grabbed a stack of folded restaurant napkins.

"How'd you know those would be there?" He chanced a glance at the napkins as she pulled off her outer shirt and clapped a folded stack against the wound.

"All elderly people and young mothers have napkins in their glove compartments. It's a rule. And a lot of older folks keep salt and pepper there, too. Just in case." She jammed her shoulder against the locked door to keep the bandage in place and withdrew a miniature salt and pepper shaker with her left hand. "Told ya."

"The supplies." Jim wanted to smack himself, because the captain had the sergeant pack the majority of the supplies in the back of the SUV. "He must have double bugged us. I can't believe I didn't think of that."

The burner phone rang. Salena answered it, and none too nicely, either. "Jim's tied up trying to drive through a forest to get us to safety and your friend is holding off the bad guys with a sophisticated little sidearm."

"They tracked you there?" She put Rafe on speaker so Jim could hear. "Man, they want you bad. I've alerted the feds here and in Miami. If your info is solid, Salena, they should be picking up that flash drive in Miami about now. You should drop the other one into the mail for safekeeping, but send it to a third party address. Just in case."

"Unfortunately I'm fresh out of stamps and envelopes," she told him coolly, but when he said, "Check the back seat," she did... and found a padded envelope addressed with enough postage. "How'd you arrange this?"

"Milt is former military covert ops, he's been around and he believes in preparedness training."

"Will they kill him?" She didn't want to ask the question, but she had to because she'd led these people into this situation. She fumbled for the second flashdrive, stuffed it into the envelope, sealed and addressed it with her left hand while Rafe replied.

"Not if he has his way," Rafe answered cheerfully. "He's also equipped with a medical alarm button because of his age and the minute things got dicey, he would have hit that button. My guess is their local sheriff is already on site and wondering who's opening fire in his jurisdiction."

"I hope you're right." She wanted the words to come out strong.

They didn't, and when she glanced right, the blood-soaked bandage said she might have underestimated the wound.

Dizziness gripped her.

"That's not a scratch." Jim's grim face matched his tone. "Rafe, Salena's hurt."

"How bad?"

"Upper arm. I thought it was a graze. Oops." She tried to keep her tone light but failed. A simple flesh wound wouldn't bleed this much, would it?

"We need to get it looked at," Jim decided. "Rafe, gotta go."

"I'll be in touch. Be safe, Dimi."

"Will do. Once I get Salena put back together." Grim-faced, he ended the call and turned hard left, determined to find medical help, somewhere, somehow.

CHAPTER FIVE

"WE ARE NOT ABOUT TO risk our lives hunting up doctors," Salena scolded. She used her good arm to double the rest of the napkins, tossed the used bundle onto the floor, and re-padded the wound. This time she kept her hand clapped tight against it to staunch the flow with additional pressure. "I didn't use enough pressure. That's all."

"We need medical help." He sounded fierce and protective, which was all well and good except if they ended up in the middle of an emergency room shoot-out.

"I am medical help," she replied lightly, and now that the initial sight of the blood loss was over, she felt better. Stronger. "It's funny how seeing someone else's blood doesn't bother me, but seeing my own made me go weak in the knees. It's doing better now that I've clamped down on it."

Jim glanced her way and grunted, dissatisfied. He turned hard right like Milt had told him to do, then saw the two lane open up straight ahead. Would there be cops waiting there? Were they a jump ahead of them?

He prayed they were because if he came face-to-face with a police contingent right now, he wouldn't know if he was facing friend or foe and that was a rude awakening for a deputy that bled law-enforcement blue.

He slowed slightly before committing to a direction, quickly scanning left and right and saw nothing.

No cars, no SUVs, no presence of either kind. He turned right, swung by a roadside mailbox in a one-stop-sign sized village and pulled up to the box. He took the mailer, tossed it in the blue box, then headed northwest. For five straight minutes they were able to breathe, and then a roughed-up blue pick-up truck careened to a stop in front of them.

"Get down!" Jim ordered, but Salena already had that part figured out. He grabbed his weapon, but stopped when a voice hollered, "Follow me, deputy! I ain't gonna shoot no one, Ernie Fallon's my boy and he said you were caught in a mess up here."

Jim straightened slightly, and the gap-toothed grin of the older man looked like Ernie if you added a quarter century and no dental care. "How'd Ernie find out where we were?"

"Your cousin, I take it, but this ain't exactly the ideal spot for a conversation, know what I mean?"

Oh, Jim understood all right.

"My place is up that trail, to the left and since I wasn't 'spectin' company I'm low on groceries, but the missus has a pot of bean soup on and there's always fresh bread."

"I'd kill for either," Salena whispered, and when she did, he turned her way. Pale gray had replaced the golden tint of her skin, and while she clamped her left hand tight against the gunshot wound, she had the look of someone who was about to faint.

And then she did.

"She's hurt, Mr. Fallon. Maybe we should chance a doctor or a clinic nearby."

"You head up. Help's waitin'."

Jim hesitated, but not for long. Yes, Salena needed help, but there was no way she'd be fully protected in a hospital situation right now. He knew that. He also understood that until he was cleared of being a suspect, any law enforcement stumbling on to him would be required to treat him as an armed and dangerous criminal. He made a quick decision and headed up the treed hill in a series of long, winding, unpaved back roads. If nothing else his awareness of rustic, rural living in this sector of the state had just been raised. He pulled Milt's car alongside a small, brown, natural-sided wood cabin, aimed the nose toward an upper fork in the drive, climbed out and hurried over to Salena's side. "Hey, how we doing?"

Her eyes had opened, then she scowled, disgusted. "I'm fine. I'm a ninny who can't stand the sight of her own blood."

"Well, let's get you inside and find out if there's anything else going on."

"There's not," she insisted. She went to stand, and when her knees went weak, Jim scooped her up and carried her up to the house.

An older woman opened the door, saw the bandage and didn't pause to worry about blood on her floor or her sofa. "Put her right there, on the couch, lay her flat, no pillow, she needs to get her equilibrium back, poor thing. She's had a rough day, from the look of it."

The understatement of the century, Jim thought, but when the stout, little woman brought out a medical bag along with a sizeable first-aid kit, he realized he needed to stop jumping to conclusions. "You're a doctor."

"Was, back in the day," she told him as she opened the bag. She nodded to his left. "Bring that small table by, won't you? And slide it in right here, so I can brace her arm. Yes, that's right, exactly there. And let's have a look-see, darlin'..." She made short work of Salena's sleeve with a pair of short, sharp scissors, instructed Jim to find and aim the bright-beamed flashlight in her bag, and grunted when she saw the wound. "In and out, that's why the blood loss, dearie. We'll get this taken care of, no worries." She sent Jim a quick look as she barked off a list of things for him to put on the table while she draped the couch and floor with plastic, then thick, cotton flannel. "I'm retired now, have been for a few years, but I like helping out here and there as needed for folks down on their luck. In the wilds, there are plenty of those."

"I didn't realize," Jim admitted. He'd have labeled a good part of his county rural, but it was positively populated compared to the back-woods hamlets in the hills.

"You know Ernie." She talked while she worked, and Jim realized she did that matter-of-factly to relax the patient, a skill he'd learned working with people in tough situations. His calm became their calm.

"A good man. He's quick to respond to danger and he helped save Salena's life yesterday."

The doc slanted him a look that said she wasn't any too sure about the situation. Salena took a deep breath and sighed in relief. "Why are medical people the worst patients?"

"You're in medicine?"

"I'm an R.N. out of Nashville."

"You're a long way from home."

"For a while. I had a job to do and there are a few folks in Florida who aren't any too pleased with my success."

"You crossed some big bucks people it sounds like."

"Well, money should never be more important than life," Salena said softly. "And sometimes you've got to jump in and do what you've got to do. If you want to look yourself in the mirror, that is."

"Life's a test at times," the doctor agreed as she flushed the wounds repeatedly. "I'm going to put you on an antibiotic I have here. It's not the one I'd normally choose, but I don't want to be tipping anyone off that you're up here and if I call in a prescription right now, there are folks who might put two and two together with Ernie all over the TV saying you folks aren't guilty."

"Ernie's doing that?"

She nodded, grim. "Like you said." She dipped her chin toward Salena. "Sometimes you've got to do what you've got to do and we figured if Ernie's willing to stick his neck out to call out the sheriff's department on national news, we'd like to do what we can to help keep him alive."

"I owe him," Jim maintained. "He's taking a lot on his shoulders right now."

She made a face at that, then smiled his way. "He wouldn't see it that way. Neither do we. When you're doing the right thing, that's reward enough."

"Mother, I got fresh milk, bread and some sausage for that stew. And cookies because I bet the young lady would like some cookies when she's feelin' better."

"You stopped at Miller's."

"Gave 'em some business. Grabbed some berries too, while I was there."

"I had a hankering for fresh berries." She finished off Salena's wound and smiled up at the old man. "You must have read my mind, Scoot."

"The soup smells amazing," Jim said. "Soup and fresh bread. It's like coming home to Mima's or my mother. Always something cooking in the pot."

"And you're likely starvin' to death and worryin' about your friend. I'll set you up a bowl to cool, it's mighty hot right now."

He nodded thanks to Scoot, but then inched closer to Salena.

Her color looked better. Her eyes seemed brighter, and he had to deal with the shot of dread to his heart when she'd keeled over in the car. How could he care about someone he'd only just met?

"When it's right, it's right."

"What?" He stared down at the doctor as she tossed used gauze into the small, plastic-lined garbage can.

"It's how we know so many things," she told him. She stood, breathed deep, eased a kink out of her right shoulder and smiled. "Most of us married for a while will tell you. When it's right, it's right and there's not a lot of rhyme or reason to it."

His grandmother would be the first to agree, but that didn't make a bit of sense. Did it?

And yet hadn't his heart stirred the minute he met Salena's gaze through the car window the day before? As if her soul spoke to his?

Ridiculous.

Or was it?

"Soup's cool enough now."

The common sense words helped. He'd focus on food and coffee and how to keep them both alive until this mess got straightened around. Despite this momentary calm, he'd been close to calm earlier, then got shot at, so he wasn't convinced they were out of the woods until they were actually out of the woods. He sat down next to Scoot and had to ask. "Where did you get a name like Scoot?"

The old timer laughed. "When I was a kid they called me Scooter. When I got tall, they shortened it. No real reason, just a nickname."

"And I'm Helen," Dr. Fallon said as she came back into the kitchen after washing up. "Nice to meet you, deputy."

"I'm grateful."

"Me, too." Salena struggled to sit upright and when the doctor scolded, she gazed at his soup bowl with longing. "If I promise not to get sick or faint, may I have some, too?"

"You feel up to eating?"

"Starved, actually, which is a good sign."

"It is." Helen scooped Salena a bowl of the soup while Scoot sawed off a hunk of bread. "An appetite says the body isn't quite so shell-shocked as we might have thought at first."

The phone rang.

Everyone stopped and stared as if they could be seen, until Scoot stood up, grabbed the phone and barked 'Hello' into the hand piece. He listened, staring at Jim with grave intent, then grunted. "I hear ya'." He hung up the phone and scowled. "That captain guy was just on TV asking anyone who's got family in the hills to notify them about two armed and dangerous people who might be holed up in an empty house or with a neighbor. He asked them to be vigilant in pursuit of justice."

"Will folks come looking up here?" Jim wondered.

Scoot met Helen's gaze and shrugged. "Most folks up here are particular about mindin' their own business and we return that favor. But if they believe what the captain is squawkin', there might be a few who start to poke around."

"We should go."

Helen cleared her throat, and Jim got the feeling that when Helen Fallon spoke, people listened. "You'll stay right here, I won't hear of anything else."

"We can't."

Jim shifted his attention to Salena and she scrunched her brow as she stared at the soup, then them. "Ernie's been on our side. They'll figure out where you live. They'll come looking."

"You're right." Jim stood and sent the soup a look of regret.

"Eat the soup." Helen stood, arms folded across her chest, and stared point blank at the pair of them, first one, then the other. "I'll pack food for you. You're right, with Ernie raising a ruckus, they'll figure this out. Finding us is no easy task, and that's on purpose, but someone will cave if they wave enough money in front of them during these hard times. Scoot, can you make sure the way up is clear? I'll put a hamper in the back seat, you should be fine as long as you avoid more bullets and take the antibiotics I'm giving you. No heavy lifting. And eat fast."

CHAPTER SIX

SALENA DIDN'T NEED TO BE told twice, and by the time she'd polished off the soup, Helen had food tucked in the car and Scoot had called from the upper mountain road. "All clear."

"Thank you." She hugged Helen quickly, and the older woman returned the embrace gently.

"Go with God, but go with speed. And I'll be praying this all gets cleared up swiftly."

"I'd appreciate that." She felt stronger now, with the arm properly cared for, food in her stomach, and a clean bandage.

"Here's a pair of coffees to go," Helen added, bustling out behind her. She waited while Salena climbed in, then handed the to-go mugs in through the side window.

"I don't know how to thank you." Jim leaned down to see Helen's face beyond Salena.

"Just did. Now go before company comes."

She was right. The thought that Ernie and Jim's family were besieging the news outlets with counter-suggestions was wonderful but until the BOLO was lifted or the arrest warrant vacated, they would be sitting ducks to any law enforcement that stumbled onto them, and if it was someone crooked, in league with the captain?

The morgue might be their next stop and that couldn't happen because she had every intention of raising that sweet baby.

Jim crested the upper hill. Scoot was pulled off, into the trees, and as he pulled up close, Scoot held up keys. "Change up cars again. I'll put this one out back and it'll take 'em a while to find it. And then awhile before they figure out what you might be driving since these are my buddy Travis's wheels."

"Scoot, you're a lifesaver," Jim told him as he transferred supplies from one car to the other. "We're so grateful for everything. Having Salena hurt, then we show up at your door and your wife's a doctor, well…" Jim scraped a hand to the nape of his neck. "I'm guessing that's God's hand at work. Thank you."

Scoot grinned. "Well, we try. You head out, sorry my pants are a little short on you, but not too bad, are they?"

"A lot less noticeable than my uniform," Jim assured him. "Thanks, Scoot."

He pulled out onto the thin, mountain road, headed west and wondered where they could duck off. "Can you check where we are?"

Salena turned the map every which way and frowned. "We're not here, it seems."

"Unmarked roads."

"Until we get to a marked one."

"So what do you think? West or east?"

She pursed her lips, deciding. "East."

"I agree." He turned east, snugged Scoot's Yankee cap down further on his head and when they got to a narrow crossroads, he shifted his attention to Salena again. "Promise Road and Morton Road."

He drove through while she scanned the map. "Aha!"

"So we're finally someplace?"

"We're not far from two campgrounds and the town of Murphysville."

That gave them a starting point, at least. It was tough to figure out where you were going if you had no clue where you were or where you'd been, and when a county sheriff's car passed them going in the opposite direction, an adrenalin surge shoved Salena's heart into overdrive. "Do you think he noticed us?"

Jim had been careful to drive as if he hadn't a care in the world, but Salena noted his drawn brows as they moved beyond. "No way of knowing. I'm going to head north and find a place to lay low until dark. No sense taking a chance like this in daylight even though the chances of being recognized are slim."

Were they? Salena wondered.

She wasn't sure, but traveling at night would be the smarter thing to do. "We'll catch a nap in the woods, then drive tonight. I'll keep watch first," she told him, then yawned.

"Let's reverse that. You sleep now, save your coffee and drink it when you wake up and I'll sleep while you drive. Okay?"

It sounded better than okay because either the shock, wound or blood loss had left her exhausted. "Okay. I probably won't really sleep, but a rest would be good."

"Rest, then." His comforting smile was better than the softest blanket. "I'll be here when you wake up."

She put the seat back, grabbed the pillow Helen had given them and was sound asleep in seconds, and when she finally woke up, hours had passed, and dusk had fallen. "I slept for more than three hours."

"You needed it."

She blinked at him, then rubbed her eyes. "So it seems. Okay, let's change seats."

"Once we get on the open road," he told her.

Concern hit her crosswise. "You're worried."

"Guarded," he corrected as he laid his gun on the panel between them and started the engine. "If that deputy made us, then they're watching for us and if we have to make a run for it, I want to be at the wheel. Once we're beyond the general area, you can take over."

He expected trouble. She heard it in his voice. Was that because he'd had hours to sit, wondering and stewing? Or because his cop instinct forewarned him?

Instinct, she decided, because in the thirty-six hours they'd been together, Jim's instinct had been spot on. She withdrew her own gun and set it in her lap.

"Can you shoot straight with that arm?"

"Straight enough to miss you."

He laughed softly, then sobered. "Here's the thing, though. The regular guys don't know we're the good guys. All they know is that I've gone off with what they think is a gun-toting kidnapper."

"Accurate so far!" She reached over and put her hand on his knee. "Neither one of us wants to hurt someone. We just want this over. Maybe we'll get lucky, because I'm really not cut out for the Bonnie and Clyde scenario."

"Me, either. I haven't gotten word from Rafe about Miami."

"I was hoping we'd hear something."

"Me, too." He hauled in a deep breath, got to the road's edge and turned left, then right. "If there's going to be a commotion, I'd prefer that it's not around innocent people."

"Agreed. If you take this about two miles north, you'll end up at Jackson Settlement Road. Hang a left and that will take us to a two-lane running parallel to the Interstate."

"Got it."

He didn't need the directions because two minutes later a flash of blue caught his eye in the distance. "Roadblock."

"It couldn't just be someone pulled over, getting a ticket?"

"Not on a dark, going-to-nowhere road this time of night. Which means they've probably got them set up on all the routes heading out of this area."

"We shouldn't have stopped."

He pulled the car off the road, jumped out and grabbed her hand when she rounded the car. "Old news. We made a choice to give the FBI and the MPD time. Let's get as deep into the woods as we can before they realize we're here." The sound of car engines rolling said they'd figured it out, which meant they'd had a spotter in the village. Smart cop move. "Come on, let's move."

His phone buzzed with a call from Rafe. He pulled it out as they made a mad dash through new growth vines and brambles, and once they got fifty feet in, tree litter from an old ice storm made quick movement impossible. With Salena's bad arm, they were in a rough situation. "Rafe, we're in trouble," he said quickly. "We're on Morton Road, in the woods, surrounded by roadblocks. I'm not concerned as much about giving it up and going in, but I'm real concerned about being someone's target practice to silence witnesses."

"The feds made a move in Miami. A big one. That's all I know."

That should mean the gig was up for the captain, but did he know that? Did these officers and deputies know that, as they hunted Jim and Salena? And what could he do to buy much needed time? Nothing. He stuffed the phone back into his pocket as they made their way forward. They needed to find a place to hold up until daylight, when it would be a lot less possible to mistakenly shoot them. "Salena, give me your weapons."

"Huh?' She paused for breath as she navigated another broken tree limb. "You're kidding, right?"

"Nope. Give 'em over. If for some reason they take us out, I want there to be clear evidence that we had no ill intent in their direction. Quick, give me your stash."

She did it, but he could tell she wasn't happy about it. Or maybe not thrilled with his pronouncement that they might get taken out anyway, but it made sense to him. If their weapons were found well away from their bodies, then clearly someone took a purposeful shot. One way or another, in life or in death, Jim was determined to take the bad guys down.

A mix of flashing lights crested the tall hill, then convened above and below the borrowed car. Multiple vehicles converged from both directions, then came to a screeching halt, mid-mountain. "You take the east woods," barked a command. "We'll go west."

A bullhorn.

Flashing lights.

Spotlights, aimed in multiple directions. And probably night vision goggles on some of the officers.

Jim pulled Salena down next to him as he ducked into the deepest brush they could find and went perfectly still.

Loud voices mingled at the roadside, and then the approach of trackers sent Jim's blood pumping so hard, he was sure it was audible. He slipped an arm around Salena and tugged her close, then realized she was praying softly.

Pray! Pray hard, Dimi, when things go bad or things get rough. Pray hard!

He took Mima's words to heart and bowed his head. *Our Father, who art in heaven, hallowed be thy name. Thy kingdom come. Thy will be done...*

The lights grew closer. So did the noise. The tree litter made it rough going. Trying to grapple a drawn weapon and climb through dark, dangerous forest made a bad situation worse, and just as he thought that, someone's weapon discharged. A scream followed.

Jim's heart raced, wanting to help while helplessly watching the shadowed figures clambering their way.

"Duke shot himself!" The raised voice of an approaching lawman rang out. "Hold your fire, he shot himself in the foot, we need help here!"

A scramble from the road's edge ate up long minutes as they tried to move the injured officer. The criss-crossed fallen limbs made it almost impossible and right about then Jim was sorry for the guy's injury and blessing the effects of the ice storm because it bought them what they needed most: time.

Noise from the road said the gathered lawmen were re-strategizing. Flashlights and spotlights swept crazy arcs through the late-spring trees, and when a light rain began to fall, the sound of rain on trees made hearing more difficult. Which meant it was more difficult for the trackers as well.

He removed his left arm from the sleeve of his jacket, then pulled it up and over Salena's head to shield her from the rain. When she tucked herself beneath his shoulder and against his heart, it felt like the most natural thing in the world to lean in and kiss her. So he did.

She kissed him back and for a few short moments the nearby drama was put on hold. When she eventually drew back, she tucked her face into his neck and whispered, "It would be a crying shame to find such a wonderful man and have that be our first and last kiss."

He couldn't argue because he'd enjoy more of those kisses himself, but the team at the road started re-approaching their side of the forest. "They're moving in again."

"Well." She reached up and kissed him again, long and lingering, then settled back against his chest. "Let 'em come."

His heart went tight. The last thing he wanted was for someone else to get hurt on his account. He understood the danger of manipulating dangerous terrain with a weapon drawn.

Could he do it? Stand up and declare their presence so no one else got hurt? Or would doing that put Salena and him in someone's crosshairs?

The rain came harder now, chilly, soaking, wind-driven drenching rain. A clap of thunder followed a flash of lightning, and when the next flash seemed to sizzle through the trees, a call from the roadside halted the hunt. Navigating the tree-strewn woods in the daylight would be tough enough. At night, in a driving thunderstorm a hunt could turn into a suicide mission of slick grips and moss-covered wood.

The combined law enforcement forces pulled back. They

climbed into waiting cars while a few milled around in rain gear, but the slick apparel made climbing through the woods more dangerous yet. Stymied by Mother Nature…

Mother Nature and God, he decided. Rain sloughed off to their right and left, but the bough of vining kept them mostly dry.

"Stay or go?"

She whispered the words in his ear, and he'd been weighing the same question. The storm would cover the sound of their movements. Should they do their best and slip deeper into the woods or up the mountain?

He grabbed her hand to help her up when a light caught him full in the face. "Come out with your hands up and if you make one bad move, I'll shoot."

The glare of the light erased Jim's vision. He stood, blocking Salena and put his hands high. "We're unarmed. If you shoot the ensuing investigation will show you shot two unarmed people running for their lives because of bad cops. So weigh that carefully before you make any rash decisions, deputy."

"You're the bad cop," scoffed a second voice, and another flashlight blinded them. "We'll give the orders here, Karralis. Turn around, hands behind your back after your little honey does the same thing."

Salena stepped around him, hands held high. "I'm unarmed and a witness in a federal prosecution."

"Save it for the judge, sweetheart."

Jim winced as they cuffed Salena. He heard her gasp of pain and knew the wounded arm must be on fire about now. Every instinct within wanted to lash out and protect her.

Pray hard, Dimi!

He closed his eyes as the deputies cuffed his arms behind his back, and when one shoved him forward and he fell to his knees, he thought of Calvary and that long walk uphill, carrying a cross.

He struggled up. The second deputy reached out a hand to help him. "Let me help," he insisted when Jim pulled away. "This is tough enough with two hands and two feet. Come on, Jim, I've got your back."

A familiar voice, a fellow deputy from his sector, but could he trust him not to fake an accident in the rough terrain and put a bullet in his back?

Right now he couldn't trust anyone. He stumbled forward, through the barkless debris, and when he finally got to the side of the road, the spotlights helped him assess the situation. Two deputies were shoving Salena into the back of a familiar car and when Captain D'Martino stepped into the light, his heart sank.

After all this time and effort, the attempts to keep a wonderful woman safe, and in the end, the crooked cop was about to win because Jim was pretty sure that Salena would never make it back to the station house. "D'Martino!" He yelled the name as two unmarked cars came up the road and pulled off to the side below the car the Fallons had loaned them.

The captain turned, faced him and shrugged him off.

"The second flash drive is in safe hands, Captain."

His words made his superior officer pause, and drew the attention of the lawmen surrounding him.

"And the third one is in the hands of the feds right now. We sent them the information earlier today and I hear they're rounding up the Vaccaros and various members of Los Hermanos as we speak. Which means no more sweet payments, Captain, and probably a very long jail term. Just in case you thought this was over. If you hurt her, D'Martino? You'll answer to me, and every Karralis with breath. Got it?"

"Shut up!" An unfamiliar office got up in his face. "You're the one in handcuffs. You're the traitor. Leave the captain alone!"

"I'd let him talk," advised another voice, unfamiliar, as a group of trench-coat wearing federal agents moved into the mix. Two of them went straight for D'Martino and as one faced him, the other wrenched the captain's hands behind his back and slapped cuffs into place. "Ralph D'Martino, you're under arrest for conspiracy and aiding in human trafficking, racketeering and aiding and abetting a drug dealer. Anything you say…" He continued to Mirandize the captain, and then a second set of agents moved closer to Jim and repeated the action with the deputy in front of him.

Two more men moved forward and pointed to the restraints holding Jim's hands behind his back "Uncuff him. Now. And get her out of that car."

The deputy who'd offered to help Jim moved forward quickly. "With pleasure." He released Jim's cuffs, and when Jim turned to thank him, the other man grabbed his hand. "I knew it was a set up. We all did, Jim. But then the trick was to get you out alive and find out who was bad and who was good."

Jim understood the conundrum. As the feds opened the back door of the cruiser, he hurried down the hill and hauled Salena into his arms. "You're okay."

"Well, that whole cuffing thing didn't make my arm any too happy." The bandage Helen had so carefully set was oozing red through her shirt. "I think a trip to emergency would be in order."

"We've got you, Miss Ramos. Come this way, we'll get you taken care of and then if you and Deputy Karralis don't mind, we'd like the chance to talk to you. And may I just say?" The man swept his gaze from one to the other. "I'm real glad we got you out of this alive. You're a gutsy pair. We're mighty glad to have you on our side."

Jim helped Salena into the back of the agent's car, then climbed in the other side. He wrapped his arm around her, glad it was over, but the sight of her blood-soaked shirt made his breath catch harder. "Hang on, okay? We'll get you fixed up again in no time."

"I've learned not to look." She peeked up at him, avoiding the sight of her arm. "I'll stare at you the whole way as I ignore the situation on my arm, because it seems I'm a wuss when it comes to my own blood, a lesson I learned the hard way."

"Well, that's the only thing you're weak on, Miss." The agent smiled at her through the rearview mirror as he switched the light on momentarily. "Because you've managed to almost single-handedly bring down a large-scale trafficking ring, and with the Vaccaros and their buddies locked up with no bail, I don't even think you're going to need witness protection."

"Really?" She sat up a little straighter, smiled, then looked back at Jim. "So I might get to have a life after all, Dimi?"

"I like the sound of that," he whispered, then tugged her back against his chest. "If you're willing to calm things down a little, woman. Because I'm a picket fence kind of guy and I think that baby boy deserves at least that. Don't you?"

She nodded against his chest, and when tears of happiness blended with his rain-soaked shirt, he barely noticed. "I do. And I expect they need nurses around here. What do you think?"

He smiled and kissed the top of her head. "I expect they do, honey."

CHAPTER SEVEN

HER ARM FELT BETTER AND the chances of having anyone tug, pull or handcuff her appeared to be over as they gathered in the small convent living room the next afternoon. Salena was grateful for that. She accepted a steaming mug of coffee from one of the agents and sat back against Sr. Kathy's sofa while Sr. Anne rocked the baby. "I have to thank you guys again for acting on the flash drive tip so quickly. I don't know where Jim and I would be right now if you hadn't shown up."

"Your info stash knocked it out of the park for us," Agent Diller explained. "They've been trying to put a lid on the Vaccaros for several years, but every credible witness ran into lethal bad luck. Not this time." He aimed his gaze straight at her. "This time we have the flash drive, we have the evidence surrounding your sister, we have names and dates and we have an insider who jumped at the opportunity to help us. Someone, it seems who was helping you from inside the organization."

"Gloria."

The agent scoffed. "Trust me, Gloria Vaccaro Miccitelli doesn't help anyone but herself. No, there was a woman working for the Vaccaros in their private residence, she didn't know what was going on behind the scenes at the compound until she saw your sister by accident. And when she realized who she was and what was going on at the second complex, she decided she needed to do something to help."

"And then you came on the scene and she realized what you were doing," added a different agent.

Salena stared at the two agents, confused. "I don't understand.

Who could have been there that recognized Roslyn and me? There was no one in that birthing wing I recognized, believe me."

"She took pains to remain incognito because if you recognized her, you could both be killed, but she sent you a message." Diller pulled out a small notepad. "To my beautiful Salena Patricia, I send my utmost apologies for not understanding and acting sooner. I have never forgotten my first two beautiful babies, Salena and Roslyn, and the kindness of their father. May God bless you and may he forgive me for my lack of understanding. Tante Dolores."

"My nanny." Salena breathed the words softy. "Dolores was working for them?"

"She was the nanny to Julio's two daughters and had no idea what his business was, but she said that one day she had taken the children to a show and saw two of Julio's men escorting a young, pregnant woman into a vehicle. She recognized your sister, and started her own investigation."

"She didn't understand the extent of what she saw," the second agent reported as Jim took Salena's hand. "And by the time she realized, your sister had disappeared but Isaac had been brought to the family wing. She said she looked at him, and it was like seeing Roslyn again, as an infant. And that made her realize she was holding your sister's child. She had more freedom with Isaac than they would normally allow because his presence caused fights between Julio and his wife. Julio's wife didn't want to raise some-one else's child and he wanted the son she never gave him. And so he took Roslyn's child as his own. But Dolores had already put two plus two together and became aware of the evil around her. She decided she needed to help, but wasn't sure how, and then you showed up."

"I'm numb." She squeezed Jim's hand as she stared at the baby, his fist shoved snugly in his mouth, his sweet, soft cheek pressed against Sr. Anne's cotton shirt. "But I'm ready for a new beginning. A new chance to be the family my father always wanted us to be."

"Are you heading back to Nashville?" Diller asked and before she could answer, Jim shook his head.

"Not unless I transfer to the NPD or the Davidson County sheriff's office," Jim answered.

Salena gripped his hand tighter. "I don't think that's necessary."

"No?" He smiled right into her eyes and lifted their linked hands for a kiss.

"I like the south and I love Nashville. It's a wonderful city, but I have no family there. The only family I have is here." She smiled across at the sleeping baby. "And I think raising this baby in Pennsylvania would be a wonderful thing, don't you, Deputy? If you wouldn't mind my staying around, that is."

He leaned down, kissed her cheek and looked deep into her eyes. "I think that would make me about the happiest man in the world, Salena. In fact, while we were at the hospital, I happened to grab hold of a list of documentation you need to apply for a job there."

She raised a brow, impressed and amused. "Did you now?"

"Well, just in case." He smiled at her, just her, then crossed the room, lifted the baby from Sr. Anne and brought him over to Salena. "I think you and Isaac need time to get to know each other, and I know a great place to stay while that's happening. Right, Aunt Kathy?"

"It's the perfect arrangement until Salena's on her feet financially," declared the aged sister. "Or married."

Salena cuddled the baby to her chest, relaxing for the first time in long, tiring weeks. "Well, my trust comes to me in a few years. Think you can beat that, Dimi?" She smiled up at him, teasing, but the sincerity in his gaze went beyond humor and straight to her heart.

"I'm going to do my very best, Salena." He leaned down, palmed the infant's head and then kissed her cheek gently. "And that's a promise."

After a lifetime littered with broken promises, Jim's words hit home. She reached up, gripped his hand, and smiled back at him. "I'll hold you to it."

And she did.

EPILOGUE

"JIM, CAN YOU ZIP THIS please?" Salena hurried out of their shared bathroom, fastening an earring as she eyed the clock radio next to the bed. "We've got to hurry, if traffic's bad we'll be late. It's a long ride to Philly."

She turned so he could zip the dress and when he hesitated about going up or down, she laughed and slapped his hand. "Rafe and Tasha will be here any minute to watch the kids and we can't keep the lawyers waiting."

"Raincheck?" he whispered against her neck.

"Always." She turned, kissed him sweetly, then pointed down the hall. "I hear Nick which means Isaac probably climbed into his crib."

"I'll get Isaac. You get Nick." He grabbed his sport coat and followed her down the hall. "Are you feeling all right? You were restless last night."

She picked up eighteen-month-old Nick while Jim lifted four-year-old Isaac out of his little brother's crib. "Braxton Hicks contractions, nothing real, and if this baby can just wait a few more hours to join her big brothers, I'll be happy. I want this trust stuff done and over. It seems like it's been going on forever, and I'm ready to put it behind me."

"Multi-million dollar trust funds aren't anything to take lightly," he agreed as they took the boys downstairs. "Does that mean I get a bigger rowboat for fishing? Because I'd be okay with that."

She laughed, kissed Nick's brow as she tucked him into his high chair and sighed. "Will it change us, Jim? Who we are? What we do, what we want?"

"Why would it?"

His words seemed innocent, but she'd witnessed the dark side of having money first-hand. The temptations, the shallower mindset, the egocentric lifestyle her mother and sister adopted when little was expected of them. And then their downturn to drugs. "When things come too easy, it's hard to develop a good moral base, isn't it? Doesn't character come from struggle? From being forged in the fire? If we get everything handed to us, to them," she let her gaze rest on their two boys, different as night and day, both beloved. "How do we teach them to be strong? Maybe we shouldn't go get the money. Maybe we should just shrug it off, pretend it doesn't exist and keep living our lives here, like we've been doing."

"You're scared."

She didn't deny it because it was true. Her father had died driving too fast in a souped-up car. What if he hadn't been able to afford a crazy fast car? Would he have lived to raise his daughters? To love his wife? Would her mother have slipped into despair and depression? Would her sister have died?

"You're looking for trouble, honey." Jim's arms slipped around her, and he folded his big, strong hands over their baby daughter, still in the womb but almost ready to make a grand entrance. "Money only changes people if they let it. Look at Rafe and Tasha." His cousin's mini-van pulled into the driveway as he said it. "Rafe's got a boatload of money, but he works at the restaurant a few days a week, molds chocolates and makes people smile. And Tasha's still helping fight cancer at the University of Pennsylvania. Life doesn't have to change. Although I'd still like a bigger boat," he confessed as he tickled her ear with his chin. "But we can discuss that later. And funding "Seeds of Grace" could become a huge help to people in need."

"Which reminds me," Rafe announced as he came through the back door with a box of Mima's pastries. Both boys immediately lost interest in their cold cereal and clamored for the box in Uncle Rafe's hands. "Tasha and I are going to match your start-up fund for Seeds of Grace. Had I mentioned that before?"

"No." Salena hugged him awkwardly as her rounded tummy got in the way. "That's a lot of money, Rafe."

"A drop in the bucket if it saves some kids from Roslyn's fate. If we can catch them early and set them on the right path, there's less chance of falling astray."

"You're all right," Jim told his cousin as Rafe's daughter Lexie came through the kitchen door, followed by Tasha with their toddler daughter Miriam.

"Miri wants to thank you for putting the dog's water bowl at the bottom of the back steps because she was very, very thirsty. Here." She handed the soaking wet girl to Rafe, kissed Isaac and Nick good morning and tapped her phone. "It's late, get out of here, we're already tempting fate with this baby." She swept Salena's tummy a measured look. "At least you'll be surrounded by hospitals should the need arise.

"I told her tomorrow is a better day," Salena patted her tummy as she gathered her purse. "But we'll see."

"What do you mean?" Jim stopped in front of her, thwarting her progress. "Are you having real contractions now? Because we can change the appointment. Or just have them come to the hospital instead."

"I'm fine, you'll be the first to know when I'm not," she scolded lightly. She took his hand, kissed the kids goodbye, and moved to the door. "Let's get this done before I realize I'm scared to death of being rich and growing stupid."

Jim stopped her at the bottom of the stairs. He caught her face in his hands and settled a long, slow, gentle kiss to her mouth, then laid one hand atop her swollen middle. "We're already rich, honey. The rest is just money. It doesn't mean a thing and I promise you it won't change a thing, except, of course…"

"A slightly bigger boat."

He smiled as he led her to the SUV and opened the passenger door for her. "Well that and a way to change the world for the better. Every kid that gets helped by Seeds of Grace will have a chance they might not have had otherwise. And that's a pretty darn good scenario in my book. Every kid that stays away from dangerous choices is one more I won't have to arrest some day. And I'm very okay with that. You ready to do this?" He held her hands loosely but put the ball in her court, letting her make the call.

She took a deep breath, squeezed his hands and nodded. "Let's go."

He pulled out of the driveway and headed south, past pretty country homes on quiet, rural roads until he merged into light traffic on Rt. 476. He turned toward Philly and a new fork in their road. Sister Anne had passed away the year before, but Aunt Kathy had decided that sixty-seven was too young to retire. She agreed to relocate to Philly and help get Seeds of Grace off the ground. Tante Dolores and two women who'd run a homeless shelter for women in South Philly would help staff the charity. Working together, they were determined to make a difference. And one by one, funded by Roslyn's trust, they would help people see their way to a better tomorrow.

Salena couldn't have imagined this outcome when she went undercover to save Isaac from the Vaccaros, but now, looking back, it was as if God's road had been mapped out all along...

And it was a good, solid path unwinding before her, with a house full of kids and the man of her dreams at her side.

DEAR READER:

REMEMBER THAT LINE FROM "PRETTY Woman"? When Edward asked Vivian what happened when the prince climbed the tower to rescue the princess and Julia Roberts looks him right in the eye and says, "She rescues him right back."

And that's how I wanted this book to roll, two strong characters, caught in the web of cartel and mob mentality, a web that stretches too far and wide in our beautiful country. And then I wanted them to break through that web and meet their destiny of "happy ever after". I hope you enjoyed this newest Karralis hero story… we had Rafe in "Longing for a Miracle", and now Dimitrios "Jim" Karralis, the deputy sheriff willing to risk his life to save hers… and in the next story "Home to His Heart" we meet Jake, another Karralis cousin, as he meets the love of his life when he least expects it. But isn't that so often the case?

THANKS SO MUCH FOR TAKING the time to read this! I'd love to hear from you. E-mail me at *loganherne@gmail.com* visit my website/blog at *http://ruthloganherne.com* or hang with me on facebook where I laugh and pray and exploit cute pics of small animals and small children to sell sweet books! Wishing you every hope and blessing as your days go on.

Home to His Heart

Ruth Logan Herne

CHAPTER ONE

TESS COSGROVE STARED ACROSS THE street, shaded her eyes, then peered harder.

Two little boys, twins, maybe? From where she was, she couldn't be sure. The pair sat on the front step of a closed-up house, looking hunched and lonely, behind the spreading oak. Fading leaves littered the ground, while others waved above in gold-red splendor, ready to fall at the next strong wind. Heads down, the pair glanced right and left, then at each other, but when their eyes met, they jerked their gazes apart, as if making eye contact was too real.

Tess turned toward her Aunt Theodora, the only relative crazy enough— or guilt-ridden enough— to help tackle Tess's crazy, cluttered childhood home. "Who lives across the street?"

"Jake Karralis." Auntie's tone sparked with disapproval, but that wasn't exactly unusual. Auntie hadn't approved of much in a very long time. And in typical Theodora-fashion, she switched from disapproval to sympathy and didn't bother with transition. "He bought the place after he lost his wife when those two were babies, so sad. His aunt and uncle moved to Arizona a few years back."

Jake Karralis. The school heartthrob from days she'd rather forget, but as long as she needed to be in Ashton, Pennsylvania, there'd be no forgetting. "He's got kids?"

Auntie grunted. "Two. Boys. Twins. Bah."

"How old are they?"

"Little. Naughty. Always making a fuss in church, so I go to a different service now. Loud children are an annoyance."

Kids were kids, weren't they? "You used to like kids, Auntie. Remember?"

Dora peered at her over a pair of the ugliest glasses Tess had ever seen. "There is a great deal I used to like. I'm old. Naughty boys are no pleasure when one is old. Mark my words. And what my sister was thinking, saving this, collecting that, hoarding all this—"

"Auntie."

Dora wove her brows together about as close as a body could get them. "All right, all right, I won't say it. Heaven knows you're old enough to fill in the blank."

Tess was plenty old enough. She'd seen thirty the year before and decided that if sixty was really the new forty, the laws of mathematics made thirty the new twenty. Now if someone could just explain that to her biological clock.

"It's preposterous, isn't it?" Auntie glared at her late sister's Dutch colonial on a well-treed street full of gracious old colonials. "I thank God every morning that Stella might have the peace denied her in life, but then I have to look up and shake my fist, and ask her what was she thinking, hanging on to all this schlock? Leaving it for us to do? And then I thank God she has *one* daughter who knows her duty and is willing to come back to her hometown and make sense of this. Ach."

Tess's twin sister had little to do with Tess, their mother, and the family in general. The Cosgroves had put their own special label of "fun" in the word dysfunctional, but that was a long time ago. Faith and forgiveness went hand in hand, whether her sister believed it or not. Tess had made the drive up to Ashton with a purpose. She intended to face the upcoming holiday season with a clean heart, all old guilt expunged. Her mother had allowed no help, and precious few visitors those last years. Now there was a job to be done, and Tess intended to do it, with or without assistance. Her mother's will had named Dora as co-executor, which meant way too much talking and not enough doing.

The boys continued to sit on the stoop, then one stood up. The other followed. Tess watched as the first boy tried the door.

Nothing.

The second one did the same thing, then tried to wrestle the big, sturdy front door open using two hands.

Still nothing.

They exchanged looks.

The first one wrapped his arms around himself and shivered.

The second one stepped closer, and hugged his brother.

The hug did it.

Whatever was going on at number one-ninety-nine, she needed to make sure those two boys were safe and sound. And warm. A cold front had chased the afternoon sun into oblivion and thick clouds darkened the horizon. She glanced both ways at the curb out of habit, not need. Outside her Manayunk townhouse, street traffic was a given. Not so much in Ashton. She crossed the neighborhood street and approached the boys matter-of-factly. "Hey, guys."

They turned and stared at her. One was wary. The other was curious.

"My name's Tess." She paused on the concrete walk and smiled. "My mom used to live across the street."

The nearer boy scowled. His look-alike followed suit, but with reluctance. Then he sat down hard, looking close to tears, and her heart melted a little more.

"Having trouble getting into the house?" she asked and indicated the broad hickory door with a glance. "Is Dad inside?"

"Dad's at—"

"Be quiet, Ben!" The scowler took charge as if he had to ward off strangers on a regular basis. "Dad will be right out."

"Ah." Tess shrugged as if she expected that answer. "Perfect. I'll wait."

The boy's eyes went wide. Clearly he wasn't prepared to deal with that response. "You can't."

"Really?" She locked eyes with him, then took a seat on the front step, next to his brother. "Who says?"

The boys exchanged glances. Ben looked from his brother to her, then back. "I'm gonna tell her, Jonah."

"Are not!"

"Am too!"

"Are not! Squealer!"

"Stop it." Tess raised a hand to defuse the escalating back-and-forth, a tirade that took her way back in time. Two little girls, born the same day, different as night and day, always bickering. "Is Dad at work?"

Ben thrust his chin into his hands. "I'm not supposed to tell."

"You didn't tell. I guessed. That's different."

"Oh. Okay." He brightened, faced her and ignored his brother's threatening look. "Yes, and he was supposed to be home at four-thirty and Brenda said she had to leave at four-thirty and he promised, and he never keeps his promises so she dropped us off and left."

"Brenda is—?"

"Our nanny."

"Your nanny left you here alone?" She didn't try to hide her astonishment because who in their right mind would do such a thing? "How old are you guys?"

"Five."

"Five," she repeated, unbelieving. "Who would leave a pair of five-year-olds anywhere on their own?"

"She said it was Dad's fault for never being on time, and then she just took off," Ben continued. "Jonah said she shouldn't go, but she didn't listen."

Oh, man.

Tess eyed the two boys, then stood. "Come across the street with me. It's going to be dark soon. I'll see if I can hunt up a number for Dad and let him know where you are."

"You know our dad?"

She did, yes. Would he remember the cruelty of fifteen years ago? The mean tricks and slights of his band of buddies, the football players and the cheerleaders? Would he even remember she existed?

It would be okay if he didn't. It might be better all around if he didn't. She took a boy's hand in each of hers and led them across the street. As soon as Aunt Dora spotted them, she threw her aged hands in the air as if the last thing on earth she needed was a couple of kids hanging around. "Why are they coming here?" she demanded. Her cranky old woman voice made Ben shrink back.

Not Jonah. He furrowed his brow and stared at her. "I'm supposed to be nice to old people."

Dora peered down her nose at him. "Says who?"

"My daddy."

"He's right."

"Maybe he is, and maybe he isn't, but I think old people are supposed to be nice, too. My Mima is nice all the time."

"Oy." Aunt Dora blew out a breath as if nice Mimas weren't all that smart.

"And she said you used to be a real nice girl, a long time ago. When you were pretty."

Tess gasped.

Ben looked about to cry, and Dora's considering expression said she might be contemplating murder, but then the boy moved closer, reached up and clasped her hand. "But I think you're real pretty, so maybe my Mima is wrong sometimes."

A reprieve.

Jonah's respectful compliment put a smile on Aunt Dora's face, and that hadn't happened since Tess rolled into town. "Thank you. Which one are you?"

"Jonah."

Her eyes went soft. Coupled with the smile, Tess wondered if her aunt was on a new prescription medication, because this was undocumented behavior for Theodora Anastas. "Well, Jonah, why don't you and I go inside this mausoleum and see what's what. There's some very special cookies in here, from my friend Leah's restaurant—"

"Half-moon cookies?" Tess had been thinking of Leah's half-moons since she arrived earlier that afternoon. "You brought half-moons and didn't tell me?" Tess scolded her aunt, laughing. "The nemesis of my childhood."

"And now you, so thin, almost bones," Dora fussed, frowning. "It is all right for a woman to look like a woman, Teresa. That's all I'm sayin'."

"Yah, yah, yah." Tess waved her off as she held the front door wide for the boys. Talking about weight, food addictions and eating disorders was off-limits, and a big part of the reason she'd stayed away from Ashton. In Manayunk, no one knew the obese girl she'd been. No one in her medical practice knew she'd been in therapy for four long years, fighting an eating disorder through college. She'd been a hot mess of crazy for too many years and now, she looked— and felt— great.

But there was always a ghost of past indiscretions dogging her trail, as if waiting for a misstep.

"Wow!" Jonah stopped inside the door and stared at the wall full of clowns in front of him. Big clowns and small clowns lined the floor to ceiling shelves. "Those are awesome! Ben, did you see these?"

Ben didn't look as impressed with the clown collection and Tess couldn't blame him. She found them fairly nightmarish herself, and she'd grown up around them. "My mother collected clowns. And a whole lot of other useless stuff."

"Scar-eee-y!" Jonah told her, and he made a face of mock fear.

"We went to a circus once with our dad and they had elephants and dancing dogs and clowns and I wet my pants," Ben confided.

"Bathroom's right over here if you need it." Dora pointed to her right. "I'm not a bit fond of all this myself, boys, so I hear you, loud and clear. Here are the cookies."

Half-moons, dark chocolate cookies slathered with rich chocolate frosting on one side, and creamy vanilla buttercream on the other. Dora's friend, Leah Stavros, baked for her family restaurant and bakery, and Leah's half-moons were a village staple. Everyone ordered half-moons for holidays, birthdays, picnics, showers, and for good reason. They were the perfect blend of everything sublime.

Dora cut one in half, and handed each boy a still-huge chunk. "There you go. We don't have milk, Tess just got into town, but I've got cold water in the fridge."

"No, thank you."

"Yes, please."

"Well, you do have nice manners," Dora decided as she retrieved the water, poured some in an expensive china teacup and handed it to Jonah.

"Ben wanted water, not me. But thank you."

Charming, when they wanted to be, and Tess was about to compliment them when Dora beat her to it in a slightly different manner. "So. You *do* know how to behave. Let's see if you can manage to follow directions the next time your father drags you into church, all right? No reason on God's green earth to disrespect your father or the house of God." She peered at them individually, then as a unit. Ben stared, wide-eyed. Jonah gulped.

"Yes, ma'am."

"Okay."

They exchanged quick looks, as if wondering how far she'd go, but then they tried a bite of cookie and all was forgiven. In an instant they became two hungry boys, gobbling one of the best confections known to man, shedding crumbs across her mother's prized Aubusson. If her mother saw the atrocity of two hungry waifs eating in her far-too-ornate living room, she'd throw a fit, but her mother wasn't here…

And the boys' obvious joy gave Tess a moment she'd never seen before. Unbridled happiness in her mother's house, and for a few, fleeting moments it almost felt like a home.

CHAPTER TWO

JAKE TOOK THE CORNER ONTO Maple Road too quickly, but the thought of his two precious boys being left alone drove him to panic, if not murder.

'Had to go, dropped boys at house at 4:30 as promised. Won't be back. Ever.'

The text had come through at four-thirty on the dot, but he hadn't looked at his phone for nearly forty minutes. Which meant his sons had been sitting in the yard for over an hour.

He careened into the driveway, shut off the car, jumped out and bellowed their names.

Nothing.

He hollered again, running from one side of the yard to the other, then wondered if she'd had the presence of mind to at least unlock the door for them.

He tried the handle. *Locked.* But that didn't mean the boys weren't inside. He turned his key, opened it and yelled. "Ben? Jonah? Where are you?"

Silence greeted him.

Panic set in, a feeling worse than anything he'd experienced since burying the boys' mother. She shouldn't have died, not in this day and age. No one dies at age twenty-seven.

Joy did, and with her all his plans and dreams of growing old together. Raising the boys.

The boys. Where were they? How far could they have gone? Or had the local sheriff's department found them and put them in protective custody because their father was too stupid to take care of them properly?

He raced back outside.

"Dad!"

"Daddy!"

His heart rate surged with a power-thrust of adrenalin. "Ben! Jonah!" He squatted low and opened his arms. When they barreled into his embrace, Jake was pretty sure the whole world tipped more upright, even as he fell back. "Hey, hey. I'm sorry, fellas, I'm sorry. Are you okay, are you all right?"

"We're fine!" Ben told him. "We went across the street and we met the lady Mima doesn't like but we like her just fine because she gave us half-moon cookies and we don't even need dinner now!"

Quiet Ben, talking up a storm for the first time in a long time. "Really? Well, that's an adventure."

"And they've got all kinds of things in that house, Dad, like some really strange things, and clowns and jack-in-the-boxes, all old and kind of just weird-looking."

"You're home." The soft, melodic voice drew his attention beyond the busy boys.

Ethereal and gorgeous.

He stared up, into the mist of patchy fog, a common enough late fall occurrence, but the woman approaching him wasn't one bit common, and he was suddenly tongue-tied. "I'm home."

Duh.

He tried to stand, but it took effort with two scrambling, grappling boys hanging off his arms. "I got out of work late and had no idea the sitter dropped the boys off to an empty house until a few minutes ago. And then I drove here as quick as I could."

"Tess let us play with toy soldiers."

"And I built a plane out of plastic bricks."

"And then he shot my soldiers."

Jonah shrugged as if the answer was obvious. "They're the enemy, stupid. Of course I'm going to shoot them."

"I'm not stupid, lizard-breath!"

"Are too!"

"Am not! Who got picked to be line leader today?"

Jonah paused, stricken. "I might be line leader tomorrow."

"Probally not, because you don't stop bossin' people around," Ben told him outright. "Line leaders set a good 'zample all the time and you're too noisy."

"Knock it off."

The boys turned. They sent guilty looks to the woman, and got quiet, real quick, which was a great trick, one Jake hadn't been able to accomplish very often.

She stooped to meet them on their level, something Jake forgot to do, even though the child therapist explained it was a smart move. Oops. "You're being mean."

They stared at her, then each other, then her again.

"Is that how you want to live your lives? Being meany-pants?"

Ben shook his head quickly. "I want to be nice."

Jonah scowled at him. "Me, too!"

"Well, to be nice you have to stop." She held up her hand, then pointed to her eyes. "Look." The boys nodded in unison, as if she was really, really smart. "And listen." She cupped her ear with her hand. "If we all stopped, looked and listened to each other, there would be a lot less fighting and a lot more fun. And there's no reason to be brats." She leveled them a look they both accepted, as if she was something or someone special, and Jake needed to learn that trick because if he could get these two to simmer down now and again...

That would be a marvelous thing.

She turned to go.

Jake reached out and touched her arm. "Excuse me, before you go, I don't know how to thank you. I was beside myself with worry."

"Are you gonna have Brenda 'rested, Dad?" Ben's eyes rounded. "And put her in jail? Her auntie," he pointed at the ridiculously beautiful life-saver, "said we should throw books at Brenda, but I don't think that's very nice. Do you?"

A part of him wanted to blow in the twenty-two-year-old college student, but the other side of him—

The side that recognized his part in this fiasco—

Knew he should leave it alone. He'd made Brenda late for way too many of her college classes, and that wasn't fair. "Not something I'm going to discuss, and she did text me right away."

"She left them alone."

He lifted his attention back to the woman, just as she tossed her mane of dark hair back, over her right shoulder.

"They're five," she continued. "Anything could have happened."

"Yeah, like you could be a kidnabber, Tess!" Jonah's nod added oomph to his declaration. "And you could have stolen us away and put us in a dungeon—"

"Wif no food."

"And left us there."

"Well, I'm a doctor, not a kidnabber," she told them, and bent to their level again. "I didn't even see any kidnabbers in the general vicinity, so I think we're okay, boys. I gotta go help Auntie."

"Thank you, Tess!"

"Yes!" Ben grabbed her legs in a hug. "F-F-Fank you for wes-cuing us!"

"Tess?"

Tess heard the note of surprise in Jake's voice. The question. She swallowed past a small, hard ball of old angst and met his questioning gaze. "Tess Cosgrove. I've come back to settle my mother's estate."

"I heard she passed," he said, but he stared at her with grave intent. "I hadn't seen her outside in ages, and didn't even realize she was living there last winter. I'm sorry I didn't know. I could have checked on her more often."

The compassion in his words came as a surprise. The Jake she remembered, the self-centered, always-in-the-limelight athletic hero wouldn't have gone out of his way for much of anything. Or anyone. "She wouldn't have answered the door. She ended her life the way she chose to, on her terms. In her house, alone."

"That's so sad."

He looked like he meant it, darn it. He looked actually bothered by her mother's choices. "Everyone's different."

"I suppose."

He supposed it, but doubt deepened his tone. "Anyway, thank you. Thank you so much. I don't know how to repay you for keeping these two monsters safe for me. I owe you."

He did, big time, but because he didn't seem to remember any of that, she had to let it go, too. "Not at all. Boys." She smiled down at the rambunctious pair. "Be good."

"We will!"

"Thanks, Tess!"

"See ya'!"

She turned to go but Jake took hold of her arm in a firm but gentle grip. "Have you had supper?"

The boys cheered. Jake shushed them with a finger to his lips, then asked again, "You must be hungry. Let me take you out for supper. Me and the boys. They do a mean spanakopita at the diner and I think Aunt Bella made baklava today."

"Another time, perhaps." She gave him her smoothest tone and most polished line. "Your simple thank you was more than enough, of course." She turned and strode away, wondering how anyone could be that obtuse. Did he really forget how mean the group was to her back then? Or was he like so many other good looking guys, thinking if he batted his lashes and offered that to-die-for crooked smile, she'd fall at his feet?

Fifteen years ago, she would have.

No more.

Now she was immune. She'd faced the enemy within, the self-destructive wounded ego that self-comforted with food, food, and more food. And she'd conquered that internal demon with faith, hope, therapy and learning to love herself, just as God made her. But God hadn't made her with an extra sixty-five pounds, so she'd taken that in hand along with the therapy.

"Auntie." Dora was preparing to leave as Tess came back up the walk. "Thank you so much for helping me assess everything today. I'm going to call an estate liquidation firm tomorrow and see what they have to say."

"And just sell it all?"

Tess saw no other choice. "I can't be here for months clearing this out. And if Mom had allowed us to help consolidate things the last few years, we could have been ahead of the game, but that wasn't possible."

"Your mother had her problems."

She sure did. "Well, no one's perfect."

"You're a good girl, Tess." Dora peered into her face as if wishing she could say more. "My sister was not an easy person in many ways, and she was not kindly to her children."

Another understatement. "That's in the past now, Auntie. We can't change what was, so we look forward to what will be."

"You've got a good heart, *kopela mou*. This comes from your father's side, he was such a good, kind man, gone too soon. Perhaps your sister is more like her mother than we suspected."

"Or perhaps Dee Dee is more hurt," Tessa suggested softly. "A child expects a mother's love as the norm. Not having a mother's love to count on leaves scars, Auntie. Deep ones."

"I won't judge, you are correct in what you say. I only know I pray for you, for you both. For Dee Dee to realize the wonderful person she has in her sister, and for you to be at peace as you handle," she sighed out loud and raked the house a fierce, long look, "this monstrosity."

"I'll call you and tell you when the liquidators can come by. I'll get a couple of estimates so they won't low-ball us."

"Until then." Auntie reached up and gently took Tessa's cheeks in her hands. "May God's blessings rain on you, my child."

"And you, as well."

Auntie climbed into her car and pulled away as Tess studied the neighborhood. The trees had thickened over the years, and the flowers of her youth were gone with the chill winds of November. Sparks of color remained in the occasional mum or late-season rose. Fallen leaves dotted well-kept yards. The last few hung in shadowed color now, past prime, waiting to meet their fate with the next strong wind or blast of cold.

Soon it would all disappear under a blanket of cold, white snow. Winter would sweep in, and with it, the higher elevation would deal with mounting snow piles, slush, and ice.

She'd never played outside as a child. It wasn't allowed. She'd never built a snowman or gone sledding. She'd been caught in the house, gazing out, wishing things were different.

Now they were.

Forget the wounds of the past, lay them to rest and embrace God's grace for the future. Your future. Your choice.

Four years of therapy taught her to believe in her own power, and God's love. Now she'd turn that grown-up courage into the same prayers for her twin sister. She turned and went inside, refusing to look left or right at the hideous living room. She'd gotten almost to the less invasive kitchen when the doorbell rang, about the same time the sound of quick, drumming rain sounded along the back porch roof.

She went back to the front door and eased it open. Jake Karralis stood there, under an umbrella, the boys by his side and a small pizza box in his hand. He thrust it her way and lifted his shoulders. "You've got to eat, I had to feed the monster-munchkins, and it just made sense to order a personal pizza for you. Hope you like pepperoni and sausage!" He handed her the box, then raced the boys through the raindrops. They paused at the road, looked both ways, and dashed across. In short seconds his door was open, then closed, and she was alone again.

With pizza.

CHAPTER THREE

HE'D DROPPED OFF A WHOLE pizza. Not big, by any means, but way more than any five-foot-four-inch woman should eat.

She stepped back inside, out of the rain. The yeasty, zesty fragrance teased her senses. She moved to the kitchen, determined. She could do this. She could open the box, eat one piece, two if they were cut small, then close the box.

She'd been able to do that for years now. No memories or regrets haunted her through medical school, residency and now, her private practice. But here...

Oh, here...

Anxiety started somewhere around the polished hardwood and crept upwards. She stared at the box, feeling out of control. She tried to separate the emotions from the memories.

The smell called her, tantalizing. Tempting. A normal person could just smile, open the stupid box, and have some pizza. And she'd been doing just that for years, successful, at last.

Examine your emotions. Look for triggers. You're not crazy, you're sensitized. Figure out what's causing the reaction, then bottle it.

She didn't have to examine this too closely. Being in her mother's house was bringing up too much, too soon, and Jake's kind gesture added to the melee. She eyed the pizza box and realized she needed to change her surroundings. She grabbed her fleece-lined hoodie and the pizza box. She walked outside, crossed the road, and knocked on Jake's door.

He might think she was crazy.

She didn't care.

He might think she was flirting with him.

Nothing could be further from the truth, but with limited choices, she needed to create a controllable situation. Eating with others gave her better options, and right now the only others she knew were Jake and his two heart-grabbing little boys.

The door opened. "Tess?" Jake looked from her to the house across the street, then noticed the pizza box in her hand. "Is something wrong with it? Come in, it's getting crazy cold out there."

She shook her head and slipped the hood down. "I realized that eating alone was about the last thing I wanted to do. May I eat with you guys?"

"Yes!" Jonah fist-pumped the air from his chair in the kitchen.

"I'm glad!" Ben grinned at her from the seat opposite Jonah. A smear of red sauce made him look even cuter than before, and Tess hadn't thought that possible. "I love havin' company, Tessa!"

"Works for me." Jake led the way into the kitchen and reached for her jacket. "I'll hang this by the fireplace."

"I won't be here long enough for it to dry, but warmed would be good."

"Warm it is, then." He hung the jacket over the metal gate in front of the fireplace. "Let's eat."

She didn't worry that he might think her weird. She was weird. But she wasn't crazy or over-indulgent anymore. She was delightfully normal in many ways and odd in a few, but wasn't everyone?

She opened her box and almost sighed with delight. Pizza, one of those rare treats she allowed herself because the smell, taste and satisfaction of it worried her a little. Okay, more than a little, even though she hadn't had a weight problem in a long time. She blessed herself for grace and was surprised when Jake set his piece down. "Guys, we forgot to pray. I'm sorry."

Jake Karralis prayed with his kids?

The Jake she knew skipped religion classes to go make out with Mandy Chatterton under the Creek Street bridge. Or was it Christina Smith-White? Both, she remembered. Consecutive years. Mandy as sophomores, Christina as juniors. Whatever.

He reached out for Ben's hand, then hers.

Well now she'd started something unexpected. She gripped Jonah's fingers, then laid hers in Jake's outstretched hand. Skin to skin. Warmth to warmth. A buzz of something that felt like live electricity hummed through her system.

Maybe she was crazy, after all.

His hand closed around hers and for the love of all that was good and holy, she would be okay if he never, ever let go.

He said a simple blessing, sweet and reverent, not overdone... and not underdone, either.

She was surprised, and when he let go of her hand and nodded to the pizza, she grabbed her first piece. "This smells wonderful."

"I'm on my second piece, and it tastes as good as it smells," he told her.

He was right, and when she allowed herself a second piece, she knew that would be enough. She finished it, happily, chatting with the boys about kindergarten.

They seemed content and joyous, the way childhood should be. She noticed a picture collage on the dining area wall. Jake and the boys, playing. Jake and the boys, riding scooters. Jake and the boys, having a catch.

Two pictures were centered below the others, low enough so the boys could see them easily. Ben and Jonah as infants, with their mother. Ben and Jonah being baptized, their mother holding one while Jake held the other. And then there was one last picture of the boys with their mother, and big #1 birthday cake sat before each boy.

And then nothing.

"We lost her two months after the boys turned one."

"I'm dreadfully sorry." She winced, imagining the pain, wishing she couldn't see it so clearly. "That had to be awfully hard."

"It still is in lots of ways. Most times?" He shrugged. "We're doing okay. But then I do something dangerously stupid like today and I realize how easily I could mess this up. Mess them up. Or lose them."

"What are you going to do for daycare tomorrow?"

He shook his head. "Don't know. I can get them on the bus, but there's no one here to get them off the bus. I can probably make temporary arrangements with wrap around care for the last couple of days, but they'll want a commitment to make it long-term, and I'd prefer having a nanny here so the boys can come home to their own place. Their own space."

He cared. It showed in his words, his gaze, the quiet undertones of his voice. He'd do what he had to do, not because it was foisted on him by fate, but because his choices truly mattered. "I can be here in the afternoon."

He looked at her then, more carefully, as if realization struck. "We know each other, don't we?"

Dread poked a hole in her spirit. "You were a year ahead of me in school, yes."

"I remember the voice. But we weren't in any classes together, were we?"

"I was accelerated, so yes, we were. We had several classes together."

"Smart."

Now it was her turn to shrug. Was she smart or had she spent every waking moment trying her best so she could be good at something? Probably that.

"Well, clearly I'm getting old because I'm not putting a face with the name."

"Fat Terri."

His face paled. He held her gaze, then swept her body a look, and heaven help her if he made a crude or stupid joke, she'd punch him right here, right now, just to help even the score. He drew his brows together and reached for her hands in one of the nicest, kindest moves she'd ever witnessed. "Please forgive me."

The request was so sweetly sincere that she stared. What could she say? *No. You and your moron friends made my life a living torture chamber for my entire junior year.*

Leave the past in the past. Approach the future with joyous jubilation.

She opened her mouth to speak, but he shook his head. "Think about it, please. I never realized you lived across the street from Aunt Judith and Uncle Sam. But now." He raised his gaze to the front windows and sighed. "Now it makes sense. Aunt J. used to say there were two girls who lived across the street, and other than catching the school bus or being dropped off, she never once laid eyes on you."

Tess went into informational overload. Too much, too soon. Being back in Ashton, back in her mother's house, seeing Jake—

Too much.

She wasn't sure she said goodbye. If she did, she didn't remember it, but she remembered the cold, hard rain pelting her head, her cheeks, her skin. She'd left her hoodie behind, draped along his fireplace screen, but the cold beat of the pouring rain brought her back into the present. A present *she* owned, *she* directed, *she* chose.

She got inside the house, breathed deep, and didn't look left or right. She went straight upstairs, shucked off her wet things, grabbed a nightshirt from her bag and went to bed. Things would look better in the morning. In the morning, the stark look of realization in Jake's eyes wouldn't sting so fierce.

Fat Terri.

Her eyes stung. Her fingers tingled. A part of her was tempted to race to the bathroom and get rid of that pizza. She knew how. Anyone with an eating disorder or food addiction knew how.

Is that where you turn in times of trouble now? Or to God? Where does your help come from? Your help comes from the Lord, the maker of heaven and earth.

God, yes.

Not dangerous old habits, brought back by proximity.

God, first.

She took a deep breath through her nose, curled up in a bed that smelled of musty lavender, and couldn't wait for sleep to claim her. But just before it did, the image of Jake's face came back to her, a mix of disbelief and shock, when she reminded him of the wretched name they'd used.

She hated stepping back. She hated doing it without Dee Dee here. She'd always pictured them facing this together. But her sister refused to answer her calls, e-mails and letters. Dee couldn't hide. The Internet made that virtually impossible, but Dee had no compunction to deal with anything once she left for college, and knowing what their life had been like... Tess couldn't blame her in the least.

CHAPTER FOUR

FAT TERRI.

Shame put a merciless claim on Jake as he tucked the boys in, heard their prayers, and kissed them goodnight. Behind the goodness of normal was the shadow of how a group of stupid, stuck-on-themselves seventeen-year-olds mocked anyone who didn't fit their narrow-minded list of cool. Tess Cosgrove had been a prime target.

He'd been a jerk. He owned that, and he'd asked God for forgiveness when he finally grew up, but facing Terri tonight— Tess, now— shoved old reality into his new life. How could he have been that cruel? What were they thinking?

He called Aunt J. once the kids were asleep. "Hey, it's Jake. I was hoping you could fill me in on the family that lived across the street from here. The Cosgroves. What was going on there?"

Judith snorted. "Who knows? The old lady was a real piece of work, and she kept those two girls more secluded than any convent could. I never saw them out, never saw them go anywhere together. For all the years I lived there, those girls were kept under lock and key until they left for college. It's a wonder they're able to function in the real world."

"Well, Tess is a doctor, so she's functioning at a fairly high level," Jake replied. "No reasons why they were kept home? Or anything about the mother?"

"She collected things. I only know that because her sister filled me in. They weren't close, except when the Cosgrove woman needed something. She collected everything, like an obsession. UPS would pull into her driveway daily, sometimes other delivery services, too. She got boxes and boxes. At first I thought she was shopping for those girls, but they'd wear the same clothes onto that school bus, day after day. They were clean, but while their mother clearly had money to spend, she didn't spend it on those girls."

J. painted a bleak picture. Ben and Jonah had told him about the scary clowns and lifelike birds. The thought of being surrounded by all that stuff as a kid… and never having a reprieve… smacked of cruelty.

And then he'd been just as bad at school.

He hung up the phone, disgusted with himself. He could pin it on his friends back then, but that was the coward's way out. He'd learned a lot the past decade-and-a-half. About being a man, a husband, a son, a father. Somehow he had to turn this old wrong around, if only for his own peace of mind.

He walked to the front window, tipped the curtain, and looked across the street. No cheerful lights shone in the yard. No tiny candles, typical for these century-old colonials, brightened the windowpanes. The Cosgrove house was cloaked in darkness, inside and out. Sad. So sad.

Come unto me all who are weary…

He wanted Tess's forgiveness. He didn't deserve it, but he wanted it. If she was here to close up that museum of a house, maybe he could help. His help was probably the last thing a beautiful woman like Tess wanted, but if he could find a way to make amends, he'd do it, because that's what real men did. They fixed their mistakes, regardless of cost.

He stopped by her house once the boys were on the bus the next morning. He knocked on the front door.

No answer.

He rang the bell.

Still nothing.

He was about to scribble a note when she came jogging up the driveway looking way too hot for a cold, windswept November morning. "Anyone who runs down the road looking that good should be labeled a traffic hazard."

His words surprised her. She looked happy, then worried. She dropped her gaze, breathed deep, bent over, stretched, and took another deep breath. "I'm sorry I ran off last night."

"Don't be. Please."

She didn't look at him, she looked at the house, and her troubled expression said more than words ever could. "Coming back here stirs up old emotions."

"I wish they were good ones."

A tiny smile flickered, then faded. "Me, too." She breathed deep again, then tapped her running watch. "The boys' bus is at three-forty, right?"

He nodded.

"I'll be here, but why don't I watch them at your house? My mother's house isn't the kind of place where children feel welcome."

She didn't call it 'home', he noticed. "I'm sorry that's the case, because it's a great old house. The Dutch Colonial styling makes it seem inviting. Family-oriented."

"It should be that way, and I want the next owners to see it just like you do. A beautiful place to raise a family." She breathed deep again, then moved up the walk. "I've got to get cleaned up. The estate sale companies are coming back-to-back this morning. I wanted to do some comparison shopping to get the best deal. And the quickest liquidation. I won't be sorry to see all the stuff inside just plain gone."

"Do you need help?"

The quick shake of her head said that even if needed, help wouldn't be accepted. "I'll manage fine, thank you. I'm smart enough to turn this over to experts. My expertise is in family practice, and I'll thank you for not noting the irony in that."

"You sure you don't mind grabbing the boys?"

She turned her back on the house in a deliberate move. "By then I will be welcoming the reprieve, and I'll enjoy being surrounded by normalcy once more."

"They're somewhat manic when they get home." Jake grinned and waved as he moved to his car. "Let's see how normal you feel after two hours of that. I'll grab supper on the way back." She made a face and he added, "I'll include a low-carb selection, okay?"

"Yes." She opened the front door with a look of reluctance. "Thank you."

"You're welcome, Tess."

Her heart stutter-stepped when he smiled her way, and not just one of those lame, little dance steps. This was one of those big, bold salsa moves she'd seen on dance competitions. She met with three liquidation firms. The third one got the nod when the company owner offered to box everything, sell it off-site, and give her a check for eighty-five percent value. "I'll have everything out of here, except necessary furniture, by noon on Friday."

Tess couldn't sign that contract quickly enough. No sooner had he left, than the doorbell rang. Tess answered it, hoping the fourth estate liquidation company had gotten her cancellation message.

A young person stood on the narrow, covered stoop, but for a young person, she seemed absolutely old-ish. "I've brought it back, Mum, and in good condition, too."

Tess frowned. "I'm not Mum and I have no idea what you're talking about."

"For the Nativity, of course, the one so beloved."

A beloved Nativity? Tess had never seen a Nativity or a Bible or any vestige of religion or faith in her mother's house. "I'm sorry, perhaps you have the wrong house."

"It be two-oh-two, right?"

The quaint British accent was adorable. "It is, yes."

"Then this be yours." She handed over a tiny sack, and in the bag was a wrapped-up angel done in a lovely, old-world style luminous paint. "He'll no doubt be happy to be back among his friends."

"It's a him?" She lifted the angel, skeptical. "I thought angels were androgynous."

"Oh, it's a him, all right, he's an archangel and he'd naught let you forget it. If he was here, of course. But he ain't."

"Of course." She played along. The young person— boy? Girl? She wasn't sure and nothing the child wore offered a hint. Anyway, he or she seemed sweet and sincere, and quite determined that the statue should live here. Which meant the luminescent angel would be packed and sent off with everything else over the next three days.

She tucked the statue aside, called a local house painting firm, and then a carpet installer. The Realtor had told her to empty everything not needed for staging a warm presence, paint and re-carpet.

Within a few weeks this would all be done. She'd spend Thanksgiving here in Ashton, finish this job and put her mother's house on the market. Now that she had a plan and an end game, she'd be okay.

"I can't thank you enough for doing this," Jake said as he walked through the garage door that night. He set down a bag filled with take-out food, noogied Jonah's head, bumped knuckles with Ben and smiled over their heads at Tess. "Were they good?"

"Tolerable." She handed Ben four plates and gave forks and knives to Jonah. "No juggling the knives. Got it?"

He grinned up at her. "Yes."

"Good."

"Have they been juggling knives again?" Jake reached into the bags and pulled out to-go containers. "Because I've told them not to."

"Hmm." She smiled at him when he handed her a lovely, fresh chicken Caesar salad. "You just made my day. Thank you. And I only let them juggle the sharp ones. I find they learn faster if we up the danger ante."

He laughed. "That's more true than you know. How'd your estate thing go today? Any luck?"

"Go wash your hands," she told the boys before she answered, and when they started to balk, she pointed to the downstairs washroom. "Now. Doctor's orders."

"I can't get over that you're a doctor."

"And slim."

"Look, Tess, I—" He was all set to apologize for being a jerk in high school and not realizing who she was yesterday, and for anything else he may have done wrong when she raised her hand, palm out, to stop him.

"No, my bad." She frowned as she tipped her salad out onto a plate. "Being back here has made me too sensitive. I do look different, I know that and logic dictates it will surprise others. That doesn't make it easy, but I should know better than to over-react. And the appointments went well today. I contracted a company who promised to have the sale off-site, and everything will be packed and gone by Friday."

"That quick?"

"So they said. Then I can have the painters come in, order the new carpet, and list it."

"Can you stay here that long?"

"My partners are covering for me over the holidays. We knew this was coming and we hired a temp doctor to come in. My sister has no interest in getting this done."

"I don't remember your sister. Was she older? Younger?"

She winced. "Twin, actually. You wouldn't remember Dee. She went to private school."

"While you went to Ashton High?"

She gave him a dubious look. "No one said we were normal, Jake."

Who did that? Send one kid to a private school and the other one to public school, especially a really smart girl like Tess. He was saved a comment when the boys came rushing back like a pair of starving pups. "Have a seat, gentlemen."

"I wanna sit near Tess."

"Me, too!"

That meant he couldn't, and when the boys claimed their territorial rights, Jake realized he might want to sit next to his new neighbor, too. He sat opposite her and smiled. "Then I get to look into her pretty blue eyes."

"I had blue eyes when I was a baby. Like my mom's." Jonah pointed to the picture on the wall, the one of them with their mother.

"Me, too," piped up Ben, the used-to-be quiet twin. Until he met Tess Cosgrove. "Then they turned camo."

"Camo eyes?" Tess leaned closer. Ben lifted his brows as high as he could so she could inspect his pupils.

Gentle excitement warmed her features.

Was there such a thing? There was, right there, across from him, in Tess's sweet gaze. She tipped her head and nodded. "Gold, brown, a hint of green. I like that, Ben. I bet your baby eyes were beautiful."

"You knew who I was and I didn't even tell you," he exclaimed. Happiness lit up his face. "I have to tell most people again and again!"

"How did you know?" Jonah asked, and he sounded a little suspicious. "Did Dad tell you?"

"Ben's cowlick goes clockwise." She put her hand on the crown of Ben's head. "Yours goes counter-clockwise. The opposite way," she explained when his forehead wrinkled. "So if I can see the tops of your heads, it's easy enough to tell you apart."

"Wow."

She winked at him. "I am pretty smart."

"You sure are! I kind of knew that yesterday when you came over, so I'm pretty smart, too."

"You're very smart, Jonah. And precious." She said the words softly, like gentle rain on a warm afternoon.

"He's too smart sometimes, especially when it would be better to do what you mentioned yesterday, Tess." Jake looked at Jonah straight on. "Stop, look and listen."

"You paid attention."

"I did." He kind of hoped for a gold star, or some form of recognition. Even a pat on the head would do. "How's your salad?"

"Marvelous. You never got this at a Chinese restaurant."

"I stopped by the diner for the salad. And baklava, but don't feel pressured."

She laughed, and it felt good to see her laugh like that. She had a vibrant laugh, the kind that drew a person in. Not boisterous, but bright and sincere.

"I will have a piece when I'm done. I promised myself some baklava while I'm here because no one makes it like Rosa and Betty at the diner."

"True words. Once everything is out of the house, you'll need to move furniture for the flooring makeover, won't you?"

She made a face. "Yes. Although I think I can hire them to help me."

"Don't waste money. I'll help you. And if we need extra muscle, my cousins Dimi and Rafe can jump in."

"If all three of the amazing Karralis boys are in my house, I could probably sell tickets to the local ladies."

"Except two of the three are married," he told her. "Dimi just got married and Rafe got snagged by Tasha Sorkos last winter."

"Born Greek, marry Greek?"

He laughed out loud. "Dimi's wife is Latina, but Tasha, yes.

They're expecting a baby in the spring and if Rafe comes by he will tell you all about what a miracle it is, so prepare yourself."

"Wait." She set her fork down and held his gaze. "Wasn't Rafe's daughter one of the first patients to be cured of leukemia with immune-therapy technology?"

"You know about that?"

Her eyes grew wide as she ticked off the magazines that covered the little girl's treatment, then added, "Half the world knows about it. That program is huge news. Breakthrough treatment. What an amazing story."

"Well, there you go, Rafe and Tash will be happy to tell you all about it. It was miraculous, I just didn't realize it was that well known."

The boys scrambled to get down just then. Her comfortable expression indicated their busy antics and noisy chatter didn't bother her. That pleased Jake, and he didn't have to wonder why.

"You've been pretty busy, Jake."

He had been busy. Work had been a bear, but was that the over-extended boss's fault or his for not drawing a firm line in the sand? "I have, but that's no excuse for messing up priorities."

"What do you do?"

The boys disappeared into the huge side room, not fighting for the moment, but that could change quickly. "Architect."

"Really?" Genuine surprise lifted her brows.

"I took Computer Aided Drawing my senior year because we were required to take a minimum of classes. I loved it. I got into Cornell's undergrad, then did grad studies at MIT. That's where I met Joy."

"She was in school at MIT, too?"

He shook his head. "Bartender, working her way through a community college degree while taking care of her little brother. Rough life, all around, but she was the kind of woman who rose to the occasion. And she kept me at arm's length for quite a while, which only made her more interesting."

"Gotta love the chase." Her attention drifted back to the pictures. "I'm sorry you lost her so young. No one's ready for that."

"We were devastated. Me, her brother, the boys, although they don't remember it. But the longing." He cringed, remembering. "They'd wander the house, calling for her."

"Oh, Jake." She reached across and laid her hand over his. "That must have been so hard."

"My aunt and uncle were ready to head south. They'd retired, and I always loved this old neighborhood. So I bought this place from them when the boys were two. We needed to do something just to break that cycle of looking for Joy around every corner."

An analogy on life, Tess thought. Looking for joy around every corner. She'd been doing that for a long time, and she'd found true happiness in her work. She loved her job, she loved her practice, she was blessed in multiple ways. Had she found true joy?

Not as yet, but she was closer to peace and wellness than she'd been in a long time. "I must go. I want to get some work done tonight, tag things to go when the liquidators get here tomorrow. I've gone through a whole lot of sticky notes." She stood and took her plate to the sink. "Does it sound weird to say I'm almost giddy about seeing the house uncluttered? Without all the stacks of collectibles?"

"Not at all."

She laughed. "Comparatively, I guess that's the least odd thing about us."

"Families aren't perfect, Tess."

She knew that, but she also understood ratios. On a spectrum of family dysfunction, hers tipped toward a solid nine out of ten.

"Where's your sister now?"

"Married, living in Illinois. She's an adjunct professor at the University of Chicago."

"Two illustrious careers." Jake brought the silverware over to the sink and faced her. "There's a lot of positives to be said for producing two brilliant young women."

"There is," she admitted. "But this particular road less chosen has little to recommend it. Whereas your boys are living a marvelous existence filled with life. They're delightful kids, Jake. You're doing well with them."

"I've messed up. But I'm trying. Yesterday's near disaster made me realize that I have limited opportunity to make things better at work, but limitless ways to ensure the boys' futures. I'm going to start looking for another firm after the holidays."

"You're not happy there?"

"I was." Concern shadowed his face. "But I'm being asked to do things now that compromise my principles. Not illegal, but not always in the customer's best interests and that's not a comfortable spot to be in. Although you have good reason to doubt my sincerity in that department based on my stupid past."

"We grow up."

"Thank God for that." He put the few dishes into the dishwasher and closed it. "Come on, we'll walk you home."

"Across the street?" She seemed amused by the idea.

"It's dark and cold. The boys will think it's an adventure and that way I'm sure you get home safe."

Home safe.

The words curled around her like hands framing a hot cup of tea.

Her mother's house wasn't home. There wasn't a home in her vocabulary, not really. Oh, sure, she had her townhouse overlooking the river, but it wasn't home. Not like Jake's house, strewn with toys, a fridge covered with little boy artwork and meeting notices. "You missed the parent-teacher's meeting."

He stared at the date, then took down the notice, crumpled it and frowned. "Oops."

"Important?"

"Naw. I just thought I should get more involved in school, but then I realized that by spending more time with the boys, I was getting more involved, especially if it means fewer trips to the principal's office as they get bigger." He turned and hollered into the front room. "Boys? Grab your jackets, let's walk Tess home."

"Okay!"

"I gotta go to the bathroom!"

"Hurry up, and stop waiting so long."

Jonah rushed by them, and returned a few minutes later, grabbed his jacket off a hook and stopped right in front of Tess. "I will like walking you home! It's not too far, and just close enough."

Tess had moved toward the door. Jake unhooked his sweatshirt and tugged it over his head. He turned at Jonah's words, and there he was, close. So close. Close enough to see the tiny individual whiskers dusting his chin, the little mole on his lower right cheek, the flecks of honey gold surrounding the pupil in his dark brown eyes.

Electricity hummed between them, eyes locked, and then Jake smiled down at her, right into her eyes. "Not too far, just close enough." He whispered Jonah's words and Tess was pretty sure her heart melted. That was silly and reckless and she made it a point to never be silly or reckless.

Part of her wanted to be. She stepped back, sent him a scolding look on purpose, and reached for Jonah's hand. "I'm most grateful for the escort, my young friend."

"My escort, too?" Ben grabbed her other hand, and the feeling of these two little boys made the night more memorable.

"All three?" Jake supposed, but he didn't look her way. He shoved his hands into his pockets and trudged alongside, in the grass because the sidewalk wasn't wide enough for four.

"Three handsome escorts is more than any girl could possibly hope for," she assured them, and when they climbed the steps to her mother's door all too soon, she plied the key and swung it open.

"See, Dad? I told you it was filled with stuff!"

She stooped to their level. "Tomorrow some worker men are coming to move all that stuff, so when you see it tomorrow night, it will look very different."

"No more scary statues?" Ben shrunk a little further into his father's side as he whispered the words.

"None," she promised. "Thanks for being good boys today."

"I liked having you at our house." Ben gave her a shy smile, but stayed close to his father, and with the number of clowns facing the door, Tess didn't blame him.

"Me, too. Can you come again tomorrow?"

"Guys, we can't expect Tess to come watch you every day."

"Not every day," she supposed. "But honestly, I'm here the next few weeks, and I kind of like bossing these two around. I'd be willing to work a trade."

"Bartering is one of my favorite things in this world," Jake told her.

"I watch the boys. You come home on time. And bring supper."

His eyes crinkled. "I'm getting the way better end of that deal."

"I like seafood, chicken and salad. And grilled veggies."

"You never had baklava tonight."

"Tomorrow," she promised. "That will be my treat for getting this part of the house taken care of. Save me a piece, okay?"

"Consider it done." He glanced around what should have been an open, spacious living room. "I can't wait to see this done."

Her, either. She took a deep breath and stepped back. "Me, too."

CHAPTER FIVE

TWENTY-FOUR HOURS OF NOT SEEING Tess was too long, Jake decided on Saturday night.

She'd watched the boys from four until six the past few nights, then had supper with them. He'd gotten out his Lego collections, separated into bins, and she'd helped the boys build a castle any king would be glad to claim.

She laughed with them, scolded them, and looked properly shocked when they misbehaved... which made them want to behave better, a neat trick, all told.

But today the boys had been invited to a birthday party, and he and his cousins were taking down a couple of stressed trees in Jake's mother's yard. They'd made good progress, but his thoughts kept straying to number two-oh-two, even with chain saws buzzing all around him.

He called her once the boys were in bed, not even sure why, just because he wanted to. "Tess? Hey, how's it going?"

"I'm kind of freaked out, actually."

His protect-o-meter went on high alert. "Why? What's wrong? Do you need help?"

"It's just so weird, being in this house, and having all that stuff gone." She spoke softly, almost a whisper, as if worried to speak out loud. "Things echo. My voice echoes. I'm honestly thinking about going to a hotel because this is quite..." she sighed, and it hurt his heart to hear it. "Abnormal."

"You're not abnormal, the situation is."

"And yet, it looks normal and so much better as if to be unbelievable. So why am I a bundle of nerves?"

"Because emptying the house is a huge step forward, but to do it you had to take a big step backward. Coming here, facing the past, making decisions. It's tough, Tess, and harder still when you're doing it on your own. Any word from your sister?"

"No." Her voice, still soft, hinted longing. "It's complicated. She's complicated. I think in some ways being the favorite made things even harder for Dee. She saw the discrepancy, but couldn't do a thing about it. And it wasn't as if my mother fawned over her and not me, she barely provided new clothes as we grew, but she made it clear that Dee was expected to succeed and I was tolerated."

"Does it bother you to talk about this? Because if it does, we can stop." He hadn't called to stir things up. He'd called because... he tightened his jaw and grimaced... he missed her. One day apart and he missed her.

"No, not anymore, not really." That sounded more like Tess. More normal, and self-confident. "Being immersed in stuff bothers me, but just talking? No, I'm fine, and I don't want to be Debbie Downer because this is really a big step forward, like you said. The painting crew is coming Monday to start their work, and that will give me time and motivation to really get a handle on things."

"What are you doing tomorrow?"

"Church in the morning. We never went to church when I lived here, so I thought I'd try Guardian Angel."

"That's our church. Can we go together? It's kind of silly to go separately, and think of the gas we'd waste."

She burst out laughing, exactly what he'd hoped. "The church is a block and a half away, but sure. I'd like that, Jake. Are the boys good in church?"

"Not even close, but they'll be better when double-teamed."

"Team Karralis, it is. I was thinking the nine o'clock Mass because I need to have time to move things around."

"Then how about this?" Jake suggested. "We go to church together, I help you move stuff, and you come over to Mom's with me mid-day. The weather's supposed to be pretty decent for November, Rafe is making a bonfire, and we're clearing debris from a couple of bug-infested trees. Food is simple, burgers and dogs and whatever anyone throws on the table. That way your work is done and a little down time surrounded by my gang should make you appreciate your solitary existence by nightfall."

Huge steps.

Tess Cosgrove wasn't taking prescription-formula baby steps anymore. Hanging out with Jake and his boys, going to church together, spending time with family... Those weren't basic moves, they were giant leap for mankind kind of moves. But it felt good, it felt right. "I'd love that, I think. Will I be able to keep the boys from pitching themselves into the fire while you're being manly and felling trees?"

"Possibly not, but with Mima, Aunt Rose and Tasha there, the boys will be herded tighter than prize-winning cattle."

"Deal." She yawned and realized she was tired. "I must hang up. I need sleep, which is funny because I wasn't a bit tired twenty minutes ago."

"You're okay with sleeping there?"

She was, actually. Funny how a simple conversation turned that around. "Yes. Yes, I am."

"Good. I'll see you in the morning. Good night, Tess."

He didn't say goodbye, like most people would. He said 'good night'. She breathed softly. "'Night, Jake." And when she plugged in her phone to charge overnight, she didn't feel the stress of the now-empty shelving, the lack of boxes, stacked six feet high. She breathed deep, and it felt like the spacious living room breathed relief right along with her.

She slept, and woke up surprised that she'd slept so well. They took the boys to church, cleared out the first two rooms for the painters, then stopped by the diner to pick up a tray of hand-rolled cannolis. Fifteen minutes later they pulled up to Jake's mother's house set along Renschuyl Creek. Butterflies didn't claim her gut. It was more like small birds, darting this way and that. She'd stayed away from Ashton to avoid reminders. Meeting Jake's family hadn't exactly been on the agenda.

"Jake, send the boys this way and gear up! Rafe and Pete are waiting for you!"

"Rafe and Pete are doing no such thing." Unperturbed, Jake called back to his mother once he climbed out of the SUV. "I have farther to drive, two crazy kids and we had to help Tess out for a little while after church. Mom, this is Tess Cosgrove, she's in town for a little while to settle her mother's affairs. Tess," he drew Tess forward and smiled before he threw her to the wolves. "This is my mother, Norma Karralis. I promised Tess you guys would help her watch the twin terrors."

"With an iron fist!" declared Norma, but when the boys barreled into her, Tess realized Norma was more talk than action. "Boys, I believe you've grown since last week. This is not possible, yes?"

"Mima, can I help cut down trees?"

"Daddy said it was up to you."

"Daddy needs a switch to his behind to put his beloved mother in such circumstance, and of course the answer is no, men's work will come soon enough, but you may go play with Lexie. And no grimy hands on her now that she's the picture of health!"

"I'm fine, Auntie, a little dirt won't hurt me!" A girl of about seven or eight laughed at Norma's directive and raced off, into the nearby grove with the boys, but south of where the men were dropping trees.

"You see this line?" Norma put her hands on broad hips and pointed to a line of snow fencing stretched through the woods, hastily erected. "You go past this line and you are out of the woods, and get to be watched all day. By me."

"We won't, Mima!"

"We promise!"

"We'll be good, Auntie!"

"Do they mean it?" Tess asked Norma. "Or is this token appeasement until our backs are turned?"

"Both, no doubt!"

"We call my aunt "auntie", too. Ever since I was little. I think for a while I didn't realize her name was Theodora, because she was always just 'auntie'."

"Theodora Anastas?"

"Do you know my aunt?" Too late, Tess recalled the boys' initial conversation with Auntie Dora. Oops.

"We were good friends a long time ago. And then we weren't." Norma frowned, but Tess didn't sense any negativity. Just remorse. "Time and circumstance do strange things over decades. If I could have seen the future forty years back, life might be different now. Better, worse, who's to say?" She shrugged and Tess did, too. "But it would have been different."

"Auntie, do you want the salads in the fridge?" A woman about Tess's age came their way.

"Oh, that reminds me." Tess zipped open the striped cooler bag she'd carried from the car. "I'm not home so I couldn't make anything, but we stopped at the diner and grabbed a tray of cannolis for later. I hope that's okay?"

"Later, schmater, life's short." Norma helped herself to a chocolate-filled cannoli from the tray. "Eat dessert first, which is why I look like I do and you look young and beautiful and slim. How long has my son known you, Tess Cosgrove?"

"And the questions begin." The other woman strode forward, grabbed the tray of cannolis— after Norma had hers, of course— and scolded the older woman with a frank expression. "If you scare her off, those grandsons of yours might never get a mother. Stop. Behave yourself."

Tess was pretty sure she'd fallen into an alternative universe because no one would talk to one of the elder women in her family like that. Ever. She glanced from Norma to the younger woman and back.

"So now it's wrong to ask questions of our guest? I should, perhaps, be silent?"

"Discreet, Auntie." The younger woman winked at Tess and smiled at her aunt. "Let us pump her for information throughout the day, then report back to you later." She held the cannolis with one hand and extended the other. "Tasha Karralis, Rafe's wife and mother to that one," she pointed to the brown-haired tomboy scaling trees above the little boys. "And this one." She dropped her gaze to the very obvious baby bump. "I'm so glad you could come."

"Me, too, and thank you for the quick intervention." She smiled at Norma, who humphed in reply. "I'm Tess, I lived across the street from Jake's aunt and uncle while I was growing up."

"You are Teresa Viktoria, one of Stella's girls."

The birds in her belly began a soar and dive pattern. She inhaled slowly, willing her nerves to stand down. The Greek community in Ashton was close-knit, even the ones at odds with one another. "Yes." She changed the subject by turning back toward Tasha. "I work in Philadelphia, and we all followed Lexie's story with great excitement. And the successes that have followed have us hopeful of a cure."

"Awesome, right?" Joy made Tasha seem even more beautiful and Tess hadn't thought that possible. "Two miracles. There." She pointed Lexie's way. "And here." She indicated her rounded belly. "And another one if these clueless men don't end up in the E.R. by the end of the day." She said it loud enough for the men to hear during a chain saw break.

"Tess is a doctor," Jake called over. "She can stitch us up and have us back to work in no time."

"A doctor?" Approval raised Norma's brows. "Well, how nice, Tess. You have done well, so I will add smart to beautiful and willow-slim!"

"Well, thank you."

"Tess, coffee or soda? Or iced tea?"

"Coffee, now, tea later, and may I help?"

"Yes." Tasha led the way into the kitchen. Once inside, she softened her voice. "Of course you can help if it gives you a ten minute respite from Auntie!"

Tess laughed. "Oh, she's fine. I think it's kind of sweet, actually, how you teased her. There was never any teasing that went on in my house. Or in our family."

"Well, prepare yourself, because it's non-stop over here. And Norma's a good woman, just a little overbearing."

"Well, she's Greek."

Tash laughed out loud. "There is that."

"I love this old house."

"This house has been in Norma's family for three generations. When her husband left her high and dry, her father signed the house over to her."

"Jake's dad left them?" Tess hung her small purse and the travel bag on a hook inside the door. "I didn't realize that."

"Jake's dad was killed in service."

Tess frowned. "I thought—"

"Norma remarried. Big mistake. He was mean to Jake and Katy and when he left, he bilked all the money he could out of Norma's accounts. She spent their teen-age years working two jobs to make ends meet, and that's when Jake's grandfather gave her the house."

So Jake had been dealing with his own brand of family "crazy" back in high school. That realization offered new insight into his choices, his behaviors. "Grownups make such a mess of things."

"Selfish grown-ups affect a whole lot more than themselves," Tasha agreed. "It was a hard bunch of years. I wouldn't go back and re-live those years of high school insanity for anything."

See? It isn't just you who looks back on those cringe-worthy years. A lot of folks do. Her therapist had told her that repeatedly, but Tess hadn't let herself delve until now. Until Jake, she corrected herself. "Me, either. And I can't believe we don't need more than a sweatshirt on the Sunday before Thanksgiving."

"It's the perfect day to hang Christmas lights." Norma bustled into the kitchen. "Tess, can you watch the kids while Tasha and I bring out the lights and decorations?"

"Tasha gets to watch kids." Tess set her coffee down. "I'm not pregnant, I get to be pack mule."

"Adding a kind heart to the list of fine qualities!"

"Does she really have a list for each woman Jake brings home?" Tess whispered the question before Tasha went back outside.

"You're the first."

Her words brought Tess's head around right quick, but one look at Tasha's face confirmed the words. Tasha grinned as she opened the door. "The pressure's on."

It sure was, but Tess forgot all about it as she and Norma brought boxes of holiday decorations to the back porch. The kids gathered around, excited.

Tess manned the ladder, framing the front of the bungalow-style house in lights. Lexie helped keep the string untangled, and by the time the men realized what they were doing out front, the job was almost complete.

"Tess." Jake sounded as exasperated as he looked when she peered down from one-and-a-half stories up. "You don't need to be on a twenty foot ladder fixing my mother's house. Get down, I'll finish up. I thought Aunt Rose was coming over to help with this project."

"A sick grandchild took precedence," she called down. "And you need to hush." She pointed the end of the fifth light string his way. "I am perfectly capable of doing this and a whole lot more."

"But—"

She pointed to Lexie next. "Do you want this amazing girl raised thinking women can't do anything more than make soup and do laundry?"

"Well, no, I—"

She affixed the last short section and climbed down the ladder. With three rungs to go, Jake grasped her around the waist and lifted her the rest of the way, then turned her, straight into his arms. "You talk too much." He smiled into her eyes, a real smile, the kind a girl could get lost in for, oh, say... forever? He held her gaze, his strong hands firm at her waist. "I'll stow my protective instincts as long as you don't do something ridiculously dangerous. Okay?"

Oh, it was more than okay. Being here with Jake, gazes locked, his steady brown eyes offering assurance and maybe more... it was the most okay she'd ever been. "Okay."

She meant to sound tough and decisive, a well-practiced trait.

She didn't. The words came out in more of a wondering whisper as his gaze traveled from her eyes to her mouth, then back. His smile deepened and he lifted his gaze to the lights. "Thank you for helping Mom. She likes everything done for Thanksgiving so we can have the house and the yard all lit up. She hasn't had much money for Christmas for a long time, but she fires up those ovens in a storm of bakery love. And that's enough."

Regret and yearning filled her.

She'd have given anything for a mother like that, but she couldn't change the past, and she was free to choose her future. If she ever became a mother, she'd be that kind of mom. The kind she saw in TV commercials, the kind who worked with kids, laughed with them, disciplined them and made cookies for them. "It sounds wonderful."

"Well, come to Thanksgiving this week and see." Jake hoisted the ladder and brought it around the driveway side of the house. He set it up just as Norma came out of the house carrying the biggest and possibly most garishly decorated wreath Tess had ever seen. "I've got lead on this one. You can do the window lights. The wreath is ugly and heavy, but it was my grandma's, so it gets a place of honor every year."

He climbed the ladder, and when she and Tasha lifted the ginormous and weighty wreath up to him, he winked at her.

Tasha said nothing, but the "told you so" look she shot Tess brought heat straight to her face. He climbed down, grabbed coffee, and headed back to the woods.

"Whoa." Tasha looked at him, then her.

The heat rose further, claiming Tess's cheeks. "Whoa, nothing."

"He's smitten, Tess."

Tess waved that off as she sorted through the lights. "He's nice. Big difference."

"That, too," Tasha supposed as she handed Jonah and Ben a box of somewhat tacky candy canes to line the walk under Norma's eagle eye. "It's good to see that expression on his face. Rafe says it's been a long time coming."

A toughened part of Tess's heart went soft at the thought. Her presence had never brought joy to anyone. Not her mother, not her sister, and she'd never known her father. He'd died when she and Dee were young, so she and Jake had that in common. The idea that being with her— *Tess Cosgrove*— made someone happy, added a particular blessing to the day.

Be careful. Don't set yourself up for failure. Heartbreak and disappointment can mess up all the progress you've made.

She shoved the internal caution aside. She was strong and healthy now. An overcomer, to the max, determined to do whatever she chose.

"And now the manger." Norma bobbed her head in approval and went back inside, a woman on a mission.

"We get to help!" The boys raced in behind her, kicked off their shoes and hooked their coats. Tess and Tasha followed. "Mima, did you get the box?" Jonah peered into the living room, excited. Ben joined him and Lexie laughed at both of them.

"Right here." Norma lifted a box onto the couch while Tasha cleared a few things from the old-fashioned sideboard. She centered the heavy-duty wooden stable as Norma lifted out pieces for the children to place. "Animals, first, of course." She handed each child an animal to place until the stable was half-filled with cows, sheep and little lambs. "And hay, to assuage their hunger."

Jonah and Ben tucked hay into the stable, as if each animal was being fed.

"The watering trough."

Lexie put the watering trough off to the side.

Then Norma handed each child a figure. Mary, Joseph and a donkey. When the children took the figures and placed them on the piano in the corner, Tess turned, surprised.

"The journey begins next Sunday," Norma said softly, and then Tess understood. Mary and Joseph hadn't sat in a stable for four weeks, awaiting Christ's birth. They'd traveled, far and long, a rugged journey for the young mother, great with child. "Each day, they will process around the room, arriving at the stable in Bethlehem on Christmas Eve."

"This is a beautiful tradition." She breathed deeply, seeing the children's faces of anticipation, and their excitement, but it was more than a coming holiday. Norma's efforts were teaching them the true meaning of Christmas, without words, without lessons, just by using the simple things in her possession.

"What about the angel, Mima?" Ben looked around. "Where is she?"

"Here, of course, and we'll put her on the mantel. That way she can keep an eye on things as Mary and Joseph find their way to Bethlehem of Judea."

"She's so beautiful." Lexie whispered the words as Norma withdrew the angel. The kids weren't tall enough to set the figurine on the shelf, so Norma did the honors, and when she moved her hand away, Tess stared.

Pale pink luminescence shimmered in the angel's robes, and the angel's outward look seemed to be searching— or watching, as Norma intimated— from above.

Her heart stuttered, then beat harder. This angel, the angel watching over Norma's Nativity scene, was like the one that had been dropped off at her mother's house a few days before.

She stared, then moved forward and reached for the angel. "May I look at this?"

"Of course!" Norma's smile went wide. "She's so beautiful, isn't she? I've had her ever since I was a little girl, so little I don't even remember where I got her from."

"Not part of this Nativity set, then?"

Norma waved a hand. "No, so different, of course, but I made her part of the Nativity because an angel *would* be different, wouldn't they? No one would expect an angel to wear clothes others would wear. She gives a heavenly presence, I think."

"She does." Tess set the angel back on the mantel with care. Maybe the angel wasn't an oddity at all. Maybe lots of folks owned pearl-glazed statuary decades back. Just because she wasn't familiar with it, didn't make it extraordinary. Still...

The thought that she'd had such a similar angel dropped off at the house seemed like more than a coincidence, but that was silly.

"Time to grill some burgers." Jake didn't come through the house with his boots on. He stood on the porch and called through the door. "Mom, we're done out here except for some burn-off that Rafe's got under control, and there's a weather front due to hit in about ninety minutes. Let's eat before rain and snow chase us inside."

"Good idea!" While Norma gathered the tray of hamburgers, the boys rushed their dad.

"We got to do the manger!"

"And Mary and Jophes will start on their way to Befflehem soon!"

"Jo-seph." Jake stressed the pronunciation for Ben.

"Beth-le-hem," said Tess, at the very same time.

He looked at her. She looked at him. And when Jake's grin swept her and those two blessed boys, warmth claimed her. Oh, it was silly, she knew that. Jake and his family were here, they belonged here and Tess would have been okay to never lay eyes on Ashton, Pennsylvania again. She was in town of necessity, nothing more. Her life was an hour away in Philadelphia, with a vibrant, wonderful practice and the respect of an esteemed medical community.

But that look and that smile hinted what could be with a man like Jake Karralis, and his fun family.

"I'll toast rolls in here, you kids head back outside." Norma pushed the back door open and held it while the kids dashed out. "Before you know it, rain and snow will be keeping you indoors way more than you should be."

Tess helped set the food out for the casual dinner. Norma and Tasha chatted naturally, comfortable in their own skins, comfortable with each other.

Tess had never had that, but working in the cozy kitchen made her realize she longed for that very thing. A family to be part of, to spend time with. And by the time they got the boys home and into bed, it had been a long, busy, beautiful day.

"They're wiped out." Jake turned off the boys' light and mostly shut the door. "Me, too. But." He reached down and took her hand. Just that, her hand, letting his fingers lace with hers. "It was the best day I've had in a long time, Tess."

"For me, too."

"Yeah?" He took those laced hands and drew them around to bring her closer. "Extra nice?"

She should walk away. She should re-claim her hand, step back and politely thank him for the best day she'd ever had.

But she couldn't because being here, being close to him, with his arm circling her middle felt so right. "Yes. Extra nice."

"You know the only thing that would make it better?" he whispered. He brought his left hand up and grazed her cheek lightly. So lightly.

She glanced at his mouth, then into his eyes. "Baklava?"

"After," he whispered.

The kiss started soft, then grew. His hands cradled her face, then her shoulders, then her. The scent of him wrapped around her, wood shavings and grilled meat and a hint of that morning's after-shave with a side of coffee.

She broke the kiss reluctantly. "I have to go."

"I know." He dropped his brow to hers, then sighed but smiled. "I know. I haven't kissed anybody like that in a long time."

She never had, so that put him one up on her.

"Baklava first. Leah made a chocolate walnut variety and she sent it along just for you."

"I love her more than life itself right now, but let's share a piece, okay?"

He didn't tease her or try to talk her into eating more. He nodded, looped an arm around her and led her into the kitchen. "Sounds good."

And when she opened her front door thirty minutes later, she turned and waved to him across the street.

He waved back, and when he blew her a kiss, sweet thoughts tumbled through her. Was she crazy, falling for this man this quickly? Was she rash? She knew the brat he'd been. Had he really changed or was she setting herself up for sadness and disappointment? In Tess's world, sadness and disappointment equated themselves with food.

Stop fearing. Start living. Now.

She loved the more pragmatic side of her conscience, so she

blew a kiss right back, went in and shut the door.

The painters would come tomorrow. In a week they'd be gone and the floor experts would take their turn, and then it would be time to list the house. Her mission would be accomplished, but never in her wildest dreams had she considered what it might be like to stay in Ashton.

She was being silly. She and Jake barely knew each other, but right now she felt romance-novel ready to love and be loved. Of course it didn't work that way in real life.

Did it?

She went to bed thinking of him. The way he cared for his boys, for his mother, for his family—

She loved that, and if she wasn't a whole lot more careful, she'd love him, and what would people think? Fat Terri hooking up with Jake Karralis.

Her conscience scolded her for being negative, but old habits die hard when stirred up. Fifteen years ago, Jake and his buddies ridiculed her and broke her heart. Maybe Jake had changed. She'd seen that first-hand.

But had everyone?

Probably not, and after dealing with her mother's brand of crazy for so long, Tess had no desire to thrust herself back into the middle. All those years of being shrugged off by her hometown had been more than enough.

CHAPTER SIX

WEATHER REALITY HIT WITH A vengeance that night. Rain, wind and cold brought down the last lingering leaves by mid-Monday. The painters were focusing on the upstairs for two days. Tess holed up in the kitchen with her one-cup coffee maker and her laptop. She'd had wifi put in her first day here, because being stuck in a house without it wasn't going to happen. Her phone rang mid-afternoon. The estate liquidator's number flashed in the box and she took the call.

"Dr. Cosgrove?"

"Yes."

"We've got everything set for the sale, we're going to hold it at our auction barn the second week of December and there are just a few items of note I need to run by you."

"Run by me because?" His answer surprised her.

"Value. Now and again we find high-ticket items and need the owner's guidance about how to proceed. It's stipulated in the con-tract where we talked about lowest acceptable bids. We have an online network that markets items of value internationally."

She remembered Mike mentioning that, but hadn't seriously considered anything her mother collected as valuable. "All right. Do you need me to come down there?"

"No, verbal permissions are fine. We have an unopened set of Christmas in a Teacup ornaments, the complete set of twelve and in pristine condition those are going for around four-hundred an ornament. For the complete set would you like a starting bid of four thousand?"

"Four thousand dollars? For ornaments?"

"It was a short-lived collection but in retrospect has become very popular. We could also sell them individually and possibly get even more money for them."

Tess had no idea, and she'd never seen these ornaments because they'd never had a Christmas tree. The stinging irony of that hit deep and low. "I'll leave that to your marketing expertise, okay?"

He laughed. "Fine. The double set of fine china from Halston, Smith and Company is the other high-end collection. Nothing you want, I take it?"

Those she remembered, sitting in four big boxes, piled high, and a picture of the beautiful dishes marking the shipping box. They'd never been allowed to open them, much less eat off of them. "No, I'm fine with selling them."

"And then one last thing. There is a Stavros angel here, a single piece, the archangel."

"I want that." She blurted the words instantly, and had no idea why, except that maybe Norma would like this angel to go with hers. "It's considered valuable?"

"Very. Magda Stavros created this trio of angels. The archangel, the seraph and the cherub."

"And suddenly there was with the angel a multitude of heavenly host…"

"Exactly. Magda's work became world-renowned post-Holocaust and she'd only produced about a hundred of these sets. Most were lost in the aftermath of World War II and the Greek Civil War, but a few have survived. A single piece in mint condition can net a cool ten thousand. The whole collection, with Magda's stamp on the bottom, is valued at five times that."

An astonishing figure. She couldn't imagine it, but regardless of worth, she wanted that statue. Something about it, or maybe it was the odd way it was delivered to her, teased at her. "Mike, I'm going to come down there and pick up the angel statue. There's nothing else I'm interested in, other than getting this all done. I'll be there in ten minutes, okay?"

"I'll have it wrapped and waiting for you."

She picked it up and drove straight to Auntie's house on the opposite side of town. Dora swung the door wide before she made it up the broad steps. "Ach, you're here, and what if you catch this?" She coughed three times, accentuating her concerns. "It's like the death of colds, it's so bad, your uncle, now me, although I think we're both getting better today. Possibly better. I say this as your uncle, God love him, still thinks he should be waited on, hand and foot over sniffles while I struggle to draw a normal breath."

For someone struggling to breathe, she'd rambled on for over a minute.

Dora shrugged and shut the door behind Tess. "Whatever. You don't smell like paint, do you?" She leaned close to Tess's coat and inhaled. "No, so that's good, you know I'd have been over to help more, but me being so sick, and Uncle down like he was, oy! The very thought of smelling enough paint to make that crazy house presentable put knots here." She patted her stout middle. "Big knots. Come in, come in, what did you need, darling girl?"

Typical Auntie, her mouth going a mile a minute, her heart ready to help with anything that didn't include wet paint or wet dogs or noisy kids. "Information, I think." She sat down at the kitchen table and unwrapped the angel. The estate liquidator had put it into a padded box, and when she withdrew the angel, Auntie sat down, hard. "I didn't think I'd ever see that again."

"Was it yours?"

"Not mine, no, but they were ours. There were three, and they were put aside for us as we grew older. Mine disappeared a long time ago, as did your mother's. I always wondered if she got rid of them, if they bound her too much to a past she couldn't remember and couldn't forget."

"What past?" Tess leaned closer. "I don't understand."

"Because it is not spoken of, *kopela mou*. As so many things in life back then were not spoken of." She frowned, then sat back. "Our country was at war with itself. I was small, very small, as was your mother. I don't remember much, but I remembered being driven far, far away. And crying, crying out, wishing my mother could hear me and come get me. And then there is nothing of much import until a big plane brought many of us here. To America. To our new families."

"New families?" Tess raised her hands, confused. "I don't get it. You were born here."

"We were not," her aunt said softly. "We pretended we were, because we were told to, but there were secrets back then. So many secrets. And your mother and Norma and I were part of those secrets."

"They smuggled children into this country?" Tess couldn't imagine such a thing. How could that happen? How could they possibly get away with it, and keep the secret for two long generations?

"They said at first it was to keep us safe. Later, we knew different, but we'd been with our American families for so long. And many in Greece had died. The queen had us taken, rounded up, like cattle, and put in a children's camp, but from that camp, they sent many children here, to America. And told no one what they were doing. Families here that wanted us, took us, named us, made us their own. And back in Greece mothers wept and fathers raged and it didn't matter because the country was at war with itself."

"You were given up for adoption because of a war?"

"A civil war," Dora explained, "and we were not given up. We were taken by order of the queen. Of course, none of this I knew until I was much older, all I recalled was being without a parent, a mother. A father. And then I was here and had a new mother and father, but different. So different."

"Of course." Tess understood how childhood trauma could dog a person. "You never saw your parents again?"

"Never. I believed them dead. And through all that fear and change and sorrow, no one ever told us the truth. If they did, we might fight to go back, to go home, and if there was no home, why would we fight? We would adjust, in time. But a kindly soldier accompanied us on the plane and made us laugh, although your mother was not easy to amuse, even then. But little Norma laughed and played and patted his cheeks, so happy. So full of life. And the soldier had these three angels, he'd found them at a little shop in Rome. They were so shiny and pretty. We ooed and ahhed over them and he gave one to each of us. Well, to our parents for us," she amended the story, "We were too young and busy to be trusted with breakable things."

"So Norma was adopted as well."

"To such a nice family, the Barous, such good people! And it was like a miracle that your mother and I stayed together, most siblings were split up, but your mother could never find a way to be happy here." Dora frowned and sighed. "She made it hard to love her, always angry and picking fights, although our new parents tried.

But she did not make it easy, and when we were teenagers there was a big fight. She left, went off on her own, and we didn't see her for over ten years. The angels were gone, too, so we thought she must have taken them. But why would she do that? And where have they been all this time?"

"I don't know. Do you think she took them? Why would she do that?"

"To sell, we thought. Or to be mean."

Tess knew her mother well enough to know either scenario could be true.

Theodora held the smooth-as-glass angel. "This one was your mother's. Mine was the most innocent looking angel, almost a babe."

"Cherubim."

"Yes." She smiled. "I've had a soft spot in my heart for them ever since. I've got a dozen little angels that will go up on my tree, but none quite as special as that one."

"Norma still has hers," Tess told her. "She gives it a place of honor on her old sideboard, watching over the Nativity throughout Advent."

Auntie's expression softened, a rare occurrence. "I'm glad. I envied Norma when we were young, she was so sweet and joyful and everyone loved her. Your mother and I were different. Darker. More subdued."

"But you were loved. Mima and Papa loved you."

"Oh, yes!" She smiled but then she frowned. "But we had been taken from love first, so it was always hard to trust the love."

Hard to trust the love.

She'd sensed that about her mother, as if she harbored some vacuous hole inside, always trying to fill it with something special, and never succeeding. "And my mother never really reconciled to anything."

"Well." Dora shrugged. "She came back with a wealthy husband and pregnant with twins. When he passed away, she was left with plenty of money, a big house, and beautiful daughters. But no heart. It was as if she couldn't risk loving people, so she tried to love things. Really awful, ugly things, much of the time," she admitted. She sighed, then stroked the edge of the luminescent angel. "But she brought you to us, Teresa. And Delia. And for that I am ever grateful, although I wish I had been a better aunt. A better person. Maybe if I'd stepped in, things would have been different. I am sorry about that."

So much to be sorry for, but the thought of small children, taken from their homes, squirreled away and then sent to other countries…

"Harsh times bring harsh choices." Auntie stood and hugged her, hugged her tight. "But then we put our shoulders back and we move on. As you have done. As your sister has done, but how I wish we could just be family again. Normal and nice, before I die."

"Well, then you better stay alive for awhile." Tess returned her aunt's hug. "Because we've got our work cut out for us."

"That we do."

Sunday had been the best day he'd had in years, and all because Tess came along with him and the boys.

You kissed her.

He sure did, and he'd do it again if given the chance. Repeatedly, if allowed.

Jake tried to bury his head in his work, but images of Tess laughing, Tess on the ladder, Tess calling the boys, Tess looking knock-out amazing in her blue jeans and lightweight hoodie. What man in his right mind found a coral hoodie amazing?

Him, when it was Tess Cosgrove wearing it.

He finished putting together a presentation for a local developer and sent it up to the front office, happy with the results. A beautiful sub-division with social amenities like green space, a playground and a community pool, a bedroom community midway between Allentown and Philly, attractive to workers from both cities. He began to set specs for an adult living community in a Philadelphia suburb, but every time he thought of Philly, he thought of Tess.

Tough and fragile, an odd mix, forged by her confined childhood. And yet, so natural with the boys, as if made to mother them. How could that be, though, without any kind of normal example? And what about that fragility? He'd be foolish to discount emotional problems when it came to something as imperfect but perfectly wonderful as his boys. He'd lived the downside of a bad step-parent, first-hand. He'd felt his stepfather's wrath far too often.

Anyone could pretend to be good with kids for a short while. His stepfather had played the part well when he dated Jake's mother. And then it all turned bad.

When in doubt, seek God.

He'd learned that lesson the hard way, after years of seeking nothing but his own personal gratification. He drove home, thoughtful.

Twinkle lights had started appearing here and there this week. By the following weekend, his drive home would sparkle, which meant he needed to think about Christmas and the boys. They were doing a kindergarten play called The Journey, a play that brought the animals and Mary and Joseph to Bethlehem.

He wanted Tess to go with him. He recognized his attraction to her. And he was pretty sure it went both ways, but nothing should be more important than how things went with the boys. His mother had been fooled by a good act.

Jake would never allow that to happen. He parked the car and hurried inside. He came to a dead stop inside the kitchen, struck dumb by the scene before him.

Jonah and Ben were standing on the table. *The kitchen table.*

Ben was in tears. Jonah looked scared to death.

And Tess stood facing them, a stern look on her face and a heavy, wooden rolling pin in her hand.

Jake didn't take time to think. In retrospect, that would have been a good idea. No, he reacted first. He grabbed the rolling pin out of Tess's grip, put it on top of the refrigerator, spun around and threw his hands in the air. "What is going on here?"

Jonah's eyes went wide. Ben stared at his over-reaction, then cried harder. Tess looked at him as if he was some kind of crazy person, grabbed her warm jacket and headed for the door.

Twin mice dashed out from beneath the counter. They parted ways at the table leg, one heading east while the other went west.

Ben shrieked.

Jonah squealed. "Tess, there's more!"

"I assumed that from the size of the first ones." She leveled a hurt but chilled look at Jake from the foyer. "I would suggest glue traps and well-hidden poison because from the size of these guys," she noted the direction of Mouse #1 with a glance, "they're pretty close to breeding age themselves. Remember the old saying, if you see one mouse, you've got seven more. Well, you're infested." She swung open the door. "Good luck."

"Tess."

She closed the door and walked away.

He'd hurt her feelings. He didn't have to hear the words to know the truth, he'd seen it in her eyes. He'd let old emotion about his stepfather taint his judgment. He wasn't a yeller. Well, not much, anyway. Which probably explained why the boys tested him frequently.

He bit back words of self-recrimination and lifted the boys off the table. He grabbed their coats, had them get into the car and then he drove to the hardware store. He followed Tess's advice, because most people living in Philly had experience with mice.

He'd forgotten to get supper.

He'd ruined everything with Tess because he assumed the rolling pin was for the boys, not the vermin, as if Tess would ever do such a thing. He'd let thoughts of his stepfather wreak havoc with his mind. What kind of a moron was he, anyway?

The kind with a less-than-pretty past.

He sighed.

He'd messed up royally, and now he had two hungry boys, a house full of mice, and Tess had no supper. And she thought he was a jerk. Well, he'd acted like a jerk, so she was correct.

He bought a bucket of chicken with two side dishes, and showed up at her door. She might toss him out. She might ignore the doorbell. She might—

"Yes?"

She surprised him. She no longer looked wounded, she looked great. Tough and hands-off, but great. "I came to apologize. And bring supper. Which I'd forgotten on the way home because I was thinking of other things. Can we have supper here?"

She shook her head. "It's probably best if we don't, Jake." He started to speak, but she held up a hand. "Two people with some serious old issues are probably the least likely scenario for success at any level. Let's call it a day, okay?"

"No."

She looked surprised, as if most people listened to her common sense edicts. Well, not him and especially not today. "Everyone has issues. The healthy adult thing to do is talk them out. Over original recipe chicken and cole slaw."

Her eyebrows lifted slightly. "You got original recipe?"

"Yes. It's my favorite."

"Mine, too."

"Then let me in and we'll eat and psychoanalyze our respective triggers."

"It can't possibly end well," she told him, but she looked less stern as she swung the door open. He waved the boys out of the car and they rushed the steps.

"I smell paint!"

"I love that smell!"

"I hate that smell!"

"Wow, it's so different over here!"

"Look, we can run!"

They kicked off their shoes and peeled off their jackets as they raced into the fairly empty rooms.

"Can we check things out?"

"We won't touch anything, promise!"

"Go ahead." She smiled at them, but they dashed off too quickly to see it.

Jake saw the smile and felt even more ashamed of his earlier reaction. "Listen, Tess."

She winced instantly. "Really, we don't have to do this. Let's just eat with the boys and move on, okay?"

He set the tote bag on the table, turned and cradled her face in his hands. "No, it's not okay." Where should he begin? With the basics, he realized, because truth was always better. "I had a really mean stepfather."

Her gaze met his.

"But he wasn't always mean. He was the nicest guy when my mother was dating him, and he took us places, and did nice things for us. It was like the perfect answer to our family because my real father died when I was little." He paused, remembering. "He fooled us all, and when they got married, his true colors came out. He hurt me, he hurt Katy, he hurt Mom."

"Jake, I'm sorry."

"Me, too. It's all old news now, but every once in a while, something hits a button and I over-react."

"To mice?"

He paused, then admitted, "To you with the rolling pin."

Her jaw dropped open. She stared up at him, dumbfounded. "You thought I could—"

He shook his head and didn't let her finish. "No, there was no thought involved. I saw and reacted. If I'd thought about it, Tess, I'd have been rational. It just hit those old buttons."

"Triggers."

"Yes," he admitted. "I'm sorry. I'm usually better equipped to handle things, but the boys looked scared..."

"Attack mice playing field hockey with spilled cereal in the kitchen will do that to you."

He grimaced. "I know, and I heard little noises a week ago and meant to put out traps, then forgot over the weekend." He met her gaze and held it. "Forgive me, please. I try not to be overprotective of the boys, but today I was."

She studied him. His expression, his eyes, his words, and then she shifted her attention to the bag. "You did get original recipe."

"It's incomparable."

She smiled softly. "Since we're talking about triggers, let me just say that no one gets to yell at me. Ever." She pointed up the stairs where the noises of curious boys darted from room to room. "Children are the exception to that rule because they're children. But no one else. Got it?"

He'd been a fool to over-react, and one look at her face had told him he'd crossed a big line. "Got it." He hugged her then, hugged her tight.

Maybe she was right. Maybe there was too much baggage in their pasts, but wasn't that part of being an adult? To recognize that baggage and deal with it? "I like holding you, Tess."

He whispered the words near her ear, her cheek. "I like it a whole lot."

She didn't answer for a few seconds, but when she drew back, met his gaze, then kissed him ever-so-gently on the mouth, he had his answer even before she whispered back, "Me, too."

CHAPTER SEVEN

THANKSGIVING WITH THE KARRALIS FAMILY.
It couldn't be happening, but it was, and Tess wasn't sure if she should race forward or walk the other way, but when Jake was around, the last thing on her mind was retreat.

"Are you sure one pie is enough?" she asked as Jake backed the SUV out of her driveway.

"Yes, because Katy's bringing one, too. And Tasha and Rafe are stopping in for late-day coffee, with a bunch of other Karralises. They'll all bring a dessert, and Mom will have two or three herself. By the time we get out of there tonight, we'll all need a diet plan."

"Don't let me bring anything home, okay?"

He cringed.

"I mean it, Jake. When I say no, back me up, okay?"

"I'll take twice as much and keep it at my place," he promised, and then he smiled. "What's your favorite part of Thanksgiving? If you weren't here, with us, what would you be doing?"

"Serving hundreds of nice dinners at a homeless mission in Philly."

"That's where you spend Thanksgiving usually? For real?"

"Every year since I went into private practice," she told him. "Great food, a good effort and a chance to thank God for what I've been given. A second chance to be all I can be."

"That's beautiful, Tess."

"Don't give me too much credit. It was a reciprocal action," she explained. "I did no harm," she continued, citing the Hippocratic Oath, "and I didn't have to spend my holidays alone thinking about how things coulda/shoulda/woulda been."

He'd been tapping a finger on the steering wheel. Now he stopped, but stared straight ahead. He was weighing her words, feeling sorry for her, no doubt. But he didn't need to. She'd become adept at examining situations and removing herself from anything dangerous or depressing. Volunteering was a great way to get through the holidays. Helping others made her feel normal and magnanimous, and she couldn't find anything wrong with that.

"Do you wish you were there now?"

It did feel funny not to be there. Not to be serving up potatoes and gravy, making corn casserole. Filling punch bowls and chatting with people who'd fallen on hard times. She was about to answer when Ben called her name, excited. "Tess! Do you see those reindeer up there?"

A plywood sleigh with reindeer was fastened to the top of a barn, as if waiting to take off. "Ben, that's awesome!"

"It lights up at night." Jonah leaned forward as far as his booster seat would allow. "I remember from last year."

"And the front reindeer has a red nose!" Ben grinned, then clapped his hands with such exuberance. "Rudolph! Can you believe it?"

Endearingly perfect. The beautiful simplicity of holidays through a child's eyes... She shook her head at Ben. "I'm amazed, Ben. Truly amazed."

He nodded as if he expected her to be amazed, and then she put a hand on Jake's arm. "I'm exactly where I would like to be today, Jake."

"Yeah?" He sounded relieved. "For real?"

"Most assuredly."

He breathed deep, smiled and covered her hand with his for a few short seconds. "I'm glad to hear it."

The holiday dinner was fun, crazy, cozy and chaotic, and Tess wasn't sure how any one house could claim all that, but Norma's did. By the time they got to dessert, the rooms were full of Jake's relatives. Laughing, talking, shouting over one another, she watched the back-and-forth like a sideline spectator, but Jake's family wasn't the kind to let anyone sit and watch. At the end of the day, she'd scored two handwritten recipes, the keys to someone's house, an address and an instruction in how to layer baklava just so— and don't skimp on the butter!— so she could make her own version every holiday. And bring it to share, of course.

The hour grew late and it was time to get the boys home to bed. "Norma, thank you again." She smiled at Jake's mother. "I've never had a family Thanksgiving like this. It was the best ever."

"Oh, honey." Norma hugged her. Tess wasn't a hugger by nature, but Norma's hug felt good, like the kind she used to imagine as a child. The kind of hug Tess never had and never knew. "I'm so glad you were here! Now, Jake—" She began to turn, but Jonah's words stopped her.

"Hey, Tess, did you tell Mima you've got a angel like ours?" He peered up at her as he struggled into his coat. He scowled, tired and exasperated, until Jake pulled his sleeve right-side out and helped him find the armhole. "Mima, it's really, really beautiful like yours, only different."

"Really?" Norma turned back toward Tess, looking curious, as if Jonah's innocent words made her think of something. She frowned, glanced up at the angel, then frowned again. "Was it your mother's?"

Auntie had said Norma was younger. Perhaps she didn't remember the angels as a trio? "Yes. Aunt Dora said there were three of them, given to three little girls on a plane."

Norma made a face. "I was small. So small. I remember nothing of the time before, although your mother tried to make me remember." She shrugged. "When she wouldn't let things go, my parents stopped going back and forth with your grandparents. I remember being sad that we couldn't play together, but kind of glad that Stella wasn't scolding me all the time."

Tess understood the truth in that.

"Mine is the seraph," Norma indicated the angel statue, sitting proudly on the sideboard, overlooking the wooden crèche. "The masterful wings tell us that."

"And mine is an archangel."

"Leaving the cherub." Norma looked suddenly thoughtful. "Has your Aunt Dora seen the angel?"

"Yes. She told me the story of the soldier and three little girls, taken from their homes and brought here."

"All of which meant nothing to me. Stella was two years older, and Dora another year more. When you're little, those years can make a big difference. Dora and I, well… we adjusted. But when we moved on, your mother, well…"

She didn't have to finish the observation. Tess had lived her mother's idiosyncrasies. "Stayed kind of frozen in time."

"Yes." Norma reached out and touched the angel. "She never forgave and never forgot anything. And that's a long, lonely way to live a life."

It was. Tess was determined to keep herself clear of a similar fate.

"Gotta go." Jake came in from starting the car. "One of us has to work tomorrow."

"Two of us," Norma reminded him, smiling, but she glanced back at the angel once more. "And Tess, you don't mind watching the boys? Usually I take them on Black Friday, but overtime shifts are a wonderful thing."

"Watching them is way better than watching paint dry." Tess rumpled Jonah's curls. "Thank you for a wonderful day, Norma."

"Thank you, Mima!"

"I love you, Mima!"

"I love you more, now go, get into your father's warm car and be so good, all right?"

"We will!"

The quiet ride back to town gave Tess time to mull the day. Warmth, love, family, food, friends and discipline. Spending the day with Jake's family was like living in a greeting card commercial. How often had she peeked out her window at the neighbor's lighted homes, wondering if there was truth in the shows, the movies, the commercials? Lack of joy had forged a hard road for a long time. She'd lost herself in the wonder of stories, the ones she made up and the ones she read. The library at school became her best friend, and when the staff there realized she had no access to the public library, they relaxed the rules and let her bring more books home.

She'd lived in those books, determined that someday, somehow, she'd recreate a normal life for herself and Dee.

Her phone buzzed a text. She pulled it out and checked it quickly. Every holiday, she hoped and prayed Dee would answer her texts, and every holiday, without fail, the phone stayed empty.

The text wasn't from Dee, it was from one of her medical partners, wishing her a great day. Praying for her.

"Bad news?" Jake kept his voice soft. The boys were tired, and keeping things low-key on the drive home was probably a smart idea.

"No. Just... no news." She flashed him a wry smile. "I always hope Dee will call."

"And she doesn't."

"No. A part of me wants to respect her privacy, but another part wants my sister back."

"We pray for healing, then."

"And forgiveness."

"What could she possibly need to forgive you for, Tess?"

"I don't think it's me." She stared out the side window. "I think she just has a hard time forgiving family for not stepping in. Not making a difference."

"Could they have made a difference? Or just made things worse?"

This was a problem she'd examined from multiple angles, and each time, she came up with the same answer. "I have no idea. It could have gone from bad to worse, but we'll never know because no one tried."

They got the boys home, got them into bed and Tess yawned, then laughed. "I have never been so totally exhausted in my life, including med school and maybe including residency and double shifts. But I've also never been happier, so that's a win."

He helped her slip her coat back on. "Do you really have to go?"

"Yes. Before I fall asleep, sitting on that sofa and give the neighbors ammunition for gossip."

"We can't have that," he whispered. He pointed to a small stack of boxes. "The boys were hoping you could help us decorate for Christmas this weekend. Are you up for that or am I taking advantage of a wonderful thing by putting you to work?"

"I'd love it!" She would, too. "I've never had the chance to get ready for Christmas with kids, so this is awesome."

He slung an arm around her as he walked her to the door. "How'd you get so good with kids, Tess? I know you've got a family practice, but that's a whole different thing. How'd you get so good at knowing kids, when you were never around them?"

"Books."

He made a face. "Parenting books?"

She laughed softly and shook her head. "Story books. Books about families. Childhood favorites, then sweet romances with happy ever afters. The mothers in those stories always seemed to know their way around kids. It might sound lame, but I copied their common sense."

"That's not lame. It's brilliant."

"Well. Thank you."

"You're welcome." Firelight from the gas fireplace flickered behind him. Quiet air filled the night, unusual for Jake's house. A fun-filled, crazy day, a peaceful night. Greeting card perfect. And when Jake drew her close, and ended a wonderful day with a perfect kiss, Tess was pretty sure she'd found her dream come true, in the place she'd least expected. Ashton, Pennsylvania, in Jake Karralis's arms.

CHAPTER EIGHT

TESS WAS ON A SATURDAY mission to buy twinkle lights. It seemed odd to doll up a house no one would really live in before it sold, but the Realtor had talked about staging, and what better way to stage a holiday showing than with festive lights? Planning it, and following through on the thought seemed right, as if by making the house seem more home-like, she was laying the specters of the past to rest.

She drove into the two-block business district, parked and walked the half-block to Jim Gordon's hardware store. For once her old childhood home was going to look at least a little festive for the holidays. She picked up a hand basket, spotted the holiday display, and headed that way. It might seem foolish to others. She'd be gone in a few weeks, the house would sell, and this was a waste of money, and Tess never wasted money. But the thought of seeing the uncluttered old colonial looking cheerful grabbed hold of her. She was going to help Jake and the boys put up their Christmas decorations. Her heart danced with excitement at the prospect, and despite her stern, internal warning, a spark of hope kindled within.

She loved being with Jake and the boys. And when she was with them, nothing seemed impossible. She felt… invincible. Silly, yes. But true.

She'd help them decorate, then ask them to help with hers. The very thought made her almost giddy, a ridiculously sweet emotion she'd never expected on her drive north from Philly almost two weeks ago. She got to the corner display and took a minute to examine her choices. Colored lights, white lights, blue lights, LED lights… And all kinds of fasteners to affix them to the house and the windows. Kids would like colored lights best, and she wanted the boys to smile every time they looked at her house. She reached out to fill her basket with hundred-count strings of merriness, when a voice stopped her cold. Real cold.

"Oh my gosh. Can you believe it, Mandy? It's—," the old familiar voice paused just long enough for Tess to fill in the blank with the word "Fat". "Terri Whatever-her-name-is, from high school."

"It can't be." Mandy Chatterton didn't feign surprise as Tess looked up. She stood off to Tess's right and stared in cruel disbelief, then said softly, "Well. Half of her, anyway."

"Isn't that the truth?" Christina raked Tess a cool, long look from the only other escape route to her left. "I heard you were back in town, but if someone hadn't told me, I'd have never guessed."

"It's like that fairy tale story," Mandy added, as if she wasn't already mean enough. "The one with the ducks and the big bird egg that finally ended up looking like something."

"It just took way longer than most," Christina added. She looked smug, self-righteous and snotty at once , a remarkable combination, all told.

Tess wanted to punch her. Punch them both. Mental red flags didn't pop up in her brain, they sprang up, waving in agitation.

Therapy had taught her to recognize triggers and defuse them.

But this was ten times worse than her first reckoning with Jake. Then she'd had a way out. Right now she was trapped in the corner of the local hardware store, next to a twinkle light display.

She wanted to run. She longed to run.

But there'd be plenty of time for that later, so she sucked in a quiet breath, thought about her choices… discounted a couple as jail-worthy, and faked a smile. "It was a fable, not a fairy tale, Mandy. Fables were designed to teach morals. Sadly, not everyone takes that premise to heart. I find it quite interesting to see that the two of you haven't changed a bit." She made a face of happy surprise, an obvious pretense, but figured the subtlety would most likely be lost on them. Her heart jumped in her chest, an answer to the adrenaline rush, but they'd never know what their cruel words and tone did to her. "And it's *Doctor* Cosgrove, girls." She stressed the title intentionally. "Luckily, not all of us stay trapped in high school for fifteen long, non-productive years, wearing jeans that saw their best days sometime in the previous decade." She should have resisted that last, little dig, but she didn't because they were brats, they put her in 'fight' mode, and their jeans were ridiculously tight and ugly.

She pushed her way through their little blockade, past a con-cerned-looking middle-aged woman, set the basket down and left the store.

She didn't run.

She gave herself extra points for that.

But she wanted to, which meant she wasn't nearly as healed and healthy as she made out.

She went through the motions of helping Jake that day. She tried to find joy in the boys' antics, in Jake's long, warm looks, Christmas music on the radio and the pressure of his hand when he held hers.

She couldn't, though. Not anymore. Too much of her lay wasted in Ashton. Yes, it was a beautiful little town, tucked at the edge of a valley, shaded by Pennsylvania hills. But she couldn't just be Dr. Cosgrove here. She saw that clearly this morning. Here she would always be Fat Terri in the eyes of some, and even one was too many.

She sent the Realtor an e-mail, asking her to list the house as soon as the flooring was complete. She didn't care if there was better staging to be done, or things to be arranged. She had the money to hire professionals, and that's exactly what she'd done.

She climbed into her car early Sunday morning, drove back to Philly and went to her own church. No cute little boys grabbed her hands or tugged her attention, and she missed the wonder of that, but staying whole and healthy had been her goal for a dozen years. Being in Ashton… even with Jake and his family around… showed her how tenuous a hold that could be.

Tess was gone.

He read the scribbled note again while his heart pinched tight in his chest.

"Jake, had to return to Philly quicker than expected, sorry to rush off. Kiss the boys for me, and have a very merry Christmas! Tess"

Just that. Nothing more.

He took the boys to church, and couldn't keep his mind on the service. Having Tess around had been more than fun. Her presence had been healing, and he didn't even know he needed healing until she strolled up his sidewalk with her kindness and common sense.

He tried calling her that afternoon, but the call went to voice mail. He texted her, then waited. Surely she'd text him back.

She didn't.

He stared at the phone, then the Christmas lights brightening the family room and the front windows. He couldn't cross the kitchen without facing the cool Christmas pictures the boys made. She'd made paper "frames" for their drawings and hung them on the wall. He would have never thought of that finishing touch. She did, and the boys loved it. And when they asked about her during half-time of the early game, what could he tell them but the truth? "Tess isn't across the street anymore, fellas. She had to go back to Philadelphia real quick."

Ben frowned. "I don't know where that is."

"Me, either." Jonah stared across the street, then swallowed. "Tess isn't going to live there anymore?" His eyes looked sad. His whole face looked bereft as he gazed out the front window. A dusting of snow covered the grass. It would melt by tomorrow according to the forecast, but right now the Sunday chill painted a pretty winter landscape in the old neighborhood. "I thought she liked living near us."

A hard lump formed in Jake's throat, because he thought that, too. It was silly of him. He'd witnessed the emotional insecurities she dealt with. He'd been hesitant for that very reason. And then he'd gone ahead and fallen for her in the couple of weeks she'd been around.

"I miss her a lot." Ben slid his hand into his father's. He didn't stare at Tess's house. He averted his gaze as if it was too painful to look. "Can I write her a letter?"

Jake smiled, but it wasn't a happy smile. "Bud, you kind of have to know how to write to do that, don't you?"

"Well, we can make pictures." Jonah met Ben's gaze. "You and me are really good picture draw-ers. Tess said so!"

"She did." Ben nodded. "We can do that, right, Dad? And we can sign our names and then she'll know it's us, and we're missing her so much."

"And maybe she'll come back to see us sometime."

Jonah's whispered hope broke Jake's heart. This is why he didn't date, and didn't bother with relationships. It wasn't just his heart involved anymore. It was theirs, and their well-being was more important than anything. He almost said no, wanting to cut ties instantly. A sharp wound heals better than a jagged one, he'd read that somewhere, but then he thought of what Tess would do.

She'd say the boys needed closure. A chance to transition themselves from one scene to the next, and she'd be right. "I'll help you get the art stuff out." The Eagles were playing a late game on the West Coast. He'd pictured them all there after church, cozied up with a pot of chili and hours of football.

He didn't want to bother with chili, so he baked chicken nuggets for the boys, handed them each a banana, and watched as they created five-year-old art for their long, lost friend.

He mailed the pictures the following day. He didn't have her home address, so he mailed the thick envelope to her medical office.

He called again on Monday evening. Maybe she hadn't gotten his texts. Maybe her phone had messed up.

No answer, again.

He shoved it aside, shoved it all aside. He went to the boys' Christmas play with his mother the following week, and refused to think of how nice it would have been to have Tess there, by his side. His bad, for letting her creep into his heart in such a short time. He got things ready for a simple Christmas with his boys and his church, trying to stay focused on the beauty of a faith-filled holiday, but every time he glanced north, the dark, empty windows of Tess's childhood home stared at him, and darned if their emptiness didn't make him feel like the guilty one. That was ridiculous, of course.

But that's exactly how he felt, every time his glance strayed that way.

Tess cut her leave from work short. Her Ashton Realtor oversaw the last of the painting and the new carpet installation, then listed the house at a competitive price. Soon it would be a done deal. That should have made her happy. She wanted it done, nothing lingering, nothing pulling at her, tugging her back to foolish thoughts and dreams. She went back to work because she needed to keep busy or go crazy. Work seemed like the better solution.

"Tess, this came for you while you were out." Carolyn Sanders handed her a large, padded envelope. "I was going to drop it by your condo when you came back, but since you're here, you saved me the time. Now I'll just stop by and watch crazy romantic Christmas movies with you."

Jake's return address stared her in the face.

Jake's scribbled writing addressed the envelope.

Emotions rose up from somewhere around her toes. "When did this come?"

"Over a week ago. I didn't realize you'd come back that quickly, mostly because you didn't tell anyone."

"Sorry." She held the envelope in two hands, studying it.

"Most people open envelopes, darling. You know, that little zip strip along the back?"

She flushed, and tucked the envelope under her arm. "Later. We don't want to get backed up first thing in the morning with cold and flu season on us."

"True enough." But Carolyn looked at her closely, then sighed. "You go tuck that away and we'll talk soon."

Carolyn meant well, and she was a good friend, but Tess didn't want to talk. Talking about Jake and the boys made the loss more real. She'd had enough 'real' in that stupid hardware store encounter. That glimpse of reality showed the thinness of her façade— no pun intended.

And when Carolyn came by on Friday night with stuff for a salad, she didn't push for information. She turned on a Christmas movie they'd seen before, tossed the salad and noticed the angel on Tess's faux mantel. "What's this?" She picked the angel up, studied it, and smiled. "That's so pretty, Tess. Where'd you get it?"

Tess recounted the story of the angel drop off, then mentioned Norma's.

"So you guys have two of the three?"

"Well." Tess shrugged. "We've got two, and there were three in a set, but who's to say if they're even from the same set?"

"Right." Carolyn deadpanned a look in her direction. "The likelihood that there are multiple sets of rare angels being handed around a small town like Ashton makes more sense than assuming they're from the same original set."

Put that way, it was a silly thing to consider.

"Well, let's see if we can dig up a little more info." Carolyn took a couple of shots of the angel, clicked into social media on her phone, and posted the pics under the banner "Looking For Third Angel, Ashton PA".

"Did you seriously just do that?" Tess rinsed the dishes and shook her head. She'd stayed away from social media purposely, except for her medical practice presence. Too many people, too many possible blasts from a past she'd like to keep shelved.

"I did, and it's on my personal page, and my friends will share it. You don't have to worry about a thing. Except whatever it is you're worried about that you're trying so hard to hide, Tess."

"You know me well."

Caro's look of sympathy agreed.

"Well enough to know some things aren't worth talking about. Sometimes it's just better to shrug things off and move on."

"It can be." Carolyn held the angel, thoughtful. "But that's not always the case, Tess, and if you need to talk… I'm here. Always. And I'm covering for Tina at the front desk tomorrow morning, so I'm calling it a night." She hugged Tess. "I'm glad you're back, but I'm sorry you had to do all that stuff back in Ashton on your own. I wish—"

Tess knew what Carolyn meant. They'd both hoped Dee would contact her. Offer to help or at least break the code of silence.

"It's done. That's the main thing. Now we can both move on."

"Yes."

Carolyn left, and Tess turned toward the angel.

Maybe she should sell it. She could donate the money to a good cause, and that would sever one more tie to a past she thought she'd dealt with. Facing those two spiteful women showed her otherwise. She may have shelved the past and moved on, but constant reminders would never be good. Facing their animosity could wear her down like water along a creek bank. She couldn't afford to put herself in that kind of situation. It was good to recognize her frailties.

She lifted the angel. The glossed paint glowed in pastel shades, as if lit from within. So pretty, so special. Maybe she'd send it to Jake's mom after a while. That way the two angels would be together, overseeing the quaint Christmas traditions in Norma's humble, kindly home.

She wasn't sure when the tears started, but they lasted a good, long time. Tears for foiled chances, old losses, and spoiled beginnings. She was tempted to put the angel away, out of sight, out of mind, but that didn't seem fair to the angel. And it was Christmas time, after all.

She sighed, decided she probably *was* going crazy, set the angel back on the mantel and went to bed. Viruses ran amok this time of year. She'd be busy the next few weeks, too busy to think a lot and that would suit her just fine.

Bill Crenshaw had purposely padded Jake's professional complex proposal, raising the profit margin significantly, while doing nothing for the client.

Jake examined the draft in disbelief. Yes, the client could afford the changes, that wasn't the point. The point was honesty and integrity. How long could a business go on adding layers to the bills before someone caught on and went elsewhere? When had ethics become obsolete? Bill strolled into his office just then. "I made a few changes, as you can see."

Jake saw all right. "This raises their cost considerably."

"Life's expensive these days." Bill shrugged as if none of it mattered, but it did. It mattered a lot. "And Nottingham Properties can absorb the difference. They're flush."

"They're flush because they're not afraid to examine the bottom line of everything they do, and they appreciate being treated with similar courtesy." Jake met Bill's gaze. "Are we in such dire straits that we need to do this?"

"We're stupid not to do that," Bill answered. "It's not about bringing everything in at the lowest cost. We already have the job. It's about doing the best job to be able to show off what we've done and gain more jobs when potential clients see it."

Jake understood the concept of good work bringing in more work, but he knew a pad job when he saw it, and the nearly sixteen percent increase in costs was shady. Was Bill getting a kickback from the contractor?

Most likely, and the thought of that churned Jake's stomach.

"Make sure you pretty that up." Bill indicated the marked up proposal with a quick wave of his hand. "And have it to me by the twenty-third. You do a good job here, Jake, and your end-of-year bonus will reflect that."

He was being bought off. He knew it. Crenshaw knew it. Whatever was going on behind the scenes, he was expected to play along. "You'll have it, Bill."

"Good." Crenshaw left the room, whistling softly.

Jake looked down at the proposal he'd put together with razor-sharp precision. Such a beautiful new complex, well-proportioned and inviting, slated for a Philadelphia suburb. Retail storefronts mixed with professional offices, a fun mesh interspersed with garden-terraced parking and outdoor seating for nice weather lunches and dinners.

His phone reminded him to leave. He had to grab a new timer for the outside lights, and he'd have just enough time to swing by the hardware store before picking up the boys at wrap-around care. They weren't one bit happy staying at school these past couple of weeks, but there was no time to interview nannies right now, and with Tess gone, his option for short term care had gone with her. He drove through the town, parked in the municipal lot, and crossed the street to the hardware store.

Twinkle lights wrapped every lamppost lining Main Street. Lighted wreaths hung off the ends, while more lights looped through the deciduous trees lining the road. A light snow accentuated the snow-globe feeling. Crossing the road, Ashton's visual was the unspoiled portrayal of waiting for Christmas. The sweet town, the beautiful layout, the pristine snow. Picture perfect.

He strode into the hardware store, found the holiday display, picked out a timer and moved toward the check-out area.

"Jake." Gladys Gordon smiled wide as he approached. "So good to see you, and weren't those boys of yours precious in that Christmas pageant last week?"

"They were. And your little granddaughter made a very good sheep."

"She did, didn't she?" Gladys laughed softly, then frowned as her husband finished a transaction at the back of the store. "And then there's some that never see the good in anything around them."

Jake followed the direction of her gaze as Mandy Chatterton

exited through the back door.

"I don't speak ill often, Jake."

She never had in Jake's presence, so he figured she was probably being upfront.

"But that woman and her wretched little friend sure did a number on your neighbor a few weeks back. Oh, she handled it all right, I'd a probably burst into tears the way they ragged on her, but why folks think it's okay to be mean, I'll never know."

Jake frowned, perplexed. "Gladys, I have no idea what you're talking about."

"The Cosgrove girl, the one that leaned toward weight back in the day."

"Tess?"

"Teresa, yes. Such a nice girl, always polite and kind the few times I ran into her."

"Mandy was mean to Tess? Recently?"

She peered at him over her rimless glasses, as if wondering why he wasn't getting the gist of her conversation. "Two weeks back, on a real busy Saturday. Calling her fat, making fun of how she used to be. I regret to this day not stepping in and saying something, because I should have. God would have wanted me too, and I didn't. Every time I see Mandy and Christina now I get so mad I could spit, and it's as much my fault as theirs for not speaking up for her. I'm ashamed of myself for not acting faster. Folks like that put a bad mark on a real nice town."

Emotional fragility.

He'd witnessed it in Tess. It had raised some questions, but more than that, it made him long to look after her, while she was looking after him. Realization broadsided him. Tess hadn't run from him and the boys.

She'd run from a mean-girl attack in a local store.

He lifted his eyes to the picturesque view outside the twinkle-trimmed window. Currier and Ives-style beauty lay before him, but a town was more than a two-dimensional postcard print. A town was the three-dimensional grace of people looking after people. Being kind and neighborly. Doing their best.

Bill Crenshaw had been his first wake-up call of the day with his blatant disregard for another business's solvency, and now this— a frontal attack on a wonderful woman of substance, a woman who'd gone the distance to make herself whole and healthy.

"Here's your card back, and thanks for stopping in here, Jake. I know the big stores have all this stuff, too, and Jim and I sure do appreciate your business."

"Thank you, Gladys. And I don't need a bag, this is fine." He picked up the timer. "Merry Christmas."

"To you, too, Jake! And those boys!"

Jake's heart took on renewed spirit as he picked up the boys. He took them home, made grilled cheese sandwiches and hot chocolate, and tucked them into bed with a lighter heart. He'd spent two weeks grumbling internally, and now...

Oh, now...

New choices lay before him. He pulled up his resume on his laptop, updated it, then sent it to a job recruiter. By the time he got to bed it was late, real late, but he didn't care. He'd made a bold, positive step toward fixing things he'd slapped bandages on for too long.

On Wednesday, he sent Tess flowers to her office. He heard nothing, but he didn't care.

On Thursday, he had a box of chocolates delivered the same way, with just three simple words: *Thinking of you...*

On Friday he sent four passes to the Winterfest ice rink and lodge, with one short note. "We're taking the boys skating on Sunday, we'll pick you up at eleven AM... No regrets allowed. Ever again. Jake."

He was taking a risk, a big risk, involving the boys, but life was full of risks. He'd discovered that the hardest way possible when he lost his beloved wife. He didn't know what the future would be with Tess, but he understood what the future *could be* with a woman like Tess... and that upped the game plan exponentially. Taking risk for that kind of gain made perfect sense. Now if he could convince the woman in question.

CHAPTER NINE

THE GORGEOUS BOUQUET OF FLOWERS got the entire office talking and speculating about Tess's secret romance, which meant she might have to kill Jake Karralis. She'd been fine, perfectly f-i-n-e, moseying along her quiet existence until he stepped into the picture, and now here he was, stepping back into the picture as if he belonged there.

And oh, how she wished he did!

The chocolates raised Jake's status in the office to Favorite Person of the Year.

And when the packet of passes arrived, Tess had no choice. She had to call and warn him off. She couldn't avoid it this time, because he was involving the boys, and how could she shrug him off with those precious boys around? She sent him a quick text: "Sunday impossible."

Would he text her back or turn the tables and ignore her text like she'd done to him? She didn't have long to wait, because a return text came right back. "With God, anything is possible."

She stared at the text. Her fingers itched to zing something back to him, something disputing his words, but how could she when he was right?

Her heart buzzed. Her throat went tight. She'd gone off the deep end in classic neurotic style by running away when those women surrounded her. They'd hit her triggers with point-blank aim, and she'd reacted in full self-preservation mode.

Now, with a few weeks of distance, clarity reigned. She'd never given Jake a chance to help. Or a choice to help. She'd run, fast and furious, a cowardly reaction.

Now she had another chance. Another choice.

With God all things are possible.

She knew that. She believed it. And so she tapped out a short, to-the-point message. "Sunday. 11:00 AM. Yes."

His reply was instantaneous and made her smile. "Good thing because we weren't taking 'no' for an answer. See you then."

In less than forty-eight hours she'd see him. She'd see those boys, and they'd wonder why she ran off, out of their lives. She'd explain it, somehow, in terms they could understand.

Adrenaline made her pulse beat stronger. Excitement put a silly smile on her face, and she found herself humming off and on for the rest of the day at work. Silly, maybe.

But in less than two days she'd see Jake and the boys for an entire afternoon, and that was worth being silly for.

"Tess!"

"Tess! We missed you so much, and we sent you pictures. Did you get them?"

"Mine was the one with the biggest Christmas tree I could make," Jonah bragged. He raced up the walk alongside his brother, grabbed hold of her middle and hugged her tight.

"And mine had so many lights, I couldn't fit them all on!" Ben had his arms wrapped around her from the other side, so when Jake strolled to a stop before her, she couldn't move. And when he leaned in and feathered her mouth with the sweetest kiss ever, she melted inside. Totally. Lovingly. Completely.

"Missed you." He touched his forehead to hers, and the whisper only made a beautiful start more special. "Every day, every moment, every hour."

"Me, too."

He smiled then, laid his big, brawny hand against her cheek and left it there. "Good. Go grab your stuff, adventure awaits."

"I've never skated." She made a face. "But I can't wait to try."

"That's the spirit."

The boys tumbled into the condo and spotted their pictures first thing.

"Tess, you hung up our pictures!"

"And you put them in those wooden things!"

"Frames," she explained and squatted to their level. "Because I wanted to keep them nice, always, so every time I look at them, I think of you."

"But if you just looked at us all the time," Ben faced her with a reasonable question and a slight frown, "wouldn't that be even better?"

She hugged him, and then Jonah, together, because seeing them all the time would be two hundred percent better. "Way better." She tipped her gaze up to their grinning father. "Did you coach them to say that?"

"Didn't have to. I think they fell in love with you that first day, when you rescued them from possible kidnabbers."

"I knew they were smart boys."

"And faster than their dad," he supposed. He reached down a hand to help her stand back up, and when she did, he twirled her in close. Real close. "It took me at least a week, Tess."

"Jake."

He winked, bumped foreheads with her and stepped back. "We've got all day to talk. Let's get these guys to the rink."

"Okay."

They skated. They drank hot chocolate and ate really good food, a surprise for a pop-up tent neighborhood and a riverside rink. They showed the boys Penn's Landing, but it was too cold to do too much sight-seeing. And when they finally got back to Tess's condo, she hated to see the marvelous afternoon come to an end.

"Do you have a kids' movie channel?" Jake asked as he moved a dining room chair over to the furnace vent on the near wall. He hung the boys cold jackets there to dry before the sixty-minute drive home. "That way we can distract the rug rats for a few minutes."

She pulled up a Christmas movie with her remote, and settled the boys in with a bag of microwaved popcorn. When Jake took her hand and led her into the kitchen/dining area overlooking the Schuylkill River, she knew the moment of reckoning had come. He'd ask why she ran off, and she'd have to reveal her hyper-sensitivity, aka: deep-seated neurosis. Then he'd head for the nearest exit, understandably. She took a deep breath, ready to explain, but Jake's first words swept the plate clean. "The next time there's a blast from the past that sends you running, Tess?" He cradled her cheeks between his two beautiful hands and held her gaze. "Run *to* me. Not away. Okay?"

She swallowed hard.

The look in his eyes… that look… of love, of devotion, of promises she'd never in the world hoped for… aimed at her. "How did you know?"

"Mrs. Gordon filled me in. She was ashamed she didn't step in and say something. She felt bad. But she said you handled it well, considering. But then you ran." He leaned in and kissed her, long and slow, the kind of kiss a girl could grow old loving and never, ever get enough of. "Please don't do that, Tess, darling. Ever again. Okay?"

Okay? It was way more than okay, it was over-the-top, to-die-for marvelous. "I wasn't running from you. Or from them, not really," she explained, and then she shrugged. "But I realized I couldn't handle a steady onslaught of that kind of thing, running into people who knew my mother was unstable, who knew my life was whacked. I knew I couldn't choose that purposely, Jake. And Ashton is your home. Your town. Your livelihood." She winced. "It all seemed so impossible at the moment."

"Well, the moment's a thing of the past, and I think the prospects for my future look a whole lot rosier if I join a Philadelphia area development firm."

Did she hear him right? Was he talking about changing things up? For her?

"I've put out my resume with a recruiter and there are already three interviews lined up for the week between Christmas and New Year's." He looked calm and confident. "The recruiter assured me no one does interviews then, which means she's expecting offers because they don't want to risk losing me."

"Jake, really? But what about the boys? And your mother, your family?" Engaged in the antics of Dr. Seuss's grumpy creation and the Who's of Whoville, the boys didn't appear to have a care in the world.

Jake smiled in the boys' direction. "They're five. I think they've got some flexibility left. And if we find a place to live midway between Philly and Ashton, then we're thirty minutes from work and thirty minutes from family. In the grand scheme of things, thirty minutes is nothing, and there's a dozen nice areas that have great neighborhoods for fun young couples." He kissed her cheek. "And a couple of kids." He kissed her other cheek. "And whoever else God sends our way."

The thought of being with Jake and the boys, the chance at building a family of their own in a nice, normal neighborhood, filled her with the sweetest anticipation. "Don't tease me, Jake." She pulled back and gave him her most serious look. "I've always wanted a happily ever after, the happy ending that seemed so real in movies. And I'd love," she glanced back at the two boys, mouths rounded with wonder as the Grinch directed poor little Max to pull the sleigh up Mount Crumpit, "to help raise these two in a neighborhood with other kids, some old trees, some new friends and whatever else happens along."

He laughed down at her, picked her up and twirled her around. "Well, they've been asking for a dog, but maybe a brother or sister would do."

"Or both." She reached up and kissed him thoroughly. "I've never skated before, I've never had a pet, and I've never been a mom, but I'm open to the idea of trying new things, Jake." She leaned back against his arms and smiled, fairly crazy with love. "As long as I try them with you."

"I'm in total agreement, Tess." He kissed her once more as the credits rolled across the big screen. "I've got to get these guys home. What's your Christmas schedule look like?"

"I'm off Christmas Eve and Christmas Day."

"Will you come up to Ashton long enough to spend it with us? Or if you want us to come here, that's fine, too, Tess. As long as we spend it together."

"I'd love that. And I'll come there," she told him as he gathered the boys' coats. "The boys should have the holidays at home, and at Mima's house."

"All right. Christmas Eve Mass, then dinner, and Christmas at Mima's."

"Perfect."

He tossed the boys their jackets, ignored their tired grumblings and hugged her one last time. "See you Wednesday."

"Okay. Jake?"

He'd started down the steps, but turned quickly, looking crazy handsome and endearingly hopeful. "Yes?"

"I—" She hesitated, then sighed softly. "I love you, Jake Karralis."

His face split into a wide grin. He moved back up the two steps and kissed her soundly. "I was being sensitive to your sensitivity and didn't want to push you too soon. Remind me to never do that again, okay?"

She smiled against his mouth and his chin, covered with five o'clock stubble. "Okay."

"I love you, too. And I think God put you there, across the street, or he put me there, when I bought Aunt J.'s house. In any case, I think this," he motioned between them, "was meant to be. And I've learned to never, ever argue with God." He sprinkled a few last, light kisses to her cheeks, her hair. "Wednesday seems like a long way away."

"Dad! I thought we were going!"

"Dad! Are we staying here?"

"Go." She gave him a little shove toward his boys… his beautiful, wonderful boys. "And thanks for not giving up on me, Jake."

He headed toward the car but his single word answer floated back on the wind. "Never."

EPILOGUE

"THIS WAS THE BEST CHRISTMAS ever."

Jake sighed against her hair. "It was. Are you as tired as I am?"

"More because I was crazy excited every single step of the way."

"You were." He laughed softly. "It was fun to watch, like having three kids believe in Santa."

"Today? I do believe." She'd had her head tucked between his shoulder and his chest. Now she leaned away to look up at him. "I am a true believer in all things good."

"Me, too."

Her phone jangled on the end table. She frowned up at him, then the phone. "Who calls on Christmas night?"

"Emergency, maybe?"

"Maybe," but as she reached for the phone, another thought struck her: Dee. She scrambled across the sofa, grabbed up the phone and saw the readout. Her fingers fumbled as she swept the phone's face to answer the call. "Dee? Dee is that you? Merry Christmas!" Her heart raced, and she had to remind herself to keep her voice soft because the boys were in bed. "Oh, gosh, how are you, Dee Dee? I miss you so much."

"I'm good." Her sister's voice sounded hesitant and surprised. "I'm good," she said again, firmer this time. "And I miss you too, Terri."

Tess didn't correct her. There'd be plenty of time for that later, she hoped. "I'm so glad you called. Every holiday, every special time, I pray you'll call just so you know I love you." She flashed Jake a look of pure excitement mixed with high emotion. He rolled his eyes, teasing, got up and handed her a box of tissues. She swiped a couple to her face, and had to swallow hard. "That I'll always love you." The words broke in the middle, and it took several seconds to finish the phrase.

"Me, too." Dee's voice broke to match hers. "I want to come see you. *We* want to come see you," she corrected herself. "Matt wants to meet you. I'm off until the third week of January. Can we come to Philadelphia for New Year's? Would that be okay?"

"Okay?" She smiled through her tears and gave Jake a thumbs up. "That would be wonderful! Yes, absolutely. I can't wait to see you, Dee!"

"Me, either. And I'm sorry I was such a jerk and left you to do that stupid house. That was weak of me, and I shouldn't have done it. The minute I saw the angel that matched mine online, I realized you and I should always be together. That I was being stupid and over-sensitive."

"You saw the angel Carolyn posted? How?"

"A friend of a friend of a friend from back there. I have one a little different, I found it at a garage sale last year."

"In Chicago?"

"Joliet, actually, an old house," Dee explained. "The owner said he didn't recognize it, figured it was something of his late wife's, and it was just so pretty, sitting in the sunlight. I decided it was worth the two dollar price tag, and now... well, now, she's just become priceless. Because she brought us together."

"I'm stunned."

"Because of the angel?"

Tess thought hard. Real hard. Should she go into the explanation of how she got her angel? Or of Norma's angel? Maybe it wasn't even from the same collection and she'd just sound weird. With this first beautiful, wonderful phone call, she didn't want to take the chance on sounding weird and scare her sister off. Time enough to sound weird next Christmas! She laughed and said, "The phone call and the angel."

"Where are you now? Are you in Philadelphia?"

Tess smiled, sank onto the sofa beside the love of her life and said, "No. I'm in Ashton where I've fallen madly in love with Jake Karralis and his twin sons. You'll get to meet them next week, okay?"

"I can't wait. And I want to tell you before you see me… We're expecting."

A baby.

Her sister was expecting a baby.

Could this day possibly get better? Tess was sure it couldn't, and then Dee said, "I'd like for you to be her Godmother when she's baptized. Would you do that, Terri? Help me teach this baby all the good things in life?"

Would she? "Yes. Absolutely. I'd be honored. I'm only sorry we're so far apart, Dee."

"Well, here's the other thing. I've been offered a position at Haverford, a private college outside of Philly. I don't miss Ashton, but I miss Pennsylvania. The hills, the mountains, the trees. I miss the feel of it. I want to come home, Terri. Does that sound odd, considering?"

Tess had felt the exact same way, so she shook her head, unseen. "Not odd at all. It sounds wonderful. I would love that so much, Dee."

She heard her sister's breath of relief through the phone. "Good. Me, too. I've got to go, but I'll e-mail you our flight stuff, okay? And we'll book a hotel near you so we don't waste any time. I've already done enough of that."

"I can't wait. I love you, Dee. Merry Christmas!"

"Merry Christmas back!"

She hung up and turned toward Jake, swiping her eyes with fresh tissues. "She called."

He hugged her, hugged her tight. "I'm so glad."

"Me, too, but it wasn't my messages that made her call, Jake. It was the angel. Somehow, someway, Dee ended up with an angel similar to mine. She saw it on Carolyn's post and realized hers matched."

"The third angel?"

She shrugged. "Maybe. Is that even possible?"

"God works in ways mysterious."

He did. She'd believed that for years, unseen. And now…

"And suddenly there was with the angel a multitude of heavenly hosts…" Jake whispered. "Why wouldn't he spare one for you, darling Tess?" He kissed her, long and slow. "And while we're making all these nice plans for the future, I'd like to make a suggestion.

Actually, it's more of a question, Tess."

"Yes?" She pulled back, and when she spotted the tiny velvet box in his hand, she hugged him. "Yes!"

"I didn't get to ask the question."

"You don't have to. The answer is yes." She pulled back again. "Wait. That is a ring in that box, isn't it? Because if it isn't, I just embarrassed myself beyond belief."

"It is a beautiful ring for a beautiful woman." He withdrew an emerald ring surrounded by diamonds. "Tess Cosgrove, will you make me the happiest man in the world by becoming my wife?"

"Yes, again."

He laughed and slipped the ring onto her finger, then held her hand in his. "I love you, Tess. And I promise I'll be the best husband I can be with the possible exception of out-of-control fan behavior during football season."

"And I promise to make you behave, especially during football season, so the boys grow up knowing to be kind and good and keep things in perspective. Deal?"

He didn't bump knuckles with her. He kissed her instead, a beautiful, long,

DEAR READERS,

CHILDHOOD SCARS CAN GO MUCH further than "skin-deep". They can pierce the heart and the soul. In "Home to His Heart", Tess realizes her mother has psychological problems, but that doesn't lessen the impact of a really poor home environment, where things matter more than people, and one sister is pitted against the other. The ingrained sadness of that scenario could make history repeat itself, but Tess refuses to succumb to the darkness. She fights her way through, emerges triumphant, and then, when her happy ever after is on the horizon, she gets tested… and she chooses not to subject herself to toxic people.

Sometimes we forget that we hold the power in our hands and our hearts, that with faith in God, we can conquer anything.

Tess has battled so much in her life. At some point in time, we all want to lay down the armor and just draw water joyously. And that's a great goal!

Jake has deep regrets. He knew the heavy hand of a mean step-parent, so he bears his own scars, but Jake's aren't as deep as Tess's. He's willing to lead her into the fullness of life. That's a true hero. A man who sees the sensitivity of a scarred soul, and longs to cherish that soul anyway.

We face so many daily choices. If we can choose kindness and valor over meanness, we can make the world a better place. If we choose sacrificial love over self-serving indulgence, we can make ourselves better people. And that's the example Tess brings back to Ashton, the grace of sacrificial love to a family in need of just that!

THANK YOU FOR READING "HOME to His Heart"! I love to hear from readers, so feel free to e-mail me at *loganherne@ gmail.com,* visit my website *http://ruthloganherne.com* visit me on facebook where I love to chat and pray and swap stories, or stop by the Yankee Belle Café where we can talk kids, recipes, dogs, cats,

kittens, romance and God! God bless you, and may he hold you
most graciously in the palm of His hand!

For the Love of Sophie June

Ruth Logan Herne

CHAPTER ONE

JUST WHEN YOU THOUGHT THE day/week/month couldn't get worse…
Carrie Sullivan pulled her wreck of a car into the looped, farm-style driveway marked 17014 Lake Road. To her right stood a huge, unpretentious, sprawling gray barn. On her left was her late aunt's house, an inheritance from an old woman's kindly heart, a bequest that could be the new beginning she'd been praying for.

But when she spotted the stuffed-to-the-rafters back porch, she realized Aunt Elsa's lawyer hadn't exaggerated. Her aunt had spent decades piling up this and that, never throwing anything away. Now the task to undo those decades fell into her hands.

Thoughts of the crazy year she'd just endured swamped her. She was sorely tempted to pull right back out and keep on driving.

She didn't, of course, because snugged in an outdated, cast-off car seat was the dear little child she'd promised to love, raise and call her own for all time. And when Sophie June lifted big brown eyes to hers in the rear-view mirror and squealed, Carrie had little choice. She put the car into park turned off the ignition, and hopped out.

Sophie scrambled out of her booster seat, an expert at clasps at the ripe age of five. She dashed around the car, one eye tipped toward the sky. "It's going to rain, don't you think? We better get inside!"

Eyeing up the chock-full back porch on the aged and faded pink house, Carrie wasn't sure that inside was a better choice, but she found the key on her ring and put it in the back door as a clap of thunder followed a bright, jagged fork of lightning.

The key didn't appear to like the lock. Or vice versa. In any case, it wasn't working. She frowned and tried again, jiggling the door.

Nothing.

"Maybe that's the front door key," Sophie suggested.

"Could be. You stay right here, okay? The front is too close to that busy road and if I get in, I'll come through and open this door from the inside."

"Okay!"

Sophie's expression said trying to break into Great-aunt Elsa's house was an adventure. After traveling for nearly three days, proving to the town attorney who she was, and having nothing but a rattle of change in her pocket and keys to a house that might could make it onto a hoarders reality-TV show, Carrie was beyond the term adventure and headed straight for chaos. She dashed around the front of the house, prayed and inserted the key.

The quick click and easy turn made her heart beat easier, right until she tried to open the door. It went about six inches and stopped.

She put her shoulder to it and shoved, hard.

An inch. Maybe. If she was using a ruler and being generous.

She tried again, but whatever lay behind the door— hopefully nothing that may have breathed oxygen at one time—

Refused to give way.

Nothing moved with her pressure and the heavy wooden door didn't open far enough for her to reach a hand in and assess the situation by feel. Which might not have been the smartest thing to do, in any case.

The sizzle of lightning and the quick, reverberating crash of thunder said she needed to make a decision fast, but there was no decision. She had no money, no job, no credit and no way to stay anywhere else. It was here or… homeless.

The big gray barn stood back, behind the house. It was in good repair, and hey, if Jesus was born in a stable and laid in a manger, how bad could it be? She yanked the front door shut, fought the urge to say bad words, and raced back up the driveway.

Maybe she'd open the barn and find a 1963 Corvette in mint condition sitting inside. Red, of course, with leather seats.

She grabbed the smaller key, inserted it into the padlock and turned it. It took a few seconds, but the arm of the lock popped free and she slipped the lock off. Grabbing hold, she pulled the right-hand barn door toward her, hoping and praying nothing big, hairy and fast hustled out.

Sophie dashed up beside her as she tugged the door wide, and they stood together, looking inside as Carrie hit the light switch to her right.

There were no vintage cars inside the barn. In fact there wasn't much of anything inside the well-maintained, cavernous space. Lean-to styled sheds lined the south wall, and the eastern wall held three attractive horse stalls, all clean. On the front left, a curving staircase led up to the hayloft.

Only it wasn't a hayloft. From below, it was hard to tell exactly what was up there, but from the looks of it, the upper reaches of the barn had been finished off into rooms. "Stay here, honey. I'm going to check this out."

A gust of wind whooshed around the western edge of the barn. The sudden force jerked the door half-closed. Sophie screeched a little, then laughed at herself. "Oh, man. I thought the door was going to get me!"

"Doors don't get people unless they're silly enough to stand in doorways on windy days," Carrie called down to her. "So don't do that, okay?"

"I won't!" Sophie clutched her kitten-shaped purse in one hand and a small, soft ragdoll in the other. "Tell me when I can come up, okay?"

That all depended on what Carrie found at the top of the stairs. Another locked door? Most likely, and as she looked at the circular key ring, she eyed up the lock and the door handle. When the manufacturer names matched, she thanked God for modernization and thrust the key into the lock. The door swung open, and she found herself staring at a galley kitchen that stepped out of the sixties. A film of dust covered everything, but not forty-year-old dust.

Year-old dust, which meant that Aunt Elsa had kept this apartment swept and cleaned on a regular basis. But, why, if she lived in the pack-rat house up front?

"Mom? What's up there?"

A sweet, humble home, suitable to raise a child.

That's what she thought, but what she called out was, "Come

see! It's darling!"

Sophie scrambled up the stairs behind her and laughed when she walked into the quaint kitchen. "Oh, it's so nice!"

Regret speared Carrie because Sophie had lived the downside of not nice for too long. Maybe now… *perhaps this…* was their new beginning. Their trek upward and onward. "Let's see the rest." They walked forward together, and when Carrie reached out and hit a switch, the front room flooded with light. "Oh. Wow. This is awesome."

Old furniture outfitted the big, rectangle room, but six massive windows overlooked the back acreage Aunt Elsa sold off years ago according to the attorney. A hillside creek wandered down from higher elevations just east of them, and the tree line following the water cut a swath through the sloping farm field. Acres of alfalfa hay stretched toward the cloud-darkened sky. "That's a gorgeous view," Carrie whispered, half afraid that if she spoke too loudly, someone would hear her, rush up the stairs and tell them this was all a mistake and they'd need to leave the barn.

But the barn— and this apartment— were part of the property she inherited, and therefore hers.

Sophie plopped onto the couch and a puff of dust raised a small cloud into the air. "We need a vacuum cleaner and dust cloths, some cleaning solution, water and elbow grease," Carrie announced. "And then?" She turned, grabbed Sophie up and swung her around. "We've got a home, kid!"

"I love it! I love being way up high instead of down low where the snakes could get us."

Carrie cringed, and held back her celebratory dance because Sophie was right. She'd been so excited to buy her little house out west, so happy to be independent and building a life for her and Sophie. But then they realized they'd been swindled by the former owners, that the house was uninhabitable. They had no recourse but to renege on the mortgage.

She lost everything, including her credit rating and the hard-fought level of respectability she'd earned through years of effort and forward progress. Being thrust back to "start" when you were so close to the lollypop forest had been a rough reality.

And just when they might have become one of the uncountable homeless dotting city streets, the letter from Aunt Elsa's lawyer came, saying she'd left her home and all of her belongings to her two grand nieces, Carrie and Miranda Sullivan, a magnanimous gesture from a woman she'd never been allowed to meet.

"How soon can we start cleaning?" Sophie wondered. "Can we sleep here tonight?"

They had no other choice, so Carrie nodded, but then she paused, listening.

A voice—

A man's voice—

Was calling from down below.

Carrie didn't know a soul in this town. And no one knew she was here except for the nice lawyer that handed her the keys when she walked into his office earlier that afternoon. Concern danced up her spine, but as the voice grew louder she turned, offered Sophie a quick smile and said, "Stay here, honey. Let me go see who that is, okay?"

"But we don't know anyone here," Sophie offered sensibly. "So why would anyone come looking for us?"

Right now she wished the beautiful girl wasn't quite so smart. "That's what I'm going to find out. Stay here, okay?"

"Daisy and I will stay right here and make up stories about princesses in towers with long, long hair. Which is why I intend to grow my hair forever and ever. Okay?"

"Okay." Carrie blew her a kiss, opened the door, shut it behind her and wondered what was worse? Leaving Sophie in strange, new surroundings with potentially lethal things lurking behind cabinet doors or facing a potential stranger/killer/nice person on ground level?

Poison won, hands down. "Hello?" She walked to the door and stepped outside. The first rainstorm had passed, but the western sky said the summer day might stir up another. A police car sat in the driveway, lights flashing, engine running. She looked around just as a uniformed man came around the front corner of Aunt Elsa's house. "Can I help you, officer?"

"Deputy, ma'am." He walked forward and while he wasn't huge by any means, he walked huge and the glare from his badge said he was pretty darned official. Carrie forced a smile. She'd walked around the Midwest with no shadows dogging her steps, a respectable woman in a responsible position, a teacher, close to being tenured in a small, suburban Omaha school district.

And yet here was a deputy sheriff at her door her first day back in New York. The irony of that wasn't lost on Carrie.

"We had a report of suspicious activity and I wanted to swing by and check it out. Do you live here, ma'am?"

"I do, now." She carefully didn't make mention of Sophie. "This was my great-aunt's house, Elsa Thurgood. I inherited it after her passing and just picked up the keys this afternoon. I'm Caroline Sullivan."

"Welcome to Kirkwood Lake." His smile went wider, and his face relaxed. "Mrs. Thurgood was mighty nice to me when I was a kid and when I was grown, too. She was good to a lot of us in Kirkwood. We were sorry to lose her. I'm Deputy Seth Campbell."

"Nice to meet you," she told him and indicated the faded pink house with a glance. "I didn't know my aunt at all."

He looked surprised. "But she left you a house and a barn and everything inside? Mighty nice of her."

Carrie cringed and his left brow winged up. "Family stuff," he supposed wisely.

"She and my grandfather never got along, mostly his fault," Carrie explained. "He wasn't a nice guy. And he wouldn't let any of the family have anything to do with her. Once I grew up, it just stayed that way, which was stupid, so I feel guilty walking into all this."

"Things happen." He turned as a second sheriff's patrol pulled into the yard. The second deputy climbed out, strolled forward, and was about to greet her when he stopped and stared as if he knew her.

Which he didn't, of course.

But she'd faced this reaction whenever she'd visited Clearwater, the small city at the southern tip of Kirkwood Lake. She and her cousin had been mistaken for twins— or each other— before, they looked that much alike. And like most polar opposites, the people who thought she was Miranda weren't generally happy to see her again.

This was why she tried to stay away from Western New York. There weren't many places to go where someone didn't see her and make an assumption, and judging by this deputy's face, that assumption made her an undesirable character.

CHAPTER TWO

WADE PRESCOTT STARED AT THE face that had haunted him for almost six years.

Miranda Sullivan, a woman he thought he loved when he was younger and stupider. A woman who left him high and dry with never a word until the state of New York started garnishing his wages three months ago, saying he had failed to pay child support. When his lawyer notified the state that he had no children, the state corrected them with documents saying he'd fathered a little girl nearly six years before, and that various states had been paying benefits to the child's mother, Miranda Sullivan.

And here she was, standing in front of him, looking as if she'd never seen him before.

Anger and disgust vied for first place, but he was a cop, on a call, and duty would always come first. "What are you doing here, Miranda?"

She sighed as if the question was troublesome.

"Miranda?" The first deputy glanced from Wade to the woman, "You said your name was Caroline, miss."

"It is." She waved toward the barn. "My purse is inside with my identification. I'm Caroline Sullivan, this is my place now, and," she shifted her attention to Wade with a concerned expression. "Miranda was my cousin."

Wade shot her a look of disbelief. "I knew Miranda real well. I know who I'm talking to."

She shook her head. "A lot of people make that same mistake. But I'm not Miranda, I'm Caroline, I'm seven months younger than Miranda, and Miranda…" she breathed deep, and the compassion on her face was more sincere than anything he'd ever witnessed in his time with her six years before. "Died earlier this year when she went against medical advice and checked herself out of a rehab center down south. I haven't seen her in years."

Miranda was dead?

This woman wasn't her?

None of this added up, because the state had assured his attorney that they'd been making regular payments to Miranda for the care of Sophie June Sullivan, a child she claimed was his daughter. They sent copies of records dated through December of the previous year. But right now he had the upper hand because whoever this was didn't have all the facts. Or lied well, and if it *was* Miranda?

She lied quite well. "The resemblance is startling."

"I know." The woman shrugged. "It created numerous problems growing up. My cousin didn't exactly live a pristine lifestyle."

"No?"

A slight noise sounded behind her and she took a step back. The look of concern etched deeper lines into her forehead. "Gentlemen, I've got a ton of stuff to do before I can settle in for the night. I'm sure you understand."

Another slight noise pulled Wade's attention toward the barn, and the woman's reaction to the noise, as if wanting to mask it, tweaked his suspicions. He took a step toward the barn, to see what she would do.

She stepped left, blocking his way.

"Mom?" A childish hushed whisper came from the barn. "Can I come down now?"

Chagrin marked the woman's face, then she turned slightly and nodded. "Come here, Sophie. You can meet the policemen."

Sophie.

Wade stopped breathing as the little girl emerged from the shadows. She didn't creep out, shy and afraid. She bounded, curls bouncing, dark brown eyes—

His eyes—

Bright and shining.

She skipped to the woman's side, a tattered rag doll clutched in one hand, while she grasped the woman's hand with the other, then looked up at them, grinning. "Hi! I'm Sophie and this is Daisy." She held up the faded doll and sighed, delighted with life.

"And this is my mom and this is our new house."

And this is my mom…

Wade swallowed hard at the innocent proof of the not-so-innocent woman before him.

Sophie June. The child Miranda claimed was his, and judging from the little girl's face and hair, Miranda had spoken truth about that.

The woman in front of him watched him with caution.

She claimed she wasn't Miranda, and sure, there were slight differences he'd noted while studying her, but six years could account for that. And Miranda had always been a great actress. He'd found that out too late, his fault for trusting too soon, and taking the relationship too far. "How old are you, Sophie?"

She held up five proud fingers but explained, "But I'm really almost six. My birthday comes in October, when the leaves all turn color."

Wade had no trouble doing the math. Miranda had walked out on him in February and had a child eight months later. The math and the resemblance added up. "That's a great time for birthdays. Pumpkins, scarecrows, decorations, Halloween."

The little girl shrugged lightly. "The leaves make it pretty enough, don't they?"

He spotted the woman's quick flash of pain before she masked it. "We haven't had an opportunity to do a lot of home decorating the past two years." She put her arm around the girl's shoulders and drew her close for a quick hug. "But I'm hoping that's all behind us now."

"I expect you've got a lot to do." Seth acknowledged the next wave of approaching thundershowers heading across Kirkwood Lake and took a step back. "If you need anything, Miss Sullivan, just call." He handed her a card with his number on it. "Learning your way around a new town can be tough."

"*Is* this a new town, ma'am?" Wade stood his ground as Seth started to move away because how could this be happening? To have Miranda here, right here, with the child, pretending she didn't have a clue who he was. Except that she wanted money from the state which they were now taking out of his paychecks. And what was she doing with that money? Because it sure didn't look like she was spending it on the sweet little girl or her banged-up car.

"Yes and no." He thought for a moment she might be truthful, but she blew that theory out of the water instantly. "I grew up just south of Clearwater, near the Pennsylvania border, in a little place called Eagle's Ridge. I knew about Kirkwood but I've never visited until today."

Wade stared, wondering what to do. Should he call her out?

Common sense and training reminded him that the first act of police work was to gather facts. That's what he needed to do here, and quickly, because whatever game Miranda was playing probably wasn't in the best interests of that beautiful child. A daughter. *His daughter.*

He called Seth as soon as they were in their respective cars. "Meet me at the Pelican's Nest."

He got there first and ordered coffees from Tina Campbell, Seth's sister-in-law. By the time Seth rolled into the parking lot, Wade thought he might burst. Seth sat down across from him, grabbed the coffee like it was a lifeline and sipped. "Fill me in."

Wade told his story, point by point, then planted his hands, palms down, against the faded wooden table. "I don't know how to handle this."

"She didn't appear to know you," Seth offered mildly. "So maybe she isn't Miranda. Maybe she's Caroline, like she said."

"What are the chances of two cousins the same age, looking so much alike?"

"No predicting genetics," Seth replied. "But the bigger problem is that sweet little girl, Wade. You've got a daughter and she doesn't know you exist."

He'd thought of that, the moment he saw her, pigtails swinging, curls bouncing.

A daughter.

His.

Hidden away for over five years. Who did that kind of thing? *Miranda.*

And now she was here, playing more games. He pulled out his phone and hit Mike Silver's number.

"Who are you calling?"

"My lawyer. The irony of me protesting I don't have a child only to have that child appear a few months later won't be lost on him."

Seth's frown pushed Wade to hang up the phone. "What?"

The older sheriff rimmed his coffee cup with one finger. "I was married before."

"I know that. Tori was from your first marriage, right?" Seth's teenage daughter was often seen around town, pushing her baby brother and sister in their twin stroller, or helping out at Campbell's hardware store now that she was older.

"It's complicated, but let's just say it took a while before Tori's mother was willing to put Tori's best interests first."

"How'd you get her to do that?"

A tiny muscle in Seth's cheek jumped. "Prayer and patience."

Wade snorted, but when Seth raised his gaze to his, he frowned. "You're serious."

"When you're dealing with kids, it pays to be serious. And calm. And patient. Sophie doesn't appear to be unhappy."

That was true enough. The girl beamed with happiness.

"And while their clothes and shoes are a little scuffed up, they both look healthy."

They did. If Wade was truthful with himself, the woman's gold-and-green eyes— *Miranda's eyes*, he corrected himself— held a softer, sweeter look than he remembered. Of course the fact that she left him high and dry after cleaning out his small bank account might have shaded his memory a little. But those eyes were what got him into this predicament, nearly seven years back. "What are you saying?"

"Give it time. Check things out. And whatever you do, don't go rushing in there, guns blazing, making accusations. Kids trust easy, but if you lose that trust right off, it's mighty hard to earn it back. Let's uncover what we can. We start by finding out everything there is to know about Caroline Sullivan." He stood and left a generous tip for his sister-in-law Tina on the table. "Starting with does she actually exist?"

"I'm on it." Wade followed Seth outside, and when Seth got to his cruiser, he turned back. "Don't forget the other part of the formula. Prayer. I'd have never gotten through that whole mess with Tori if I didn't have God on my side." Wade must have looked guilty because Seth smiled as he got back into his squad car. "No time like the present to start."

Wade considered Seth's words as the older deputy pulled out of the parking lot.

Prayer and patience. He'd been a complete zero on the first, and the second quality could use a little work, but not as much as the first. His mother would love to see him drag himself into a church pew every Sunday, and if he did, it might lessen the shock of telling her she had a secret granddaughter.

After she killed him, of course.

CHAPTER THREE

"MOMMY, THE POLICEMAN'S HERE AGAIN," Sophie called from the front window the next morning. Which one, Carrie wondered?

The nice one with the easy smile or the suspicious one that made her feel like she should check her pockets for stolen silverware? She finished wiping down the kitchen counter and hurried down the loft stairs when she heard him call. "Coming."

Yesterday's rain had given way to warm, welcome sun, but she was pretty sure the weed population had taken a greedy drink from nature's generosity and grown a foot overnight. She added "weed everything" to her mental to-do list that started with finding a job. Elsa's legacy had included a small bank account, and her elderly great-aunt had paid a year's taxes ahead, but even with that, Carrie needed to find work quickly. Now that Sophie would be entering first grade, she'd have reduced child care expenses and that was a huge plus. She stepped out of the barn quietly and found Wade Prescott glancing around. The disparaging look on his face made her want to smack him. She desisted, but barely, because no one should walk through life being a downright grump. This guy had other ideas, apparently. "Deputy, good morning."

He turned and met her gaze, and when he did, she had the distinct impression he was struggling mentally. "Seth mentioned you couldn't get into the house yesterday. Are you staying in the barn, ma'am?"

"There's an upstairs apartment, so yes. It's actually really nice, and totally necessary because I'm not even sure what to do in there," she pointed to the house and moved a few steps in that direction, "when we get a door open. It looks jam-packed, doesn't it?"

"It does. I can help you get the door open, if you'd like. You might need a locksmith to re-do the lock when I'm done, but there's really no other way around it, unless you call a locksmith in to do the job. Or if I break it, we can simply go to Campbell's hardware store, buy a new lock and replace it once we get in."

With money almost non-existent, she wouldn't be calling in a locksmith any time soon, so she accepted his offer and decided to overlook his surly attitude. "If you wouldn't mind, that would be great. I got the front door unlocked, but I couldn't budge it. The back door wouldn't work with either key, unless I wasn't doing it right." She pointed to the loft behind them. "Let me get Sophie and the keys. She'll love to be part of a breaking-in adventure."

She hurried to the loft, told Sophie to come down, and grabbed her keys before she dashed back down. She crossed the yard, held out the keys and started toward the back door. "If you can figure this out, I am forever in your debt."

His face darkened slightly, but he moved ahead, picked out a key, and tried to unlock the door.

No luck.

He tried a second key that appeared to fit, but also refused to engage the lock.

He scowled, and was about to try a third key, when Sophie raced up behind them. "Mommy! Do you think we'll get in? Oh, that would be the most exciting actual adventure, ever! I wonder what's in there?" Eyes round, she grabbed Carrie's hand and pumped it. "Probably not toys, because you said Auntie was old, but there might be," she stretched up and dropped her voice to a whisper, but loud enough to include the sheriff's deputy in on the secret. "A buried treasure."

"That would be exciting," Carrie agreed, laughing, and when the deputy shot her a strange look, she took a step back. "Sorry, I didn't mean to laugh in your ear, deputy."

He stared at her, then at Sophie, then bent to try the lock again, silent, but something in that exchange raised Carrie's curiosity.

He didn't like her. She'd sensed that instantly, a common enough reaction from people who knew Miranda. And yet he'd come back today to help.

Why? What would motivate him to do that? Was he feeling

sorry for her? More likely he was feeling sorry for Sophie, and that would only make her mad because she and Sophie June had been a pair for a long time. Nothing was about to separate them, no matter how they came to be together. And that was that.

A tiny *click!* spelled success.

Sophie cheered and Carrie laughed, delighted, but Wade held up a hand of caution. "This has been vacant for a long time and Mrs. Thurgood hung onto most everything, it seems. Can I go in and have a look around to make sure there's nothing dangerous inside?"

"That would be very nice. Thank you." She picked Sophie up and swung her around because saving the cost of a locksmith was a huge bonus. "Sophie! Our very own house and apartment, and yard! Oh my gosh, Sophie, aren't we the happiest ever?"

"Yes!" Sophie squealed in her arms, her brown, curly pigtails sailing in the breeze, and then she grabbed Carrie in a big, ginormous hug. "Mommy! I just love you so much I could burst into a bajillion pieces!"

The faith of a child, simple, heartfelt and true. Sophie's faith in her gave Carrie faith in herself, despite how rough the past two years had been. Today, here and now, they'd begin anew. She grabbed her precious girl close and said, "I love you too, June-bug."

Sophie's innocent declaration knifed Wade's heart. Her proclamation of love, so sweet and pure, aimed at a woman who was either a drug-using thief or an imposter. Either way, there was no way on earth his child belonged here, with her. But he had work to do before delving further into the possibilities before him. He walked around the interior of the house, surrounded by stacks of this and piles of that, every horizontal space filled with mounds of junk. He took a deep breath, gazed heavenward, and decided it was time he and God had a little one-on-one. *Do I leave her here? In this crazy, hoarder environment? How do I keep her safe when she has no idea who I am?*

Nothing but muted sunshine through blocked windows answered him. Tall stacks effectively blocked any chance of natural light. He moved back outside and faced them. "I don't see anything too crazy, but there's so much stuff that it's probably not a safe environment for a child."

"I can peek though, right?" Sophie sparkled up at him, her head tilted just so, utterly charming. "Just to say I saw it before Mommy gets it all cleaned out!"

Mommy would be working serious overtime to accomplish that task, and Wade was pretty sure it would require a dumpster... maybe two... and a back hoe. He didn't say that, though. Instead, he said, "Do you mind if I check out the loft, ma'am? I don't expect there's been a fire inspection on it in a long time, and if there are bad wires or loose connections, it could be dangerous."

He hadn't exactly been on his best behavior since meeting her, so he was pretty sure the blond was going to tell him to take a hike, but she didn't. Instead she reached out, still holding Sophie, grabbed his hand and headed that way. "That would be perfect, thank you! How did you know I was worried about that? I don't know anything about hardware and electric and repair. I intend to learn but what if I missed a problem and something happened?" She darted a quick glance down to Sophie, who seemed to enjoy being carried up the stairs. "I would never be able to live with myself."

His feelings exactly, and they were the very reason he asked. Hearing her voice and the immediate concern she had for Sophie June's safety, doubts pushed forth again. Miranda would have had to change laughs and personality to be this woman... so maybe this wasn't Miranda. Maybe the woman's story would hold true. He'd know more later that day, but in the meantime, whoever she was, his duty was to keep his daughter safe, even if she had no idea who he was.

The woman dropped his hand at the top of the stairs and opened the loft apartment door.

He strode into the kitchen, expecting disaster.

Sparkling clean counters and cupboards greeted him with the fresh smell of soap and water. He moved through the small dining area and into the living room, bending to check sockets and outlets.

Everything was up to code, solid, and screwed in tight. "I had no idea there was an apartment up here," he said as he moved toward the back corner bedroom. "Do you mind?" he asked, feeling odd to be walking into her private space.

"No, it's fine."

They hadn't had a chance to clean in here, yet. Dust hit his nose as he inspected the wiring and overhead ceiling fan and light combo. Checking carefully, he found everything in order.

"Actually, would you mind helping me open that window?" She pointed to the east-facing window overlooking Luke Campbell's grazing land. Two young horses browsed the fenced area, back-dropped by big trees lining the creek bank. "It doesn't appear to be painted shut, but it's stuck tight and I can't budge it. And this room needs a good cleaning, washing and vacuuming before we can use it."

"Sure." He moved forward. So did she. She grabbed one side while he grabbed the other. "On three."

She nodded.

He counted and when they got to three, they both shoved... and the window moved up. It groaned in protest, but it moved. She laughed as fresh air poured in through the tight screening, happy with so little.

Miranda had never been happy with a little of anything. Hence the bad habits. This can't be Miranda.

"Yes!" She high-fived him and when she did, her foot caught the edge of the bed. She stumbled forward, ready to pitch face first, but he caught her before her head hit the footboard rail.

"Hey, steady. You okay?" He gripped her arms, just enough to hold her up. When he looked into those pretty hazel eyes, eyes that brought out the gold in her blond hair, his heart went into pause.

But then it started again, because wasn't that how he got into trouble the first time? He let go too quick, and she almost fell again, his fault. "Come here." He grabbed her hand and led her out of the narrow end of the bedroom. "Is there a washer and dryer here?"

She shook her head, then paused. "Wait. I bet there's one in the house!" She grabbed his hands, excited, and something about the innocence of her excitement made him excited, too. "I can take all this bedding over there and wash it while I'm cleaning here! Oh, that's the perfect solution."

"Money's tight?"

She winced, and he felt like a crumb for extracting information he might use against her. "Very. We were doing all right but then I made a couple of bad decisions that left us virtually homeless, but now." She waved her hand around the nicely appointed apartment. "I don't know whose this was, or why Aunt Elsa had an apartment she never rented out, but Sophie and I are absolutely blessed to be here. Aren't we, June-bug?"

"Yes!" Sophie waved a book from a stack about two feet high. "I'm picking out two books to read later, Mom, and I don't care if we have to wait a little while, okay?"

"As soon as I get the washer going over at the house," Carrie promised. She went back into the bedroom, pulled off the comforter and moved toward the door. "Deputy, thank you so much for helping us with the door and the window."

"Those were little things."

She shook her head as she moved down the stairs ahead of him. "Not if you can't do them. Sophie and I are used to being on our own, but I love it when God sends along help just in the nick of time."

He wasn't her help.

He might, in fact, be her enemy. She didn't know that. He did. "God might laugh at the notion that I'm the answer to prayer, Miss Sullivan."

"Carrie," she insisted and she smiled when she said it as if calling her by name was the most natural thing in the world. It wasn't, of course, unless he called her Miranda, because in his head, that's the name that went with her face, her eyes, and the soft, honey-blond hair.

"Well, Carrie, I was glad to help."

She accepted that with a shy dip of her chin, absolutely engaging, except the last thing Wade Prescott could do was become attracted to whoever this was.

He sighed, climbed into his car and met Seth and Luke Campbell back at the section house. "Any luck?"

"Here you go."

He stared at the two pictures, side-by-side, and if one of them wasn't marked with Miranda's name, he'd have no idea which one was Miranda and which one was Carrie. "That's unbelievable."

Seth shook his head. "It's not. They're double cousins."

"Which makes them as close genetically as full sisters," Luke added. "Brother and sister married brother and sister and had baby girls seven months apart. Miranda lived in Clearwater, Carrie lived thirty minutes south of the city in Eagles Run. Miranda gave birth to a female child five years ago on October fourth. Two weeks later, Carrie shows up in Nebraska with her master's degree in education and a brand new baby girl named Sophie June. She subbed for various districts for nearly two years, then was on the tenure track outside of Omaha. Budget cuts made them release eight percent of the staff the year she would have been tenured. So it was back to subbing day by day."

"Where was Miranda all this time?"

"Moving," Luke told him bluntly. "She bounced from Michigan to Illinois and then

Florida while using a New York address, accepting benefits for a daughter who lived with Carrie in Nebraska."

"She gave her the baby."

"Considering her lifestyle, not a bad choice," Seth offered quietly.

"But what about me?" Wade stared at Seth, then Luke. "Why not tell me about the baby?"

"The fact that she stole nearly two thousand dollars from you might have had something to do with her reticence," Luke reminded him. "That's a punishable crime."

"But to hide a baby from her father." Wade stared at the pictures, as if looking harder might tell him more. It didn't. "That's callous and underhanded and just plain wrong."

"So what are your intentions?" Seth asked. "My guess is that Carrie has no idea who Sophie's father is, and came back here to start a new life."

"Why does she need a new life?" He glanced back and forth between the brothers. "You said she was a teacher."

"Something happened in Nebraska," Seth told him. "I'm not sure what, and the time frame isn't exactly clear, but somehow in the last year she lost her house, her credit tanked and her bank accounts went to nothing."

"Drugs. Like her cousin."

Seth groaned. "If ever a person didn't have a drug problem, it's the young woman we met yesterday. It doesn't say what happened here, but it's clear from the figures that something pulled the plug on her financially. And then she inherited Mrs. Thurgood's place.

And now she's here."

Wade dropped his head into his hands, then sat back and stared at the two deputy brothers. "You've both got kids. What should I do?"

Seth looked at Luke and laughed. "Marry her and give Sophie brothers and sisters."

Luke fist-bumped his older brother. "My thoughts exactly. Win/win, everybody's happy."

"That's the dumbest idea I've ever heard," Wade roared the words, drawing the attention of the four other deputies in the broad, long room. "Let's get serious."

"I was." Seth filed his paperwork and stretched. "I'm heading home, boys. Can't wait to hear the next chapter of this little melo-drama. Keep me in the loop, okay?"

"If he doesn't, I will," Luke promised.

"You guys aren't funny." Wade stood, rolled his shoulders and faced them down, but the Campbell men didn't back down read-ily. "First thing on Monday I'm going to talk to my lawyer and establish my legal status."

"While that's not necessarily a bad idea," Seth called back, walk-ing away. "I like my idea better. Lawyers are expensive, and being married has its own share of built-in benefits."

"Yeah. Like taking out the trash. Cleaning gutters. Scrubbing garage floors," Luke teased as he pulled his Kevlar vest into place to get ready for the evening shift. "Although I can't say I mind those now and again. Considering I've got Rainey to go home to every day."

"I'm calling your wife and telling her what you said," Wade threatened, and when Luke left the room, he shifted his gaze down to the two look-alike pictures.

Sophie didn't look like either of them. She looked like a femi-nine version of him, but he knew lawyer would request a paternity test. He'd have to get Sophie's DNA.

Which meant either getting it quietly or telling Carrie Sullivan who he was and what he was doing. Seeing how much she loved the child, and how much Sophie loved her, he couldn't risk her fleeing the area.

She's got no money, and she's downright nice. Why not just tell her?

Not yet, he decided, and then felt like a crumb for making the decision. He'd find out for sure if Sophie was his child, and then confront the situation. Because what if for some peculiar reason she wasn't his child? Miranda wasn't exactly the true-to-heart, trustworthy sort.

No, it made sense to be certain first. And then?

He'd go from there.

CHAPTER FOUR

"**H**E WAS SO NICE," SOPHIE said for the fourth time that afternoon, singing Wade Prescott's praises as they drove into the school offices. "Wasn't he, Mom?"

"He was." She couldn't argue the point, but Carrie wasn't a five-year-old. While she appreciated the good-looking deputy's help, mental caution flags had popped up during his visit.

You're being silly. It's because he's a deputy and you feel guilty being back here with Miranda's child. Stop beating yourself up and enjoy what God's given you. You know what Sophie's life would have been like with Miranda.

She refused to weigh Sophie's outcome if Miranda had kept her. She'd been Carrie's child from the day Miranda was released from the hospital, and that's how it would stay. She'd explain the truth to Sophie when she was old enough to understand it. Until then, she was one hundred percent Carrie's little girl. She went inside the central office entrance, got Sophie registered, then they took a quick tour around the elementary school side of the building.

"This is bigger than my first school." Sophie stared at the long halls and her breath caught. "Way bigger."

"It's pretty big," the principal said as they walked along the kindergarten-through-fourth-grade wing. "Kids from all over come here to learn, but these two halls will be the ones you use most of the time. And of course, Miss Garrett will look after you and your classmates." The principal exchanged a smile with the first-grade teacher as they approached her door. "Sophie June, this is your teacher, Miss Garrett. She'll be hear waiting when you start on Wednesday."

Sophie glanced around, then smiled up at the copper-skinned teacher. "You're beautiful," she whispered, then grabbed Carrie's hand tighter. "I think I'll like coming to your school even if I miss my mommy."

Miss Garrett brought herself to Sophie's level. "Everyone misses their mommy sometimes," she admitted. "But we have so many fun things to do and good things to learn, that the days pass quickly. And if Mommy has free time, she can come in to help sometimes." She looked up at Carrie for guidance and Carrie winced.

"Once my job situation is straightened out, we'll do just that," she promised. "We just got into town yesterday, but I wanted to get Sophie registered before Labor Day weekend so we wouldn't be rushing to do it next Tuesday."

"Good planning," the principal commended her. "Tuesday will be a busy planning and meeting day here. So, Sophie June Sullivan." She stuck out her hand and shook Sophie's littler one. "Welcome to Kirkwood Lake Elementary."

"Thank you." Sophie whispered the words, but she didn't look daunted by the school's size. She looked inspired, and Carrie hoped she'd continue to love school, like she did. "See you next week!"

They walked outside and Sophie spotted the playground instantly. "Mommy! Can we play for a few minutes? Please?"

Carrie refused to think of the huge amount of work waiting in Aunt Elsa's house. In a few days, Sophie would be gone all day, and until she had a job, she'd have extra time. She'd dropped off her substitute teacher application in the Central Office human relations room, and if they added her to the call list, that would be a huge plus. The elementary school had wrap-around care, so if she got called to sub for a district teacher, she could drop Sophie off early and pick her up after school.

But in the meantime, she needed to find some way to supplement their meager bank account.

Hasn't God provided, right along? It wasn't chance that brought you here, to Kirkwood after so many years out of New York. Who besides the Holy Spirit nudged your aunt to leave you her entire estate? God has blessed you, and he'll continue to do so.

She believed that, whole-heartedly. Her faith had taken a beat-down in Nebraska, when everything fell apart the past two years. She'd been so close to the simple gold ring she'd always wanted. A clean, respectable little house, a good job and the chance to make a difference in children's lives.

Then a major manufacturer went bankrupt, the local economy took a brutal hit and the school budget cuts forced newer staff out of a job. She'd hung on, subbing again, hoping something would open up in an adjacent district. And she and Sophie would have managed if she hadn't invested everything she had in that cozy-looking, snake-infested house.

She'd clung to her beliefs, to God, even in the darkest hours. The county health department had given her little choice when all was done: They'd condemned her five-room house, pinned a notice out front where everyone could see, and changed the locks. And when they intentionally burned her house to the ground to excise the snake pit, her heart felt the crash and fall of every timber.

God had leveled the playing field again, with Aunt Elsa's bequest. She'd hold that tight and run with the realization.

A sheriff's cruiser curved slowly into the school parking lot, did a perimeter scan, then pulled to a stop in the corner near the playground. Wade Prescott climbed out of the cruiser, slid his sunglasses up, and headed her way. Her heart jumped into a quick, staccato rhythm, tap-dancing its way in her chest.

"Hey." He smiled at her, but when he caught sight of Sophie climbing up the rungs to the fire pole, his smile went even wider. "She likes to climb?"

"Born to climb is more like it," Carrie replied, and when he took a seat on the bench next to her, she had to will her heart to calm down and behave itself which was silly because she was pretty sure the good-looking sheriff's deputy didn't like her. Or maybe he didn't trust her. Or both. And that made her reaction ridiculous, didn't it? "She was climbing before she was walking. And once she started talking, she hasn't stopped. It's funny how a child is born with a personality intact, isn't it? Stubborn or sweet? Tough or anxious to please? So many combinations, and Sophie seems to have gotten all the best ones. Do you have kids, deputy?"

Wade was ashamed that he dodged the question so easily. "I'm not married," he hedged, even though marriage was clearly not required to have children. "But my cousin has four kids, and you're right. They're born to be themselves and they give their parents a run for their money."

"Sophie June!" She stood and cupped her hands around her mouth. "Ten minutes, then we've got to go home."

Wade watched as Sophie's head popped out of a wood-slatted tunnel. "Okay! Mom, I met two friends over here, Sally and Athena!"

"Wonderful!" Carrie sat back down and laughed, and that laugh tugged Wade's heart once more. Contagious. Light. Open. The kind of laugh that brought sunshine on a dark day, and with the change of seasons coming, they'd have plenty of those. "She makes friends so easily. People gravitate to her, kids and adults. What a great personality trait, right?"

"Does she get that from you or her father?" Wade asked smoothly. Her face did an instant freeze. He read her reluctance. But she handled the question with the skill of a master diplomat, and his respect for her climbed higher.

"Both, I'd expect. I adopted Sophie when she was a newborn, so I don't know all of her family history, but enough to say I expect her wonderful personality comes from both sides."

She'd admitted adopting her. Did that mean they'd filed legal papers? Then how was Miranda extracting money from the government all that time?

Really? You think it would be all that hard for Miranda to score paperwork to scam the government?

In truth, no. He made a mental note to check that out, because if Sophie had been legally adopted and Miranda had swindled the government, he couldn't be financially liable for the government's mistake, could he? Another question for the lawyer. "She is adorable."

Carrie's eyes met his, and once again he was drawn, but this time there was no confusion about the Carrie/Miranda resemblance. This time it was the sweet, honest, caring sincerity in *this* woman's eyes. The light-toned capris and the green ruffled tank top weren't a bad combo, either, bright, eye-catching summer wear on a beautiful woman. "Do you need someone to watch her while you look for work? I'm free the middle of next week, and I know it's hard to find child care when you're new in town. I could take her to visit my cousin's kids. They live just up the road from Deputy Campbell and his family off of Main Street."

"What a nice offer."

Her smile hiked his guilt exponentially because he figured that would be the easiest way to get a DNA sample.

"But no, we're fine. I dropped off the substitute teacher application packet a little while ago and they won't be calling for an interview until after they do a background check. By then Sophie will be in school all day and I can schedule around that. Thank you, though."

"So you're a teacher," he noted, as if he didn't realize it and now he felt like a bigger crumb. But if she was willing to apply as a substitute in the district, and go through the interviews and the background check, she couldn't have done anything wrong in Nebraska, and that was a weight off his mind.

"Yes, junior high science and math." She grinned when he made a face of disbelief.

"That's crazy. *They're* crazy. Why did you pick that age and those subjects?"

"I love science and math, I love absolute answers and unending discovery and adolescents are certifiably insane, but weren't we all at that age? So I think of it that way and I keep them so busy in class they don't have time to cause trouble."

"You make it sound sensible. And easy. Why do I suspect it's neither?" he wondered as Sophie and her new friends jumped down from one of the built-in ledges and raced for the swings. "And if you're working when will you have time to clear out the house? That's a monumental job."

She made a face, then shrugged. "I'll take it as it comes. We're going to stop by the church today and meet Reverend Smith and his wife. I talked with Mrs. Smith on the phone yesterday and they seem really nice. With church and school taken care of, and the beginnings of a job search, I figure the rest will take care of itself. I'll start hauling things out of Aunt Elsa's tomorrow. The weather looks great for the holiday weekend, and there's no time like the present, right?"

"Do you want help, Carrie?" He thought it would feel weird, using her name when her face reminded him so much of Miranda, but it didn't feel weird. It felt nice. And the more he talked to her, and listened to her upbeat, optimistic nature, the less she resembled Sophie's biological mother.

"No, but thank you. Tackling into this project is kind of exciting, actually. A chance to start anew."

"I would have said intimidating, but hey. That's me," he teased. "You've got a pretty tough nature behind that smile if you think tackling all of this is no big deal. Most people I know would be overwhelmed just looking at Mrs. Thurgood's place. What made you give up teaching out west and head this way? Was inheriting the house enough of a draw? Because I've seen the house and I'm thinking you might have been sold a bill of goods."

"It's not that bad," she told him, then shrugged lightly. "Timing brought us here." She said it as if she still had a hard time believing it herself. "We were solid in Nebraska, living a nice, normal life. I bought a house on a small lot in the country with a beautiful view. It was just the sweet kind of place you'd want to raise a child, like a page from a Laura Ingalls' book. So we moved in, I was teaching and Sophie was in pre-school, and then we ran into serious trouble once the weather got warm." Her expression darkened, remembering.

"What kind of trouble?"

"Loss of job and snakes."

He hadn't been expecting that, so it took a moment to digest. "Snakes? Real snakes?" The thought of Sophie having to deal with snakes tightened every muscle in his body. He might be a big, brawny sheriff's deputy, but if there was one thing he hated, it was sliding, slithering snakes. "I don't understand."

"Our pretty little house turned out to be infested, a fact we discovered not long after the district I'd been teaching in had to cut staff."

His skin crawled and Wade could do nothing to stop it.

"At first I thought it was no big deal. Everyone sees a garter snake or two in the spring, when the ground warms up. I was raised in the country and snakes never bothered me."

"This was more than a snake or two, I take it?"

Her face crinkled in disgust. "The house was either built on a den, or the den formed beneath it at some point in time. We tried exterminators, glue traps, everything I could think of or afford, but we barely made a dent in the population. Then the school district had to eliminate some staff because of the WestLand Ag bankruptcy and I wasn't tenured yet."

"So you lost your job and had a snake house."

She nodded, grim. "When I realized there was nothing I could do, I let the house go. No one would want it, I couldn't do the same thing that was done to me, and sell it to someone knowing what was wrong with it, so I let the bank foreclose, I ruined my credit, had no job and we were bordering homelessness. But when I look back on it, it's kind of amazing, isn't it? Like a miracle."

Wade saw nothing miraculous about snakes, unemployment and homelessness, especially where Sophie June was concerned. "I don't see how."

"The letter from Mr. Silver, Aunt Elsa's attorney came right before we would have been out of a home," she told him. "I had no money for another month of apartment rent, we knew we had to move out, and then the letter came. What if I'd already left the apartment in Lyons? There would have been no way of finding me. I had no forwarding address. It was amazing, really, like God and Aunt Elsa were both watching out for us and the notice came in the nick of time. Perfect."

"If you say so."

The doubt in his voice made her laugh. "Well, the snakes and job loss weren't perfect, but the chance for a respite was. And that's the miracle part." She stood and called out for Sophie.

Sophie said goodbye to her new friends, called "See you next week!" over her shoulder and skipped their way. "That was so much fun! I think I will like it here a lot, Mom! Did you know there's a farm that sells ice cream right down this road?" She pointed toward the town of Kirkwood and her eyes went wide. "Sally and Athena both go there sometimes and I said maybe we would too, once we were here awhile and have some money."

"That was absolutely the best answer," Carrie declared. "How'd you get so smart?"

Sophie June lifted her shoulders and blushed in a little-girl shrug. "Because I'm like my mom."

Carrie hugged her. "I'll take that as a compliment although I don't think I was ever as cute as you are, kid. But we'll let it ride. Can you say goodbye to Deputy Prescott?"

"Wade," he insisted, realizing he should have done this when they first met. "Just call me Wade, please."

"I will." She smiled up at him, one of those slanted, 'the sun's too bright' looks, and when his gaze met hers, the sun did seem brighter. The day seemed nicer. And the soft breeze through the trees blew sweeter.

"It's silly to say goodbye if he's walking with us," Sophie supposed as she skipped ahead, and since he was walking the pair to their patched-up car, he figured she was right.

"Were you patrolling the school yard?" Carrie asked as they crossed the broad, green school yard and the attached athletic fields.

"Yes."

"For wayward eight-year-olds?" she asked in a teasing voice.

He made a face. "Every now and again some of the older kids pick this area for stuff they shouldn't be doing. If we patrol regularly, they take their bad habits to other places."

"Bad habits such as?"

"Smoking. Drinking. Drugs. The typical."

"Here?" She stopped and looked around at the pretty school setting in disbelief. "I don't believe it. Everything here seems so far removed from anything like that."

"It is, mostly, but every town's got a few bad apples, don't they?"

She hugged her arms around herself as a cloud slipped in front of the sun, casting a chilled September shadow. "I suppose. I was hoping that wouldn't be the case here, but you're right. If it was all perfect, you'd be out of a job because no one would need a sheriff or his deputies. Well." They'd reached her car and she checked through the back window to make sure Sophie had put her belt on correctly, then bumped knuckles with her when she did. "I love how independent you're getting, June-bug. It's awesome."

"Thanks." Sophie grinned, proud as could be, and Wade wondered at all he'd missed over the years. True, he knew nothing about babies, but he knew himself. Given the chance, he'd have been a great father to this little girl. But he wasn't given a chance, and even if that wasn't Carrie's fault, he wasn't in the frame of mind to forgive almost six lost years of his child's life. "Goodbye, Wade! Thanks for taking care of us!"

"We do what we can," he told her, smiling, and then he reached up and tipped his sunglasses back down. "See you soon, Sophie June."

"It rhymes!" She laughed up at him, and he wanted nothing more than to bend down, grab her into a huge hug and tell her who he was, and then go on hugging her forever. He couldn't do that, of course, so he stepped back, closed the back door, and pulled Carrie's door open for her. He, closed it gently once she'd gotten in behind the wheel.

"Thank you, Wade."

"My pleasure." He stepped back and watched her go, his thoughts clogged by the overload of information.

She'd fallen on tough times and gotten through.

She appreciated everything she'd been given, including the blessed child riding in the backseat, although a newly graduated teacher couldn't have anticipated being a mother. But she'd stepped up to the plate and gave Sophie June a wonderful example of faith, thrift and humor, all qualities the child seemed to embrace.

She rose above calamities and accepted change with patience and expectation. Watching her drive away, he realized he could learn a lot from Carrie Sullivan, but as her car spit and sputtered its way out of the lot, he knew that once she discovered his true identity, she'd hate him. His very being was a threat to life as she knew it, her life as Sophie June's mother.

He sighed. He didn't dare wait until he was able to do some form of clandestine DNA testing. He needed to talk to Mike Silver ASAP, because he needed to understand his rights and responsibilities before something happened and Carrie discovered who he was by other means.

Although how on earth he was going to face Carrie Sullivan and tell her the truth was beyond him at the moment. The thought of erasing the joyous smile from her pretty face made him feel lower than that den of snakes she talked about.

A shiver ran up his spine at the image of Sophie co-existing with a clutch of snakes, and as he passed the church, he spotted Carrie's car parked there, dutifully following her plan of action.

A home, church and school, the kind of life every child deserved, and if he followed through with his intended actions?

He'd be the guy responsible for taking it all away from her.

CHAPTER FIVE

"MOMMY, WHAT ARE WE DOING today?" Sophie asked first thing Saturday morning.

Carrie bent low. "First, hang up your towel, put away your jammies and did you brush your teeth?"

"I almost did."

"Well, take care of that and then come see me, but I'll give you a hint, June-bug. Saturdays are meant for adventure."

"Adventure?" Sophie peered up her, skeptical. "For real?"

"Possibly a treasure hunt."

Her big, brown eyes went wide. "I love those so much!"

"Me, too, June-bug. You and me, with the help of two of your most trusted toys—"

"The pillow twins," Sophie interrupted instantly. "Pink and Purple, at your service!"

"Ideal! Soft, cuddly and if you need a nap, they're the very best friends to have on hand. Go brush those pearly whites and meet me back here in three minutes."

"Okay!" Sophie rushed to the bathroom and grabbed her pink-and-gold flecked toothbrush. What she lacked in time she made up for in vigor, and when she was done, she gathered her trustworthy pillow dolls, a gift from an elderly neighbor in Lyons, Nebraska who loved to sew. The stamped-cut, stuffed dolls had been constant companions since Sophie was big enough to walk. Their faded faces and thinning seams did nothing to lessen their worth and beauty in their little owner's eyes. "Got 'em!"

"Okay, we're going to start with the back porch. It's lovely today and this way we've got a head start on the weekend."

"Remember when we used to go to parties sometimes?"

Guilt hit Carrie crosswise because of course she remembered. When she was working and Sophie was in daycare, there was a flurry of birthday and holiday parties at friends and neighbors outside of Omaha. That seemed like so long ago. "I do, and I expect that will happen again once we've been here a while. It takes a little time to make friends in a new spot."

"Like when I go to school, I'll make friends," Sophie decided. "Absolutely. And when I start teaching, I'll make new friends, too." She crossed the yard

with Sophie, set her up with a water bottle and her toys on the back lawn beneath the shade of a spreading maple. "I'll be working right here on the porch, so if you need me, I'm just a stone's throw away. Okay?"

Sophie spread out the pillowed dolls against the base of the tree, propped a book in front of each one, and waved Carrie off. "I'm the teacher and I'm teaching Pink and Purple how to read."

"Oh. Okay, then." Carrie faced the porch, refused to be daunted, and charged up the stairs. She propped the door open with a sturdy brick for two reasons. Opening and closing the door would be awkward with her arms full. Second, if there were any furry friends living on the porch, she wanted to have a clear path of escape for them— and her.

It didn't take long to have a stack of boxes filled with old papers and magazines. She toted each full box over to the barn and started filling a corner. She couldn't put them out for recycling until the following Thursday, but this got her a step ahead.

One day at a time.

With an open corner, she spotted two old, metal signs tucked beneath the windows. She pulled them out one by one, and smiled. "Farm Fresh Eggs," she read as she ran a finger over the deep blue enamel of the first one. The second sign was broader and longer, and when she pulled that one free, she smiled at the old-fashioned lettering. "Fresh Dairy Products Sold Here."

An idea took root quickly. If she thought the signs were charming, maybe other folks would, too. She hauled a picnic table bench out to the grass alongside the driveway and propped the vintage signs against it. She grabbed a piece of cardboard from one of the recycling boxes and jotted *$20, Your Choice* on the sign. She set the price between the two signs and went back to work. Less than half an hour later, a voice drew her attention to the side yard.

"Hello?"

"Hi!" Sophie darted up from the blanket they'd spread on the ground and waved, excited. "We're back here!"

"I see that."

A woman approached the back yard as Carrie brought a stack of old hangers off the back porch. Carrie set the hangers down, stuck out her hand, then eyed her hand, the porch, and the dust and withdrew the offer. "I guarantee you don't want to shake my hand right now. I'm Carrie and this is my daughter Sophie. Can I help you?"

"You already did." The woman waved toward the picnic bench. "I'm going to buy those signs from you."

"Both of them?" Carrie should have pretended nonchalance, but the thought of a quick forty dollars in her pocket when every penny got counted at least three times meant a lot. "That's so nice of you."

The woman handed her a fifty-dollar bill. Carrie grimaced, then motioned to Sophie to come with here. "Come here, June-bug, we've got to run upstairs and get this nice lady some, change."

Sophie's frown said Pink and Purple's lessons shouldn't be interrupted, and the woman helped by shaking her head. "I won't hear of change, honey, they're priced too cheap as it is."

"That's a lot of money." Carrie held up the fifty dollar bill as if the kindly woman would understand better by seeing it again. "I can get you change, I just have to run upstairs."

"Not needed, but you could do something for me."

"Yes?"

"My name is Jenny Campbell," the woman told her with a smile. "My son Seth stopped by your first day here."

The slightly older, married deputy she'd met first. "The really nice deputy."

"I'd like to think so!" Jenny told her in a pert voice. "Anyway, Seth mentioned you had a little girl. I've got a bunch of grandkids here in town and we're having a Labor Day picnic on Monday. I would be honored to have you and Sophie come over and have a picnic with us. We're just up the road at seventeen-nine-forty-one. That way Sophie could meet Dorrie and Sonya and Aiden.

They're a year or so older than she is, but friendships have to start somewhere, don't they? And it's always hard to get started in a brand new town."

When Carrie hesitated, Sophie skipped across the lawn and grabbed Jenny Campbell's left hand. "I would love a party with other kids! We were just talking about missing parties and things like that, weren't we? And then you came here and invited us to a party, so I think that's kind of perfect, don't you, Mom?" Joy brightened her features, and how could Carrie say no? Sophie asked for so little, wise beyond her years.

"What time should we come over? And what can I bring?"

"Any time after eleven," Jenny told her, "and if you'd like to bring some marshmallow crispy bars, they're always a crowd-pleasing favorite."

Delicious and not too expensive. "They're crowd-pleasers here, too." Carrie smiled at Sophie. "We'd love to come. You're sure I can't get you change?"

Jenny waved her off as she gathered up the two signs and tucked them into the back of her SUV. "I'm considering them a bargain at this price, honey. And I'm so glad I drove by and spotted them! My daughter-in-law runs an old-fashioned dairy on the other side of the lake and these are perfect for the store. See you Monday!"

Fifty dollars.

Carrie tucked the money into her pocket, and considered the porch. Crammed full except for a narrow walkway into the house, she'd have her work cut out for her, but as she re-strategized where to put things, an idea began to blossom.

Some of Aunt Elsa's collection *was* junk, but a lot of these old things had value. When she uncovered an inlaid tile table beneath a stack of moth-eaten old clothes, she put the woolens into a large, plastic garbage bag, then loaded the table into a nearly ancient wheelbarrow, and hauled it over to the barn. Piece by piece, she salvaged saleable items from discards. She stopped long enough to make Sophie a quick peanut-butter and jelly sandwich mid-day, and when she'd gained about a quarter of the porch by mid-afternoon, she took a quaint old table and a lamp to the side yard, then planted a fifty-dollar sign on the pair.

They sold within the hour and that's when her seed of an idea began to really take root.

She had a barn. She lived on a road that circled the long, slim circumference of Kirkwood Lake and she had no job at present. If she could sort through things once Sophie was off to school, a few more sales like this would provide gas and grocery money. By four o'clock she was ready to call it a day. "Sophie! Come on over here."

Sophie dashed across the grass and hurled herself into Carrie's embrace. "Pink and Purple have been very, very good!" she noted as she hugged her mother.

"It looks like they've been joined by a few friends," Carrie observed, and Sophie made a face.

"Well, they got kind of bored, so we invited some Ninja turtles and little people to a party."

"I think that was very smart of you and because you and your buddies were so good, how would you like to go get an ice cream?"

"Really?" Hope bloomed in Sophie's eyes.

Mixed emotions gripped Carrie. Should going for ice cream be that big a deal?

Eighteen months ago she wouldn't have thought twice about stopping for a cone with Sophie, or grabbing a treat from the ice cream vendor. And then she bottomed out financially and every-thing changed.

A soft breeze washed her face. The late-day sun blinked through deep green leaves and the thought of living on Aunt Elsa's land in this sweet, small lakeside town seemed ripe with opportunity.

Was this the answer to her prayers? During those dark, cold months of struggle, when everything seemed bleak, she'd prayed for a second chance to thrive. Maybe this was it, here in her aunt's hometown, the new beginning she and Sophie craved. "Shall we go?"

"Yes! But first I have to put my babies away. And their friends. Because what if it storms?"

"Better safe than sorry," Carrie agreed. She reached for a corner of the blanket. "Head over there and pick up that corner."

Sophie followed the direction while Carrie walked to the second corner and lifted it. Then she walked toward the center, clutching the corners. "Hand me your corner."

"This is such a good idea, Mom!" Sophie's enthusiasm made Carrie feel ten feet tall. "We won't hardly have to make any trips at all! We're almost done!"

"Well, we will be if you hand me that last corner, June-bug." Once Sophie walked that corner in, Carrie bundled the blanket like a big sack, tossed it over her back and carried it to the barn, then shut the main door. "We're good."

"Can this be an ice cream supper?" Sophie wondered as she bounced into her seat.

"I think that sounds marvelous." She checked Sophie's seat belt, bumped knuckles with her for getting it just right again, and climbed into the car. "An ice cream supper is just the thing for two hard-working girls."

CHAPTER SIX

"**W**ADE, YOU'RE JUST IN TIME." Cathy Prescott waved her son toward the backyard before he'd even climbed out of the car late Monday morning. "I can't move these last two rocks and my goal is to get them all in place today. Would you mind?"

"Of course I wouldn't mind, I can't believe you moved the rest of these," he scolded as he hauled the last two worm rocks into place. "What if you threw your back out?"

"Well, I didn't so there's no sense worrying about it now," she told him. "And just so you know, I like taking care of myself. Dad's been gone for nearly two years, so pulling the big, strong, sheriff's deputy act will get you nowhere with me. If I called you to come over for every little job that needs doing, you'd get sick and tired of it pretty quick."

"I hate that you're right, but you probably are," he admitted. "I stopped by to see if you wanted to drive to Campbell's together."

"I'd love that. Give me ten minutes, and don't let me forget those lemon bars in the fridge. Summer parties are always best with lemon bars."

"I love 'em no matter what the season." He snagged one from the plate, then crossed to the wall of pictures in the living room while his mother was upstairs. He and his brother, growing, laughing, competing, grinning. But it was the first part of the wall he examined most closely. The pictures of him as a little guy, riding a trike, then a bike, running and playing, a male version of Sophie June Sullivan.

"I love looking at that wall, watching you boys grow up."

He turned, startled. "I didn't hear you come down."

"You were engrossed." Cathy Prescott crossed the room, and swept the photos a fond smile. "It all goes by so fast, Wade. Too fast. I look at you and your brother and you're all grown up, but there's a part of me that will always see the little child within the grown man. The little boys I raised. The boys who aren't afraid to test lemon bars as needed."

"I can't possibly resist them. Best things ever, Mom."

She laughed as she picked up the tray. "You and Mick have done that since you were knee high. It didn't matter what I was cooking, you were right there helping. And tasting."

"I do what I can." He turned away from the pictures, thinking hard. *It all goes by so fast,* she said, and he'd already missed the first five years of his daughter's life. The realization angered him.

Miranda had no right to make that call on her own. And yet, according to the attorney, his parental rights were limited because she'd never named him as the father before giving Sophie up for adoption. Even with DNA testing, his paternal rights had been decreased by decisions Miranda made years before, and that wasn't right. He might still be in the dark if she hadn't gotten greedy and swindled the government for additional monthly funds in Sophie's name.

Wanna talk right? His conscience mused. *She didn't have to go ahead and have that baby. You wouldn't have known the difference, would you? So maybe you shouldn't be so quick to throw stones because your own behavior back then wasn't exactly Gentleman-of-the-Year.*

He opened the door for his mother. She smiled up at him, pleased by his thoughtfulness, but he realized he hadn't always been this thoughtful. He'd been fairly self-absorbed when he dated Miranda. He'd matured in the last half-dozen years. Serving as a deputy had offered a dose of realism. He needed to face this current situation with that maturity. He just wasn't sure how when the injustice gnawed at him.

He parked along the road's edge and walked into the broad, lakefront front yard with his mother. Campbells of all sizes milled around, along with some neighbors and friends, a typical Campbell get-together, but different, too. Charlie Campbell had passed away. Mrs. Thurgood was gone, the sweet, elderly woman that had owned the house Carrie lived in now. And this was the second year his father had been gone.

It all goes by too fast.

The absence of three special people cemented his goal. One way or another he intended to be part of his daughter's life, and he'd no more than had that thought when Sophie June raced by with Luke and Rainey Campbell's three oldest kids. "Hey, Wade!" Dorrie waved to him, then his mother. "Hi, Mrs. Prescott! Yikes! She's fast!" She pointed to Sophie and made a wild face as she ducked left, then streaked toward the sandy beach fronting the property.

"Dorrie! Not by the water!"

Dorrie banked right and Sophie tagged right after her, agile and quick. "She's fast," Wade noted, meaning Sophie, with a purely male surge of pride that his kid could run fast. Was that pathetic or delightfully normal?

Normal, he decided.

His mother followed the direction of his gaze. "They both are, but that little one's a spitfire, isn't she? Who is she? She's adorable." Talk about awkward. A prickle of unease tightened Wade's collar.

Would she recognize her own granddaughter? Would she see the resemblance to him? "A new family, they moved into Mrs. Thurgood's house last week. I was Seth's back-up when someone reported activity there."

"Oh, how nice that someone's moved in so quickly," his mother said. "I hate to see properties sit empty. That's good news, although Elsa wasn't exactly neat as a pin."

"Carrie's got her work cut out for her."

"Carrie?"

"Sophie's mother. She's—" he scanned the group until he spotted her just beyond the small grove of swamp willows south of the boathouse. "Over there. With Gianna and the twins."

"Exactly where I'm heading," announced his mother. "I've been dying to see these babies and you know how busy summer's been." She made a beeline for Seth and Gianna's twins, paused to hug Jenny Campbell and didn't hesitate to introduce herself to Carrie once she reached that group. "Gianna, they've gotten so big! I can't believe it, it's only been two months since I've seen them, which is totally my fault for spending too little time in the village this summer. Hi." She turned toward Carrie as Wade came up from behind. "I'm Cathy Prescott. Wade's mother."

Carrie shook Cathy's offered hand, and smiled. "So nice to meet you. When Jenny invited us to come over today, my daughter was thrilled with the idea of meeting new friends, but I have to say I think I've gotten the bonus end of the deal. Gianna, Rainey, Piper." She ticked off her fingers. "And their assorted spouses. How nice it is to meet people."

"You'll love Kirkwood," Wade's mother assured her.

Wade knew better. There was no way Carrie would love Kirkwood. Not once she discovered the truth.

"We're small enough to be friendly, and big enough so we're not tripping over each other," Gianna added. She raised a hand and waved across the yard. "Tina! Bring that baby over here so we can spoil her."

Cathy pulled up a wooden rocker, sat down, and extended her arms. "I'm willing to hold a sweet child for any young mother who'd like a break."

Tina Campbell gently laid Charley into Cathy's arms when she reached the group. "She's tired so if she dozes off, Mrs. P., you just relax and hold her. She's teething now, so quiet moments are always appreciated, and you have such a nice knack with babies."

"A lovely compliment on a frustrating subject," Cathy teased, and she indicated her son standing nearby.

Wade grimaced purposely because he knew his mother's wish for grandchildren. Little did she know that her firstborn grandchild was busily downing a frozen strawberry juice bar with her new-found buddies.

She caught his expression and laughed quietly. "I won't pester you, it's quite annoying when parents do that, and luckily Jenny is willing to share her grandchildren with me."

His mother was true to her word, and Wade loved that about her. She teased him and Mick now and again, but not too much because she believed that things happened in God's time. Well, he'd messed up God's time frame about six years ago, and the proof of that stood across the yard, having a wonderful time.

"Sophie's too cute for words," Gianna said to Carrie as little Michael tried to kick an over-sized soccer ball to his mother. He missed it completely, went down on his diapered bottom and stared at the ball, as if perplexed before he righted himself and tried again.

"Thank you." Carrie nudged the soccer ball back toward Mikey, and when he laughed, so did she. It was a warm, carefree laugh, and yet Wade knew she wasn't carefree. In fact, if he'd been caught in her position, caring for a child in wretched circumstances, he wasn't sure he could have done it. That meant she was strong, and he admired strength. "She's been my joy and inspiration for five years, and when we fell on some hard times, she rarely complained about anything. It's as if she was born with a strong, stoic nature. She rolls with the punches and that helps me do the same. Kind of a backwards twist, isn't it?"

"Wade was like that," Cathy offered innocently.

Wade's internal tension spiked.

"Accepting. Easy going. Mick was frenetic, planning this, trying that, a 'type A' personality from the time he could walk. He pushed Wade into things, and then Wade became the voice of reason. I love how God makes us a pretty complete package by the time we're born."

"You knew me before I was knitted in my mother's womb," Carrie quoted softly. "I love that verse."

Cathy's smile deepened. "Me, too. And Tina, you're right, this little one is nodding right off," she whispered, glancing down. "This is my idea of a perfect holiday, right here. Watching kids, rocking a baby. I'm in my glory."

"Mom!" Sophie sped their way, faintly purple and smelling of fresh, ripe berries. "I'm sticky."

"Shh." Carrie put a finger of warning to her lips and bent down. "You sure are, June-bug. Hold still." Gianna handed her some wipes from a nearby pack and Carrie made quick work of cleaning up Sophie's face and hands, but she made a face at the bright red dots on the t-shirt. "You are officially speckled, my dear."

"Is that all right?" Sophie looked down, then up. "Can I still play?"

"I think speckled shirts are the very best, so yes. Go, have fun and I'm glad you've got new friends."

"Me, too! Dorrie said I can come visit and go up in their tree house and I told her I would love that so much!"

"Well, who wouldn't?" Carrie asked as Sophie raced off. "She was born to climb," she told the others. "She was up and out of her crib before she was a year old. I'm pretty sure she's part monkey."

"Isn't that dangerous?"

Four sets of female eyes stared at Wade when he asked the question with a little more bite than needed.

"The climbing?" Carrie asked. She shrugged. "Well, I wasn't all that sure she was going to live to see her second birthday, but she did. She's fearless, which can be good and bad."

Irritation mixed with the consternation Wade had been fighting once he realized Carrie and Sophie were here. "Isn't it hard to take that lightly? When a child's life is at stake?"

"Wade." His mother spoke softly, but there was quiet rebuke in the single word.

Rainey rolled her eyes at him and hooked her thumb toward her husband. "Do you remember how over-protective Luke used to be?"

Wade nodded, because Seth's younger brother had been a true helicopter parent, hovering over Aiden constantly. "But he had reasons to be protective, and isn't that a father's right? To protect the ones he loves?"

"Sure," Gianna agreed, but he noticed Carrie took a distinct step back as if uncomfortable, and that was his fault for challenging her. "But pretty soon you realize that kids will be kids and they need roots and wings. It's mighty hard to grow wings if you're never allowed to flex them."

"Can you imagine you and your brother if I'd tried that?" Cathy whispered as she rocked the sleeping baby girl cradled against her chest. "There would have been daily battles and no one needs that. Sometimes you have to teach them to climb… and teach them how to fall."

"Exactly." Carrie smiled at his mother. "And it can be hard to know where to draw the lines."

"Well, we all survived," noted Piper as she picked up Mikey and headed toward the house. "This one needs changing so I'm going to take care of that and possibly sneak a tray of cookies out of the kitchen. Including some of Cathy's lemon bars."

"Homemade?"

The hope in Carrie's voice made his mother smile. "Yes."

"Be still my heart." Carrie put her hand to her chest as if ready to swoon, and his mother laughed softly, delighted. "But first I'm going to see what those urchins are planning over there. Too much silence is never a good thing."

"I'll come with you." Wade fell into step beside her. She didn't look all that thrilled by his company, and why would she? He'd just challenged her in front of others. He'd have to think twice before opening his mouth about things because the last thing he wanted to do was spook her. But how could he stay silent when Sophie might be endangered? What kind of father could do that? Aiden spotted them first, and intercepted them with a finger to his lips. "Shh."

"Okay," Wade whispered. "Why are we being quiet?"

"Uncle Seth is putting up the bounce house in Taylor's yard."

Wade's funny face of confusion made Luke's son grin. "Are we hiding?" he asked softly, and crouched down low.

"No!" Sophie giggled, then clapped her hands over her sweet mouth to keep Seth from hearing. "We're pirates and the bounce house is going to be Neverland. Just like Peter Pan! And we might never grow up," she added in a softer voice. "Do you want to play in the bounce house with us?" She put her little hand in Wade's and stole his hand… and his heart. "There's room."

"I'd love to, if you don't think I'm too big. And maybe I should go help Seth tether it to the ground. Make sure the stakes are tight so nothing goes wrong."

"Is it broken?" wondered Aiden. His question made all the little girls turn toward Wade, concerned, and when Carrie sighed, he knew he'd said the wrong thing.

"It's fine." She lowered herself to their level. "Seth is setting it up in the yard next door because there are too many trees and people over here and the neighbors gave him permission. If you were being really good pirate spies, you'd see that he's staking it to the ground right now."

"Oh, he is!"

"I see him!"

"Me, too!"

Wade stood and took a step back before he said anything else to mess up the nice day.

Carrie had impressed him. He'd created a tempest with simple words and she'd defused it capably, which meant he had a lot of learning to do. He'd have done that by now, if he'd had the chance to be a dad. But he didn't, through no fault of his own. Or hers, he supposed, but that didn't seem to make things better.

His conscience scoffed, because the choices he made then put him in this position now. He ignored it and turned toward Carrie when she blended back into the tree-line next to him while the kids stayed crouched, spying on Seth's efforts. "You handled that nicely. Thank you. I think I need more practice around kids."

She hesitated before raising her eyes to his, and he couldn't fault her for that. He was running the gamut of emotions, and how was she supposed to react? But when she looked straight at him, his heart softened, like a freeze-pop on a summer's day. "You don't have kids yet. I was exactly the same way, Wade, almost afraid she'd break if I messed up."

"She didn't."

Carrie laughed. "No," she admitted, "but it took me awhile to get into the swing of things. I ran the gamut so I do understand. And being on my own with her, I'm always second guessing myself. Am I doing the right thing? What's best for her? How do I ensure her future, while dealing with an uncertain present?"

"How *do* you do that? Because that's a trick, isn't it?"

"Not a trick. Just prayer," she confessed. "And because I've got no family to speak of, I don't even have people I can call and ask for advice. My dad passed away a long time ago and my mother shrugged off anything related to family after that."

"Is she alive?"

"I think so." Regret shadowed her pretty eyes. "But she's in her own world, a world that didn't include me. My grandma helped me during my first few years of college, and then she passed away. She was Aunt Elsa's sister, and I think Aunt Elsa understood better than anyone that Miranda and I were kind of left hanging at a young age."

"But you went in opposite directions." Talk about an understatement. Mixed emotions said Carrie didn't totally agree, and then she explained why.

"We took different paths, yes. We looked alike, but inside we were at opposite ends of the extreme. But in the end, knowing she was having a child, Miranda did the right thing. She put Sophie first. She told me she didn't use anything while she was pregnant, that she went to a ministry that helped women stay straight, and she did, at least until she came to me and handed me her precious daughter."

He didn't want to ask because he already knew the answer, but he did ask, and that drove up his guilt factor exponentially. "What about Sophie's father?"

She shrugged, but not because she didn't care. He saw that instantly. It was a shrug of confusion. "There was no record of him in the paperwork. I asked and she said she didn't know who the father was, and that she was sorry about that. I was hoping she'd stay with me awhile, hoping she'd see the chance to start anew. I mean, I look at Sophie and instantly I want to make the world a better place. Safer, kinder, stronger. More faith-filled."

"She didn't stay."

She shook her head, then laughed when the four children spilled out of their hiding spot to tackle Seth as the big castle-style house inflated. "I think it took all her gumption to stay straight long enough to deliver Sophie, and that's something to be grateful for every day. Sophie's got no issues, no after-effects, she's delightfully bright, funny, normal and fearless."

"I see that." He moved around the trees to get a better view of the kids. Eight mixed up sandals and sneakers lay in a heap outside the rainbow-toned, inflatable house. When Sophie spotted him, she waved, excited.

"Wade, come on in! You said you would, remember? You promised!"

"You did," Carrie reminded him. "She's not easily put off, and she never forgets."

More qualities they shared. He kicked off his shoes.

Seth made a face at him.

Wade ignored it. His little girl wanted to play with him. And that was that. He climbed in and immediately went off-balance, which made every one of the kids shriek in delight. "An alligator! An alligator!" yelled Aiden, and immediately, the girls started bouncing and laughing, daring him to catch them.

He did, grabbing for feet, pretending to smack his jaws, and when the kids tumbled his way, he pretended to eat them, only to lose his grip at the last minute.

They didn't stop laughing and dodging his pretend attempts at a hearty meal until he crawled out of the house long minutes later, exhausted. He stretched out on the ground, facing the bright, blue September sky and huffed out a breath. "They're ridiculously energetic."

Carrie laughed down at him, eyes bright, her soft blond hair shining in the late-summer sun.

Beautiful. Kind. Funny and understanding. All the qualities of an amazing woman, the kind of woman—

No, he couldn't go there. This mess was already too convoluted, mixing romantic notions with dire emotion would only knot things further. She would hate him when he revealed himself because her choices were already limited by lack of finances. The attorney indicated her lack of funds could help tip things in Wade's favor, but the whole thing felt wrong, mostly because it had been wrong from the beginning.

Sure, Miranda did well to stay off drugs while pregnant, but her deceit and lawlessness had put him— and now Carrie and Sophie— in a messy situation, so thinking of how winsome and beautiful Carrie Sullivan was couldn't make the short list.

CHAPTER SEVEN

"**Y**OU DID GREAT IN THERE," she told him when she offered him a hand up. He accepted the gesture, and when he was on his feet, gazing down at her, the last thing he wanted to do was let go. But he did, because there were no other options. Were there? "They'll remember this forever, how the big ol' sheriff's deputy pretended to be an alligator and made them laugh."

He couldn't look her in the eye. Not now, when her face shone with approval. Because until she knew who he was, he was living a lie. Which meant he needed to tell her, he needed to be straight. "Carrie, I—"

"Seth? Wade? Would you guys mind cooking the burgers?" Rainey interrupted him as she made her way toward them. "Luke's going to take the kids out for one last boat ride, so if you two can take over lunch in a little while, that would be awesome."

"How big is the boat?" Carrie asked. "Will it hold one more? I've never been on a boat ride."

"Never?" That amazed Wade because when you lived in Kirkwood, going out on the water was a regular occurrence.

"Nope. And it would be a great experience for Sophie. Do you think Luke would mind one more?"

"Extra hands? He'd love it, Carrie, and that way I can stay here and help Jenny get food set up." Rainey picked up a handful of life vests from a nearby hook and helped Carrie get them on the kids, then handed an adult vest to Carrie. Carrie shrugged into it, frowned at the buckles, then smiled when Wade stepped forward. "You've got the arm-strap crooked, come here." He eased the vest off, ignored Seth when he cleared his throat deliberately, then held out the vest so Carrie could slip her arms into it, unfettered.

He liked helping her. He liked being with her. And yeah, he remembered Luke and Seth's dumb advice about solving his problem with marriage, but what did they know?

"Carrie, I'm so glad you were able to come over today." Rainey reached out and gave Carrie an impetuous hug. "We loved your aunt, she was just the nicest little eccentric old lady, with such a heart for God and people and this town. When Jenny brought me those signs from your place, all I could think was how that old house and barn just needed someone with energy to love on them. I think losing her husband and son wore Elsa out, and she kind of sat for years and years, doing fancy work while stuff piled up around her. You're just what that old place needs."

"Don't get me emotional." Carrie held up her hands. "I get sentimental over the littlest things, so maybe I'm more like Aunt Elsa than I'll ever know. But I don't like clutter, so I've got my work cut out for me. Look how well it worked out, though." She exchanged smiles with Rainey. "I put the signs out for sale, Jenny shows up, buys them, and invites us here. As if it was supposed to be that way. And then a man stopped and bought the table and lamp I set out later on Saturday, so piece by piece I might be able to inch my way toward a normal comfort zone while Sophie's in school."

Signs? Tables and lamps? Wade frowned, confused. "I thought you put in your subbing application at the school offices. That will help, won't it?"

"The problem with subbing is you never know when or how often you'll get called," Carrie explained as she helped Sophie into the boat. "And teachers have their favorite subs, so they can request to have them called first. It can take time to work your way into the system, so I really won't know until school starts and people get sick. Selling some of Aunt Elsa's things will make a nice stop-gap."

"People just come to the house?" Wade asked.

Carrie nodded. "Well, sure. They drive in to buy the stuff. Like a yard sale."

"But you're alone."

She got that funny look again, like he was going too far, and he most likely was, but the thought of her and Sophie alone, with strangers driving in and out, seemed wrong.

"I'm alone in the dairy sometimes, and people come in and out," Rainey reminded him, but Wade shook his head.

"You're not really alone, because there's family moving all around the dairy area, running the farm. Carrie's there, alone with a kid, while strangers stop by."

"One of whom was Jenny, and I don't think she's very scary," Carrie whispered as if sharing covert information. She raised her brows and indicated Luke and Seth's petite, blond mother across the yard. "Although to raise all these children, she had to be tough, so maybe I should have been scared. A little."

She was teasing him. He knew it, and normally he'd laugh and agree, but the image of strangers pulling into the yard where Sophie ran and played, made him nervous. He'd been on the force for enough years to know that even a great place like Kirkwood had its share of bad apples, and he didn't want one of them to realize Carrie was on her own, and target them. Was he being over-protective?

Maybe.

But hadn't people died selling stuff online, meeting up with strangers over household goods?

Yes.

Which meant safety should be the first order of the day raising children. Not an afterthought.

"We're ready to head out." Luke's voice put an end to the conversation as Carrie climbed in and claimed a seat between two kids.

"You've got first-timers on board," Rainey reminded her husband. She aimed a warning look that matched her tone and Luke laughed.

"I'll play nice," he promised. "Queasy stomachs aren't my thing. But by next year, I expect to see Carrie and Sophie water-skiing."

Carrie didn't discount the idea. "I think that would be a blast, and Sophie's such a natural at everything, she'd love it. Which means we sign up for winter swimming lessons at the high school so you can move up a level, Sophie. That would be awesome, right?"

"Totally, Mom!"

"My dad is the best boat driver." Aiden's voice took a deep turn as Wade stepped back from the boat. "But then he takes you over waves and sometimes you fall in."

Wade's heart shoved up into his throat and refused to let him breathe.

"Once, Aiden," Luke argued, but he grinned when he said it. "We hit the wake once. And you survived, remember?" Luke shot his son a look. "Everyone gets dumped in the drink a time or two. That's life."

Wade took one look at the seven-year-old's face and decided no way was Luke driving Sophie around the lake on skis next year. If he could scare his own kid, how could he trust him with Sophie?

"If you dunk me, I'll just spit out water and try again," bragged Sophie. "Can we do it today? Please?"

"Nope. Next year," Luke promised as he gave the engine a little more gas, just enough so Wade couldn't hear them anymore, but he saw Luke exchange a grin with Carrie, and he knew what that meant. They agreed that a six-year-old could go skiing.

Over his dead body. And when they returned from their little excursion about thirty minutes later, he was right there, at the dock, ready to help the kids out of the boat. Aiden hustled out and raced to the bounce house again. Dorrie followed on his heels, Sonya stepped out much more carefully, and then Sophie barreled his way as if rocking boats and tie-lines were no obstacle. "Whoa, there, little sailor." He caught her up and set her down on the dock and couldn't help but smile. Excitement brightened her eyes. As Luke and Carrie stepped out of the boat, she hurried to Luke's side, hugged his legs, and almost pitched him into the lake. "That was the very best ride ever! Thank you!"

Luke grinned. "You're welcome. And I promise, next year we'll do it again, okay?"

"Okay!" She turned back toward Wade, eyes wide. "I think I will always like being on a boat."

"You had fun."

"The most fun," she admitted. "And there were fisher people out there, and some water skiers and some—" she frowned up at her mother, silently asking for help.

"Jet-skiers."

"Those went so fast." She made an "eek" expression. "But they looked like a lot of fun, too!"

"My little adventurer," Carrie mused as Sophie ran off to join the other kids in the bounce castle. "She's got spunk, that's for sure."

Wade was pretty sure he could do with a little less spunk. Luke read his face and gave him a friendly shot in the arm.

"She had a ball. Skis. Next year. Definitely," Luke announced, grinning. "Help her stretch those wings."

He'd punch Luke later, because Luke was tormenting him on purpose, but then he remembered how over-zealous his buddy used to be with Aiden until Rainey and the twins came along.

Aiden was a tough, sturdy, adventurous little boy now. And Luke didn't worry like he used to. Was that Rainey's doing? Or had Luke simply overcome his fear? Carrie headed toward the women as they set out food and Wade took advantage of the moment. "I had no idea I'd worry like this."

Luke laughed. "I know. I remember it well."

"But how'd you get better? I can't imagine going through life being afraid something's going to happen to her every single minute."

"Well first I was a jerk."

Wade winced because he had that part covered.

"And then I turned it over to God. I realized I wasn't in control and I had to learn to trust. Rainey wanted a man of faith, and those kids deserved the same. So I humbled myself, stopped acting like a know-it-all, and started to relax and have fun with my kids."

"That easy?"

Luke laughed, then sobered. "It wasn't easy at all. The thought of giving over control, of not micro-managing everything drove me crazy. But once I actually did it, things were good. And Aiden's gotten so much better. Of course having a sister like Dorrie pushes him constantly, so in the end, the kid didn't have much choice."

"I haven't darkened the door of a church on my own in a long time," Wade admitted. "I go with Mom on Christmas and Easter, but that's just so she won't be alone."

"There's your starting point, then. Drag yourself down to the church on Sunday. Or if you're working the weekend, St. Thomas's has daily Mass at seven o'clock every morning. There's something kind of peaceful and strengthening about going to church with others. Praying together."

He'd grown up doing that at his parents' insistence. And the minute he went off to college, he'd shrugged off traditional faith practices. Why did he do that? So he could shrug off guilt about the choices he was making?

Sophie spotted him, screeched "ALLIGATOR!" to the other kids, and they raced around the bounce house, baiting him to play again. Wade felt a surge of joy-mixed-love so powerful it made him want to be better in every aspect of his life. He kicked off his shoes and dove through the curtained entry. As the four kids shrieked their way to safety, he joined in the fun of a late-summer day. For right now, he'd stop fretting and just be Sophie's dad. Soon he'd have to tell the truth and face the music, but for the rest of the afternoon, he was determined to chill out and have fun.

CHAPTER EIGHT

CARRIE FOUGHT TEARS AS HER beloved child climbed the big steps of the school bus on Wednesday morning, and when Sophie waved from the top step, she waved back, watched the bus pull away, and let the tears fall.

She tried to stem the emotion and couldn't, which was ridiculous, wasn't it? Or was this normal? Would she do this every year, on the first day of school, or was it because this was all new?

She had no way of knowing, so she blew her nose, wiped her face and swiped her eyes one last time and got busy. If she was busy, she wouldn't dwell on the fact that her little love was starting a new path in life, much like her mother. Only Carrie's path was a lot dustier and contained the dried-out remnants of some small creature as she worked her way to the far left of the back porch.

She set out three old-fashioned chairs in good condition and a fourth that needed fixing. She put a price of twenty-five dollars on each of the good chairs, and felt guilty asking ten for the broken one, but reasoned if someone haggled with her, she'd take five and be happy.

A triangle table that needed some light work went into the barn, while a heavy duty oak coat rack with an ornate bottom was put out for sale with a fifty dollar price tag.

She carried box after box of recycling to the curb for the Thursday morning pick-up, and when she'd gotten eleven boxes moved down, a freshly washed-and-waxed SUV pulled into the driveway. She hesitated slightly.

Was Wade right? Was she foolish to have people coming to her house, a woman alone? But then she shoved those thoughts off, remembering the strong women who helped make this country great, and strode forward to meet the man stepping out of his car. He nodded quickly, crossed to the chairs, bent, examined one, then turned. "You're selling these chairs?"

She nodded. Did he seem over-anxious, or was she letting Wade's concern un-nerve her?

Both, she decided.

"And this is the price?" The man looked at her cardboard placards and lifted a brow in question.

"Yes. I'm firm on the three, but there's room to dicker on the broken one," she told him honestly, and when he smiled, she knew she'd said too much, because a guy driving a sleeked up foreign car like this could afford the ten-dollar price tag.

"Let me call my sister, she runs the tea room overlooking the lake on the west side." He stepped away, spoke for a moment, then came back and extended his hand. "I'm Paul Andersen."

"Carrie Sullivan."

"Well, Miss Sullivan, I'd like to make you an offer."

Carrie breathed deep, determined to stick to her guns about the chairs. "I'm ready to listen."

"I'll give you twelve hundred dollars for the four, and if you find any more like this, call me first. Is that fair?"

"Fair?" She stared up at him, then down at the chairs, then back. "I don't understand."

"I can see that." He laughed and indicated the card. "I deal in antiques and one-of-a-kind items, and my sister Patrice runs the Cornwall Inn on the opposite shore. Tea at Teaberry's is part of her enterprise and finding period chairs that work in the tea room or the lobby is difficult. A dealer would charge me considerably more for these chairs, so I'm getting a bargain, and you're getting more than the eighty-five dollars you had on them."

"But—" She swallowed hard, but had to be fair. "You could have had them for the eighty-five dollars. Why would you tell me they're worth more?"

His sincere smile said a lot about the man, and his words confirmed it. "Because I have to sleep at night. And cheating people just because they don't immediately recognize the value of an object isn't my style. God's provided me with a lot." He shrugged lightly. "But He expects me to be fair."

"Wow."

He laughed, and that's when Wade's cruiser pulled into the driveway. He angled the cruiser off to the side and climbed out with a dour expression, but when Paul Andersen turned, Wade's expression changed and he stuck out a hand. "Paul, how are you? How are the grandkids doing?"

"Smart as can be and they're keeping Lonnie and me on our toes. And your mother's well, I hope?"

"Quite." Wade glanced at the chairs and Carrie. "You tempted Paul in off the road, I see."

"Nineteenth century English walnut ladderbacks will do it every time," he laughed as he lifted the first chair. He eyed the car, then the chairs, and turned. "Do you mind if we tuck these into the barn and I come back later with my van? I don't want to bang them around trying to fit them in the car."

"Of course I don't mind." Carrie lifted a chair and started walking. "And don't worry about paying for them until you come back, okay?"

"Nonsense." Paul carried a chair while Wade lifted the one with the broken arm. Then Paul walked back for the last chair. They tucked them into the front corner of the barn. Paul withdrew his wallet, peeled off twelve one-hundred dollar bills, and handed them over with surprising nonchalance. "And here's what I'd like for you to do, if you don't mind." He pointed toward the house. "I know Elsa has a mix of trash and treasure in this old place, so if you find more things like those, call me. I'll cut you a fair deal on them so we both make money. Some of what she's got is just fun stuff, like that table there." He indicated the unusual triangle table Carrie had tucked into the barn. "What you need to do is develop an eye for antiques versus shabby chic."

"How do you do that?" she asked him. "I get the shabby chic, cottage-look, but how do you know the difference between something that's just old but serviceable and something valuable?"

"A great question," Paul told her. "Put the stuff you're unsure of in the barn, then call me over and I'll tell you. In the meantime, you'll be learning about value and you'll get ideas. If you go on the Internet, you'll find cooperatives with antiques, vintage and retro displays. You've got a lot of space here, and an amazing beginning inventory, once you've gone through the house. I deal in high end items, but there's a big market in Western New York for the Americana, rustic, and shabby chic." He swept the house a fond look. "There's not a person in this town that won't miss Elsa and her wisdom, but I won't pretend I'm not excited about the house being cleared out. She used to talk about some of the things she'd tucked here or there, but she couldn't bring herself to sell anything. She said they were too rich in memories to put a price tag on them."

"Am I wrong to sell them then?" The thought of her elderly aunt's wishes being ignored concerned Carrie, but Paul put those concerns to rest quickly.

"No, and not because I love the chance to buy gret old things, but because those were Elsa's memories. Not yours. You need space to make your own memories, here, don't you?"

She sure did. "Yes."

"Then you keep on. Elsa left you this stuff for a reason, and I'm sure she'd be pleased to know you're taking care to go through things one by one. Some folks would have rolled a dumpster in here and started heaving. Dealing with decades of hoarding is a daunting task. You're doing this just right, section by section. The good thing is that Elsa was a house hoarder, which means she cared about having things under cover. No rain, wind or snow damage, and that will keep the prices higher than they might have been otherwise." Paul started back toward his sleek, black vehicle. "I'll head over later. Wade, good to see you."

"You, too."

Carrie waited until he pulled out of the drive, then turned toward Wade. "Unbelievable, right?"

"What if he wasn't a nice, philanthropic antique dealer? What if he was an Internet killer?"

Carrie felt like she was taking one step forward and two steps back, but she wasn't about to let Wade's negativity stand in the way of groceries and electricity. Only people who'd never had to worry about money could shrug it off with this kind of ease. "I haven't had time to put things online yet, so there's little chance of that. He'd have to be a random murderer, on the lookout for innocent people selling chairs."

Wade started to sputter, so she raised a placating hand in the air. "When I do set up a website or facebook page, I'll let you know right off so you can come and scare me more. Geez, Louise, what's up with you, deputy? Why does anything I do matter to you? Is this from some old, unrequited thing you had with my cousin, and I'm the innocent target because we look alike?" She flung that over her shoulder as she strode toward the house to get back to work. "Because if that's what's got you all up in arms, you need to get over it. I have to be able to make a living for me and my daughter. I look around here and see amazing potential. You see danger lurking in every corner, and that's tiresome."

"The thought of safety and children is tiresome?"

She sighed extra loud on purpose and kept moving, letting him trail behind because she'd just gotten beyond saying goodbye to Sophie and firming up the day with an amazing sale. Sparring with Wade over her lack of parenting skills had little appeal. "Worry is not of God. You must have missed that Sunday school lesson. It might do you good to re-read Luke's Gospel, and the Psalms, because God wants us to trust. And don't fault me for doing just that because it's gotten us this far, Wade. And what's it to you, anyway?" She turned and faced him square, because they might as well have this discussion now. "Why are you obsessed with my poor mothering skills? Because every time I see you, that's the vibe I get and frankly, I'm tired of it."

She thought he disapproved of her.

He didn't.

She thought he faulted the way she'd raised the amazing child that was his daughter.

She was wrong. Her mothering skills helped mold Sophie into an engaging child. He stared off, over her shoulder, and decided to ignore the lawyer's advice and go with instinct and heart. "I'm Sophie's father."

She stared at him, stared hard, and when she saw it— the resemblance, the similarities, the realization— her expression changed and she took two firm steps back, then folded her arms across her chest. "How long have you known?"

"Almost three months."

She scowled instantly. "Which is impossible because Sophie and I have only been here for ten days."

"Can we sit?"

"No, I don't want to sit." Her chin trembled. She looked at him, then beyond him, toward the cruiser. "Aren't you working? Shouldn't you be saving someone instead of chatting on the back stoop, springing surprise paternity papers on hapless women?"

He touched the shoulder radio, and wished there had been some better, smarter way to do this, but it was done now, and he hoped that would make things better. "They know where I am, and that I was taking fifteen to bring you this." He finger-swept his phone and showed her a picture of Sophie, laughing and running into school with a troop of other first graders. "She looks happy, doesn't she?"

"Yes." She agreed, but the quiver in her voice said something was wrong. Very wrong. He looked up, confused. He'd brought the picture to make Carrie smile, and here she was, her lower lip out, her face distraught, staring at a happy child as if she wanted to cry. "It's good that she's happy, isn't it?"

Tears slipped down Carrie's cheeks. Because he'd dropped his bombshell on her, or because he brought the picture or both?

She swiped her face with her sleeve and faced him. "How could you have known for months, Wade? Because I didn't know who Sophie's father was and Miranda's gone."

"Three months ago I got a notice that said the state intended to garnish my wages for being a deadbeat dad."

"That makes no sense." Carrie frowned at him. "I've never asked anyone for anything. Sophie and I have paid our way from the beginning, so there's no reason for the state—" She saw his arched brow and sighed. "Miranda."

"She must have kept an extra birth certificate or something, or had one made illegally. She was collecting benefits in Florida for a child she gave up for adoption in Nebraska. For whatever reason, she must have let it slip who the father was before she passed away because I'm not on any original paperwork. When I got the notice from the state's offices, I went straight to my lawyer because I didn't think it could be true. She never said anything to me, she left me high and dry and took nearly two-thousand dollars of my money with her. I didn't press charges because I didn't want to look bad for my academy application. I kept my mouth shut, started being a better person and then a good cop. Five-and-a-half years later I got that notice and you showed up." He paced across part of the yard, then retraced his steps back to her. "I know this is a shock."

Her face said he got that right.

"And I wasn't sure how to tell you."

"Well, you've told me now."

He had, and he figured she'd hate him because he wanted to be part of Sophie's life and there was no reason on earth for Carrie to share that wish.

And then she surprised him again when she said, "We have to figure out how to tell her."

"You're going to let me tell her?"

"No," she corrected him softly. "*We'll* tell her, and we'll do it carefully, but why are you looking at me like that?"

"Shocked and surprised? Because I expected you to fight me all the way."

She stared at him and she didn't look angry. She looked like she was sorry that he thought like that, and that shamed him. "Are you going to try and take Sophie away from me?"

She surprised him with the point-blank question and Wade didn't answer quick enough to suit her.

"I see." Chin down, she started for the barn. "You've already got a lawyer and you know I'm broke."

"Carrie, stop."

She didn't, so he moved in front of her, blocking her way. "I've only got another minute, so would you listen, please?"

She paused, but he saw a tear trail down her cheek. A second one followed, and he reached up with two gentle thumbs and wiped them away. "Don't cry. I'm not taking Sophie away. You hold the cards here. Yes, I talked to the lawyer handling the wage garnishing and here's the deal. You're Sophie's mother. You have every legal right to chase me off and pretty much never let me see her. It seems that those decisions made in secrecy long ago kind of shut me out of the picture."

"Well, that's not right, either."

He glanced at his watch and grimaced. "Can we talk tonight? Can I come over? I'll bring supper to celebrate Sophie's first day at school."

She shook her head. "You've had time to get used to this idea.

I've known for five minutes and you're ready to charge full steam ahead. That's not fair."

It wasn't, so he backed off. "I've got to get back into town. Carrie, I—" He stopped, because what could he say? That he was sorry? He was, but for convoluted reasons, too many to delve into now.

He'd given life to a child, and never had the chance to be the father Sophie June deserved.

Now he did. Now he had no choice because he knew what a great father meant to a kid. He'd had the very best, and he wanted to be that loving example to his daughter.

Carrie walked into the barn and shut the big door.

He'd made her cry twice. He felt like a jerk because he was pretty sure a woman like Carrie didn't share her tears publicly as a rule. He climbed into the cruiser, headed into town, and when he came abreast of the church, he remembered seeing Carrie's car parked there the week before, keeping her word. Luke's advice came back to him, words of wisdom from a friend.

He'd shrugged off faith and church for years. He'd taken Sunday duty for extra pay and pretended it was necessary.

It wasn't, or at least he could have done "B" shift, and gone to church in the morning. Faith was another grown-up facet of life he'd treated casually.

He paused the cruiser, got out, and walked over to the small grotto on the side of the church. He paused, glancing around, deep in thought. The broad, old cemetery stretched into the upward slope, and then into the woods north of the church.

He stared at the grotto, then the graveyard, wondering when he'd grown so careless. His parents had raised him better than that. They'd sacrificed, loved and encouraged all of his dreams. Mick's, too.

And sure, he was doing well in law enforcement, but in life he'd been more foolish. That needed to stop. He was a father, and to be a good father, he needed to be not just a good man, but the best man he could be. Starting right now.

The radio stayed quiet so he stopped by Campbell's Hardware and met Jenny on the main floor. "I need ideas," he told her.

"About?"

"Mrs. Thurgood's old barn. Carrie's been selling some things by the road, like the signs you bought."

"Rainey loved them right off," Jenny told him. "Elsa's place is a treasure trove."

"Paul Andersen stopped by and told her the same thing, but here's what I'm wondering. Carrie doesn't have money, but she's got ambition. Do you think the boys could come up with a way to section off the barn like they do in those fancy shops?"

"Fancy shops?" She frowned, not understanding.

"The ones that have stuff all over the place. You know, antique stuff here, old stuff there, in little rooms."

"A cooperative."

"Yes!" He grinned, because that's what Paul called them. "Like that."

"I think between Max and Seth we can come up with a plan, sure. How soon were you thinking?"

"ASAP?"

"Of course you were." She laughed at him as if she knew something he didn't, then waved him out. "Seth will get hold of you so you guys can measure things. Nothing starts without measurements, Wade. Measure twice, cut once."

"Charlie used to tell my dad that all the time. It was usually followed by a laugh."

Jenny's smile said she remembered that, too. "Your dad was a wonderful guy, but he was a Home Improvement episode waiting to explode. Let's see if we can't get you a little more comfortable with power tools."

"Sounds good to me."

He went back to the car, humming. Carrie might not think she needed help, and she might not want help, but he'd watched Amish farmers gather together to raise barns and businesses. He'd watched the volunteer fire department put together the community light show and holiday Festival of Lights every year. He'd grown up in a community that worked side by side most of the time, so if he and the Campbell guys could give Carrie the space she needed in the barn, he'd be helping ensure her income and Sophie's comfort. No matter what else happened, this was the right thing to do.

CHAPTER NINE

W ADE WAS SOPHIE'S FATHER.
     She saw the resemblance now. It ate at her, thinking of it. The dark curls. Big brown eyes. Gorgeous lashes, like father, like daughter.

His child, not hers.

But she is yours. Yours in all the most important ways. You raised her, taught her, bathed her, rocked her, fed her. Remember Horton the Elephant and the egg?

Of course she remembered the story, a personal favorite. She and Sophie had worn the spine thin, reading it so often. Diligent and faithful, Horton cared for the egg when the mother bird took off to party at places unknown. And the egg ended up hatching a bird that looked like Horton.

Only that was fiction and Carrie was living a too-crazy-for-reality-TV drama right now, that all started with Miranda. And that had been the case for a long, long time.

A knock at the downstairs door startled her.

She couldn't see anyone right now. Her face was a mess from crying, and her emotions were in tatters which meant she better buck up and pull herself together. She stood up and peeked out the window.

Gianna Campbell was at the lower door. She glanced up, saw Carrie and waved.

Outed. Now she had no choice but to go downstairs. When she pushed the door open, Gianna took one look at her and went totally sympathetic. "Tell me who hurt your feelings and I'll go all New York on them!" She hugged Carrie, then drew back. "And

I'm not even kidding, Carrie. What's wrong? How can I help?"

"You can't." Carrie scowled, then shook her head as she drew a deep breath. "No one can. I got all emotional putting Sophie on the school bus, then got caught by surprise when Wade stopped by."

She got surprised— *wait*— *make that shocked*, when Gianna winced in sympathy. "He told you he was Sophie's father."

Carrie stared, dumbfounded. "Does everyone in town know except me?"

"Seth knows. Wade told him and Seth told me. But it's good that he told you, isn't it?" Gianna slung an arm around her shoulders. "Better to know what's going on, because that way you can plan your strategy."

"I don't have a strategy," Carrie grumbled. "I have a life that keeps getting wrecked every way I turn. I don't know how it all came to this." She sat down at the little table she'd parked inside the barn door. "Being here, all this stuff to sort out, no job, and an amazing child who may or may not be snatched away from me at any moment."

"Wade said that?" Gianna faced her, amazed.

"No." Carrie gripped one hand with the other. "He didn't say anything like that. For once, he seemed genuinely nice and sincere."

"I think he's like that ninety-nine percent of the time," Gianna told her. "He's a good guy who made mistakes." She shrugged. "Who hasn't?"

"I'm scared." Carrie drew her legs up on the chair and hugged them. "I've never been so scared, even with the snakes and the job and—"

"Whoa." Gianna scanned the ground. "You've got snakes here?"

"No. At my old house."

"Snakes at your old house?"

Carrie nodded, glum. "As bad as that was, this is worse. I was able to take Sophie out of danger's way and move. Sure, we lost everything, but we were safe. How can I keep her safe from her father when he obviously cares about her?"

"If it was me," Gianna mused, smiling, "I'd just marry the guy. Oh. Wait. I already did that." She grinned when Carrie shot her a scathing look. "Hey, it kills two birds with one stone."

"Hateful analogy."

"But apt. Okay, if you refuse to marry the guy, let's look at Plan B."

Carrie faced her, hopeful.

"The two of you live peaceably in a friendly, small town and enjoy raising your daughter separate but together."

"You make it sound easy."

"Oh, it won't be easy," Gianna stressed logically. "You won't agree on everything, but the important thing is, Sophie gets the benefit of having two parents who love her. A mother and a father. There are so many kids today who would love to have both parents on board."

Carrie had witnessed that first hand in her teaching assignments. "True."

Gianna leaned forward and clasped Carrie's hands. "Give it time. Give him time. Whatever you do, don't lose faith because maybe this broken path you traveled to get here was the road you were *meant* to travel to bring you here, to this place and this time."

She'd thought that at first, but Wade's words had brought her rose-toned imaginings to a screeching halt. She took a deep breath. "I should have been more mentally prepared. I knew Miranda hung out around the lake, I knew she'd been living in the area at one time, but it never occurred to me that bringing Sophie back here to Aunt Elsa's would open a Pandora's box. And it should have occurred to me, I suppose."

"But then you might not have come, you might not have this fun old house and cool barn and a place to make a new life with your precious daughter." Gianna stood up. "Come with me, I've got a few things that came into the vintage shop that are too modern looking for us to market. They looked to be about your size." When Carrie looked reluctant, Gianna reached over, grabbed her hand and tugged her to her feet. "This isn't charity, it's plain old girlfriend stuff. If I can't use it at the store, you get the spoils." She crossed to her mini-van, withdrew two bags of clothing and handed them to Carrie. "Feel free to donate anything you can't use, and I hope some of it fits, because it's all darling stuff."

Kindness and caring. The entire Campbell clan had welcomed her with kindness and caring. This could be so much worse, Wade's declaration aside. And maybe Gianna was right. A father had rights, a father should always have rights, unless he'd done something to lose them.

Wade was a good man. She saw that.

Grace, Carrie. Grace under pressure. It's what you've always strived for. Now is no different. She gripped the bags tightly and summoned a smile. "Thank you. Thank you so much, and I'm so glad you came by, Gianna. And that you knew. I was feeling crazy alone up there." She indicated the loft apartment with a glance. "And then you showed up."

Gianna winked and climbed into the driver's seat. "An upside and downside to small town living is that nothing gets done in a vacuum. Small town plus big family equals not much privacy but a whole lot of help."

She didn't care about privacy, not really. But help? Oh, help she could use and appreciate. "That's amazing, Gianna."

Gianna smiled at her. "That's Kirkwood. Most of it, anyway. And don't give up on Wade quite yet. Yes, he's a little protective, and he's made a few mistakes, but if I was putting the grown-up Wade on a rating scale? He's an eleven out of ten." She waved, backed around and pulled away.

An eleven out of ten.

She thought of his gaze, deep and sober when he told her. His caution and concern around Sophie, that had seemed overbearing at the time, now seemed normal because she'd been the same way as a new parent.

A soft wind waved against her face. A few early-changing leaves sifted to the ground, tiny yellow emissaries of what was to come.

Wade was Sophie's father.

She breathed deep, determined. Sophie deserved the best of everything, and if God plunked her right under Wade's nose, he'd done it for a reason: Sophie's well-being. And that should always take precedence.

Chicken nuggets, fresh apples, cider and a bouquet of flowers.

Wade pulled into Carrie's driveway, second-guessing himself. Were the flowers overkill? Was his impromptu visit going to step on her toes? She'd asked for time, and he meant to give it, but he'd hadn't been able to get her morning reaction out of his mind. The shock he read in her face. Her eyes. The quick fear, the tears.

He'd scared her.

He hadn't meant to, and he was glad everything was out in the open, but he couldn't leave it like that. He didn't have to stay, but this way they'd have a fun meal to share and pretty flowers.

He climbed out of the car, gathered the purchases, and turned when Sophie called his name. "Wade! I went to school today and my teacher is so nice, and she let me erase the board on the low part and we all got fruit snacks for being so good!"

His heart melted.

He went down on one knee and opened his arms. She raced to him...

To him...

And hugged him, excited. "And I met all kinds of kids, and I don't even remember most of them, but Mom said I will, she said give it time, June-bug, so I will!"

June-bug. Such a sweet nickname.

He looked up.

Carrie stood in the doorway of the big, old barn, watching them. She didn't look sad and wretched to see him, she almost looked... wistful. As if what she saw pleased her.

It couldn't, of course. He must be imagining it, or putting his own spin on things, but when she met his gaze, hers dropped to Sophie, to the hug and the non-stop informational network that seemed embedded in his little girl and smiled. "She's a little wound up."

He stood. "So it would seem. How are you doing?" He studied her, then apologized. "I know I wasn't supposed to come, but I couldn't stay away."

She accepted that with a look toward Sophie. "First day of school is a pretty important thing."

"Not that."

She looked up, startled. He reached out and handed her the vibrant bouquet. "I couldn't leave things the way they were this morning, Carrie." He glanced away, then back. His cheek twitched, just a little, like it did whenever he thought too hard. "I thought about you all day."

"You thought about us!" Sophie danced, then spun in a circle. "I love it when people think about us! It makes me spin-happy!"

Carrie laughed. "Too spin happy will make you dizzy, my dear."

"I wasn't sure what you two planned to celebrate the first day of school, but I brought chicken nuggets."

Sophie's face went quiet. She darted a look up to her mother and gulped.

"Oops." He faced his daughter. "You don't like chicken nuggets."

"I can try to like them." She put on a brave face, like a soldier, marching into battle.

Wade shook his head quickly. "No, no, I should have asked. I should have called your mother to find out, I just assumed that every kid on the planet likes them."

"All but one, and that would be Sophie June." Carrie faced him square. "We've got red sauce and meatballs and spaghetti all made. It's Sophie's favorite."

"Mine, too."

"Well." She reached out a hand to Sophie and Wade was about to turn and go, when she surprised him by saying, "Come on up and have supper with us. Sophie and I would love that."

He should hesitate, but he didn't want to. He moved back toward them. "Are you sure?"

She sent Sophie a look and Sophie said, "Honest, she wouldn't have said it if she wasn't sure!"

He laughed, because they'd obviously shared that phrase before. "I've got apples from the farm up the road. And cider. Do you guys like apples and cider?"

"We love both."

"I do!"

"Okay, then. Apples, cider and flowers." He turned as he withdrew the jug and the basket of apples from the car. "Three out of four isn't bad. If I was hitting like that in the majors, I'd have a multi-million dollar contract."

"Sophie and I love baseball. We're going to sign her up for a team next spring."

The thought of watching his little girl play the sport he loved, and the fact that Carrie said "next spring" widened his smile. Sophie skipped ahead and raced up the stairs. He followed Carrie, and when she turned unexpectedly, there they were. Face to face. Almost mouth-to-mouth. Close... so close he could count tiny flecks of gold rimming her pupils. So close he got a sweet whiff of strawberry-something mixed with rich coffee.

He smiled because standing there, gazing into Carrie's beautiful hazel eyes, he realized he liked staring into Carrie's beautiful hazel eyes. And when she opened her mouth slightly, as if surprised by his proximity, or maybe him, or maybe by how kissably close they were, he wondered what it would be like to kiss Carrie Sullivan, and maybe go on kissing her.

Her gaze dropped to his mouth, surprised, and maybe intrigued? Just a little?

He hoped so, then he felt silly for hoping so, but it didn't matter that he felt silly or awkward, because as wrong as it probably was, he really hoped she wanted to kiss him as much as he wanted to kiss her.

He sighed and smiled. "Are you mad that I came over?"

She shook her head. "No. I'm glad. You've already missed so many firsts, Wade. I was going to call you and tell you to come over, then I chickened out. I didn't want you to think I was flirting with you."

He reached out one hand, and it was awkward because he held a half-peck of apples in one hand and a half-gallon of fresh-squeezed cider in the other, but he grazed the lower section of her cheek with one finger. "I'd be okay if you flirted with me, Carrie. Real okay."

"Except." She breathed deep and backed up a step. "We have an amazing child who stands to get hurt in romance gone bad, and that's not something we can risk. Keeping her world sweet has been my main objective for almost six years. And I can't let anything mess that up. And in my experience, Wade?" Her face and her eyes showed regret. "Adults mess things up far too often."

He was living proof of that so he nodded, but just when she resumed walking up the stairs... and looking really good as she did... he paused her again by saying, "Then you and I have to make sure we don't mess anything up, Carrie. For her. Or us."

Her heart beat harder.

Her palms grew damp.

His words, his tone, all said he was looking down a road she'd never imagined, and she certainly hadn't imagined it nine hours ago when he dropped his bombshell on her.

Go slow. Calm and steady. Sophie first, always.

She knew that. She believed it. But when she glanced behind her, the sincere warmth in Wade's expression weakened her knees. Ridiculous.

What if he was just trying to weasel his way into their lives only to gain information to take Sophie away? Was she trusting too easily? Was her judgment trustworthy, or was she so hungry to love and be loved that she'd fall for come-on looks and great smiles?

She didn't know, and until she did, she needed to take a step back and analyze the situation, but every time she met Wade's gaze over supper, the last thing on her mind was analytics.

CHAPTER TEN

A MID-MORNING KNOCK ON THE SCREENED porch door drew Carrie's attention on Friday. "Ma'am?"

"Yes?" Carrie crossed the porch and spotted a man with a clipboard. In her experience with banks, mortgages, liens and snakes, men with clipboards were rarely a good sign. The minute this one opened his mouth, she knew she'd called the game correctly.

"Are you Miss Caroline Sullivan, the new owner of this address?"

The Midwestern debacle with her former home had schooled Carrie in the fine art of silence. "Who's asking?"

"I'm Roy Burrows, the town building inspector."

Carrie crossed her arms and waited, still quiet.

"I'm here to examine the dwelling for your C of O."

He probably thought she had no clue what he meant, but she understood him just fine. A certificate of occupancy was required for buildings that had fallen into disrepair or a dangerous situation... or cute, country homes infested with snakes. "What is the purpose of your examination?"

Her question surprised him. He hesitated, then gave the house a frank look of disdain. "This place is a mess, Ma'am. Probably not a safe environment for children."

"Do you see a child here?" She maintained a cool expression, but inside her stomach went tight. Why was he mentioning safety and children? They weren't living in the house, so what was his point?

"No, but you have a five-year-old daughter registered for school, and there's some concern that this isn't a suitable environment for a child."

Who would complain about something like this? Who would share concerns with the town regarding Sophie's safety? Only one person she could think of, and that thought was like an anchor to her heart. "You said you were a building inspector, correct?"

He nodded.

"And as such do you have jurisdiction to be checking up on children?"

He flushed a little. "Safety is our first concern, Miss Sullivan."

"My daughter is safely in school. I am busy cleaning out the property I inherited from my aunt, and if you weren't overly concerned about an infirm, elderly woman living here, I'm having a hard time understanding why you're here now. Who sent you?"

"That's not for me to say, but it was brought to our attention—"

"By whom?"

He held up a hand. "That's confidential information, but I can see we've got code violations all over the place."

"Code violations that have existed for years, according to locals."

"Well, we may have ignored some of this and a little of that while Mrs. Thurgood was alive. Now that the property is changing hands, it's up to the town to ascertain that it's brought up to standards. And until then, I'm sorry, but you'll have to vacate the premises."

"What?" She couldn't have heard him right. She came through the door, not one bit happy, unwilling to back down. She'd been dealt a bad deal in Nebraska, but she'd learned a lot about town governments, small-minded officials and standing her ground. She and Sophie were perfectly fine here, and no trumped up local politician was going to push her out. "Do you have a notice of eviction?"

"Well, no, but we can't possibly issue a Certificate of Occupancy with this house in this state of ill repair."

"First." Carrie ticked off her fingers, "There's no way to tell what state of repair this house is in until I get it mucked out, which is what I'm doing as you can see. Second, we are not living in the house, we're living in the loft apartment above the barn. Third..."

She never got to third because his brows jumped like crescent moons. "A barn apartment?"

"Yes."

"I've got no record of a barn apartment on this property, and it's zoned for single family residential."

"Perfect. I'm a single family and I'm living here."

"Now see here, Miss…"

"No, you see here." Carrie had enough. No, wait, scratch that, she'd had enough back in Nebraska when all her hopes and dreams went up in puffs of intentionally set smoke. "This is my property. My home. No one is inhabiting the house at the moment, and when we're done with the clean out, we certainly want a safe, wholesome environment for both of us. At that time, I'll gladly let you inspect any upgrades to make sure they're done safely. But until that time, I want you to leave my property."

"You'll regret this, Miss."

No, she wouldn't. "On the contrary, it feels rather good." She pointed toward the road. "Now, go. And don't come back with any trumped up issues. I actually know my rights, and I'm not afraid to claim them in front of every local media source available."

The word 'media' got his attention. He scowled, turned and strode away. He slammed his car door, then backed into the road, quickly.

A cool breeze swept up from the lake below. She crossed her arms again, not in defiance, but to warm herself as she considered what just happened. Had someone targeted her specifically? The only one who would raise a fuss about Sophie's safety was Sophie's father. Did Wade go to the town to make trouble for her?

No. He wouldn't do that. He seemed so sincere on Wednesday night. Unless he wasn't one bit sincere, and was setting her up for a fall.

She stared at the road, then the house, wondering who to trust.

Trust God, her conscience reminded her. *He's brought you this far.*

But to what? she wondered. She'd lost the rose-colored glasses when everything fell apart in the Midwest She didn't like doubt and suspicion, but her trusting nature had cost them their home and their credit standing. That was penance enough. Nothing— and no one— on earth was going to cost Carrie her daughter.

"I applied for the necessary permits," Wade told Seth. "If you guys have time, I've got a free weekend in two weeks. We can get that barn revamped for a safe, warm shop for Carrie and Sophie."

Seth and Luke exchanged a look. Seth grinned first. "I do believe I called it."

"What do you mean? I said it first," answered Luke.

"You're a pup," Seth told him, laughing. "But if you want credit for this one, take it."

"There is no credit for anything," Wade insisted. "I just want to make sure they're safe. That's a father's prerogative."

"Of course it is." Luke grinned at Seth.

"I couldn't agree more," declared Seth, but he was laughing as he spoke. "On a more serious note, will we have enough help on hand to get it done in a couple of days?"

"Max is on duty, so he won't be around to help," Luke noted. Their brother Max was a former military special operative, now a New York State Trooper.

"Normally, the three of us should have no problem with it," Seth noted, "but I'm working Saturday overnight, so you guys will be on your own on Sunday and we're limited to after-church time. I know Zach's got that weekend off." Zach was married to Luke's sister-in-law, and a New York State trooper like Max. "I bet he'd step in."

"Or Zach's dad," Wade suggested. Everyone in town knew Marty Harrison, even though he'd only lived there a couple of years. A master-of-many-trades farmer, when Marty put his hand to a task, it got done.

"Marty. Yes. The perfect solution." Seth withdrew his phone and dialed the western shore farmer. He explained the plan, and when Marty agreed to help out, Seth hung up the phone and grinned. "Consider it done. We're meeting at McKinney Farms on Monday night to do a quick layout sketch which, knowing Marty, he'll have all done when we get there."

"He can work me under the table seven days a week," Luke admitted.

"Ditto. Which means, Carrie and Sophie will get the surprise of their lives when we're done."

"Perfect." Wade bumped knuckles with both Campbells. "I don't think Carrie takes too kindly to charity, and I don't want her to feel rushed, but this is a whole lot easier to do before the weather changes."

"Amen to that. And keeping the little woman happy is never a bad idea," Seth noted.

Luke's grin offered approval. "He's learning quick."

"I always thought Prescott was a quick study." Seth laughed as he headed for the door, leaving Wade and Luke to the evening shift.

The little woman.

The quaint, old phrase sounded nice. Of course, Carrie would probably pop him in the jaw if he said something like that, but the thought of being a couple, building a partnership— a partnership that revolved around Sophie and love— seemed tempting.

He'd never longed to be seriously involved. His fling with Miranda had been just that, the foolish decisions of a hormone-driven young guy who didn't think first.

He wasn't that guy anymore. He hadn't been in a long time, and now he was glad he'd straightened up years before. Because now he had a daughter, and he wanted everything he did, every choice he made, to bless her because she was the most wonderful and unexpected blessing of all.

Jenny Campbell stopped by Carrie's place the following week with two sacks full of fresh veggies from her overflowing hillside garden.

Rainey Campbell dropped off glass bottles of fresh milk, and pretended it was farm policy to build business. She also left Carrie and Sophie a melt-in-your-mouth tres leche cake, and mentioned the upcoming fall festival on the western lake shore.

Tina Campbell happened to be passing by with an apple pie in need of a home, and Piper Harrison, Rainey's step-sister, dropped off fresh ground beef in one pound packages, perfect for freezing.

By the following Thursday, Carrie realized she was living in the nicest town ever. She'd volunteered to help in Sophie's class for their apple farm field trip, and when she came home, the borders of the house and barn had been transformed. No longer were thirty-inch weeds hiding thick stands of hosta and bleeding hearts in the shade, and black-eyed Susans and coneflowers in the sun.

Someone had come through and weeded everything, then layered thick mulch to help retard future weeds. A note on the back door said simply: "You've been visited by the Kirkwood Lake Weed Stealing Society! Have a Blessed Day!"

She cried.

She sat right down on the old stump that had been covered in wild morning glory and some kind of sticky weed a few hours before, and cried.

She wasn't used to this. She hadn't expected it, and it felt so good, so nice, so right to be cared for like this, that she wasn't sure what she could do in return. She had no money. She hadn't even been called for a substitute position, yet. She had enough in the bank to cover September's bills, and part of October, but people were letting her know they cared.

No one had ever cared in all her life, not really... and when Wade pulled into the driveway about two minutes later, he saw her crying and charged out of the sheriff's cruiser, a man on a mission. "What happened? What's wrong? Who hurt you?"

No words came. She tried to swallow and talk, but blubbered instead.

He grabbed her up, pulled her in for a hug and, oh...

It felt wonderful. It felt marvelous. It felt perfect-beyond-perfect when he wrapped her into a big, strong, comforting embrace.

"It's all right. Whatever it is, Carrie, whatever's going on, it will be all right." The whispered reassurances helped her relax, and when she finally pulled back, she swiped a bunch of tissues from her purse across her face.

"I'm sorry, I don't usually get crazy emotional."

Sympathy and concern deepened his expression. "How can I help?"

She laughed, and her reaction surprised him. "They were happy tears. Mostly."

Now he frowned, confused. "So I just hugged you for happy tears?"

"Yes. But it was a great hug. And a good hug is never wasted."

"Was it good, Carrie?" He drew closer, lifted one hand and tucked the left side of her hair back, behind her ear, then left his hand there. Right there. "Because it felt pretty darn nice to me."

"Did it?" She half-whispered the words, looking up into the most beautiful, deep brown eyes she'd ever seen.

Tiny laugh lines edged his eyes when he smiled. "Mm hmm. And I wonder if—"

He didn't wonder long as his mouth met hers with the barest

of kisses. Soft, fleeting, sweet… A teasing kiss, testing uncharted waters. And then he drew her back into his arms, and deepened the kiss.

Time vanished.

The earth stood still and silent, or maybe she just lost all contact with normalcy because kissing Wade was the most beautiful and wonderful thing that had happened to her in a long time.

"Well." He didn't let go when he paused the kiss, he held her close, his forehead touching hers. "Is your heart racing like mine? Because if this is all one-sided tell me now."

"And you'll quietly walk away and we'll just be friends and no one gets a broken heart?"

He laughed softly. "No way. I'll increase my efforts to win your heart exponentially. Prescotts play to win. So, truth, Carrie Sullivan." He leaned back slightly and gazed into her eyes, then smiled. "Ha, no words needed." His smile turned into a somewhat smug grin. "I'm glad this goes both ways."

"Except we need to tread more carefully than most because we have a daughter."

"Whereas I would say that should just speed the process up." He grazed her left cheek with his right thumb.

"Are Prescotts also somewhat impatient?"

He winced and nodded. "Guilty. So." He dropped his hand, and sighed, but looked happy. Really happy, and that made Carrie happy, too. "May I escort you and Sophie to church this weekend?"

"Taking a girl to church in a small town is like a billboard on I-86."

"One that says, 'hands off, she's taken'," he agreed. His radio cut in. He paused, took the message, and leaned in to give her a quick kiss goodbye. "Gotta run. Talk later."

"Okay."

He hurried to the car, then turned quickly. "You never told me why you were crying."

"Somebody weeded the gardens. All of them."

He grinned, waved, and climbed into the cruiser. The tires spit stone as he sped out of the drive, and when the sound of his siren pierced the quiet afternoon, she realized he was on his way to help someone in trouble.

She looked around the yard, and smiled. Everything looked so much better. Cleaner, clearer, and even though the back porch was really only half done, at least she could see through a couple of windows.

Wade kissed her.

She'd cautioned herself about this non-stop once she'd recognized the attraction. In her life, happy endings were the exception, not the norm. Her family had broken up when she was young, and from the time she was sixteen, she'd pretty much fared on her own. Taking a chance on traditional happiness raised the risk potential, but God wanted his people happy. He said so, repeatedly.

But happiness and dependence brought risk, and risk worried her. She raised her right hand to her mouth, remembering the feel of Wade's kiss. The scent of his clean uniform, the hint of leather from his utility belt, the spiced scent of his aftershave.

That spicy smell alone was enough to put her over the top.

Was he sincere?

He seemed so. But she couldn't forget that he had a vested interest beyond romancing a single mom. He had a daughter he'd just discovered, and she'd glimpsed his protective side. Sure, she wanted to trust him. She longed to trust him. But life had shown her the downside of trust too often, so the words "proceed with caution" had become her mantra. But when Wade was around, caution was the last thing on her mind.

CHAPTER ELEVEN

*M*AN UP, WADE'S CONSCIENCE REGALED him that Saturday morning. *Walk back there, explain the situation and get it done.*

He heard his mother laugh at something his brother Mick said, took a deep breath, and walked around back.

"Wade." His mother sounded delighted to see him, but that might change in a heartbeat once she heard his news.

"Hey, ugly." Mick hailed him from a ladder halfway up the back of the house as he scraped paint. "I expect with the two of us working, we can get this side done today."

"Perfect. But first." He faced his mother. "I've got something to tell you both."

"Oh, man." Mick stared at him, then the house, then back at Wade. "There goes the work day."

"Wade, what's wrong? What is it?" His mother moved closer. Her look of concern and love melted his heart and raised his guilt-meter.

Should he ask her to sit? Should he be ready to duck? He frowned, stuck his hands in his pockets and said, "I have a daughter."

Mick's brows shifted up. Way up. "Well, you're right. This is news."

His mother stared at him, but not for long, because he saw the moment she figured things out. "The little girl at Campbell's on Labor Day. Sophie."

He nodded slowly. "Sophie June is my daughter."

"Then you and this Carrie girl…"

"No." He shook his head and motioned to the porch chairs.

"This is where it gets complicated. And stupid on my part, I know. But no, Carrie and I just met when she came to town."

"Well, I might be a simple, church-going country woman, but I don't think that's how it works, Wade." His mother's grim look said he better come up with a better explanation, right quick.

She sat. So did he. Mick came down off the ladder and took the seat between them. Wade explained his relationship with Miranda, how they parted, and how Carrie ended up with Sophie.

Mick cut right to the chase. "Are you *sure* she's not Miranda?"

"Yes."

"And I'm not talking gut instinct here, I'm talking DNA or fingerprints," his brother added brusquely.

"Well, no, but her story checks out. I was able to follow the paper trail of her college, her master's degree, her job, and the adoption. Then everything falling apart came through on her credit report, so I'm sure she's who she says she is. And besides," he made a face and shrugged. "Carrie's different. So different. They look alike, but this is definitely not Miranda."

"You're attracted to her. Whoever she is."

His mother turned toward Mick, then back to Wade. "Are you? Is this true?" And when he hesitated, she frowned. "You are, I can see it, and she seems nice, Wade, but are you sure you're not being taken for a ride again? You fell for this girl once, and it brought nothing but trouble, and then a beautiful child who looks just like you that she kept hidden. How can you fall for her again?"

"I'm not falling for *Miranda*. According to Carrie, Miranda passed away this past year, and we're still checking that out. But I am attracted to Carrie, as odd as that does sound. And the fact that she's Sophie's mother should be a positive, shouldn't it?"

"Your child was hidden from you, then given away as if you were a non-entity." Mick's low tone oozed disapproval. Wade had expected that. Mick had dealt with his own share of troubles the past two years. They'd left him with a pretty grim outlook on life and love. "I don't see anything positive in this."

"I felt the exact same way at first."

"When you were being sensible." Mick stood and grabbed up the scraper he'd set down. "Listen, we all make mistakes, and I'm going to love being an uncle, but you've got to be careful Wade. This woman or her look-alike cousin, whoever she is, either way… she made a fool out of you. Yeah, you were younger, but remember that old saying: Fool me once, shame on you. Fool me twice, shame on me."

Carrie wasn't trying to fool him, or anyone. She was the most sincere, sweet and kind woman he'd ever met, and right now he felt like punching his brother.

His mother touched his arm. "I would like to meet them both again, now that we know. May I do that?"

"Yes, but we haven't said anything to Sophie, yet, so we have to keep this to ourselves for the time being. Can we handle that?"

"Of course we can. Protecting children is what we do best."

Relief eased the weight in Wade's chest. This sounded more like his mother's typical reaction. "I'm going to church with them tomorrow. Maybe we could have breakfast together after?"

"You check with Sophie's mother, of course. And then let me know."

"I will. And Mom?"

She faced him, and he hated himself for putting that look in her eyes, for giving her reason to be concerned. "I'm sorry."

He expected her to berate him. To scold and remind him of all the lessons he'd been taught as her son. Goodness and caring, love and responsibility. Honesty and integrity.

She didn't do any of those things. She cradled his cheeks with her two, hard-working hands and kissed him. "This woman, this Miranda. She had choices, Wade. Choices she didn't make. She could have erased this precious child and no one would have been the wiser."

"She didn't."

His mother's expression recognized the grace in Miranda's choice, the choice to have the baby. "Which means for all her faults, there was God's essence of good in her. And for that, for the gift of a beautiful child, I will be ever in her debt."

"So you're not going to kill him?" Mick had gone back to the ladder, and he sounded genuinely disappointed. "Because I was kind of looking forward to that, Mom."

"I'm keeping my options open," she declared, and she shot him a fierce look that said she meant it. "But first, I must meet my granddaughter and thank God for bringing such beauty into my life. And then I will tend to the father."

"I love you, Mom."

She tapped his cheek and pointed to the second ladder. "I love you, too. And I'm glad you told me before I heard from others. That would have made me mad. Go help your brother while I make tea and think about being a grandmother at long last. And if her mother has no objections, I would love to take my grand-daughter out shopping for back-to-school clothes. Shopping for you boys was fine, but I have always wanted to take a little girl to the mall and just have some fun. Perhaps Carrie and I can take her shopping together."

He'd have to warn Carrie today so he didn't blindside her tomorrow. He climbed the ladder and began scraping the far end of the small Cape Cod. If he had time, he'd stop by Carrie's place on his way to work that afternoon. If not, he'd call. Either way, she needed to know that Catherine Prescott was now a grandmother, and a grandmother with a debit card was never a bad thing to have.

"Nervous?" Wade whispered the word late the next morning as he angled the car into his mother's driveway.

"Scared to death," she whispered back so Sophie wouldn't hear. "This isn't the first time I've wished Miranda and I didn't look alike, so that when people see me, they see Carrie, first."

"She never met Miranda."

Wade had an intimate relationship with her cousin, and never introduced her to his family? The shallowness of that made her cringe as she climbed out of the car. "I see."

"I hope so." Serious eyes sought hers over the roof of the car. "I was young, stupid and self-centered." He said the words softly as he opened Sophie's door. "I grew up, Carrie."

His mother's voice interrupted just then. "I love Sunday company! Come on in!"

Wade took Carrie's hand.

A part of her wanted to snatch it back. Another part wanted him to hold it forever, and she wasn't sure which instinct to trust. "Mrs. Prescott, so nice to see you again."

Wade's mother took her hand, and met her gaze. She studied Carrie, as if looking for what? Reassurance? Deceit? The whole thing was quite simple and yet so convoluted, a hyped-up mix of crazy, but then Wade's mother covered Carrie's hand with her second one and squeezed lightly. "Thank you, dear. Thank you so much."

She didn't hate her.

She didn't seem to hold the whole messed up dynamic against Carrie. She looked down as Sophie spotted the calico cat lounging in a mid-day sunbeam.

"A kitty!" Sophie didn't screech the words and wake the cat. She said them softly and thoughtfully, then peeked up at her grand-mother. "May I pet her, please?"

Quick tears filled Cathy's eyes. She blinked them back and nod-ded.

Carrie handed her tissues from her purse and Cathy pulled her-self together before Sophie looked up again. "She's so soft. I love kitty fur. Someday we might get a pet," she leveled a happy look up to her mother, "but I have to help and right now we're really busy. But maybe someday."

"I think that's a sensible and good plan," Wade's mother replied. "Who's hungry? I wanted to have a special brunch to welcome you girls to town."

"I think that's so nice!" Sophie sprang up and smiled wide. "There are *so many* nice people in this place, and in my school, and Dorrie can run faster than me, but I can beat Sonya and Aidan and I can climb higher than all of them." She eyed the huge, towering spruce behind Cathy's house. "I'm a really good climber."

Cathy looked at Wade and he raised one shoulder. "I love to climb too, kid. Being up high never bothered me."

"Me, either." Then she smiled up at him, right into his eyes, a father/daughter connection, and Carrie thought Wade would melt right there on the spot. He didn't, because his brother pulled into the driveway just then. As he approached the porch, his cool, hard expression indicated it would take more than little girl charm to win his trust. "You must be—" he drew the blank out purposely, Carrie was sure, trying to shake her. "Carrie," he said finally.

"Mick." A note of warning deepened Wade's voice.

Carrie met Mick's gaze dead on and held it. "Caroline Mary Sullivan. I can supply you with more information if you need to do a background check."

He shook his head, cool and protective. "No need. Wade's taken care of that already."

Wade's chin came up. His hands clenched, and Carrie was pretty sure he might turn around and punch his brother, and wouldn't that be the perfect ending to a brunch that hadn't even begun? "I know," she told him and kept her voice even with effort. And when Wade's brother looked surprised, she nodded toward Wade. "He told me. I think it was the prudent thing to do."

She'd surprised him, but she was tired of surprising people. Tired of having to prove herself repeatedly. Maybe coming here, to Kirkwood, was the worst mistake ever, and not because she'd stumbled onto Sophie's father. In so many ways, that was a blessing.

But she'd left the area because she didn't want to have to prove herself to others, worn out by her cousin's misdeeds. She wanted what she'd found in college and in Nebraska— apart from the snake debacle— she longed for people to look at her and see Carrie. Just Carrie.

Cathy had prepared a lovely brunch, a table laden with simple, good food. Sophie ate French toast, bacon, a scoop of fluffy, scrambled eggs and a full glass of milk.

Carrie couldn't eat.

She pretended because she didn't want to hurt Cathy Prescott's feelings, but between the lump in her throat, a knotted gut and the urge to possibly smack Wade's brother, food ranked last on the morning agenda.

"Sophie are you loving school?" Cathy asked, and her kindly voice broke the awkward silence.

"I do!" Sophie's eyes danced as her curls bobbed. "It is so much fun, and I love learning things, and I love being teacher helper and I want to be line leader someday and maybe that will be soon, don't you think?"

"Gotta love the enthusiasm." Wade smiled over at her.

"I hope so," Cathy told her. "I expect you'll be a very good line leader."

"I'll try." Sophie said the words with childlike seriousness. "But I do like to talk and line leaders are supposed to be so very quiet." She put her finger to her lips in demonstration. "And that's hard for me."

"Sophie has loved to talk from the beginning," Carrie told them. "I love that about her."

"Does she get that from you?" Mick asked. The obvious rudeness of his question made Wade and Cathy frown.

"Knock it off, Mick." Wade said it easily, but there was steel in his tone.

"Kids normally inherit their traits and tendencies, right?" Mick went on as if Wade hadn't spoken. "If Sophie doesn't get her talkative nature from her father, then it must come from her mother."

Carrie had options. She could explode. She could launch a hissy fit and let Wade's brother have it, but instead she turned his way, met his somber gaze and shrugged. "I'm a science teacher, and I love the mysteries of genetics, so actually, Sophie's tendencies are part nature, part nurture, and science has been debating that line for decades. I just take great delight in the amazing child she is, and the wonder of God, setting her in my lap, letting me mother her. Right, June-bug?"

"Right!" Sophie fist-pumped the air. "Me and my mom just love being together, no matter what. I'm her little buddy and she's my best mom ever."

"And no one else at this table finds it amazingly coincidental that you two landed here in Kirkwood within a few months of Wade being notified by the state?"

"Mick."

"Michael Thomas."

Wade stared at his brother, stood and held a hand out to Sophie. "Hey, kid, we've got to head out. I promised your mom I'd take you to the zoo today, and we don't want the afternoon to slip away, do we?"

"I love the zoo!" Sophie slipped out of her chair, wiped her face with her napkin, then hugged Wade's mother. "Thank you for my delicious food! I loved it so much!"

"Wade." Mick stood, but he didn't look repentant. Doubt and concern molded deep lines in his forehead and between his eyes.

"You've said enough." Wade reached out for Carrie's hand and when he clasped it, she felt good and bad. Why wasn't any of this easy? How could someone else's past mess up the present with such a vengeance? "Mom, thanks for a great brunch."

Carrie glanced over at Cathy.

She looked so sad, so caught between the normal existence she'd enjoyed up until yesterday and today's harsh family reality.

Wade strode toward the door behind a happy Sophie. Carrie pulled her hand out of his, turned and walked back to Cathy. She took her hands and gazed into the other woman's worried, tearful eyes. "God has sent us an amazing gift." She turned her attention toward the front porch where Sophie had paused to pet the cat once more. "And the best gifts in life are meant to be shared. While some might see this as a coincidence." She aimed a pointed look at Mick as she stressed the word, "I try to see God in the broken roads that lead us places. Sophie will be blessed to have you," again she looked at Mick, but she kept her expression more cautious. "All of you, in her life. She's an amazing child."

"Thank you." Cathy gave her a quick hug. "You've given me hope."

"And joy." Carrie smiled at her, then followed Sophie out onto the front porch.

"Wade, listen—"

Wade didn't answer his brother. He came through the screened door behind her. "If we head straight up to Buffalo, we might get there in time to see the baby rhino. They bring him out for about two hours every day."

"I love baby anythings!" Sophie stood and waved a quick good-bye to the grandmother and uncle she didn't know she had. "Bye! Thank you so much for such delicious food!"

"Goodbye, honey." Cathy's voice sounded wistful.

Mick stayed quiet, which was probably a good thing. And when Wade started to apologize in the car, Carrie held up a hand and gave Sophie a quick look in the back seat to quiet him. "We'll talk later. Let's just enjoy today, okay?"

He didn't look like he bought the scenario, but he nodded. "I'm okay with that."

So was Carrie. Mick Prescott had stirred up a host of old doubts. She couldn't blame him for wanting to be careful, for wanting his brother to be careful, but she was done taking the fall for Miranda's misdeeds. And if that meant leaving Kirkwood Lake, then she'd do just that because proving herself day after day wasn't just tiresome. It was a ridiculous way to live.

CHAPTER TWELVE

CARRIE WAS CALLED IN TO sub at the junior high three days in a row. She was ecstatic, and the prospect of regular money coming in seemed to ease her mind. Wade stopped by late Wednesday afternoon as he made a regular patrol sweep of the eastern shore. "You look happy."

"So far beyond happy as to be delighted," she laughed. "Three days of work, and they've already locked me in for three days next week to help cover teacher development days."

"And cold and flu season hasn't even begun," he teased.

"I know it seems silly," she began, but he didn't let her finish.

He hugged her, laughing, and Wade couldn't remember the last time he'd laughed this much. Being around Carrie and Sophie lightened his days. Lightened his spirit. "I don't think it's silly at all. Being employed is a good thing, and making money pays the bills. And this yard looks so much better now that the Weed Stealers have stopped by."

"There is so much to love about this town." Carrie swept the yard a quick look. "There's a lot of goodness here."

"There is. And I have to admit I took it for granted, like that's how it's supposed to be."

"Isn't it?" She looked up at him as Sophie's bus rolled over the hill south of them.

"Yes, sure. But I didn't notice it until I started seeing things through your eyes. And hers," he added as the bus rolled to a stop. "Knowing you and Sophie has been my wake-up call."

"I'm glad."

Sophie hopped off the bus just then. She turned, waved to the bus driver, blew him a kiss, and then dashed up the driveway. "I had the best day ever!"

"No way."

She nodded, triumphant. "Yes, way! I got to be line leader ALL DAY."

"No."

"Yes!" She twirled, then hugged her mom, then hugged Wade and his heart stretched

wide. "Miss Garrett said I did a great job!"

"That's some pretty solid praise, right there," Wade told her. He looked at Carrie,

mouthed the words "thank you" then smiled when she bit back emotion. "Hey, do you gals want to go into town and have supper at The Pelican's Nest on Friday night?"

"Is it a fancy restaurant?" Sophie asked, eyes wide. "Oh, Mom, you know I love going to eat at fancy restaurants! Can we go? Please?"

Carrie tweaked one of her curly-q pigtails. "I'd love that, and you don't have to worry about getting up for school the next morning, so yes. Thank you, Wade."

He pointed to the barn behind them. "I'm going to interrupt your sleep on Saturday, though. I want to install a fire-escape system from the back of the apartment, okay?" He didn't have to tell her that wasn't all they planned to do. He wanted the makeover to surprise her, and Rainey and Piper had promised to keep Carrie and Sophie busy and out of the way on Saturday.

"We're actually spending the day on the farm on Saturday, and then the bonfire at Campbells' on Saturday night."

"Perfect. Then my hammering and sawing won't bother you."

"It wouldn't bother me, anyway, Wade."

The way she said it, as if having him there, working around the place, helping her, was a welcome thing, made him smile. "Well, good." He bent low, hugged Sophie goodbye, then did the same with Carrie, but managed to feather a few soft kisses to her ear, then her cheek. "I'll see you Friday, okay?"

"Okay."

He went back to work, humming.

Yes, it was too soon to talk about commitments.

Or maybe it wasn't.

He had no idea, not really, but what he did know was that he felt better than he ever had when he was with Carrie and Sophie, and that said a lot.

Carrie drove into town on Friday morning to buy some touch-up paint for three sets of shutters she'd found stacked in the far porch corner. Using the bright-toned sampler sized paints, she'd scroll vine-work up the sides of the dark red shutters, splashed with a few eye-catching flowers. The whimsical look was sure to draw a buyer for them, and she wanted them on display in the yard before the busy fall weekend. She didn't even linger to talk with Jenny Campbell, because time was of the essence for a working mom.

The thought of that made her smile. It felt so good, so wonderful to be teaching again. And to have a sweet home, clean and neat, for Sophie to come home to. A lake west of her, and a rolling horse pasture behind her... so many wonderful things to celebrate in Kirkwood.

She started to make the turn into her driveway, then stopped.

A big red sign emblazoned with a white "x" was tacked to the front of her house.

Her heart ground to a stop while her pulse raced.

Not again.

This couldn't possibly be happening again, not when she'd already gone through the condemnation process in Nebraska and watched hopes and dreams turned to ash before her eyes.

She pulled up the driveway, and there, on the back of the house, by the porch door was another big red sign had been nailed into place, a sign that meant "hazardous materials".

She didn't stop to think.

She reacted. She got out of the car, marched across the yard, grabbed up her hammer and pried both signs off her house. She tossed them into the back seat, and got behind the wheel.

She pulled that car back onto the road and drove to the town offices on the lake's western shore. She pulled into a parking space, and didn't walk into the building.

She stormed.

The town clerk looked up, saw her, saw the red signs she was waving and picked up the phone.

At that moment, Carrie didn't care if she called the police, the troopers or the county sheriff's office, because no way in this world was she about to watch her hopes evaporate again. "Who do I see about this preposterous sign I just found on my house?"

"You moved into Elsa Thurgood's place, didn't you?"

"Yes."

The clerk didn't look unfriendly. In fact, she looked almost pleased to see Carrie. "The town supervisor isn't in his office, but the building inspector just returned."

"Holding a hammer, I expect. Where is his office?"

"He's coming up the hall, right behind you."

Carrie turned, and there he was, Roy Burrows, the same man who paid a visit the week before. He looked smug, but the sight of the two red signs now laying on the clerk's counter wiped the smug look off his face. "It is illegal to remove those signs, young lady. Under New York State law we have a duty to our local firemen to advise them of unsafe conditions they might encounter in case of a fire. Those signs are not lightly placed and need to be put back on your house."

Carrie faced him, arms folded. "This is a hack job, and you know it. What's more, I know it."

His slight flinch told her she was on the right track, but why would the town be against her efforts to clean up Aunt Elsa's property? Most towns embraced improvements. No one wanted eyesore properties.

"That old house is a hazard. You can't live in it. No one can live in it. And if it becomes more lucrative as an insurance payout than as a domicile, our firefighters need to be aware of unsafe conditions."

"Arson?" She stared at him, dumbfounded. "Did you just suggest I might burn Aunt Elsa's house down for an insurance payment?"

He folded his arms. "It's been done before, and I'd be remiss not to ensure the safety of our first responders."

She glanced at the clerk, then back at the inspector. "Why would you think that? How dare you think that?"

"How dare I?" He took a step closer. "When a county sheriff comes in to find out about permits to make a property safer, we consider that a valid warning of unsafe conditions. Deputy Prescott's concern ran big red flags up the flagpole, so I followed with big, red signs. And considering that your last home went up in smoke, well—" His look of disdain indicated his suspicion. "We might be country, but we're not stupid, Miss Sullivan. We look after our own."

She zeroed in on one phrase, one soul-searing, heart-breaking phrase. "Wade Prescott came in here?"

The clerk's hesitant nod said yes.

"Our law enforcement takes safety just as seriously as the town of Kirkwood does. Knowing Wade was concerned alerted us to chronic adverse conditions. If you want to protest our move, you must do so through the proper means afforded you by law. You can file a grievance and we'll be happy to look at it next month."

Next month.

So cool, so callous, as if people's lives could go on hold for a month here, a month there.

She turned and walked out.

She didn't cry there. She *wouldn't* cry there. No matter what else happened, she wasn't going to let a self-inflated, small-town official get the best of her again.

She let the tears fall all the way home. She let them fall when she texted Wade that she couldn't do dinner that night. When he offered to get take-out and bring it by, she refused. And when Sophie got off the bus, she tucked her beautiful daughter into the car and drove down to Clearwater. She didn't want to see Wade if he came by. She needed time and distance to figure things out.

How could she have been so foolish?

How could she have been so blind? Was she that needy? That gullible?

By the time she got home and got Sophie tucked into bed, the apartment seemed quiet. Too quiet. The chilled night air had silenced the late-peeping cicadas and frogs, a hush that hinted of colder things to come.

She'd been so excited to come here. So full of enthusiasm, full of dreams. Aunt Elsa's generous bequest had seemed like a wonderful opportunity for a second chance. The thought that Wade could act so kind and benevolent to her face, then go behind her back to stir up trouble, scared her. She was nobody in this town. If he decided to fight for Sophie, even though she'd been legally adopted, a bad town record might move things in his favor. Even the appearance of unsafe conditions could be enough to tip a judge's ruling.

She couldn't sleep.

She tried, because she knew the coming day would be filled with fun, kid-centered activities, but her mind refused to settle down.

How could he do this? How could he have fooled her this completely? Was she that gullible and needy?

No.

Yes.

Maybe.

She dozed off about the same time Luke Campbell's rooster greeted the pre-dawn hour, and when Sophie woke her two hours later, the last thing Carrie wanted to do was crawl out of bed and pretend to have fun. But that's exactly what she did, because no matter how self-serving adults were, Sophie needed her best and brightest for a joy-filled Saturday on the farm.

Berto, Rainey's uncle and milk barn manager, had taken the kids out on a hay ride when Jenny Campbell pulled into the driveway separating the farmhouse from the barn mid-day.

"Uh, oh." Rainey looked at Piper. "Are you in trouble?"

Piper shook her head. "Not that I'm aware of."

"Then it must be her." Rainey winced and pointed to Carrie. "She's been too quiet all morning, so there's clearly something wrong."

"And she's trying to be brave," Piper added.

Carrie frowned at both of them. "When someone's trying to be brave, you're supposed to respect their privacy and let them be brave, especially if they weren't able to sleep all night because they came to a new town and trusted the wrong people."

"Tell me who it is, and I'll thrash him/her/it for you, honey." Piper's expression said she'd do it, too. "Although in my condition, I am somewhat limited."

"Well, I'm not." Jenny Campbell came up those steps, crossed her arms and held Carrie's gaze. "The town clerk called me last night and said the building inspector is making trouble for you. Why didn't you call me?"

Carrie glanced at the younger women. They were clearly on her side, but neither one spoke up. "Well, what could you do about it? They came and put those stupid hazard signs on my house and that's the first step toward condemning a property. And then the building inspector half-accused me of being an arsonist, plotting a major insurance payout because I'm down on my luck."

Jenny moved forward and put her hands on Carrie's shoulders. "Well, he's a moron, and there's absolutely no reason for you to listen to him."

"He's a town official." Carrie's voice squeaked on the words. "And he's the kind who likes to throw his weight around. How am I going to fight him and the town and work and be a mom and clear out that old house?"

"With a little help from your friends," Jenny declared, but she paused when Carrie reacted. "What else is wrong? And don't think you can slide by me, I've raised seven kids and helped raise more, so pretense is useless."

A tear slipped out. Just one. But soon it was followed by friends, lots of friends, and before she knew it, Carrie was blabbing the whole story of Wade and his relationship to Sophie, her nefarious cousin, and how he double-crossed her and went to the town.

"You think Wade blew you in?" Piper took a seat next to her and slung an arm around her shoulders. "He'd never do that, Carrie."

"Well, he did."

Piper looked at Jenny, then Rainey. "You're sure about this?"

"The people at the town hall said so. They have no reason to lie, they didn't know about Wade's history and Sophie."

The three women swapped looks, then Rainey stood. "You know, maybe he is a creep and we just didn't know it."

"Could be," Piper chimed in, looking a little too quick to change sides.

Carrie had the sudden urge to leap to Wade's defense, but that would be ridiculous. Wouldn't it?

"Well, nothing we're going to solve now," added Rainey, "and here comes Uncle Berto with the kids, so how about we get those hot dogs ready for our fire pit barbecue? My mom made crispy treats, and homemade lemonade, and I bet these kids are hungry."

"Starving!" Piper stood, dusted off the seat of her maternity jeans and moved forward. "I'll do the barbecue pit."

"And I'll get dishes," Jenny offered.

Carrie stood, too. No matter how bad things were, she wanted Sophie to enjoy this perfectly beautiful autumn day. "And it's better to keep me busy," she assured the other women. "That way I'm less likely to kill someone, and more inclined to stay awake."

"Then busy, it is," Piper told her. "And honestly, Carrie, having been married to a cop for a couple of years now, I find that the times I'm most likely to murder him, he comes through by doing something so wonderful I wonder what I did to deserve him."

"And that's the kind of romance folks write books about," Carrie answered as she moved off to greet the wagon full of kids. "Trust me on this: No one's going to be writing one of those happily ever afters about me anytime soon. My recent past lends itself to jaw-dropping, reality TV, unfortunately. Not the inspirational channel."

"Then maybe it's the perfect time to change things up." Jenny gave her a half-hug, smiling. "And we'll be glad to tackle into that first thing next week, okay?"

Carrie wasn't inclined to think it would do much good, but longed to grab hold of Jenny's optimism and never let go. "Okay."

CHAPTER THIRTEEN

CARRIE WAS AVOIDING HIM.

She'd copped out on their date, and wasn't around when he stopped by the house last evening. Had Mick's antagonism pushed her away? Was she pulling back because he was moving too fast? But how did a man slow down, when just being around a certain woman made him this happy?

Wade didn't know, but if he needed to slow the pace so he wouldn't scare her off, he'd do it, because a woman like Carrie was worth some sacrifice.

Marty Harrison laid out his plans on a picnic table, pinned them in place and assigned jobs.

And just as they were in the process of breaking down the last, thin interior wall, Mick drove in and parked. He crossed the drive, grabbed a carpentry apron and put it on. "I'm here to help."

Wade faced him.

He read regret in his brother's eyes. And commitment. "You're okay with this? For real?"

"Yup."

Short and to the point worked for Wade. "All right, then. Marty will give you a job."

They cut, angled, hammered and re-built. For the next nine hours Carrie's barn looked like the filming of a home makeover show. One crew ran electric, another crew upgraded plumbing, and a third roughed-in rustic-looking display booths. They cut in three west-facing windows, two new exit doors to make fire code regulations, and by the end of the day, bright, western sunlight angled into the newly laid-out and insulated display barn.

"Amazing." Mick pumped Marty's hand, then punched his brother in the arm. "I can't believe we got this much done and it looks this good."

"Finishing touches tomorrow," Marty said as they packed the tools into the area slated for a cash register and greeting corner just inside the new front doors. "We'll finish the double door entry to block the winter wind, we'll hang the lights, and by next week we'll have this place ready to house old stuff. I thought it was a kind of crazy idea, at first." He bumped knuckles with Wade and smiled. "But it came out great. See you tomorrow. After church."

"I've got to go, too." Mick climbed into his car and backed around, just as Carrie's car rolled to a stop on the road. "See you tomorrow." He waved as he passed Carrie, but the sharp, late-day angle of the sun hid Carrie's reaction from Wade.

She pulled into the drive and spotted him.

Her face went flat. She stared at him, holding his gaze, looking hurt and confused… but then she turned the wheel to park the car and stopped abruptly when she saw the new, window-flanked doors.

She stared at the barn, then him, then the barn again before she climbed out of the car. "What have you been doing?"

Sophie hopped out of the back seat, eyes wide. She clapped her hands in delight. "Oh, this looks so different, and so pretty!"

"Well, it's not done, yet," Wade began.

"I don't understand." Carrie stood still. One hand came up to her chest as she stared at the barn in disbelief.

"Well, it's a surprise, but right now it's only half a surprise," Wade explained. He took her hand and drew her forward. "Your new business entry, which leaves that door as an apartment entry." He pointed to the left where a new entry door shone in the fading light.

"A business entry." She breathed the words as he pulled open the first door, then the second, and when she stepped inside, she rewarded him with a quick intake of breath. "Oh my word, Wade. You did this? All of this?"

"Well, not alone, we got a work crew together for the weekend, so by tomorrow night it will look much better. More finished."

She spun in a circle, checking out the new layout. "I'm…"

"Happy?" He came around in front of her so she had to look

at him. Just him. "Because when you ditched me last night, I was pretty sure I was in big trouble, and then you avoided me today, so that pretty much clinched it." He laid his hands on her shoulders as Sophie explored. "There are no strings attached to this, Carrie." He swept the upgrades a quick look. "I'm not doing this so you feel like you have to fall madly in love with me, although, for the record, I'm not opposed to that option."

"No?"

He shook his head easily. "Naw. I actually kind of like the idea, but I'm doing this because I've never met a harder-working, more honest person in my life and I just wanted you to have a fun, pretty workplace to show off your hidden treasures. With a security system built in, by the way."

He pointed up and she laughed, and when the laughter turned to tears, he grabbed her and pulled her in for a good, long hug. "Hey, hey, nothing to cry about. Stop that. I don't do tears, I'm not good with them. We've had this discussion."

"Happy tears, again," she reminded him.

"Happy or not, stop it." He made a pretense of being afraid. "This is supposed to make you smile. Not cry."

"Is this why you went to the town?"

Puzzled, he pulled back and met her gaze. "For permits, yes. We'll have to have some of this inspected next week, but yes, I wanted everything done by the book so the supervisor and his team don't bother you. The supervisor has been trying to buy up all the lakefront property he can get his hands on over the past five years and I heard he wasn't a bit happy when an heir showed up to live here. Why?" He looked at her more closely. "What did you think?"

"I thought stupid, that's what."

He frowned. "I don't get it."

She laughed, hugged him and took his hand. "You don't have to, let's just say I need to learn to trust my heart. It's a good lesson in faith development! And was that Mick who drove off as I was pulling in?"

"Yup. He was here helping, all day."

"Really?"

"Truth. And my mother brought food and Rainey sent cake and Jenny dropped off a pot of stew."

"They all knew."

He grinned. "Yup. The Weed Stealers aren't the only ones in town who can keep a secret. So." He slipped his arms around her waist, and nuzzled her cheek. "Tell me you forgive me for whatever I did wrong. Because honestly, Carrie, nothing else really matters."

"Only if you forgive me for doubting." She faced him, contrite. "I was so sure you betrayed me, and then my imagination did all kinds of things, and—"

"That's funny, because when I'm around you..." he kissed her then, long and sweet and slow. "My imagination goes wild, too."

She blushed and he laughed, then he took her hand and showed her around. "It will be brighter once all the new lights are installed tomorrow."

"I can use that wall over there to hang signs." She pointed to the far wall.

"Well, then, maybe we can rig a wiring harness to give you light from below."

"Oh, Wade, that would be perfect!" She hugged his arm as Sophie raced across the newly sectioned barn.

"I'm going to love this so much! We could play hide and seek in here and never be found."

"Oh, honey." Wade stooped down and picked her up, into his arms. "Mom and I will always find you, Sophie June. I promise."

She giggled, pressed two hands to his cheeks and kissed him. "And when you find me, we can play together forever, right?"

His heart swelled tight, good and tight, a weird combination. He exchanged a quick look with Carrie. "Forever sounds real good to me, Soph."

She reached out an arm to Carrie and hugged them both from the safety of his arms... a father's arms... and whispered, "Me, too."

EPILOGUE

JENNY CAMPBELL ANSWERED THE SOFT tap on the bridal room door in late November. "Cathy, come in here!" She drew Wade's mother into the room, and quickly closed the door. "Just in case there's a snoopy groom out there," she explained, smiling.

Sophie spotted Cathy and clapped her hands. "It's my grandma!" She hurried across the floor in a pale pink gown, trimmed with a deep rose sash and tiny embroidered flowers. "Grandma, do I look so pretty in this dress? Isn't it just the most beautiful thing ever?"

Cathy's expression melted Carrie's heart. The older woman squatted down and hugged Sophie to her chest. "Oh, darling, you look beautiful in anything, but yes, this dress is a very special for a very special girl. And Mommy looks lovely, too."

Sophie peeked around and grinned. "She is the most beautiful mommy ever, and she loves taking care of me. Isn't that so very nice, Grandma?"

"Oh, darling, it is." She smiled up at Carrie with a look of pure thanksgiving. "And I thank God for your mommy every single day, because she brought you to us. And now we're going to be a big, happy family."

"I know!" Sophie almost jiggled with glee. "I can't even hardly believe it!"

"Me, either." Cathy stood up and crossed the few feet separating her from Carrie. "This is for you." She held out a beautiful, old-fashioned necklace that sparkled beneath the overhead lights. "It was my mother's, then mine. And now it's yours."

"Oh, Cathy, it's stunning."

"Sweet, isn't it?" Pretty blue sapphires winked light alongside small diamonds. "My father gave it to my mother on their twentieth wedding anniversary. And she handed it to me on mine, but I want you to have it now."

"Cathy, it's gorgeous. It's absolutely breathtaking, but why break tradition? I don't mind waiting twenty years for it, as long as they're with your son."

"Nope. I've had my time and this needs to be passed on. And maybe someday, on to my precious granddaughter."

Her eyes met Carrie's and Carrie understood the emotion there.

There could have been any number of mis-steps along the way. Miranda could have ended her pregnancy, or signed her child over to strangers, or kept Sophie with her as she made repeated poor choices.

Instead, Sophie and Carrie were here, in a beautiful small town, surrounded by wonderful, sacrificial people. They'd found faith, hope and love, and the arms of a new family. A new beginning.

"We have word that there's an impatient groom waiting for his bride… and his daughter," Jenny reminded them. She tapped her phone. "Piper just texted me."

"May I wear this today?"

"I was hoping you would." Carrie turned. Cathy clasped the gold chain around her neck, then stepped back. "Perfect."

Her eyes filled.

So did Carrie's.

"Stop it, both of you." Jenny shoved a tissue to Cathy, then did the same for Carrie. "Now, here's a suggestion. Since you have no one to walk you down the aisle," she aimed her gaze at Carrie. "And you've got nothing better to do," she shifted her attention to Cathy. "I suggest you walk your new daughter-in-law down the aisle."

"Oh, I—"

"What a perfectly splendid idea." Carrie reached out and hugged her. "Then Wade will know he's truly double-teamed."

She peeked around the corner of the old, chestnut doors as Sophie stepped into the aisle. The look on Wade's face, as he watched his beloved daughter walk toward him was priceless. And then, as the music changed to the very traditional "Here Comes the Bride", Carrie slipped her arm through Cathy's.

They might not be a traditional family in the old-fashioned sense of the word, but they were a family rooted in faith, and steeped in love.

Wade's face softened when he spotted them together, and then he smiled.

Such a smile!

A smile of warmth and welcome and excitement. A smile she'd love to grow old seeing, every single day. And now, she would.

DEAR READERS,

I LOVE KIRKWOOD LAKE! I'VE HAD so much fun there, I've come to know and love the Campbell family and all of their friends, so when this idea came to me, to use sweet Mrs. Thurgood's home as a wonderful reward instead of an eyesore, I just had to do it.

My friend Mary Kay Huber gave me the idea for a "Dollar Decorator", and we all know displaced teachers, so that offered me a plausible reason for why Carrie fell on hard times... well, and the snakes (EEEEK!) didn't hurt. But out of the ashes of disappointment can come great good and noble spirits, and that's what I wanted to show with this story. How a woman's bad choices, tempered by a good one, to keep that baby and maintain a clean pregnancy, brought joy to so many.

Sacrificial love is a wonderful thing, and in this story we see it in Sophie's parents, in varying degrees. And in the end, it all works out, with the adults making good choices *"For the Love of Sophie June"*.

My wish and my prayer is to see more of that across our great nation!

You know I love to hear from readers, and I treasure your reviews, so if you've got some time come visit my website *http://ruthloganherne.com* and friend me on facebook, visit me in Seekerville or cook and laugh with me and other wonderful inspirational authors at the Yankee Belle Café! And you can always e-mail me at *loganherne@gmail.com*

May God bless you and keep you, and thank you so much for taking the time to read this delightful "Kirkwood Lake" story!

OTHER BOOKS BY RUTH LOGAN HERNE

Visit Ruthy's Amazon Author page and books:
www.amzn.to/1v26FHw

INDEPENDENTLY PUBLISHED BOOKS
Running on Empty
Try, Try Again
Safely Home
Refuge of the Heart
More Than a Promise
The First Gift
From This Day Forward

FROM WATERFALL PRESS/AMAZON
Welcome to Wishing Bridge
At Home in Wishing Bridge (October 2018)

FROM WATERBROOK PRESS/PENGUIN/RANDOM HOUSE
Back in the Saddle
Home on the Range
Peace in the Valley

LOVE INSPIRED BOOKS
North Country:
Winter's End
Waiting Out the Storm
Made to Order Family

MEN OF ALLEGANY COUNTY SERIES
Reunited Hearts
Small Town Hearts
Mended Hearts

Yuletide Hearts
A Family to Cherish
His Mistletoe Family

KIRKWOOD LAKE SERIES
The Lawman's Second Chance
Falling for the Lawman
The Lawman's Holiday Wish
Loving the Lawman
Her Holiday Family
Healing the Lawman's Heart

GRACE HAVEN SERIES
An Unexpected Groom
Her Unexpected Family
Their Surprise Daddy
The Lawman's Yuletide Baby
Her Secret Daughter

SHEPHERD'S CROSSING SERIES
Her Cowboy Reunion
A Cowboy Christmas (with Linda Goodnight)

FROM BIG SKY CONTINUITY/LOVE INSPIRED BOOKS
His Montana Sweetheart

FROM SUMMERSIDE PRESS
Love Finds You in the City at Christmas

FROM BARBOUR PUBLISHING
Homestead Brides Collection
FROM ZONDERVAN/HARPER COLLINS
"All Dressed Up in Love"

CONTRIBUTING AUTHOR "MYSTERIES OF MARTHA'S VINEYARD" (GUIDEPOSTS)

A Light in the Darkness
Swept Away

Catch of the Day

ABOUT THE AUTHOR

MULTI-PUBLISHED, BESTSELLING AUTHOR RUTH LOGAN Herne loves God, her family, her country, her dogs, chocolate, coffee and pretty gardens. Flowers don't talk back and with a houseful of kids and grandkids, Ruthy is always grateful for a bit of quiet in the garden… And a bit of quiet when she's writing books. That means she has to get up in the middle of the night because with a house full of people, a couple of dogs, a few cats, the occasional mouse (and don't even ask her about the snakes!) quiet is a cherished commodity!

Made in United States
North Haven, CT
02 May 2022